FIC
PHI

$7⁰⁰

NO TURNING BACK

"I'm so glad," Darian answered. "I was going to call you tomorrow. I never thought I would be coming home under such devastating circumstances. I can't comprehend any of it. Everything is turned upside d____ ___ _____ ___ ____ __ _____ __ will b____ 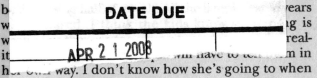 years w____ ____ ____ ____ ___ __ ng is w____ ___ ____ ___ ___ ___ ___ __ real-it____ __ ___ ___ ____ will have to tell them in her own way. I don't know how she's going to when they are so young."

Darian slipped out of her brown boots and placed them next to the sofa. "How do you tell young children about death? Are there any books that can help explain?"

"Everything is not in books, Darian. But it would be an excellent child book to write. How's life in L.A.?"

"I finally earned that promotion I told you about. I often think of all our dreams we had together about going to L.A. to start our careers. I sure miss those fun times." Darian meant it.

Also by Patricia Anne Phillips

Last Bride Standing

Nice Wives Finish First

June in Winter

No Turning Back

Patricia Anne Phillips

Dafina
Books

Kensington Publishing Corp.

http://www.kensingtonbooks.com

As always, my books are dedicated to
Arabya, Aaren, and Javyn.

DAFINA BOOKS are published by

Kensington Publishing Corp.
850 Third Avenue
New York, NY 10022

All Kensington Titles, Imprints, and Distributed Lines are available at special quantity discounts for bulk purchases for sales promotions, premiums, fund-raising, and educational or institutional use. Special book excerpts or customized printings can also be created to fit specific needs. For details, write or phone the office of the Kensington special sales manager: Kensington Publishing Corp., 850 Third Avenue, New York, NY 10022, attn: Special Sales Department, Phone: 1-800-221-2647.

Dafina and the Dafina logo Reg. U.S. Pat. & TM Off.

ISBN-13: 978-0-7582-2383-8
ISBN-10: 0-7582-2383-8

First mass market printing: April 2008

10 9 8 7 6 5 4 3 2 1

Printed in the United States of America

Chapter 1

"Well, Darian. How do you like your new office?" Bill Landers asked. "I even ordered two new chairs just for you." He stood by the large window with a view of downtown Los Angeles. Bill looked around the office; it shone like the surface of a lake. Its sparkling perfection was disturbed only on the edge of the shore, caused by the beautiful woman that stood in front of him. Bill was in his mid-fifties, medium height, with blond hair and piercing blue eyes.

Bill had just promoted Darian Cantrell to manage the buyers in five of the largest department stores from Los Angeles to San Francisco. There were other outstanding buyers that could have been awarded the position, but Darian was the best. She worked long hours and had no family responsibilities or other distractions to interfere with her work schedule. If she was needed in San Francisco, she could leave instantaneously and without hesitation, and stay as long as necessary to complete the assignment. There was no one to stop her. Bill Landers and her peers were genuinely impressed by her professionalism.

Bill had been in love with Darian for the past four

years. He held her hand longer than necessary, inhaled her perfume, and envisioned her nude, standing in front of him, her brown body glistening in a dim light. She would float to a small bed and lie on her back, hands raised above her head, legs spread apart, and locks of curly, sandy brown hair spilling over smooth shoulders. He would feel her heated juices mixed with his own. Bill would do anything for Darian, give her whatever she needed for just one night of blissful passion. He wanted to savor her, smell her sweet scent, taste her full lips, and caress every part of her curvy body. But loving her wasn't the reason he gave her the promotion. She deserved it.

Darian had graduated from Dillard University in New Orleans at the top of her class. In the office, she was methodical and respected by her peers. Darian avoided cliques, except for her friend, Yasmine, who started working for the company the same day as she did.

"Bill, I love it. I still can't believe I did it." Her eyes twinkled with delight and excitement. She gave him a dazzling smile, then clapped her hands together and bounced around her new office.

"Oh, it's just so beautiful. And I won't disappoint you, I promise." Enthusiastically, she threw both arms around his neck. "All I can say is thank you for appreciating all my hard work."

Bill tried to compose himself and felt tremors awaken his body. He needed space before he embarrassed himself, and gently took a step backward.

"Well, I have work waiting for me at my desk. So I better get back. Just buzz me if you need anything, Darian."

Bill started to the door and turned around to get one last look at her. She was facing the window. Her black suit fit perfectly, and the sun illuminated the red highlights in her hair. He shook his head as if to clear it, sighed, and shut the door behind him.

After Darian heard the door close she jumped up and down and twirled twice. "I did it, I did it," she repeated. I am the manager of five stores." All the hard work and staying late paid off. With this promotion, she could still send money to her sister in New Orleans and buy herself a town house. She was finally in the prime of her career.

Darian was thirty-five years old, smart, ambitious, and beautiful. Her mother, Shirlee, was Creole with very fair skin and light brown hair. Darian's father Ronald had dark skin. Darian's skin was the color of cinnamon. A straight nose, strong cheekbones and slanted brown eyes, the same gentle radiance as her mother's. Darian's face made men turn their heads. She worked out in the company gym daily and visited the beauty salon weekly. Her appearance was impeccable.

After Darian finished school she and her childhood friend, Vickie, moved to Los Angeles and rented an apartment together. Two years later, Vickie dated a married man and had hopes that he would leave his wife, but instead her heart was broken by empty promises. She returned to New Orleans and Darian missed her terribly.

Against her mother's wishes, Darian stayed in Los Angeles alone and focused on her career, which kept her too busy to get homesick or lonely.

Darian visited her family as much as possible until her mother married a man fifteen years her junior. The visits dwindled because of her disappointment at her mother's choice of a new mate. It was still hard seeing her mother with another man after her father's death. However, she was loyal to her family and helped Monique, her sister, financially with her two children.

She heard a soft knock on the door, posed at her

desk as though it had always been hers. Sitting in her black leather chair, she slid her hands down the arms, feeling the soft leather.

Darian knew instantly that it was Yasmine. "Come in," she yelled.

Yasmine stepped inside. "Wow, what an office," she squealed and closed the door behind her. "Your office is even prettier than Bill's. He has the hots for you." There were two chairs in front of the desk and Yasmine slumped down into one of them, feeling the soft leather beneath her. "This chair feels good to my ass. Nice and soft."

"Well, that's a good description. Come and look at this view," Darian said and hopped up from her chair.

Yasmine sucked in her breath. "I hate to get out of this chair. Goodness, you can see for miles and miles." She pointed at the tall Wells Fargo Building. "I could stay inside and sit here all day. You did it, girl." Darian and Yasmine embraced, and faced the beautiful view.

"I just love it," Darian said and took her seat again. "Can you actually believe this is my office?"

"Yes. I can believe it. You worked your butt off for this promotion. When some of us had hangovers and couldn't come in on Saturdays, honey, you were here."

"Thanks, Yasmine."

"Beverly's crystal party is Saturday. I could pick you up on my way to her house," Yasmine suggested.

Darian threw her hands up. "No, thank you. The last time we were there, those two bratty kids of hers were running and playing all over the house. They were stepping over everyone, and spilled punch on the carpet, and some of it spilled on my new shoes. Kids make me nervous. And now she's pregnant with another one. Can you believe that? I just can't be around small children very long, especially when they're not disciplined."

"How do you cope with your sister's two daughters?" Yasmine asked.

"I only see them twice a year, and believe me, twice a year is enough. They are a handful."

"Maybe when you have children you'll feel differently." Yasmine took one last look at the panoramic view.

"I'm not having any children at all. And Wade doesn't want any either. I just don't have the patience for children. Besides, I'm a career woman. I could never be a good mother. Children deserve to have parents with patience."

"That remains to be seen, honey. I've heard women say the same thing and end up with three or even four children. Anyway, I have lots of work to complete today. I'll be in the field tomorrow."

"Not me. I'll be here in my new office."

Darian entered her two bedroom townhouse on California Street in Santa Monica. Darian unlocked the door, dropped her briefcase on the sofa, and went into her bedroom to kick off her shoes, then downstairs into the kitchen to pour a glass of orange juice.

As Darian passed the television, she picked the remote up from the coffee table and flipped it on. She sighed and slumped down on the white leather sofa. Deliriously exhausted, she laid her head back and closed her eyes. Employees had been in and out of her office all afternoon. And she had attended a two-hour meeting. It had been quite a day.

Darian fell into a slumber and awakened to the shrill of the ringing telephone. She looked at the time on the cable box; it was 7:30 p.m. She had slept for an hour.

Through a haze of sleep she answered, "Hello." Darian smiled as she heard her sister's voice. They talked at least twice a week, but as Darian remembered, Monique hadn't returned her call last Thursday.

"Hey, Darian. What were you doing?" Monique asked.

"Just relaxing. You didn't return my calls last week. I left two messages. And come to think of it, Mama didn't call me back either. I'm in L.A. alone. Don't you guys even miss me?" she teased.

"Of course we miss you. Last week was hectic," Monique said, her voice lowering into a mere whisper. "I had a busy week."

Because of the distance, they always had so much to say, but this conversation seemed quiet to Darian. They weren't laughing and joking as usual. Was Monique angry with her? "So, what's going on with you, and how are the kids?" *Little brats*, Darian thought and rolled her eyes up.

"The kids are all right."

Darian frowned, cleared her throat, and sat up straight. Did she hear Monique's voice crack? And she seemed so remote. "Monique, is Mama all right?" Holding the phone for Monique's answer, Darian was getting alarmed, and gripped the phone tighter. She knew there was something not quite right. "Monique, you didn't answer. Is Mama all right?"

Unable to speak, Monique started sobbing.

"Monique, what is it. It's Mama, isn't it? Please, stop crying and tell me, girl." Darian was yelling and started to bite down on her fingernails like she used to when she was a kid and afraid.

"It's not Mama," Monique cried out. "God, Darian. Oh my God . . ."

"What, Monique! What!" The palms of her hands were moist, and she felt heat in her face as panic spread rapidly. If Monique didn't stop crying and tell her soon, she was sure that her heart would stop beating. "Monique, please, compose yourself and tell me."

"I have breast cancer. I have only months to live, if not less. And my children are so young. They need me," she sobbed. And it sounded as though she had put her hand over her mouth to muffle the sound.

Darian placed the receiver against her chest and laid her head back on the sofa. She closed her eyes tightly and opened them again. When she placed the phone back to her ear, Monique was still sobbing.

"Are you sure, Monique? Could it be a mistake?" Darian asked, her voice drowning.

"No mistake. Mama and I have consulted three doctors. All three agree on the same diagnosis. Can you come home, Darian? I need you here with me now."

"Yes, of course. I'll be there. Stop crying, Monique, please. I'll see you tomorrow." Darian hung up. In just five minutes her world had turned upside down. She ran to her bedroom. Still in a haze, she perched on the edge of her bed. "What to do next?" she whispered, trying to calm her nerves.

Darian got up and stood in the middle of the room. "Suitcase, I have to pack my suitcase."

She ran to the hall closet and pulled out her overnight bag and luggage. She swung open the closet doors and started pulling out clothes, throwing them into the opened suitcase. Then she ran to her dresser and pulled out clothes from the drawers. She stopped and ran her fingers through her hair, then realized she had pulled down slacks and dresses that weren't needed. What did she need with slacks and dresses? She hung everything back inside the closet and pulled out jeans, sweaters, boots, and a pair of brown loafers. Under the circumstances, all she needed was clothes to kick around in.

Darian stopped packing and called the airlines. Which she should have done first? she thought. She just couldn't seem to concentrate clearly. Breast cancer, it didn't seem to sink inside her head, and none of it seemed real. "Monique, cancer?" she asked out loud. But it was real.

Her reservation was for six the next morning. She would arrive in New Orleans by noon.

The phone rang. Darian jumped and answered with misty eyes.

"You should be celebrating," Yasmine said. "But since you're not, I'll take you to lunch tomorrow."

"I can't. I've got to go home tomorrow."

"Home?" she asked, surprised. "You mean New Orleans?"

"Yes. Monique needs me. She has breast cancer." This time Darian cried. Saying the word "cancer" out loud was too realistic.

"Darian, breast cancer can be cured, you know. Thousands of women are getting it every day, and today they're alive and cured."

"No. She's had three opinions and all three said the same. A few months, maybe less."

"Maybe I should come over. You shouldn't be alone."

"Thanks, Yasmine. But I have to e-mail Bill and I need to be alone to pull myself together before I get home tomorrow. Lord, Monique has two young children and they won't be any help."

"I know, and I'm so sorry, Darian. Call me back if you want to talk."

"Thanks, I will. If I don't tonight, I will when I get there."

After Darian hung up she thought about Nikki and Shelby, and wondered how her mother felt knowing she would have to raise them. Darian sat down and closed her eyes. A day can change one's life forever. She'd had a wonderful day. But after the conversation with Monique she felt as though she had taken a gut punch that left her sinking aimlessly into depression.

She looked at the clock on her nightstand and knew that Wade was home. She and Wade had been dating for a year and a half, and planned to be married in a year. He was finally getting a chance to produce a movie that would earn an income to match Darian's. Together, they could reach their goals of being a successful career-minded married couple.

Darian grabbed her purse and ran frantically out the door.

"Hi, Sweets, come on in." Wade had given her the name Sweets as soon as they started dating. It seemed so natural because she was a sweet and loving woman.

Darian followed him to the kitchen and perched on a stool at the counter. He begin filling two tall glasses of apple juice.

"I have to be on the set tomorrow morning at four. This new actress is harder to please than anyone I've ever worked with. She's a real pill," he said disgustedly. He set the glasses on the counter and turned away. "Have you eaten dinner yet? I have leftover pizza I brought from the set. It was my lunch but I was too irritated to eat it." He set two paper plates in front of Darian. But she seemed to be distracted and didn't notice.

Taking a seat next to her, Wade saw her wipe a tear from her cheek. He turned her around to face him and placed both hands on her shoulders. "Sweets, what is it? Why are you crying?" He sounded concerned and placed his arm around her shoulder, feeling her body crumbling.

Darian laid her head against his shoulder. "My sister has breast cancer. I'm leaving at six tomorrow morning.

She only has a short time left, Wade." The flood of tears flowed as he tried to comfort her.

Wade held her closely. "Has she gone to more than one doctor?"

"Yes, she's gone to three. I know my mother is grieving already. She needs me right now. I don't know how soon I'll be back."

"I know, Sweets." He held her close as though she was leaving forever. He kissed her neck, moved his hands around her waist, then slowly up her back, pulled loose her bra, and heard Darian inhale softly. Wade unzipped her pants and pulled her like a magnet against his hardness. He caressed her inner thigh as Darian moaned seductively.

Wade's full lips covered her right breast. Wade loved the sensual sweet scent of the peach lotion Darian wore. She wanted him. He knew when she was overwhelmed with passion. The familiar purr escaped her mouth. His tongue kept massaging her nipple; it stood up like a pink rosebud. She encouraged his desires, holding his head to her breast. Her hips moved rhythmically as her head reared back.

Darian had never experienced such exhilaration. Her needs were urgent as tremors radiated through her body.

Wade looked at her face; her eyes were closed. "Come on, baby. I need you before you leave." He led her to his bed. With his skilled hands she felt her pants sliding down her legs and over her feet. In seconds, she was completely naked, wanting his firm physique mingled with her own.

She writhed into another world. She quaked when he entered her, and smiled deeply as she wrapped her legs around his hips. Her anxious rhythm pulled him deeper. She felt herself losing control. It was always that way with Wade. She felt his pace quicken, his moans grow louder, and his body fully firm. She held on to him, feeling her passion intensify. They exploded like fireworks on the Fourth of July. Suddenly, they inhaled and held each other.

Darian got up first and dressed.

"I had to have you, Darian. We won't see each other for weeks."

She stood in front of the mirror. "I can come back on the weekends, and we can lock ourselves inside all day." She watched as he finished dressing.

"Are you sure that you can't stay longer?"

"No, I can't. I better go home before my mother or Monique calls me. The buyer for my car wants it tomorrow. Can you take care of it for me?" She went back to the living room and he followed.

"Not a problem. He can come to Sony Studios in Culver City. I can drive the car there and get a ride home." He went around the kitchen counter to get a pen and paper. "Here, jot your sister's address down and I'll mail the cashier's check to you."

Darian wrote the address. "Good." She pulled the keys from her pocket. "Now, can you drive me home?"

"Sure, my Sweets. I'll get my jacket."

Darian watched Wade as he strolled away. He was always so considerate and gentle to her. Wade was medium height with a perfectly round, shaved head, and a small earring in one ear. She watched the hard muscles in his thighs protruding through his jeans. She needed some air and went out on the balcony.

Wade stood behind her. "Sweets, is there anything else I can do?" He wrapped his jacket around her shoulders and kissed the back of her neck.

"What would I do without you, Wade? You're always here when I need you."

"I'm going to make sure that you never have to

know what you would do without me." He gave her a warm smile and kissed her tenderly.

After Darian arrived home she stood in the shower feeling the warm water relax her. She had finished packing and written a check for her rent. She would mail it tomorrow. Darian had no idea what to expect when she returned to New Orleans, or how long she would be there. She'd been home only five months ago, and now this. *"Only months,"* she kept hearing Monique's voice repeat. That was her thought as she fell asleep on the sofa.

Chapter 2

New Orleans, known as the most festive city in the world, the Mardi Gras City and Cajun Country, had hosted more Super Bowl games than any other city. Wonderfully romantic and historical it sits along the crescent bend of the Mississippi River. The city clung to her gracious traditions of the past, while keeping pace with the present, and planning for the future. New Orleans had sights that etched into the memory of tourists as they walked through the grand, romantic French Quarter, feeling the humid summer heat simmer through their clothing, while enjoying the vigorous unfamiliar scenery.

New Orleans would always be home to Darian. She walked through crowds and scanned the faces of passing strangers, hoping to see a familiar one, like she'd done so many times. She picked up her luggage and exited the luggage area. The cold air caused her to pull her coat tighter around her.

Shirlee was leaning against her car waiting for Darian. Remembering the constant complaints from her daughter about smoking, and all the health hazards, she dropped the lit cigarette and ground it out with her foot. "Hell, my daughter is ill, why shouldn't I smoke?" Shirlee whispered to herself, and swallowed the sob that bubbled up inside her throat. She had stopped smoking, but now she needed a cigarette to take the edge off.

"Glad to see you, Darian." She kissed her daughter on the cheek and took her overnight bag, put it in the trunk of the car along with two large suitcases that Darian dropped heavily to the ground. They got inside the white Toyota Camry and Shirlee sped off.

"How was your flight, Bay?" Shirlee asked. Like all Creoles, Shirlee used the name "Bay" as a term of endearment.

"It was all right once I was on the plane. But checking in is a royal pain in the butt. It takes at least two hours with the security and all. It's worth it to be safe, though. But in my case, I was in a hurry to get here. How is she, Mama?"

"She's taking it hard. After all, she has two young children that need her. It's hell for me to lose a child, Darian. And it's hell for Monique to leave hers behind." Shirlee cleared her throat and blew her nose. She saw the eye shadow on the tissue and dabbed at her eyes before she balled it up.

"It breaks my heart to see my child suffer the way she is." Shirlee patted each side of her hair to make sure it was still in place. By habit, everything she wore had to be perfectly matched, her hair, nails and all her clothing. She looked tired, and her skin was light and pale. Her hazel eyes were swollen and red. Shirlee appeared younger than her fifty-two years, and worked hard to keep her youthful appearance. She was saucy, and at times obnoxious.

"I know it's hard, Mama."

"No, you just think you know. She's your sister and you love her, but she's my child. There's a big difference, Darian. You'll never know until you have a child of your own. But you're thirty-five and have no children yet. I wonder if you ever will."

Darian turned her head as if she was watching the traffic. But the truth was, she couldn't look at Shirlee. She looked as though she had cried all night. And now that Darian was home it all felt so real. What do you say to your only sister when she's going to die? She wiped her eyes with the tissue she had in her brown, suede jacket pocket.

Darian had dressed hurriedly, wearing blue jeans, a navy blue sweater, brown boots and jacket. Her hair had tumbled into soft brown curls. She wasn't wearing makeup and was often told that she didn't need to.

Darian felt her heart racing when Shirlee turned the corner. "I don't think that I can go inside the house, Mama. What do I say to her?"

Shirlee parked the car and turned around to face Darian. She grabbed her hand. "Bay, all you can say is that you're here with her. Now hush up and wipe your eyes."

Monique lived in the Seventh Ward with her six-year-old daughter, Shelby, and three-year-old Nikki. Her husband had disappeared right after Nikki was born. When his mother died, the rest of the family agreed that Monique and her children should have the three-bedroom house that their mother owned. After all, Pete Jr. had left his children with nothing, and hadn't returned. After a year Monique had gotten word that Pete was killed in a prison riot. The house was made of red bricks, and was still in good shape with a large backyard the children played in.

Darian saw a football on the front lawn, and the blue Volkswagen parked in the driveway.

The grass was neatly cut, and flowers grew from one

side of the house to the other. A gray cat shot out from the flower bush and ran across the lawn.

Darian pulled the suitcases from the trunk of the car. As she walked closer to the door she could hear Miss Idele yelling at one of the children. Just the thought of having small children around at a time when Monique was ill made her nervous. The yelling, crying, and fighting among themselves. And the running through the house and touching her with their little hands that were never clean.

When Darian walked in, Miss Idele jumped from the green sofa and threw her arms around her neck. "Where is Monique, Miss Idele?" Darian whispered as she hugged her and gave her a quick kiss on the cheek.

"She cried herself to sleep. All the poor child talked about was leaving her children. Leaving them is gonna kill her before the cancer does." Miss Idele hugged Darian again and smiled, flashing gold-plated teeth.

Darian walked through the house; it was clean, tidy as usual except for the toys in the middle of the living room. She glanced into the kitchen. There were no dirty dishes in the sink, and the hardwood floors were shining. What little Monique had, she kept clean. The kitchen was small, but adequate for her and the children. There was a small, round table in the corner and yellow curtains hanging at the window. The dining room and living room were small, too.

Shirlee stuck her head in the door. "Darian, come out here and help me carry your suitcases inside the house. You left me alone. The damn things are too heavy for me to carry by myself, girl. You must have packed enough for three people."

"Sorry, Mama." Darian ran outside. Shirlee grabbed the overnight bag, and Darian carried the heavy suitcases. "Thanks, Mama. You're all heart," Darian murmured to herself.

"Miss Idele, do you think Monique is awake by now?" Darian asked.

"She will be with all this racket going on. You children stop roughhousing in here," Miss Idele yelled with both hands on her narrow hips. "I don't think they even hear me," she complained. Shelby stood in front of her and ran off again.

As Darian stood in the living room with her suitcase, Nikki ran in from the kitchen and grabbed one of Darian's hands. "Aunt Darian, did you buy me a present?"

Darian looked down at Nikki and frowned. "Sorry, honey, but I didn't have time to do any shopping for this trip. My goodness, are your hands dirty?" she asked, jumping away from the child. "Go and wash your hands before you touch me again," Darian snapped. She looked at Shirlee and Idele staring at her, their mouths open. "What?" Darian asked as though she didn't realize how snobbish she sounded.

"The child was glad to see you, Darian. Did you have to snap at her?" Shirlee asked, her arms folded across her chest.

"I know, but her hands were dirty. Doesn't anyone teach them to wash their hands before they touch people?" Shaking her head, Darian took her suitcase to the bedroom that she occupied on her visits to New Orleans. She sighed, and placed her suitcases in the corner as she looked around the room. The bedspreads were clean, the same ones that Darian had bought two years prior.

After Darian hung her clothes inside the closet, she decided it was time to see Monique. She tiptoed into Monique's bedroom and sat on the edge of the bed. She watched her sister sleep. She had gotten thinner, but didn't look ill enough to be dying. Darian touched her soft hair that lay on her face. Her face looked thinner and the deep, round eyes were closed with dark circles around them.

Feeling someone near her, Monique opened her eyes. "Darian, you made it? I'm glad, too." She pulled Darian by her arm so she could sit closer to her.

Darian took her hand in hers and realized that Monique's hands were all bones. "I told you that I would be on the next plane. Monique, I prayed that this was all a bad nightmare. Lord, I prayed and prayed it wasn't true. But it is, isn't it?" Her voice was lost in her tears as she lowered her head against Monique's shoulder.

"I know, Darian. It seems like a bad dream to me, too. But it's not."

Darian raised her head. "Maybe we should go to another doctor?"

"No, it's no use. Three times is enough. I couldn't bear hearing another doctor telling me that I'm dying. I have to face it Darian, and you do, too. I have to be strong for my children so I can leave everything in order for them."

"Did you find the lump in your breast yourself?" She inched away, giving Monique more space on the bed.

"Yes. I was in bed and turned over on my stomach." She choked and stopped talking for a few seconds. Then she continued. "There it was. I don't know why I didn't feel it in the shower that morning."

"Well, who looks for lumps in the shower, even though we should? So what happens now, Monique?"

"Well, the cancer has already spread through my body. I need intensive surgery, a lumpectomy. I also need chemotherapy. The tumor is deep inside my breast in an area that always indicates a malignancy." Monique felt Darian squeeze her hand. "I'm having a modified radical mastectomy." Monique quickly buttoned her blouse at the top. Just the word "*surgery*" was ominous to her.

Darian listened, but most of it was an indistinguishable blur of words spilling out of Monique's mouth. "Monique, I have to ask you this. If there's no chance of you living, why have surgery at all? I mean, why go through the suffering?"

"I thought of that, too. But it's my children, Darian. I may suffer but it may buy more time to be with my children. The operation is at six tomorrow morning."

She sobbed and Darian embraced her, and mustered all the strength she could to be brave. "Mama and I will be waiting for you. Miss Idele can watch the children. But you rest some more and I'll finish unpacking and talk to Mama and Miss Idele."

"Yes. I feel very tired. I didn't sleep well last night."

"Mama," Shelby yelled from the door then ran into Monique's room. Nikki ran in behind her. She took Darian by surprise, and jumped on her lap, giving her a big, wet kiss on her cheek.

Darian forced a smile. "My, you've grown." Nikki had been eating a cookie. Darian wiped the crumbs off her cheek with the back of her hand. "Be a good little girl and go with Shelby. Shelby, take her to Mama and tell her to wipe her mouth and hands." She still wasn't certain how she would deal with the children.

Darian saw the girls standing at Monique's bedroom door.

"You kids go into the living room with Mama and Miss Idele," Darian ordered impatiently. "At a time like this you need some peace and quiet, Monique."

"Young children can't give peace and quiet, Darian. You should know that." Monique wiped a tear from her face.

"Why don't you get some rest and I'll see if Mama needs help with the children? I'm here to help, you know."

Darian went into the living room. The children were

sitting on the floor watching television, and hitting each other. Shirlee and Miss Idele were sitting at the dining room table with a cup of coffee in front of them. Darian flopped down in a chair next to Shirlee.

"Too bad Pete Jr. was never a real father to his children," Darian said.

"Who cares?" Miss Idele answered. "That man up and vanished like a fart in the wind. But he's dead now and taking up residence with the devil 'cause he sho' ain't going to heaven. He left Monique and two babies without even a good-bye. Now his mama is dead and his two sisters left New Orleans. None of his family is here anymore. And no one left a forwarding address."

Darian noticed that Miss Idele had aged in the last few years. Her dresses were always too large for her small frame. She was sixty-seven but the strong corn liquor had put extra wear and tear on her face. To relax, a good piece of chewing tobacco along with a glass of corn liquor was a treat. She knew everything and everyone in the Seventh Ward. And lived in the same house all her life.

Shirlee had lived in the Seventh Ward until her husband, Ronald, Darian and Monique's father, was able to buy a nice home and move his family to a better neighborhood. Once they relocated, it was as if Miss Idele had lost part of her family.

Miss Idele was a goodhearted woman, and helped anyone that needed it. Darian and Monique were like family. And Monique's children were like her own grandchildren. She baked the children cookies and bought them toys when she was shopping. Miss Idele was always there to babysit when Monique needed her.

It was well past midnight, and the house was quiet and dark. After tossing and turning for hours, Darian sat up in bed and turned the lamp on. She looked at the empty twin bed beside hers. Thank goodness her noisy nieces slept in the next bedroom on the sofa bed. At least she had some peace by having the room to herself.

She was falling into a deep sleep when her eyes blinked, and it all came back, Monique's tearstained face, the cancer, surgery and the chemotherapy. Darian felt an ominous chill creep up her back every time she thought of it. It had been there since she stepped on New Orleans soil. Was Monique strong enough for such treatments? Darian remembered a talk show on television about women with cancer. One woman said the doctors gave her a year to live and she was still alive two years later. Darian wondered if the woman was still alive today. Perhaps the same would happen to Monique. Maybe she would live longer, Darian thought with hope. Who knows? Maybe she could even be cured.

She thought of her promotion and new office. No, she couldn't think of it now. She would have to take a leave of absence to be with Monique. Her brain was spinning fast, and she felt as though she was running on empty. She needed to relax, but how could she? Her one and only sister was dying. It was beyond belief, and incomprehensible. No one in her family had died of cancer. So why Monique?

Knowing that she would get no sleep, Darian had to keep moving, and got out of bed. She slipped into her long blue bathrobe and left the bedroom.

Walking to the kitchen, Darian heard a movement and stopped, quickly turning around. She started to turn the light on and heard Monique's voice in a low whimper.

"Don't turn it on. I prefer the darkness. It seems so quiet when it's dark. Whenever I need to solve a problem I sit here in the dark. But I can sit here forever and not solve this one. I was thinking of my children. Dying wouldn't be so sad if it weren't for them."

"I know, Monique."

"I won't be at their graduations or weddings. Lately, I've been trying to imagine their little faces as they grow older." She couldn't see clearly as the tears blurred her vision.

"They will be beautiful, Monique. Like you are."

Darian sat on the sofa next to her. In the dark she looked like a frightened child covered with a green, faded blanket, her legs curled up under her.

Darian took her in her arms, rocking her back and forth as though she were a baby. And both sisters held on to each other and cried together until they fell asleep. That's the way Shirlee found her daughters at five the next morning.

Shirlee stood in the living room and watched their faces relaxed in a peaceful sleep. They were always so close, and now one would be leaving the other behind. Shirlee felt tears bursting caused by exhaustion and sorrow, and went into the bathroom, closed the door, and cried privately like she had done for days. Not wanting her daughters to hear, she muffled the crying with a towel against her mouth. Oh God, what would their father do if he were still alive? She was married again but she still wondered what Ronald would do when a problem arrived, especially one so urgent and unrelenting.

Darian and Monique hadn't accepted Shirlee's marriage to her thirty-seven-year-old husband, Jefferson. But his being younger or not, Shirlee doubted if her daughters could accept any man other than their father.

Shirlee was only seventeen years old when she married and gave birth to Darian. Ronald, their father, was nineteen and responsible. He worked hard for his family, believed in education. He provided both daughters with an opportunity to get an education. But Darian was the one who utilized the chance and graduated at the top of her class. Ronald worked on the New Orleans police force and died from a bullet that ripped through his chest during an arrest at the Mardi Gras seventeen years ago. He left enough pension and Social Security income to last Shirlee for the rest of her life.

Shirlee loved her daughters, but from the age of seventeen, all she had been was a wife and mother. Now she enjoyed life and her marriage to a younger man. The sex was better than she had ever experienced, and like her, Jefferson was young at heart. She still had a voluptuous body and wore clothes that clung to her curves. Shirlee was five-two and one hundred and sixty pounds. At times she dressed provocatively. That was what Jefferson liked. Her nightgowns were short, low enough in front to make any man's blood run hot. She knew what to do to keep her marriage stimulating and exciting.

Shirlee was not a typical grandmother; she loved her grandchildren, but was busy with her life. She was a happily married woman, and felt younger than she had when she was thirty.

Shirlee went back to the living room to wake her daughters.

Darian and Monique jumped up and looked at the clock. "We're late," Monique said and started to panic. "I have to take a quick shower." She ran into her bedroom, grabbed some clothes from her closet, and ran into the bathroom to shower.

"I'll go next door and get Miss Idele so she can keep the children," Shirlee said.

As Darian was going back into the girls' room, Nikki ran behind her. "I want some juice," she whimpered.

"Okay, let's get some juice and you stay in the kitchen while I get dressed."

"I want my mommy," she cried as she followed Darian into the kitchen. Darian sighed. *Does the child ever stop crying?* she thought. *Poor Mama is going to have problems on her hands when she takes Monique's girls.*

Darian filled the cup and sat Nikki at the table. After Nikki gulped down her juice she went to the bedroom looking for Darian again. She jumped up and down on the bed that Darian had slept in the night before, as if it were a trampoline.

"Oh no. You stop that. Go back to bed with Shelby." Nikki gave Darian one last look and ran down the hall. "Don't wake her," Darian yelled.

All I need is to get in bed after the little brat wets it, she thought and shook her head. Young children were not her favorite people to be around, especially with so much drama going on in the family.

After Darian dressed, she found Shirlee and Miss Idele sitting at the table drinking coffee and eating doughnuts.

"Grab a cup, Darian," Shirlee said.

Darian set her purse on the table and reached for her coffee. She dusted off the chair before sitting on it. She could feel Miss Idele and Shirlee exchange glances. "Never know if one of the kids dropped any food."

"Well, I guess you forgot how bad you were when you were a kid. And, yes, you dropped food every time you ate," Miss Idele said. "So don't be so touchy, girl. You gonna have a nervous breakdown trying to make little children out of grown folks." Looking over the rim of her cup, Miss Idele watched Darian as she sipped her coffee with a deep frown across her forehead.

"What's wrong now, Darian?" Miss Idele asked.

"What's wrong? This coffee is strong enough to

grow hair on my chest." Darian grabbed the cream and sugar and dumped more into her coffee.

"I'm ready," Monique said. She stood at the table with her coat folded across her arms. "Let me kiss my children good-bye."

"Are you ready, Mama?" Darian asked.

"Miss Idele, thanks for being here."

"You're welcome, Shirlee."

Monique was in the car five minutes after Shirlee and Darian. She sat in the backseat, quiet, worried, and wondering how much pain she would be in. Maybe Darian was right. If she was going to die, why go through so much suffering? But she knew why. She would do anything for her children.

Darian and Shirlee waited nervously in the waiting room. They drank more coffee and shared stories about Darian and Monique when they were children. Darian also told Shirlee about her promotion. They avoided discussing Monique's insurmountable illness. It was as though they pretended Monique was getting her teeth cleaned.

Every few minutes Darian looked at her watch, and became tense with anticipation every time she saw a nurse or doctor coming in their direction, or walking down the halls.

Finally, Dr. Adams came out. He approached Shirlee and Darian. They were sitting and stood up. It was like slow motion as they watched him walking toward them. Shirlee rocked on her heels with anxiety. He looked fatigued as he stopped in front of Shirlee.

Dr. Adams shook his head in sorrow. "I'm sorry. But her condition remains the same. The chemo will help, but it's all we can do for her at this point. She's in the recovery room right now. It will be a while before she wakes up. It's unfortunate, but your daughter never had a mammogram. I suggest you two have one every year." He walked away, disappearing down the hall.

Darian felt faint as though she would fall in her tracks. Monique had already told her what to expect, but hearing it from a doctor made it too final, and diminished all hope. It was hard for the family to lose their father; losing Monique would be just as devastating.

Darian watched Shirlee as she sat on the sofa staring ahead as though she couldn't believe it. What would happen to her family now? Darian wondered.

"Mama, you want to go home and return when she's awake?"

"You mean just leave her alone?"

"This place is too depressing, and she's not going to wake up soon."

"You're right. She won't need us until she's awake." Shirlee moved slowly. She was so tired and afraid.

Darian and Shirlee were back at Monique's house by noon. Both of them were exhausted. When they entered the house the children were having lunch. Miss Idele had a pot of red beans, rice, and hot links on the stove.

"I know you two may not feel like eating but you have to keep up your strength for Monique and the children. Once she goes for chemo treatments it's going to be tough. I had a sister that went through it. But she died anyway."

Darian's and Shirlee's mouths fell open and they looked at each other. "Was it really that bad?" Darian asked.

"Yeah, Bay, it's horrible. Cancer is always bad. You just never know if someone will just up and die."

Darian was sitting in a chair facing the children.

Shelby had Shirlee's hazel eyes. But her hair was a lighter brown; curly with two braids dangling down her back. Her eyes were what captivated most people's attention. They were round and alert. Shelby was a loquacious child, and had been reading since she was four. She was undeniably a beauty. Nikki had red hair, with freckles sprinkled across her nose. She was her mother's twin.

Shirlee was so distraught about Monique's condition that she had only heard the end of the conversation. "I appreciate all the help you can give us, Miss Idele. I'll be here every day, too, and of course we have Darian's help."

Darian went to the bathroom and back to the kitchen to get a glass of water, and both girls were eyeing her. She wondered what they wanted but didn't ask.

"Can I have a glass of water, too?" Shelby asked.

Okay, here it goes, Darian thought.

"I want a cookie," Nikki whined and bounced up and down in front of Darian. She started to cry when she saw Darian take a step toward her.

Darian nodded her head, tired from sleepless nights and worrying about Monique. "I suppose you want something, too, Shelby?" she asked. "You guys just finished eating your lunch."

"I want five cookies, and I don't want to share." To be so young, Shelby looked mean and hadn't smiled since Darian's arrival. She made it a point to convey that Darian knew she was the intruder in their home.

"That's not a nice thing to say, Shelby. You have to share with your sister." Darian grabbed the bag of Oreos from the cabinet. "Here, you guys. Now promise you'll sit down and watch TV."

Nikki grabbed Darian around her leg with cookies in her hand. "Where's my mommy?" she exclaimed.

Darian looked at the teardrops on Nikki's cheeks. She was a big crybaby.

"Do you have to cry for everything you want?" Darian asked and moved back quickly. "Nikki, your hands are dirty. Don't touch me again until you're finished eating." She clicked her tongue in the top of her mouth. "Children," she whispered in an irritated tone of voice and hurried out of the kitchen.

When Darian returned to the dining room, again she dusted off her chair before sitting in it.

"I just called the hospital, but Monique is still asleep. She's been moved to her room," Shirlee said.

"Maybe we should wait for a couple of hours, Mama. She needs to sleep some of the medication off. And she didn't sleep well last night."

Miss Idele convinced Darian and Shirlee to eat. Darian could hardly swallow the food down. When would Monique be home? How ill would she get from the chemo? So much to worry about. And she had to call Wade before he started to worry about her.

"I know what I'll do," Darian said, jumping from her chair and grabbing her purse.

"What?" Shirlee and Miss Idele asked in unison.

"While we're waiting for Monique to wake up, I'm going shopping for her, slippers and a new bathrobe."

"That's thoughtful, Darian," Shirlee answered. "When you get back we will go to the hospital."

"It shouldn't take more than an hour, Mama."

Darian rushed out of the house. The first store she saw was on Bourbon Street and Canal. It was small but carried what she needed. Moreover, she needed to be alone and feel the air blow against her face. She needed time to think. She parked the car a block away from the store and walked, filling her lungs with fresh air.

An hour passed and she was back as promised. She had selected a dark blue terry cloth bathrobe and slippers to match. "I chose dark blue because of the kids. Their dirty little hands will stain it, but it won't show as easily," Darian said.

Shelby ran into the living room and stood in front of Darian. "When is my mommy coming home? And when are you going home?" she asked sarcastically. She talked loudly with an irritating tone that made Darian's hairs stand up on her arms. She was too young to be so insulting, Darian thought, as she watched the child roll her eyes.

"I'll be here as long as it takes your mom to get better." Darian looked down at the small girl. The rubber band had broken around her ponytail, and her hair had tumbled down her back. Shelby had the same texture of hair as Shirlee's.

"We don't like you much and you didn't bring any presents. We want you to go home today."

Darian was stunned at the expression on Shelby's small face. Shelby stood back, standing her ground, or at least she tried. As far as Darian was concerned, the child was born too soon, and too advanced for her young age. Darian heard Miss Idele and Shirlee laugh out loud.

"It's not funny and you shouldn't encourage her rudeness. I keep telling Monique that she has a mean streak in her." Darian went to the bathroom to comb her hair. And again, she was thankful that she had no children of her own. It had been a long time for Shirlee and she wondered how she would manage with two young children.

"Are you ready to go back to the hospital, Mama?" Darian asked and threw her purse over her shoulder.

"Yes, I'm ready. Poor Monique. What am I supposed to say to her, Miss Idele?"

"I can't tell you that, Shirlee. She's your child and

you'll find the right words." Miss Idele extracted a stick
of gum from her pocket, rolled it up, and flipped it
inside her mouth.

"Miss Idele, please don't let those bratty kids go into
my overnight bag. I have makeup in there and I don't
want it destroyed," Darian said, looking at the kids.
They were on the floor in front of the television.

Shelby smiled. "I will be a good girl, Auntie Darian."

With those big beautiful eyes and that sweet smile of
Shelby's, for a flicker of a second Darian almost be-
lieved her. "Do you really promise to be a good girl?"
Darian asked.

"Yes, I promise."

"Me, too," said Nikki.

Shirlee stood over Monique as tears stuck in her
throat. She looked so small, so fragile and helpless.
Her dark hair was loose like a halo around her head,
but what twisted Shirlee's heart was that Monique
looked as though she had been in pain. Even in her
sleep her face was wrenched with pain.

Shirlee looked at Darian standing at the window, her
back to Monique's bed as though she was afraid to be
too close. Shirlee knew it was because she was crying.
Darian could always compose herself in a crisis. She was
stronger and more independent than any woman
Shirlee knew. But she loved her sister, and Shirlee
sensed that Monique's illness was torturing her.

"Mama, how long have you been here?" Monique
whispered. "Where is Darian?"

"Right here, Monique." Darian rushed to her bed-
side. "Does it hurt to speak?"

"No, it doesn't. It just feels like it's hard to get the
words out." Tears rolled from the corner of her eyes,
falling onto the pillow. "I guess you know by now that

they did a mastectomy, but nothing has changed, my condition is no better. I wished I would have signed for the doctor to do a biopsy and the mastectomy at the same time: I would be home instead of being here. How's my babies?"

"Don't worry, Monique. You know Miss Idele will take care of them. You just get better so you can come home," Darian said, holding her hand. "In the meantime I'll do everything I can to help."

Monique closed her eyes and opened them again. "Mama, please stop crying. Right now I just want to get better and be with my girls."

"I know, Bay." But Shirlee's heart was bleeding, and her chest felt tight. She wasn't sure how she would get through the next few months, or year.

After twenty minutes had passed, Monique drifted back into a deep slumber. "She'll probably sleep through the night, Mama. Tomorrow most of the medication will have dissipated. We can return first thing in the morning." Darian kissed Monique on her cheek. She was asleep and didn't stir.

"Come on, Mama. Let's go." Darian took Shirlee's hand and led her outside. They stood in front of Shirlee's car.

"Could this really be happening to us, Mama?"

"I'm afraid it is. I never dreamed that I would be losing one of my girls. I don't know if I can survive this, Darian." She covered her face with both hands to mask the river of tears.

Darian held her breath to keep from crying, but tears escaped against her will. "I know, Mama."

The house was quiet that evening. It was as though the children knew their lives were about to change, but they just didn't know how, or why.

Shirlee was weary and went home to be with her husband. Miss Idele and Darian were discussing potential changes in the house for Monique's comfort. Before she arrived home they would sanitize her bedroom. Nikki's nose had been running. Monique's resistance was low, and she didn't need a runny-nose kid around her, Darian thought.

"I wonder if she will have to eat certain foods, Miss Idele? Maybe she'll have to eat soups, yogurt, or Jell-O. Oh, and she loves puddings of all flavors." Being overwhelmed with tears, Darian could no longer speak.

"She can eat the same until chemo treatments begin. Some days she'll be too weak and ill to eat very much. It's going to be a long haul, Darian, for you and Shirlee."

"I know. Our lives are turned upside down and there's nothing that we can do about it. I haven't been here for a week and I already feel like a train hit me."

"I know. I'm going home. This has been a long pain-wracked week. You girls feel like you're my granddaughters. It hurts me to see Monique so ill. Poor Shirlee looks like she hasn't slept for a week. I hope she doesn't collapse."

"I hope she doesn't either. I can't take care of everything alone. And the children are in the way."

"They're like all children their age. Do any of your friends have children, Darian?"

"No, and I work too hard to visit any of my friends. On weekends I'm with Wade. Yasmine is a good friend but she doesn't have any children. Monique didn't discipline her children is all I have to say."

Miss Idele opened her mouth to speak, then decided to keep silent. It was no use trying to make the girl understand. She was snooty and too touchy for her own good. Prancing around like she was the queen bee up in here. But Miss Idele loved Darian. Guess her uppity ways were in her blood. She'd seen it in her when she was a child.

Darian walked Miss Idele to the door and kissed her on the cheek. She went back to the living room and turned off the TV. Miss Idele had already coaxed the children into their pajamas. "It's time for bed. Shelby has to go to school in the morning."

Nikki threw her doll at Darian and it landed against her head. Darian turned around to face her. "Why in the devil did you do that?" she yelled, and stomped her feet. "One more time and it goes inside the trash can with all the garbage and dirty trash. Do you hear me?"

"Yes, and I want my mommy. I want to go to school, too," Nikki cried.

"I want you to go as much as you do, but you are still a little girl. Now, scoot, go to bed. Damn," she murmured under her breath.

No one moved. Both girls stared at Darian.

"Now what?" Darian snapped, her hands resting on her hips. "I said go to bed and I mean now." What was going on in their small minds? she wondered.

"Mama always kisses us good night," Shelby said.

Darian sighed. She would kiss them if it meant they were out of her face for the remainder of the night. She had never been so tired. She picked up Nikki, kissed her on the cheek, and then kissed Shelby. "Now, good night." Thank God Miss Idele had washed the dishes, Darian thought.

"Good night, Auntie Darian." They ran off to bed. Darian was sure they were laughing because she kissed them, which was not often. Just as she started to go to her room, the doorbell rang. She sighed and ambled back to the door.

"Vickie!" Darian yelled. "I'm so glad you came." They hugged and then, hand in hand, Darian led

Vickie to the sofa. "You don't know how good it is to see you."

"My mother saw Shirlee in the store and said you were here."

"I'm so glad," Darian answered. "I was going to call you tomorrow. I never thought I would be coming home under such devastating circumstances. I can't comprehend any of it. Everything is turned upside down. It still doesn't seem true. Losing Monique will be like losing half of myself. All the irreplaceable years we've shared. I think the kids know something is wrong but they are too young to understand the reality of the situation. Monique will have to tell them in her own way. I don't know how she's going to when they are so young."

Darian slipped out of her brown boots and placed them next to the sofa. "How do you tell young children about death? Are there any books that can help explain?"

"Everything is not in books, Darian. But it would be an excellent child book to write. How's life in L.A.?"

"I finally earned that promotion I told you about. I often think of all our dreams we had together about going to L.A. to start our careers. I sure miss those fun times." Darian meant it. She missed Vickie terribly.

"Well, I messed up big time. You were smart. I should have listened when you advised me that a married man was only a waste of time," she said, loathing her stupidity. "But once I met Bernard, I was glad that I returned home. At the rate I was going, I wouldn't have found a man as good in LA.." Vickie adjusted the pillow against her back. "I think that I will buy new pillows for this sofa. I'm never comfortable with the small ones."

"I'm happy for you two," Darian said. "And I like the pillows you have now."

"Has Monique made any plans for the children yet?"

"My mom. There's no one else. Pete Jr. is dead and he wouldn't help even if he was alive, the jerk."

"Guess who I saw last month?" Vickie asked.

Darian held her finger under her chin and pondered for a few seconds, but came up with no one. "I don't know, who?"

"Brad St. James. And, girl, he looks terrific, too. He was at Miss Brown's house. She's very ill, you know. He asked about you. Whenever I see him, he asks about you, Darian."

"Was his wife with him?"

"No, of course not. They're divorced. It happened too fast anyway. One month they were dating, two months later they were married. When I asked how she was, he changed the conversation, and fast. But he does have an eight-year-old son.

"Before we went to Los Angeles, we had run into each other twice, but there was never much to say. We haven't seen each other for a long time now. I've never forgotten Brad. He was a nice guy," Darian said with a soft, lamentable look in her eyes. "I don't really know what happened to us."

"We were young and still in college. But there was something in his eyes that told me he still cares for you, Darian. He did a lot of small talk before he asked about you, when I knew all along that was his main concern. It's been that way every time we see each other."

"That's ridiculous, you're imagining things. What happened between us was a long time ago and it wasn't serious anyway. Now, enough about Brad. What about that accounting job you were telling me about at city hall?" Darian inquired.

"I got it. I studied night and day to past the test," Vickie said with pride.

"I knew you would."

Vickie was born and raised in the Seventh Ward about four blocks from Monique's home. She had dark chocolate, smooth skin with a round, attractive face. She was five-six with long, shapely legs, and she looked good in the tight jeans that she was wearing. Two gold earrings dangled from each ear, she had a fashionable short haircut, and her full lips were lined with pink lipstick.

"So, when is Monique coming home?"

"In a few days. I don't know what we would do if we didn't have Miss Idele to help us. My mom doesn't say much. She cries often. I'm trying to be strong but it's hard, Vickie. Odd, sometimes I forget she's so ill. Then I look around and remember what's going on around me."

Darian started to cry, and Vickie hugged her. "Let it all out, honey. You're carrying too much on your shoulders. You don't always have to be the strong one."

Darian cried until there were no more tears. It was after 9:00 p.m. when Vickie left. Darian retreated to her room and undressed, and dragged herself into bed. But as she was easing into a deep sleep, she felt something crawling up her leg. She screamed, threw the covers to the floor, and switched the lamp on to see her attacker.

She saw a lightning bug jump to the floor. Darian shuddered and jumped back, then screamed again. She tripped over her shoes and grabbed the doorknob to keep from falling. Darian clutched a shoe and smashed the bug. She picked it up with a tissue and ran down the hall to the bathroom and flushed it down the toilet.

Darian sighed, taking deep breaths as her heart pounded rapidly. "There, you won't be any more trouble tonight," she said as she watched the little monster disappear down the toilet.

Darian felt her legs shaking on her way down the hall and stuck her head into the girls' room. "Stop the laughing and go to sleep. Remember, tomorrow is a school day. You won't miss school because your mother isn't home."

Darian turned the lights out and lay in bed. She had started dreaming when she heard a voice at the door.

"I want some water," Nikki whined.

"Lord have mercy on me," Darian said out loud. "Come on and get some water." She took Nikki's small hand and led her to the kitchen. "Here, drink this." On the way back, Darian stopped. "I guess you want to pee, too, right?"

"Yes. Mommy makes me pee when I drink water."

"Well, go ahead so I can get some sleep." Standing in the door, Darian sighed impatiently. "Wash your hands before you go back to bed. You should always wash your hands after you use the bathroom."

"I want to sleep with you," Nikki said, looking up at Darian's face with the most innocent eyes.

Oh no, Darian thought. "Come on, you can sleep in the other twin bed. Just go to sleep so I can rest."

"But I want to sleep with you in your bed."

"No, you're not a baby anymore, and we are in the same room. Now, once and for all, go to sleep," she hissed between her teeth. How could she live with children day and night? She wondered if this would be a regular routine with Nikki.

The alarm clock went off at 6:30 a.m. Still tired, Darian turned over in bed and reached groggily for the clock. She thought that she was home in her bed until she opened her eyes. "Lord, am I still here?"

Each morning she awoke was like coming out of a nightmare.

Shelby had to be dressed and at school by 8:30 a.m. Plus Darian had to cook breakfast. She crawled out of bed and went to the bathroom to brush her teeth and splash cold water against her face. When she finished, she placed two bowls on the table and started a pot of water to boil for the oatmeal. Darian felt like she was sleepwalking.

At seven she got Shelby up, helped her dress, combed her hair, and placed their breakfast on the table.

Shelby was grumpy and Nikki was still asleep.

After Shelby finished eating, Darian turned the TV on and instructed her to watch it until she dressed. She finished, and Nikki walked into the kitchen behind her. She touched Darian's leg, and Darian screamed, hopping away from the sink. "Don't creep up on me like that," she yelled.

Nikki's feelings were hurt and she started to bawl.

"She's only a kid," Shelby shouted angrily.

Darian picked Nikki up and carried her to the bathroom to wash her face. When she finished, she went into Monique's room and retrieved her car keys. "Come on, Shelby, it's time for school. Wait a minute, show me your hands." Darian stood in front of the children as they held their hands out.

"I washed mine already," Shelby asserted. Mommy never makes us wash our hands five times like you do." She stared at Darian and, obviously having a frustrating morning, she felt tears running down her cheeks.

"No, I do not make you wash your hands five times a day. Now come on before you are late for school," Darian ordered and grabbed Nikki's hand. They rushed outside and got into Monique's blue VW.

After Darian and Nikki returned home, Darian sat

her in front of the TV and made herself a cup of coffee. She would have eaten a bowl of cereal or a slice of toast, but she had no appetite for food. She grabbed a sheet of paper from the small desk in the corner and titled it Things To Do. The first item on the list was to buy fruits and foods that Monique could eat, and she noticed the kids had too much junk food, too many cookies, chips, and candies. Darian and Shirlee would be bringing Monique home tomorrow, and Darian would have to shop for her, too.

By nightfall, Darian's nerves had been stretched like a rubber band about to pop. Shirlee and Miss Idele came over to help her. She had already gone to the supermarket and mopped the kitchen floor.

Shirlee did the laundry, but she moved like a robot, and every time Darian looked at her, she was blowing her nose like a horn from crying all day. Miss Idele cooked dinner.

"I think we need a break and a cup of tea. It's five o'clock and we've been at it all day," Shirlee said.

"I'll fix the children's dinner. They will eat in the kitchen and we can have tea in the dining room," Darian answered.

Darian was in the kitchen when Shelby and Nikki took a seat at the table. They observed Darian as she pulled down two plates and set them in the center of the table.

"We want our mommy to come home," Nikki whined.

"She'll be home tomorrow, but you and Shelby have to be good little girls because Mommy doesn't feel well. Now eat your dinner." Darian sighed heavily. She just wasn't good at this, and had no patience with young children. She loved her life without children and no hassles or responsibilities to no one but herself.

She loved being free, her career, and the life she had waiting in Los Angeles.

Darian had placed three cups of tea on a tray and headed for the dining room.

As she walked she overheard Shirlee and Miss Idele mention her name, and stopped in her tracks. She knew it was wrong to eavesdrop, but she wanted to hear what Shirlee was saying about her. She didn't need her mother worrying about her, too. She had enough to worry about with Monique's health and the children.

Darian wondered if Shirlee was strong enough to help Monique, knowing that one day she would lose her. By looking at Shirlee, Darian could see that she was mentally and physically drained. As Darian continued her way into the dining room she heard her name again.

"Miss Idele, I've raised my two girls. I can't raise no more children. I'm sure that Darian knows she's going to raise Monique's children. There's no one else and Darian has to do the right thing by her sister."

"I don't know, Shirlee. She has no patience with children and I've heard her mention that she doesn't want any of her own. I'm sure that she can be a loving woman and maybe she's a little snobbish, but she has a good heart."

"I know, but I'm fifty-two. My husband is thirty-seven. It's time for me to enjoy life again. I set aside everything when Ronald died. No, Miss Idele, Darian has no choice. She'll have to stay." But Shirlee was waiting until Monique was home to tell Darian what was expected of her. Maybe when she saw how much the children needed her she'd grow to love them, and who knows? Monique might live longer than the doctor said.

Miss Idele and Shirlee heard the loud clamor in back

of them. When they turned around in their chairs the cups were broken, spattered in pieces, lying in the center of spilled tea. Shirlee and Idele looked at Darian. Her hands were still in the same position as though she was still holding the tray. They looked at one of the cups still rolling and then stopping against the wall, while steam floated lightly from the broken pieces.

Shirlee and Miss Idele looked at each other, their mouths open, and then they looked at Darian as she stood frozen, her eyes wide with anger and shock. The walls of the small dining room seemed to be closing in on her.

"Shirlee, I guess she knows now," Miss Idele said finally.

Chapter 3

"It's not fair, Mama," Darian shouted. "I won't let you do this to me."

"Darian, think about it. It only makes sense that you raise your sister's children. I was responsible for you and Monique, and Monique was responsible for her children. Now you have to take on some responsibility for somebody other than yourself."

Miss Idele swept up the broken dishes off the floor and said good night. This was between mother and daughter.

Darian took a seat at the dining room table and cried. "But you're their grandmother, Mama. I'm just the mean aunt they don't even like."

"That's not a good enough reason," Shirlee said and started to get up, but Darian grabbed her hand.

"Oh, please, Mama. Just think of what you're doing to me, to my life. You're stripping me of everything I've worked for. I'll take a leave of absence from my job and help get the children moved into your house. I'll even help buy you a larger home. Please, my career is booming, and I'm engaged to be married in a year. Children were not in my plans. Taking

Monique's children will ruin all my plans. Can't you understand that?" Darian pleaded. She had to think fast and make Shirlee understand.

Darian's elbows were resting on the table, and her hands clutched her head as she blubbered, but Shirlee was relentless. She just sat there and stared straight ahead.

"I will not raise Monique's children, and I have no intentions of taking one child because they need to stay together. Mama, please don't do this to me. It's just not fair." All of a sudden she felt fiery inside, her head was spinning, and her heart ached. The blue T-shirt was sticking to her underarms with sweat. She felt as though her life were exploding like a volcano.

"Darian, I'll babysit when you need me. Miss Idele is right next door when you need her. Besides, I'll be here every day. Darian, you can't place your own blood in foster homes. Listen, your sister will be home tomorrow. We'll have to finish this conversation at another time. But keep in mind, Darian, there's no one else besides you." Shirlee's elbows rested on the table and her hands covered her face. She was drained.

"I thought you cared about your daughters, Mama. But as it turns out, you care more about Jefferson than us. Why should I have to raise children that are not mine? I don't even want children of my own and Wade doesn't either." Darian felt as though time was racing past her and Shirlee was not showing any signs of changing her mind.

"They're beautiful children, Darian. Trust me, you will learn to love them as though they were your own. One day you're going to thank me for this."

Darian stood up suddenly, knocking the chair over. "That will never happen," she snapped.

Her tantrum caused her head to hurt in both temples. "I can't do it, Mama. It's Jefferson, isn't it? You're afraid that if you take the children you'll be an old grandmother. You know he won't hang around with two small children in the house. Face it, Mama; you are fifteen years older than him. Kids or no kids, sooner or later he's going to leave you for a younger woman."

Shirlee stood up, anger distorting her face. Her eyes flared like flames at Darian's insults. "You're angry now. I'll just pretend you didn't say that," she said through clenched teeth. She snatched her purse and car keys from the table.

"When Monique comes home tomorrow, I'll tell her that I can't take her kids."

Shirlee turned around and took a step closer to her. "If you do, you'll kill her." She walked out the door and slammed it behind her.

Darian sat on the sofa, thankful that the children were watching TV in their bedroom, and had not witnessed the altercation. She was shaken, afraid for her future. What was she going to do? She listened to her own breathing. She had to think of another solution and fast. *She would not raise Monique's children.*

"Nikki hit me with her doll," Shelby complained.

Darian tried to ignore her, but Shelby just stood there waiting for her to reply. "Stop tattling," Darian finally answered as she wiped the tears from her eyes with the back of her hands. No way could she go through this day after day, night after night. Darian felt her life shattering around her, and all the hard work she'd done to accomplish what she wanted was slipping away. She had to speak to Monique about her children. Not tomorrow, but they had to decide where the children would be placed. As for Shirlee, Darian had nothing more to say to her.

Darian looked at her watch. It was time to put the children to bed, and then she thought of something—

they needed a bath. So much work, and it would only get worse, she thought as she prepared their baths.

The next morning was a disaster. Darian was up at daylight to cook breakfast for the children, and each one wanted something different. Shelby wanted pancakes, and Nikki cried for cookies. Just as Darian thought the morning couldn't get any worse, she discovered that Shelby had wet the bed. The second day, Darian thought despairingly. She flopped down on the bed, closed her eyes, held her breath, and counted to ten. She exhaled and opened her eyes again.

She heard a knock on the door and rushed out of the room to open it.

"Hi, Miss Idele." Darian stood aside so Miss Idele could enter.

Miss Idele looked at Darian from head to toe. "You look wore out already, girl, and it's only seven-thirty. Child, you've got to find a routine to make it easier on you."

"No, I don't, Miss Idele. I don't care what Mama says, I won't raise any kids. But I will help Mama financially if she agrees to do her duty as a grandmother. Come on, let's sit on the sofa." All of a sudden Darian thought of Wade. What would she tell him? They didn't have children in their plans for the future. And when she had called him yesterday he was happy to hear her voice. She didn't mention the children.

Darian sat next to Miss Idele. "After I take Shelby to school I have to come back and wash the damn sheets all over again." Darian stopped and took a deep breath, and exhaled an avalanche of tears.

"Look, child, I know it seems unjust to you now, but you will learn to love the girls. They'll add joy to your life, and they are already your blood."

Darian wiped her eyes and sat up again. "How can Mama do this to me? I feel as though I hardly know her. If they were your grandchildren wouldn't you take them?"

"Yeah, honey, but they're not my grandchildren, and I'm not your mama. But I am here to help you, Darian." Miss Idele held Darian's hand lovingly as they continued their conversation. "Now, what can I do to help you?"

"Please stay with Nikki until I take Shelby to school."

"I'll watch Nikki. But, Darian, think before you speak to Monique. I know she wouldn't be able to handle the stress of more worry about her children."

"I will, Miss Idele, but I won't give up my life. Every time I come home I'm reminded of all the reasons I left. The Seventh and Eighth Wards have been neglected like abused children. I still feel the racial tension in the air when I'm around white people. I even tried to persuade Monique to come to California to live, but each time she refused."

"Have you considered taking the children to California?"

"Hell no," Darian replied. She pranced into the kitchen.

Miss Idele shook her head. *It's gonna be drama for sure. She is going to move back to New Orleans and raise Monique's children,* Miss Idele thought as Nikki jumped into her welcoming arms.

The ride to the hospital was quiet. Darian completely ignored Shirlee as though she weren't in the car.

"I hope your attitude changes by the time we get to the hospital. After all, Monique didn't ask for this illness," Shirlee said. She turned the corner looking for a parking place. But Darian kept looking out the window.

"I didn't ask for Monique's illness either, Mama," Darian retorted. She felt strained every time she thought of inheriting the children.

Exiting the parked car, Darian walked ahead of Shirlee. She had nothing else to discuss with her. As for Monique, Darian's heart pained every time she thought of losing her. Telling Monique she had no intention of raising her children would be the hardest thing she would ever do. But she had to find a way to tell her. She had to know.

Darian entered Monique's room first. She froze when she saw Monique lying in bed, her face twisted in pain. She wasn't dressed to go home, and Darian wondered if she should stay longer.

"Are you in very much pain? Should I call a nurse, Monique?" Darian asked and sat next to her.

"It's not the surgery, Darian. It's the agony of leaving my children behind. They're so young. Dying and leaving my children alone is the worst pain I have experienced. I cry every time I think about what's going to happen to Nikki and Shelby. But I'm thankful that my children have you. That quells the torture some. I feel so sorry for women in my predicament that don't have a sister like you."

"I know, Monique." Darian wanted to cry out and looked at Shirlee as she held her head down. Monique's words were so painful she could barely breathe. When or how could she tell her that she couldn't take the girls? Would it make her a disgustingly evil person by not taking her children? Shameful tears leaked from Darian's eyes.

"We'll get through this together, Monique. You've got me and Darian," Shirlee said. Her eyes met Darian's. She could see the resentment in Darian's eyes. Shirlee understood what Darian was feeling.

Trapped and frightened. She would have to persevere; Shirlee was confident that she would.

"Monique, are you ready to go home?" Shirlee asked.

"Yes. I want to go home to my children. Have they run you crazy yet, Darian?"

"Just about, but they will be happy when you get home."

Monique cringed inwardly. It was bluntly apparent that Darian wasn't pleased with her children's behavior. They could be a handful, but they were good girls. In time, Darian would get used to them. Monique tried to tie the belt around her bathrobe. Darian assisted her. Every time she moved, she frowned in pain.

"Okay, let's go. Mama, you can carry her bag, I'll push the wheelchair," Darian said with her back to Shirlee.

"The nurse is coming to wheel me out. You just park the car at the front entrance," Monique instructed. She never lifted her eyes during the ride to the car. All she wanted was for the wretched pain to leave her body.

Shirlee and Darian carefully helped Monique into the front seat of the car. Darian sat silently in back as Shirlee drove. The drive to Monique's house was somber. One would have thought that there had been a tragedy.

As Shirlee parked in the driveway of Monique's home, Idele was sitting on the front porch with Nikki on her lap. Darian helped Monique out of the car. Nikki shrieked with joy and leaped from Miss Idele's lap. She ran to Monique, her arms ready to embrace.

"Mommy's sick, Nikki. I can't pick you up, but you can sit close to me and sing the song that I taught you, okay?"

"Here, I'll pick her up and you can give her a big bear hug," Darian said.

Monique held her close as though she would never let go.

"It hurts, Mommy. You're hurting me," Nikki cried out.

"I'm sorry, baby. I didn't want to let you go." Monique cried inwardly, and turned her face away from Nikki so she wouldn't see the tears. "I missed my children so much."

Shirlee, Darian, and Miss Idele smiled, but everyone was quiet. It was such a sad homecoming, and Monique would have to say good-bye again. The doctor said that she would be in and out of the hospital until her time was up.

The expression on Monique's face was heartbreaking. How could life be so unfair for all of them?

After helping Monique to her bed, Darian hugged and kissed her sister. "I'm going to pick up Shelby from school."

When Darian entered Shelby's classroom, she was waiting, and anxiously ran to Darian.

"Is my mommy at home?"

"Yes. She's waiting for you."

On the way home, Shelby told Darian about her day at school. "I can read better, Aunt Darian. My teacher says she's proud of me."

"Good girl. Your mommy will be proud of you, too."

They were home and Shelby reached for Darian's hand and walked in with her.

Shirlee stood in the middle of the living room, looking at Shelby as she ran to Monique's room. From the sound of the child's voice, seeing her mother was like waking up on Christmas morning to a house full of toys.

"How do you feel, Darian?" Shirlee inquired.

"How do I feel? I'm angry as hell that you expect me to take care of Monique's children. You won't be a grandmother and do what's right, so you put the burden on me." Darian stormed out of the living room and slammed her bedroom door.

Instead of consoling each other, she and Shirlee behaved like bitter rivals. Darian sulked and tasted the bitter tears that dripped and made a path to the corner of her mouth as she stood at the window with a piercing stare. She could see the neighborhood tomcat lying in the driveway.

"Well, it seems she's not taking it well, Shirlee," Miss Idele said.

"No, she's not. I better go in and check on Monique." In five minutes Shirlee was back on the front porch with Miss Idele. They were sitting in patio chairs. "Miss Idele, I don't think I've ever seen Darian so miserable."

"You don't look too good yourself, Shirlee." Miss Idele straightened her dress around her knees, revealing the top of her white socks. She set a tall can of beer on the small patio table.

"I don't look good today because I was drunk as Cooter Brown last night. Jefferson's old polluted, pickled-brain brother came over with a bottle of white lightning. Now I'm sick, I can't eat nothing because I might vomit. Monique is on her deathbed and Darian is acting like she's the one dying. I'm the good-for-nothing mother. They're worrying me into an early grave, too." Shirley wiped the corner of her eyes with a paper towel.

"All I've done for my children and this is the thanks I get. Darian hardly looks at me. I'm fifty-two, my husband is thirty-seven. What would he want with me if I brought two little kids home to raise until they're grown? Darian is still young enough to work and raise the children. She could even have one of her own if she wanted to. I'm too damn old to start over with young children."

"She's angry, Shirlee, and she never wanted children. You can't expect her to be happy about it. That girl knows nothing about children and never wanted to. She's stubborn, impatient, and never kisses or even plays with them. They're your grandchildren and you won't take them. So can you expect Darian to walk around the house smiling about the situation? One day soon she'll get used to the idea, I think." Miss Idele opened the second can of beer she had in her hand, took a long swallow, and felt the bubbles crackling in her throat. "Now, this is good, cold beer on a damn hot day. Summer is coming and tempers are flaring. But this beer sho' is good, Shirlee."

"You know, Miss Idele. This is a bad time for all of us, not just for Darian. I can't eat, sleep, or enjoy sex. My baby is dying and I can't help her."

Shirlee thought of her daughters when they were children. It was easier to deal with them when they were younger. But now she didn't know how to communicate with them.

"The girls were fourteen and sixteen when Ronald died. I didn't even look at another man because my daughters were my life. I didn't have to work. But I chose to work at the sewing factory across town two days a week to teach them the importance of a hard day's work. Ronald left us with a good pension income. Then Darian and Monique finished high school. Darian graduated from college, Monique dropped out because of that no-good fool she married. They had been running around and acting like sex-crazed teenagers before they married. I can't say that I'm sorry he's dead. But it was good that his mama left the house to Monique and her granddaughters. Poor little kids."

"Darian was a handful growning up, Miss Idele. She

always knew what she wanted. She refused to be bullied or bossed around by other kids. That head is hard like granite. I'll bet if she stays with her career, four years from now she will be a vice president. That girl's got brains, although she's a fanatic when it comes to cleanliness, promptness, discipline, and she is a workaholic. She washes her hands all day. I thought that she had that cleaning disease."

"You mean the one that crazy people have? Because my old cousin, Ruth, used to wash her hands all day. But, Shirlee, she was nuts."

"Darian isn't crazy, Miss Idele. She's just a little unbalanced. Although she's acting foolish right now," Shirlee said acrimoniously.

"And she ain't short on looks either, Shirlee. You seen that tight little butt on her, and those long shapely legs are long enough to wrap around a telephone pole three times. Darian's eyes are so light you can see the reflection of yourself in them. I don't know any woman that could hold a candle to her."

"Yes, the Good Lord gave me two good-looking girls. But I was a good-looker, too, if I must say so myself." Shirlee ran her fingers through her hair, pushed her breasts out, and sat up straight.

Shirlee became serious again. "All I know is that I can't be no old grandmother and adopt Monique's children, unless Darian absolutely refuses to."

Miss Idele nodded. "God bless all of you, Shirlee."

"Thank you, Miss Idele. God won't give us any burden we can't handle."

"Amen! I'll drink to that," Miss Idele replied. "Shirlee, you know what you should do?"

"What? Any advice would help."

"Go inside the house and support your daughters. They're hurt and angry. Monique is distraught because she's dying, and worried about her children.

Darian is depressed because she's afraid of changes she'll have to make in her life. A no-win situation is what your family got." Miss Idele gulped the last of her beer.

Shirlee stood up. "I should go in and see if the soup is ready."

Darian was sitting in a chair next to the bed, watching the children snuggle with their mom.

"Nikki, be careful. Don't touch Mommy's chest," Monique whispered. Feeling a chill, she pulled her blue flannel gown up around her neck. She looked at Darian. "She's just too young to understand what it means to have surgery."

"I know," Darian answered. "Are you warm enough, Monique?"

"Yes, but I don't want the bandages to scare the girls."

Maybe she didn't want them to notice her missing breast either, Darian thought.

"Can I get you anything to eat? Mama made some homemade soup. Do you remember when we were little, Mama would always feed us her homemade chicken soup?"

Monique smiled at the recollection of those good times.

Darian blinked back tears. At that moment she felt remorse for thinking of her inconveniences with Monique's children. Life had certainly dealt the family a bad hand, Darian thought.

When Shirlee and Miss Idele walked inside the room, Darian walked out. Shirlee and Miss Idele looked at her as she passed them. It was apparent that she wasn't ready to reconcile.

"Mama, you have to talk to Darian. I know she's

concerned about me, but she looks as though she is angry at the world. It's hard for me to see her like that," Monique said. "I hate seeing her so miserable."

"I'll speak to her right now," Shirlee said hastily and left the room. She went outside where Darian was standing on the front porch leaning against a pole. "We've got to talk, Darian." Shirlee stood in back of her.

"You've said all I want to hear, Mama. Why don't you go in and act like the loving mother with Monique?"

Shirlee sat on one of the chairs. "I said we have to talk, and I mean right now. So sit," she demanded, and pointed to a chair.

Darian sighed and sat in the chair next to her. "What?" She folded her arms in front of her.

"First of all, Monique asked me to talk to you because you're upsetting her."

Darian turned to face Shirlee and looked directly into her eyes. "What did you tell her, Mama?" she asked with concern.

"I told her that you are angry with me, but it's affecting everyone. Monique is in enough pain." Shirlee started to cry, but Darian just looked stone-faced. No tears. No emotion. Just hatred in her eyes as she stared back at Shirlee.

"Darian, you are being selfish. Can't you think of anyone else besides yourself? The kids need you, Monique needs you, and you might not believe it, but I need you to help me through this tragedy in our family. Monique is dying and our lives will not be the same without her. Didn't you come home to see how you could help your sister?"

Darian stood up with hands on her hips. "Why are you here, Mama? Who are you thinking of, Jefferson? Because he makes you feel younger than you are? Well, let me tell you something, you're living an illusion.

You're no young woman, and not taking your grand-children isn't going to change that—"

Before Shirlee realized what she had done, she felt the stinging in the palm of her open hand against Darian's face. Shirlee held her hand in midair and paused, shocked. She saw her fingers still printed against Darian's face.

She couldn't remember the last time she had laid a hand on her daughters. But everything was out of control and she didn't know how to handle it. Shirlee felt dreadful. She couldn't reclaim the happiness they had felt only weeks ago.

Darian was shocked; her face burned like fire. She heard herself stuttering an indistinguishable blur of words and ran to her room. Standing against the door, Darian grabbed her purse and Monique's car keys. She felt as though she was choking and couldn't get enough air into her lungs, and slowly she was dying inside. She grabbed her sweater and ran out the door.

Shirlee ran behind Darian but she couldn't catch her before she sped out the driveway. A passing car blew the horn twice and swerved left to avoid a colli-sion. But Darian didn't look back as the car stopped suddenly.

Shirlee watched with her hand over her chest. Her eyes weakened as she saw double and was sure that Darian would be killed. She went back inside the house and sat on the sofa with chills running down her back. Her family had fallen apart.

When Darian parked her car she was in front of Vickie's apartment complex. She sat there for thirty minutes before she got out and rang the doorbell.

Vickie opened the door. "Hey, girl, surprised to see

you here. What's wrong? You look troubled, and you've been crying. Is Monique okay?" she asked urgently.

"Do you have something cold to drink?" Darian asked.

"Sure, I made some iced tea an hour ago. Think I'll get myself a glass, too." Darian followed Vickie to the kitchen and waited while Vickie poured two tall glasses.

"I had to get away from my mom. This is the worst time of my life!" Darian took a deep breath and sipped her tea.

"What's going on, Darian? I know you're having a hard time coping with Monique's cancer. It must be dreadful."

"That's just half of it."

"What could be any worse?"

"My mother thinks I should raise Monique's daughters. I don't know anything about raising children. You know that I've never wanted children."

"What? You raise kids? You've got to be kidding, girl." Vickie placed her glass on the coffee table and curled her feet up under her.

"No. I'm not kidding."

"What are you going to do? And how can Shirlee place that burden on you? After all, she's the grandmother."

"Tell her that. She's doesn't want any children to interfere with her marriage. Her man might leave her."

"Well, I'll be damned. I've never heard such foolishness. Why would she feel that way? But you know how Shirlee is. Although it would be good to have you here." Vickie laughed, and Darian stared at her as though she had lost her mind.

"I'm not trying to be funny, Darian. But would it really be so bad?"

Darian leaped off the sofa. "I can't believe you said that. You know more than anyone that I haven't the tolerance for children. Those two are rascals. Shelby still pisses in the bed, and Nikki is a crybaby." Darian held both hands to her face and sat down again. "I just can't do it, Vickie. And I don't know what to do about it. My job? Wade? I could even lose the man I love."

"What has Monique said about it?"

"Nothing. I wonder what she's thinking?"

"You better talk to her about it. She needs to know." Vickie heard the mailman placing mail in her mailbox and went to the door.

"I guess I better get back before Monique wonders where I am." She shuddered, and frowned at the thought of going back to Monique's house.

"Anytime you want to talk about it, or get out of the house, you know where you can find me."

"Bernard's out of town again?" Darian asked.

"Yes, but he'll be home tonight. I hate it when he's away."

"You married a good man, girl. I just wish it was me," Darian said sadly. She didn't know what would happen to her engagement if she took Monique's daughters back to Los Angeles with her.

"I'm going. . . ." Darian picked up her purse.

"Girl, I've missed you so much. And you better have that talk with Monique soon. You two need to clear the air and figure out a solution. Tell Monique if I can do anything to call me."

"I will, and of course you're right. Walking around pouting about it doesn't help the situation. Monique needs to know exactly how I feel. I'll give you a call in a day or two."

Darian walked outside and left Vickie standing in the doorway.

Chapter 4

As the weeks wore on, Darian had enough guilt and anger inside to make her explode. And it was noticed by anyone that was in her company. She was impatient with the children, tried to stay out of Shirlee's way, and only spoke to her when Monique was in their presence. Darian constantly paced the floor, barely ate, and couldn't sleep at night. To be alone, she spent time in the backyard. She tried to confide the truth to Monique but could never do so. Either it wasn't the right time, or Monique was in too much pain. How could she watch her sister suffer and tell her that she didn't want her daughters? After all, she did love Monique.

Darian learned to establish priorities taking care of the children. Finally, she had developed a routine with Monique's guidance. First, she cooked breakfast and helped Shelby get dressed. Nikki stayed with Monique until Darian returned, which helped immensely. It seemed as though Nikki had sensed something different about her mother. Every step Monique took, Nikki was right behind her. She cried whenever

Monique was out of her sight. Darian noticed Nikki seemed to resemble Monique more every day.

Darian observed that Monique did everything she could to please the children and avoided chastising them, which made matters worse for Darian because she had to say no to the girls and discipline them.

Darian cooked, did the laundry, and cleaned the house. She and Miss Idele would sit on the porch and talk about the good old days. When Shirlee came over, Darian would keep clear of her.

"Were you asleep?" Darian asked as she peeked into Monique's bedroom.

"No. It's so quiet and I was wondering where everyone was," Monique said and struggled to sit up in bed.

"Here, let me fluff your pillows." Darian pulled the large pillow from Monique's back and fluffed it. "Are you hungry? You're sleeping more today."

"No, I'm not hungry. But I'm glad you're here with me. I know it's a bad time for all of us." Monique frowned and sighed deeply.

"Wait, Monique. I hear Miss Idele calling Shelby. I'll be right back." Darian had heard Miss Idele and Shirlee call Shelby's name at least five or six times without an answer. "Goodness, the kids are going to get the best of her," she whispered as she rushed outside.

"What's going on out here?" Darian asked. Shirlee and Miss Idele had stepped off the front porch, and were still calling Shelby's name.

"We can't find Shelby anywhere," Miss Idele answered.

The neighbor's son ran from the backyard. "I can't find Shelby anywhere." His name was Derrick; he was eight years old and lived in the brick house across the street.

"When was the last time anyone saw her?" Darian asked.

"She was talking to that big boy. I told her to go inside because he is a big bully." He started to walk away but Darian grabbed his arm.

"What big boy are you talking about?" Darian asked, her voice intensifying. "Where does this boy live?"

"With his mama. He is big like his big old mama, and his sister is mean. She says she eats people."

"No one is going to eat anyone around here," Shirlee answered firmly.

"Come on, boy. Show me where this boy lives." Darian took Derrick's hand, then immediately pulled her hand away. "Your hands are dirty," she snapped.

Shirlee and Miss Idele sighed and lookd at each other. "We have no idea where Shelby is and she's worried about the boy's dirty hands," Shirlee said with both hands on her hips.

Darian and Derrick took off running.

"Over there. The haunted brown house is where he lives." Derrick stood back and pointed. "It's the ghost house. Everyone knows it."

Darian stopped in front of the house. To a little kid, the house would be hideous. It was made of red bricks with vines growing wildly on the front and sides of the house. The yard was unkempt and the grass needed cutting.

Darian knocked on the door and a tall, old woman answered and looked annoyed as though Darian was an unwanted guest.

"My name is Darian and I live around the corner. I'm looking for Shelby, my niece."

"Your niece isn't here, miss," the old woman answered.

She was closing the door, but Darian grabbed the doorknob. "Look, miss. Your son or grandson was seen with my niece. Where is he?"

The woman was frustrated. Her dark face distorted,

and she planted her feet apart as she folded her arms across her chest. "I said he's not here so leave me alone. My children are blamed for everything that happens in this neighborhood."

"Well, I suggest you find your son before I call the police. I am serious, lady."

Darian was fearful that if Shelby wasn't here, someone might have kidnapped her. She felt her eyes burning with tears and turned around when she heard footsteps.

"That's him," Derrick yelled, and stood behind Darian.

"Where is Shelby?" Darian asked the boy. He was as big and tall as Derrick said he was.

"Shelby walked home a few minutes ago."

"And where were you all this time, boy?" his mother yelled loudly.

"I went to the store to buy this pop." He held up a bottle of orange soda in his hand.

"Did Shelby go to the store with you?" Darian asked suspiciously. She fought off her urge to panic as she imagined her niece lying someplace dead. "You show me where you left her or I'll call the cops. Miss, tell your son to show me," she demanded.

Derrick was quiet as he listened to Darian yelling at Frederick. She didn't seem to be afraid of him or his mother.

The woman eyed Darian warily. She had rolled her sleeves up and grabbed the door like she would push it open. "Frederick, show this woman where you saw that girl and come right back. I don't want no trouble with you, miss. So after you find your niece, she won't be allowed here anymore." The door slammed in Darian's face.

"How rude!" Darian shouted, made fists, and hurried away from the door.

"Just hope we find her," Darian growled at the boy. "Come on, we better find her fast. Come on, Derrick, you're too slow."

Frederick led Darian around the corner, but Shelby wasn't there. They called her name, searched around another block, but still no Shelby. Darian was frantic, and sorry for all the insults she had said to Shelby. Monique trusted her kids in her care, and look what happened. She was more convinced than ever that she couldn't raise any children. Shelby was home, and in the next minute she had vanished while under Darian's supervision.

"Maybe Shelby ran away from home," Derrick said as he walked beside Darian. "She doesn't like you, you know? She told me so."

"Look, Derrick, you've picked a bad time to be a smart-mouth. If you don't know where Shelby is, then don't say anything, you little brat," Darian murmured under her breath. What would she tell Monique? How would she live with a missing Shelby on her conscience? Shirlee and Miss Idele were outside; didn't they see where Shelby had gone? Apparently not, she thought to herself.

Frederick was angry and walked ahead of Darian and Derrick, as they neared Monique's house. "There she is," Frederick said, and pointed.

Darian's eyes followed Frederick's finger and she saw Shirlee, Miss Idele, and Shelby standing on the lawn waiting for them. "You can go home, Frederick. Tell your mother thanks for her help," Darian said with relief.

"Yeah, right," replied Frederick and started walking in the direction of his home.

Darian let out a deep breath. *Who cares if he's angry?* she thought. She had never been so frightened in all her life. Shelby missing. *What's next?* she wondered.

"Thank you, Good Lord," she whispered and looked up at the blue sky. She felt as though the sun were shining down on her.

Apparently Shelby saw Darian across the street and ran to meet her, not noticing the oncoming car. Darian looked up quickly as she heard Shirlee and Miss Idele scream. "Stop! Stop!" Darian heard them yell out.

Darian froze in her tracks when she heard the tires screech, coming perilously close to killing . . . Darian ran to Shelby and kneeled down on her knees in front of her. "Are you all right, Shelby?" she asked, feeling her arms, her legs. "Don't you ever run across the street again, do you hear me, Shelby? And where have you been? Did anyone hurt you? Answer me!" Darian demanded and grabbed Shelby's hand. With her other hand, she ran her fingers through her hair.

"I . . . I went to Tanya's house and her mommy gave me a cookie. I said thank you like Mommy said. Then I saw Frederick and he gave me a drink of his soda. I tried to come home but I was lost."

Darian grabbed both her shoulders and began screaming. "Don't you ever leave this house again unless you ask me first. You are too young to leave this house alone. Do you hear me, Shelby? I said do you hear me? You scared me to death." Darian pulled her close and hugged her with tears rolling down her face.

Shelby was frightened and cried uncontrollably as she ran into the house to her mother. Darian went in behind her.

Shirlee and Miss Idele just stood by watching the action as if it were a movie.

"Miss Idele, did you see that?" Shirlee asked.

"Yes, I saw it. Looks like Darian loves the children after all. She was so happy to see Shelby safe at home. She's a mother and doesn't even realize it yet."

* * *

Darian wondered how she would have handled Shelby's disappearance if she were her own kid. Her hands still trembled. She could never have any children of her own. She knew that she had frightened Shelby, but maybe now she knew to stay close to home. Darian sighed and shook her head. Tomorrow, she had to have a talk with Monique. It was time she made other plans for her children.

Darian spoke with Bill Landers that morning and he said they were looking forward to seeing her soon. Wade called and said he missed her terribly. Monique needed her, though she had considered returning to Los Angeles and flying home on the weekends. But that would be money that she could use to help the children. Besides, she didn't dare leave Monique.

Darian walked outside with Miss Idele and Shirlee. She needed the fresh air, and the time to calm down and relax before she prepared the children's dinner.

"What are you cooking for dinner, Darian?" Miss Idele sat in a white lawn chair. Her legs were parted and her long green dress dipped low around her ankles.

"Miss Idele, I'm not a very good cook. They're having pork and beans, salad, wieners, and hot dinner rolls."

"That sounds good," Shirlee answered.

Darian nodded. She was still angry at Shirlee. After today she felt worse about the talk she would have with Monique tomorrow. Who would take Monique's children? Would they end up separated, and in foster homes? No. She was sure that Shirlee would take them before she gave them to strangers. All she had to do was stand her ground and Shirlee would give in.

Darian relaxed on the sofa in the living room. She lay

back and her eyes were closed. Shelby walked in softly and sat next to her and tapped her on the shoulder.

Darian opened her eyes. "What is it, Shelby?"

"I'm sorry, Auntie Darian. Are you angry with me?" she asked, her long braids lying over her shoulders.

"I'm not angry but don't ever leave this house again. Always ask me if it's okay." Darian held her small hand. She was undeniably a beautiful child, but rambunctious and stubborn. *She reminds me of myself when I was her age*, Darian thought.

Darian contemplated whether the children sensed that she didn't want to be here. Though it was true, she didn't want them to know that she felt that way.

Darian felt Shelby's small hand rub her arm. Without thinking about it she gently touched Shelby's face. She was surprised when Shelby kissed her on her cheek. Darian looked after her as she ran out the front door. Her walnut-colored face was framed with a full head of sandy hair, almost the color of . . . of her own hair. How amazing, she thought.

Chapter 5

The drive to the hospital was solemn. Monique had spoken to the oncologist earlier, and was told her visit would be approximately two hours depending on how well her body reacted to the chemotherapy treatments.

Everyone was deep in their own thoughts. Shirlee was worried about the whole family, and was thinking how hard it was when Monique's and Darian's dad died.

Darian was thinking of Wade, her career, Monique's health, and the possibility of being forced into motherhood.

Monique was afraid of dying, and worried about how her children would handle the situation when they realized what was happening. She felt like she was being punished. "God, what have I done to deserve this?" At their daddy's funeral, Shirlee had held them close and whispered (as the minister read from Ecclesiastes 3:1–8 in the Bible: to everything there is a season, and a time to every purpose under the heaven: A time to be born, and a time to die), "We are a family and we must hold on to the good memories of your father because he is still a part of our lives."

Monique looked at her mother and sister and

sighed, feeling thankful that she had them. She had been watching Darian with her daughters the last few weeks and noticed she and the kids were developing a bond. Monique knew it was because of Shelby's disappearance. It terrified her as much as it did her family because she physically didn't have the strength to go out and find Shelby herself.

"Monique, we're here," Shirlee said and looked at her daughter. She wondered if Monique had realized the car had stopped.

Darian helped Monique get out of the car; she held her hand as they walked inside the waiting area. Monique was still feeling feeble because of her surgery and lack of an appetite.

The waiting area was decorated in soft pastel colors, airy and deceptively cheerful.

Monique's name was called; she followed the nurse into the examination room. The doctor came in and discussed the pathology reports and the cytotoxic drugs that would be used. She would have a physical examination before each treatment, a blood test, and an X-ray. Monique's tumor had progressed to stage two. The prognosis was unfavorable.

Monique saw no need to discuss it any further. She had heard and lived through it all. She just wanted chemo to be over and done so she could go home.

Dr. Gamble was at least forty with dark eyes and hair. She was friendly, and knowing Monique's condition, she felt her pain. She'd witnessed enough young women with cancer. Some survived, some died, but she felt empathy for all of them. She wanted to send Monique home as soon as possible. Dr. Gamble made a note to call Monique's doctor to discuss how weak she appeared to be.

After Monique's first dose of chemotherapy, Dr.

Gamble gave her a list of the side effects that were normal, and those that weren't.

"I expect to see you here in a week, the same time. Please do not hesitate to call me with any questions," she said and gently squeezed Monique's hand.

Two hours and fifteen minutes later, Monique entered the waiting room. Darian and Shirlee jumped from their seats.

"How do you feel?" Darian asked. She had been watching the door and anticipating Monique's entrance every time it opened. "Did it hurt?"

"My arm is sore because of the intravenous drug that had been administered. But other than that, I feel fine. We can go home." She didn't want to frighten her mother or Darian about the side effects that would occur later.

Shirlee was parking in the driveway when Miss Idele and the children ran out the door. Monique climbed out of the car and kissed her children. Nikki stretched her arms so Monique could pick her up.

"No, Nikki. Mommy's arm is sore. She can't pick you up anymore," Shelby said and grabbed Nikki's hand.

"Auntie Darian, are you going home today?" Shelby asked. She looked up at Darian with a frown across her forehead.

"No, Shelby. I'm staying right here with you," Darian said and smiled as though making Shelby miserable gave her pleasure. "Now, you guys, your mommy needs rest." They went inside and Darian helped Monique get in bed.

An hour later Darian, Shirlee, and Miss Idele were sitting in the living room when the doorbell rang. Darian answered. It was Jefferson, Shirlee's husband.

"Well, look who the wind blew in," Darian commented.

"Hello, Darian. I see you're in a good mood. Always full of sunshine, huh?"

Miss Idele laughed out loud. "Now sit down, Jefferson, and take a load off. I got some white lightning at my house if you want a drink."

"Still a little early in the day for me, Miss Idele. But I might need one if I stay too long," he said with a smirk and looked at Darian. Shirlee got up and kissed him on the cheek.

"I came to see if I could do anything for Monique, or give you and Darian a hand with the children." Jefferson was medium height and thick-built around the chest and shoulders. He was dark-complexioned with a scar at the top of his cheekbone, and wore his black hair close-cut. Jefferson was a contractor with all the characteristics of a construction worker, the buffed arms, tight jeans and T-shirts with rolled-up sleeves revealing hard muscles. His voice was raspy, and he became boisterous when consuming too much alcohol.

Jefferson picked up Nikki and went into Monique's bedroom where she was resting. Her eyes were closed, and he stood there for a few seconds. Jefferson had turned around to walk out when he heard Monique's soft whisper.

"Hi, Jeff."

Flashing even white teeth, he smiled at her. Monique was the only person he knew that called him Jeff. "What's going on, kid? Is there anything I can do?" He sat in the chair beside her bed. The room was small and he didn't like tight rooms or crowds. Nikki jumped out of his arms and scrambled out of the room.

"No, thanks, Jeff. I have everything I need."

Jefferson saw a tear drop from her face onto the pillow. He cleared his throat and wiped his eyes. "I wish you had more time, Monique," It was time he got out of there. After all, men didn't cry, not strong men anyway.

A lump formed inside his throat. He had to be strong for Shirlee. She did enough crying at night for all of them. "I see you were getting some rest so I won't over-stay my welcome." He bent down and kissed her on the forehead. "Just give me a holler if you need anything."

Monique nodded her head. "I will. Was Darian nice?" she asked and smiled. Monique and Jefferson liked each other. But Darian was against Shirlee marrying a man younger than she was.

"You know Darian, sour as buttermilk." He smiled back at her and hurried out. This was all too disheartening for him. After Jefferson walked out he stood in the hall for a few seconds to compose himself. He had lost his mother to lung cancer, and all the sad memories were floating back.

It was later in the day, and Darian had cooked dinner, bathed the children, and washed dishes. She inhaled a long, deep sigh, thinking of how she missed having a dishwasher. She felt like Cinderella doing all the dirty work.

By 10:00 p.m. Monique and the children were asleep. Darian took out the trash, turned out the lights, dragged herself into bed, and was asleep before her head hit the pillow.

The noise was a choking sound that was repeated over and over again in her dream. Darian awakened and looked at the clock. It was only five-thirty. The sun was forcing its way through the faded shade in her room.

"Monique?" Darian's eyes blinked open and she jumped out of bed, ran down the hall, and stopped at the bathroom adjacent to Monique's bedroom.

Monique was on her knees, slumped against the toilet bowl. She was so tired that her head felt too heavy to hold up. She had been in that position for twenty minutes, and now there was nothing left except the bile she felt in her dry throat.

Waves of nausea coursed through her stomach and caused her to retch and cough uncontrollably. She was ill, weak, and dizzy, tears blurred her vision, and her gown was soaked with perspiration. Her body felt sticky and she needed a shower. But she knew that once she finished she would collapse in bed, if not on the floor.

Darian wet a towel in cold water and dropped to her knees beside Monique. "Why didn't you call me?" she asked, frightened. So this was the side effect after chemotherapy, she thought.

"I tried, but I couldn't. It didn't seem like I ate enough for so much to come up," she said between deep breaths, and heaving loudly. She felt Darian pull her down and lay her head on a pillow. Darian ran into her room and got a blanket to cover her shivering, thin shoulders. Monique had been dressing in pajamas and gowns, and had only had the surgery weeks ago. But Darian hadn't realized how slim she had gotten.

"Here, we'll stay in here until it stops. Do I need to call the doctor?"

"No. She told me this would happen." Monique pulled her legs under her and closed her eyes. She was still shivering under the blanket.

"Wait, let me get another blanket," Darian said and ran back into Monique's bedroom. On her way out, she grabbed the phone and dialed Shirlee's number. "Mama, you have to come over here and see that the children get breakfast and take Shelby to school—"

"Lord have mercy, what's wrong, Bay?"

"Monique is sick, Mama. She's vomiting."

Shirlee and Jefferson were sitting up in bed. "I'll slip

some clothes on and be right there. You just hold on, Darian."

"Hurry, Mama," Darian said and rushed back to the bathroom.

"Here's another blanket, Monique." Darian sat on the floor, spread her legs out next to Monique, and placed the wet towel against her forehead.

"What about the children?" Monique asked. "They have to have breakfast and Shelby has to go to school."

"Don't worry. I called Mama, she's on her way. You just lie still," Darian said, feeling the nerves in her stomach tighten. It just wasn't fair that Monique had to endure so much pain.

She sat up against the wall with Monique's head on the pillow beside her. Darian tried to make Monique as comfortable as possible under the circumstances. The small rug on the floor lay underneath Monique as a cushion. The bathroom was small and they were cramped, but Darian refused to leave her alone.

Shirlee ran to the door of the small bathroom. Darian opened her eyes, but Monique kept hers closed. "How is she?" She had to hurry and couldn't seem to shake the ominous feeling that had begun haunting her. After looking at Monique huddled on the floor, Shirlee felt as though her feet were stuck and she had forced herself to move.

"I'm better, Mama. I just want to lie here." Monique's voice was so weak. She held her head up but it fell back against Darian's chest.

"Do you need another blanket?" Darian asked when she saw Monique button her gown, and felt her thin frame tremble against her.

"No, I just felt a chill going down my back."

"I'll start breakfast for the children and take Shelby to school."

Monique felt another wave of nausea rumbling in

her stomach, and any movement would cause another eruption of vomit.

Shirlee heard the retching sound from the kitchen and came back one last time to check on Monique before attending to the children.

Monique placed both hands on her stomach, then turned over on her back. She felt a sharp pain in her side that quickly moved up her chest. The torture was unbearable as she heaved, coughed, and tried to speak, but the piercing pain was too excruciating. The doctor had said nothing about her having chest pains. The room spun, she tried to breathe to prevent suffocating and choking to death. She was paralyzed.

As Darian witnessed her sister's fight for life, a deep tremor coursed through her stomach. "Are you all right, Monique?" But Monique couldn't answer, she couldn't speak, and it felt as though her chest was crushing. She held her hand out for Darian as though she were drowning.

"What is it, Darian?" Shirlee asked as she burst into the bathroom and stepped over Darian. "Monique!" Shirlee shrieked and fell to her knees.

Monique remembered Nikki's birth as she was pulled from her womb. She blinked, tried to breathe again, and saw her two babies' smiling faces. A smile crept into the corner of her full mouth. Her babies were so beautiful, holding their arms out to be picked up and kissed by her. Monique's eyes rolled back, her face relaxed, and this time she saw the faces of two small girls, six and eight, with brown-golden curls bouncing all over their heads and blowing in the wind. "Daddy, Daddy," they yelled. It was Darian and Monique. Daddy's pretty little girls, he called them. He called their names and reached out to touch their faces. Daddy picked up Monique and held her in his arms. He walked away and waved good-bye. Monique reached for Darian's hand, but her hand fell back before she could grab it. The pain was gone, her body relaxed, and she took her last breath.

Darian's hands were trembling as tears poured from her eyes. "Mama, Mama, call 911."

Shirlee couldn't answer, or move. She felt as if time had slowed down to a crawl.

"Monique! Monique," Darian screamed, and cried. She held her sister in her arms. "Don't do this to me, Monique. Don't you dare leave me this way."

Somewhere in Darian's heart, she knew that Monique was gone.

"How could she leave me, how could she die and leave me?" As children, they had promised to be together forever. "Oh, God, how can she leave me so alone?" Darian murmured.

She would take the kids, do whatever Monique wanted, if she would just be alive. Darian laid her head against Monique's chest, rocking back and forth.

Jefferson rang the doorbell. He held his ear to the door and heard crying, and Shirlee screaming into the phone. He dashed inside the house and heard Darian and Shirlee down the hallway. Jefferson ran to the door and kneeled down on his knees. He touched Monique's hand, placed his hand against her throat to feel her pulse. There wasn't one. He laid his hand over her eyes, closing them. *"She's dead, Darian."*

"No, Jefferson, she had months to spend with us. The doctor said she would live for months to come, even a year," Shirlee screamed and placed her hands over her face, stumbling against the wall. She slumped to the floor and held Monique's hand. "My baby, my poor, poor baby," she cried out loud. "Oh no, not yet, Monique, not now." Shirlee raised both hands in the air and screamed with misery and a broken heart. The sound resonated through the house like a roaring hurricane.

Jefferson picked Monique up as though she were a baby. Darian held her hand, trying to keep up with Jefferson's long strides. "She's dead, Darian. You can let go now," he said softly and pulled Darian's hand from Monique. "It's time she rest in peace." But he wasn't at all sure if Darian heard him. And when he looked at Shirlee she was as pale as a ghost.

Darian's hands fell to her sides, but she stayed with Monique. She sat on the edge of the bed and lingered over her as if they were children again.

Miss Idele walked in. "What's all the fuss about up in here?" she yelled from the back door. The children ran into their mother's room, but Jefferson stopped them when they approached the door. "Go watch TV," he mumbled and pointed to the living room before they could protest.

"Shirlee, you in there?" Miss Idele yelled. She heard crying, the children running through the house, and Shelby asking for her mommy.

Miss Idele walked to the door and stopped as she saw Jefferson covering Monique's face with a sheet. She slowly entered the room. Miss Idele had seen enough dead people in her days to know Monique had passed on to her Maker. The suffering pain and worrying about her children were over. She moved her hand under the sheet and touched Monique's thin face for the last time. "What a beautiful, sweet woman she was." Miss Idele grabbed the hairbrush from the nightstand and brushed Monique's hair, folded her hands, and placed them over her stomach. "Now she looks peaceful," Miss Idele said, looking up at Darian and Shirlee. They were holding hands.

Shirlee was stunned. Even when the paramedics came and asked questions, she was unable to speak.

Darian answered all the questions as Miss Idele sat close to her.

"Everything happened so fast," Darian said. "The doctor said she would live for months and she had hard chest pains, and closed her eyes. My sister was gone," she said between sobs.

Shirlee, Darian, the children, Miss Idele, and all stayed home and mourned the loss of their beloved daughter, sister, and friend.

The evening descended with suddenness. Darian and Miss Idele sat on the front porch and talked about her life in Los Angeles.

"What are you planning to do about the children, Darian?"

Darian held her head up and looked at Miss Idele as though she hadn't realized that she had to make the decision about the children. Monique's death had happened so suddenly. "I hadn't thought about it. I was going to discuss it with Monique but it was never the right time. I guess that I thought maybe Mama would change her mind and take them."

"Your mama and I have discussed it more than once. She's not going to take them, Darian. Now you have no choice but to make a decision."

Sometimes Miss Idele mixed her sentences with English and French. Darian had to listen closely to understand her. "If the children were adopted, do you think they could stay together? They may be all right if someone would adopt both."

Trying her damnedest to keep calm in a delicate conversation, Miss Idele didn't answer for a few seconds. She tried to choose her words carefully and without a hint of sarcasm or resentment. Did the girl have no scruples? Miss Idele thought with disgust and pity.

"Can you live with that, Darian? Can you really love your sister and leave her children with total strangers, not knowing how they're treated, or if they are being abused, or getting enough food to eat? Can you do that?" Miss Idele knew that Shirlee would keep the children if Darian absolutely refused. She would never let her grandchildren be placed into a foster home, but first they had to do everything to convince Darian to take them. "The children need to participate in dance classes, Little League, Brownies, and Girl Scouts. And someone with the knowledge to help with their homework. They need everything that Shirlee can't provide."

Trying to hide fear, Darian turned her head. *Why must I be responsible for someone's children?* she thought. But they weren't just someone's children, she knew. They were her sister's children. They were her blood and her family.

Darian felt defeated, and she knew when she was beaten. She had been ridiculously gullible to think she could just say good-bye, pack up, and go home to continue her life where she had left off. And she wondered if Monique's children would grow up to hate her if she left them to be adopted. Of course they would, and with good reason, too.

"So, can you live with it, Darian? If you can, then what are you waiting for? Leave. Let the chips fall where they may. But, child, you will be rippin' and runnin' from your conscience for the rest of your life," Miss Idele said, her words smothered with her Creole French accent.

Darian couldn't speak for a moment. With a mere whisper she said, "I'm staying, Miss Idele. I have to do it for Monique." She started to cry and Miss Idele sat in the chair next to her and placed her arm around Darian's waist.

Darian buried her face in Miss Idele's shoulder. "I'm going to need your help, Miss Idele. I'm still getting used to washing clothes every day, cooking, bathing kids, and the whole mother thing. When night comes I'm too tired to even read a book."

"I know, child. And I'll be here."

Darian felt her heartbeat quicken with anticipation and fear. She had never felt such weight upon her shoulders. Her past life was over.

Chapter 6

"Miss Idele, do you think the children are too young to go to their mother's funeral? Maybe it's not normal for children so young to see their mother buried."

"Shelby needs to go, Darian. She needs to know Monique won't be coming back. I'll stay and keep Nikki if you like. I'm getting old and can't take all the commotion anyway."

"I appreciate that, Miss Idele. Who would have thought that Monique would be cheated out of months by a heart attack? She was too young to die with cancer, but a heart attack? I never would have imagined."

Darian had accepted the fact that she was the children's guardian, and was trying to adjust to it. But she didn't know the first thing about raising children. She had to fly back to Los Angeles and convince Wade to accept the children, too. After all, he loved her and wanted to marry her. She still resented Shirlee, and felt that Shirlee should raise her grandchildren. Wasn't it only natural?

Selecting clothes for Monique to be buried in was difficult for Darian, but Shirlee was in no condition to help with any of the arrangements. She stayed with the children, and Vickie helped Darian. Shelby and Nikki were melancholy and quiet. They were confused by all that had happened.

It was the morning of the funeral, and Darian was tense, and hadn't slept well since Monique's death three days ago. The house was tranquil that morning as though the children sensed their lives had changed.

Darian heard the doorbell, and Vickie's voice as Miss Idele let her in. Right after Vickie walked in, Darian heard the door open and close again. It was Shirlee and Jefferson. Darian stayed in her room until she finished dressing in a black pantsuit. Darian's hair was combed back into a knot at the nape of her neck. Although she was grief-stricken, she fought to stay focused.

"You look pretty, Shelby," Shirlee complimented.

"Auntie bought me my new dress. See the ruffles, Grandma?" Shelby's dress was white with ruffles on the sleeves.

Darian came out of her room with Nikki in her arms. Vickie was sitting on the sofa flipping the pages of *Jet* magazine. Darian looked out the window to see if the funeral limousine had pulled up.

The doorbell rang, and Darian flinched. "Well, it's time," she said. They all walked out slowly and climbed inside the limousine.

The service was brief. Shelby stayed close to Darian and stared at Shirlee as she wept. Darian saw two cousins sitting behind her. When they filed around the church to view Monique's body, Shelby grabbed Darian's hand. Darian was beginning to wonder if she should have left her at home.

It was worse for everyone at the cemetery. Shelby, almost delirious, wanted to know if Monique knew her way home.

Shelby turned around to face Darian. "If you weren't here my mommy wouldn't be dead. You killed her," Shelby shouted. Her small hands were balled into fists and hanging by her side.

Darian gasped. She was too stung to answer Shelby. And she was too numb to move. She trembled, still hearing the angry words ringing in her ear. But after all, she was only a little girl who had lost her mother, Darian reasoned. Still, the words hit her like a swooshing wind. She was lucky to have Vickie by her side.

Everyone looked at each other, and the pastor stopped when he heard whispers about the little girl's outburst. "God bless you, child." Then he continued, but his eyes stayed on Shelby for minutes after her big scene.

Shirlee cried on Jefferson's shoulder. He had to hold her up for the duration of the service. "Oh God, Monique," Shirlee cried out loud. Losing her child was worse than losing their father. She cried and blubbered all the way back to Monique's house.

Vickie went inside with the family in mourning, and the cousins, Vivian and Linda, followed. They attempted to have a conversation with Darian, but Darian focused with all her strength on not losing her mind. She was not prepared for losing her so soon, if ever.

Miss Idele baked chicken, greens, and red beans and rice. Miss Mary, the neighbor across the street, left a chocolate cake with Miss Idele, and Betty, the neighbor next door, left a sweet potato pie. Since the funeral was private, they didn't want to intrude on the family.

Darian and Vickie were in the kitchen alone. "You look terrible, Darian. Have you gotten any sleep since Monique died?"

"No, I can't. My head has been spinning. Mama can't help. The kids are my responsibility. Monique

died much sooner than we thought she would. I had prayed that she would beat the odds and live on."
Darian started to get up, but Vickie stopped her.

"Stay and I'll get what you want," Vickie said. "Bernard won't be home until noon tomorrow, so I can stay with you tonight."

"No. Go home so you'll be there when he returns. I just wanted a glass of water. I'm so glad you're here with me today."

"I'm going to fix you a plate, Darian. You are already too thin."

Darian started to object but Vickie shook her head. "I'll tell you what. I'll eat with you, deal?"

"Deal." Her eyes followed Vickie as she went to the dining room and returned with two paper plates. As a size 10, Vickie looked terrific. Her black hair was combed back smoothly on each side, and her full lips were painted light red. She could wear any color and look good.

"When was the last time you ate anything, Darian?" Vickie placed her plate in front of her.

"I ate a sandwich yesterday around noon. After everything that's happened, I forgot to eat. Damn, I sure missed you."

"Well, we're together again. I know you wanted to go back to L.A. and your career. But you can do the same thing here. And be happy if you just give yourself the chance."

Darian heard Nikki crying and went to the living room. "What's wrong, Nikki?"

"I want Mommy," she said and stuck her thumb in her mouth.

"I told you Mommy wouldn't be back," Shelby answered. "She'll never come back."

"No, she won't," Darian said and picked Nikki up. "Shelby, did you eat lunch?"

"Some of it. But I put the pie in the trash. I didn't like it."

Darian looked at her and shook her head. She heard her mother in the dining room talking to Jefferson and Miss Idele. Linda and Vivian had come and left. They were never too friendly anyway. Darian took Nikki back into the kitchen with her.

She sat at the table with Nikki on her lap. "I don't know what to do next, Vickie. I don't even know where the children's birth certificates are." She sighed. "So much to do. I think it would be good for the children if I redecorate this house. You know, use different colors to make it brighter. Do you think that's a good idea? Or should I leave it alone for the children since they are used to it?"

She felt anxious and nervous. "I just don't know what to do, Vickie."

"Honey, the first thing you'll have to do is find some kind of common ground with Shirlee. The children need both of you, and you need her help. This is not something that you had planned. Nothing has happened so bad between you two that you can't talk at a time like this," Vickie said seriously. She sat opposite of Darian at the round table eating a slice of chocolate cake and sipping on a cup of coffee.

"I'm just so angry with her. I don't know if I can talk to her right now." Darian stared fixedly at the picture on the wall. "Tomorrow, I'll try."

"You should know more than anyone that there may not be a tomorrow. Just do it. You are the strongest woman I've ever known, Darian. You're hurting over your only sister's death, but you are still composed. I know you too well. You'll die before you grieve in the presence of others. And you'll never ask for help. This is the best chocolate cake I've ever eaten."

"I had to be strong. When my father died, my

mother almost died with him. She was a total mess, like she is now, and I had to take care of Monique. I was only fifteen years old and Monique was twelve, and you know how wild she was. I took care of both of us because my mother couldn't. It's always been me and Monique," she said as she heard her own voice quaver. "But I'll talk to her tomorrow."

"I think you should. You can't change your mother, but she can help you. And, honey, she's not going to take the children." Vickie looked at Darian, and she looked like the woman in the picture. "Who's that?"

"It's my grandmother, my father's mother. Everyone says I look like her."

"You do. You look more like her than Shirlee."

Darian noticed that Nikki had fallen asleep in her arms. "Let me lay her in bed. And, girl, she's heavy when she's asleep."

Darian came back to the kitchen where Vickie was waiting. "Maybe I'll redecorate Monique's room for the girls." Should she sell the house and move the children to a different neighborhood? It would take some thinking about. She would have to make a lot of decisions. She laid Nikki in bed and covered her. She couldn't believe she had two children and had no inkling what to do with them.

As Darian walked back into the kitchen, Vickie was standing at the sink rinsing off the dishes and drying her hands.

"I guess it's time I leave. Call if you need me for anything."

Darian got up and hugged her. "I'll need you so come back soon." Darian walked Vickie to the door. After Vickie left, Darian sat on the sofa in front of the TV.

Jefferson walked in from the dining room. "How are

you holding up, Darian?" he asked, standing close to the sofa.

"I'm trying, Jefferson. I'm trying for the children."

Jefferson nodded. "It takes time."

"How would you know that, Jefferson?" Darian asked.

"My grandmother died when I was only fourteen. It was hard and it stayed with me for a long time."

Darian felt ashamed. "I'm sorry, I didn't know."

Shirlee was crying, and hadn't eaten since the day before. She was ill and Jefferson had to help her to the car so he could take her home.

Miss Idele sat beside Darian. "It's almost six o'clock, Darian. Do you need me to bathe the children?"

"No, Miss Idele. Tomorrow is Saturday and they can stay up later tonight. Bathing the children is the least of my worries. I have to learn simple things like what medicine to buy for colds, how do I explain when they ask why their mother died, and so on and so on. And I have to get a job, somebody to keep the children. I don't know where to start." She felt so tired, confused, and misplaced. She didn't belong here, had never wanted to move back to New Orleans anyway. Her home was Los Angeles where she was happy, smart, and had a terrific life to look forward to.

Miss Idele stood up and scratched her head. "Some things will come natural. And all you have to do is holler if you need me. You've just taken your first step. You've accepted what's expected of you. It's the right thing to do, girl."

Darian looked at Miss Idele and realized that she knew nothing about her when she was a younger woman. They had known each other since Darian was a child, and it seemed that Miss Idele was always an old woman. What kind of life had she lived before they met? "Miss Idele, do you have a son?"

Miss Idele sat down again. "Yes. His name was Melvin. But he was hooked on heroin. Took too much and killed himself. I mourned for a long time after my Melvin died." She turned her head away as though she couldn't continue. All these years and she still couldn't speak of him. She sighed and closed her eyes. Melvin was her only child, and when she lost him, she lost everything. She lost her husband, her sex drive, everything.

Darian touched her hand. "I'm sorry, Miss Idele. We don't have to talk about him."

"That's okay, child. I've accepted the fact that Melvin was a dope addict. He was young when he died. Now, I'm tired and ready to go to bed. It's been a sad day." She felt as though her heart was being carved from her chest. Every time she spoke out loud about Melvin, her heart ached all over again.

"You go home and get some rest, Miss Idele." Darian was sorry she had asked about her son. She walked Miss Idele to the door and gave her a tight hug before she left.

It was nine o'clock and Darian put the children to bed. She needed to be alone so she could think. And she was always so tired. Shelby had tested her patience every way she could.

Darian sat on the sofa alone. Trying to stave off anxiety, she flipped the TV from channel to channel. Then flipped it off again. She thought of Monique, and wiped her tears. She flung the remote to the other end of the sofa and cringed inwardly; it was no use. She couldn't hold back the tears that began to overflow. The resentment, the dread of losing Monique, it all hit her at once. She cried until she retched and tasted the bile in her throat. The room was closing in on her, and she was struggling to do the right thing for her sister. But, God, how she hated it, she hated everything about her current life, the house, the city, and most of all she hated Monique for leaving her. They had been friends forever. Now she had to return to Los Angeles to tell her boss, and especially Wade, that she was relocating to take care of her new family.

Darian lay on the sofa and cried until she had fallen into a deep sleep.

"Mommy, Mommy, Mommy," Nikki cried. She ran from room to room and into Monique's bedroom and climbed onto the middle of the bed and cried. Then she ran back to the living room and sat on the sofa near Darian's feet.

"I want my mommy," Nikki cried out again and pushed her thumb into her mouth.

Feeling the movement against her feet, Darian reached groggily for the little hand and opened one eye. Nikki was sitting there with a tearstained face that was as pretty as the doll that she held in her hand. "Why are you crying, Nikki?" Darian asked. She knew without asking but tried to say something to pacify her.

"I want my mommy. Where is she?" She hid her face in Darian's lap.

Darian gently held Nikki and rocked her.

"Look, Nikki." She held Nikki close. After all, she was only three years old. Why wasn't there a book to explain to young children about death, especially the death of a parent? That's something she had to remember. Later, she might write one herself. But first she had to learn to help Monique's children cope with their mother's death.

"Mommy is gone to heaven and she doesn't want you to cry. She said you would be a brave girl." Darian pointed up at the ceiling. "See, she is watching you but you can't see her." Darian was sure that at three years old, Nikki didn't understand any of her explanations about her mommy.

"Will she bring me some candy?"

"No, love. But she's watching because she loves you. Tomorrow I'll buy you some candy."

"Then why did she leave us with you? Why didn't she stay with us?" Shelby asked in an angry tone of voice.

Darian jumped at the sound of Shelby's voice. She hadn't heard her walk into the living room. And again the voice was angry. Darian knew that Shelby understood that Monique wouldn't be back. She just didn't understand the circumstances.

"I said, why did she leave us?" Shelby demanded again.

Darian took a deep breath, sighed as though she was ready to give up. "You guys have to remember that your mommy wanted to stay. But God needs her right now. Just always remember that she is watching over you and remember how she took good care of you," she said as she watched their solemn expressions. If only she could convince Shelby, then Nikki would believe her, too.

Shelby stood there and just looked as though she was trying to decide if she believed anything Darian had said. She took a seat on the sofa beside Darian and Nikki.

"I'm hungry. Is it a school day?" Shelby asked.

"No, not today. How about pancakes? Go wash your faces and brush your teeth." So much for the days that she could wake up and stay in bed or just turn over and go back to sleep. Now she couldn't even do it on the weekends. "Damn you, Mama," she whispered to herself.

Chapter 7

Shelby was at school, and Nikki was still asleep. Darian placed her cup on the coffee table in front of the sofa, the phone in her hand. She had tried to tell Wade about the children, but never found the right time, or words. But whom was she kidding? Wade had said more than once that he didn't want any children, and so had she.

She sighed as she dialed the phone. It rang three times and he answered.

"Hi, baby, when are you coming home? I thought you would come back weeks ago."

Darian listened to his anxious voice coated with excitement. It was so refreshing to hear someone that sounded happy. "Wade, I'm leaving in a couple of days. I hope you'll be happy to see me," she said and wiped a tear from her cheek.

"Of course I'll be happy to see you, Darian. Why would you doubt it?"

She closed her eyes and held her breath for a few seconds before she could speak again. "Because I have to raise my sister's children. Looks like we have two children before we get married. But—"

"Wait, slow down a minute here." He got up off the sofa and went to the window, not sure if she was serious or joking. All he heard was silence on the other end of the phone.

"Wade, honey, I'm serious," she said and closed her eyes, and waited for his reply.

Wade rubbed the top of his head. "You're kidding, right?"

"No, Wade, I'm afraid not. My mother says she's too old and I can't stand by while my sister's children are placed in foster homes. They belong to my only sister, and we were close. She would have done the same for me."

"Except you don't have any children, Darian."

Darian cringed at the iciness in his voice. "Baby, I know it's a shock to you. But it was for me, too. Together we can handle it. Wade, I can't just walk out on the girls." She was pacing back and forth in front of the sofa, and stopped at the window. The wind was blowing and a small branch fell from the tree.

"I'm sorry, Darian. I don't want any kids of my own, and I know that I don't want anyone else's. We've agreed no children a thousand times."

"But just think about it, Wade. I'll be home in a couple of days." She wiped another tear. He sounded so cold and remote, and it made her stomach cramp and her palms sweaty. She was losing the man she loved.

"You can come home, Darian, and we can talk. Something this important needs to be discussed in person, don't you think?"

"Yes, of course you're right. But as much as we love each other, we can do anything together, Wade," she said and listened for a similar response. But he had already hung up.

That night Darian was quiet and patient with the

children. After they went to bed, she packed and then cried herself to sleep.

It was Saturday, cold and raining outside. Darian had packed and was waiting for Shirlee and Miss Idele to come over and keep the children while she flew to L.A.

"Hey, Bay. It's quiet in here. Where are the children?" Shirlee asked as she walked inside and threw her jacket on the back of the dining room chair. She glanced in the mirror on the way back to the living room. "Damn wind blew my hair all over my head and I stepped in a damn puddle of mud."

"The kids are playing in their room, and your hair looks fine, Mama."

Shirlee looked at Darian's trembling hands. She was concerned about Darian's health; she was nervous enough to make herself sick.

"Don't worry, Darian. Everything will work out, and you have a life here. I'm glad you're home, Bay."

"Yes, I know you are, Mama. Now you don't have to raise your own grandchildren." Darian didn't wait for a reply and walked away.

Shirlee's face drained as she watched Darian's back. Would she ever forgive her? she wondered. She felt her heart palpitating and took deep breaths until she calmed down.

"Darian, Shirlee," Miss Idele yelled from the kitchen.

"We're in the living room, Miss Idele," Darian answered.

Miss Idele walked in and glanced at the luggage in the middle of the living room. "So I see you're all ready to go?"

"Yes, my friend Yasmine is going to stay with me until Monday and help me pack. I will be back on Tuesday."

"Darian, don't worry so much. Like I said, I'll be here all day, cook dinner, and give the children their baths, and Miss Idele will sleep over at night," Shirlee said and glanced in the mirror one last time. She turned from side to side, admiring her full breasts and tight jeans. "Gee, do I look like I'm gaining weight? I should be losing because I can't eat."

Darian's back was turned to Shirlee. "I really hadn't noticed, Mama. And if you are gaining you're at the menopausal stage in your life, so you should expect a change."

Shirlee jerked her head and looked at Darian, but she was already walking out of the room. "Did you hear what she said to me, Miss Idele? That was completely disrespectful."

"Yeah, try telling her that."

Darian had gone to the girls' room to say good-bye. First, she kissed Shelby on her forehead, and Nikki jumped in front of her to be kissed, too.

The ride to the airport was quiet. Darian felt she could never love another man as much as she loved Wade. They were friends, and had laughed, talked, and cried together. Darian loved Wade like Juliet loved Romeo, and she supported Wade through many trials and tribulations. He wasn't able to see his daughter as often as he wanted because his ex-wife had taken her to New York to live. There was the time he had broken his leg and gone unemployed for almost a year. Yet the last conversation with Wade was not a good omen of things to come. Contempt stirred in Darian's spirit because she felt that Wade was insensitive to her feelings at her lowest moment. It had crossed her mind more than once that Wade could have at least visited her for a few days especially during Monique's funeral.

Shirlee made a left turn following the sign that said AIRPORT ONE MILE, and reached to change the radio station as she noticed Darian biting her bottom lip. Shirlee parked in front of American Airlines. "If you need an extra day or two, don't worry about the children, they'll be all right, Bay."

"Thanks, Mama. I know they're in good hands." She hesitated for a few seconds, and then leaned over and gave Shirlee a brief kiss on the cheek.

Darian checked in and went to her gate. She bought a magazine and flipped through the pages until it was time to board the plane.

Darian's face lit up in a wide smile when she spotted Yasmine waiting at the gate.

"Girl, I am so glad to see you." Yasmine beamed. She took a step back. "You're so thin, haven't you been eating?"

"I haven't had very much of an appetite since I left L.A. I'm always busy with the children. In the evenings I'm too tired to eat."

"Well, I set some empty boxes inside your apartment on my way to pick you up." They walked through the crowd. "Oh, and I have to tell you about the new buyer at the San Francisco office." Yasmine always talked fast when she was excited. "I wish you were here to stay."

"So do I, girl."

"You know what I'm thinking?"

"No. But I know you'll tell me," Darian said and laughed.

"Maybe Wade will have a change of heart about the children once he sees you. I mean, who would have thought that you of all people would change your mind about raising someone's kids?"

"They're not someone's. They're my sister's kids."

They went to the escalator and followed the arrow for luggage pickup.

Darian shook her head. "I didn't change my mind, Yasmine. Circumstances changed it for me. Sometimes you have to do what's right. After we get to my apartment can I use your car? I have to go to his apartment right away."

"Of course."

Darian stopped. "I'm lucky to have a friend like you. Please come to New Orleans for a visit."

Luckily, Darian's luggage was the first piece that glided from the plane so she could grab it and start for the car. After they stepped outside, Darian took a deep breath and felt the warm air against her face.

"Sunny California," Darian said and smiled as they rode down Sepulveda Boulevard going north.

"We're home," Yasmine said and parked in front of the apartment complex.

"Yasmine, is it all right with you if I take the car now? I haven't seen Wade for over a month, and I can't wait a minute longer. Oh, how I've missed that man."

"Go. I can take your luggage inside, and I had already bought a pizza for lunch."

"Good," Darian said with a twinkle in her eyes. She and Wade had never been apart for so long.

She sat in front of Wade's apartment building combing her hair and applying fresh lipstick evenly on her lips for about three minutes before she ran upstairs to make long, passionate love with him. His green Jeep was parked across the street.

Darian started to buzz for entry, but the large glass doors were ajar. If she could get the tip of her fingers inside, she could get a tight grip and pull it open. Darian walked down the hall to apartment 10 and rang the bell. All she wanted to do was spill out her love for him. If he accepted her with children, she knew that she could be a good wife and mother. She rang the bell again, and he opened the door.

"Darian, I was expecting you tomorrow." He was only wearing jeans, and nervously zipping his fly. "Why didn't you call me? I would have picked you up at the airport." He ran his hand over his head, and still, he didn't invite her inside.

"I couldn't wait to see you, baby. Can I come inside?" she asked, taking a step forward.

Wade looked in back of him, but before he could answer, Darian stepped around him and was inside his apartment. She stopped abruptly when she faced a tall blond in the living room wearing Wade's brown bathrobe that Darian had bought him last Christmas. The woman stopped in the middle of the room and looked Darian in the eyes.

Darian's dreams went up in a blaze. It was quiet; everyone stopped talking in midsentence. She looked at Wade and back to the tall blond-haired woman. Seconds passed and she was still unable to speak. She just stood there as though she were a statue. She was in love with Wade and wanted so much to feel his strong arms around her, and he was with another woman. *Another woman!*

"Darian, I'm so sorry. But you really should have called first." He placed both hands on her shoulders, and before he could speak she slapped his face so hard that her hand burned.

"You liar. How long has this been going on behind my back?" she shouted.

Wade stepped back, his hand still against the side of his face. The blonde noted the wild look in Darian's eyes and rushed back to the bedroom.

Darian turned to walk away and saw Wade's hand reaching out to her.

"I didn't mean for you to see this, Darian. . . . I really didn't mean to hurt you. But I can't marry you, and, well, well, you see, Shannon is pregnant and we have to at least try and make it because of the baby."

Her head was spinning, and she saw double. "A *baby?* I know you didn't say that you had to make it with her because of a *baby*. You said after your ex-wife left with your daughter, who you haven't seen for over two years, that you didn't want any more children. Now you say she's pregnant?" she asked, both hands on her hips. "You're no man with your sorry ass." He took a step toward her and she raised her hands and pushed him away.

Wade wasn't expecting her to push him and stumbled against the small table. The lamp fell to the floor and shattered into pieces.

Darian ran to the car, got inside, and beat the steering wheel with her fist. She was crying as she drove off. "Pregnant? Pregnant? Liar," she shouted. She felt sick inside. He had broken her heart.

"What did the jerk say?" Yasmine asked.

"That I should have called first, and that he was sorry, and get ready for this. She is pregnant. I hate him, Yasmine. They were sitting on the sofa, and Darian wiped the tears with a napkin that was beside the pizza box.

"But what did he say about Monique's children?"

"What was there to say? His answer was there in front of me. Seeing this woman said all there was to say. He betrayed me," she yelled. "What have I done to have my life turned upside down?" she yelled. Exasperated, she put her face in her hands.

"One day I woke up with this big promotion that I worked my ass off for, had a man that I loved, and my sister. Damn!" Darian laid her head on Yasmine's shoulder and cried. Then she stood up and went to the bathroom to wash her face in cold water. When she returned to the living room, Yasmine was eating a slice of pizza. "Aren't you hungry, Darian?"

"I can't eat anything now. I hate everything about my life," she murmered between tears. Darian felt as though she was withering away like a flower left too long without water. "I hate that I woke up this morning," she yelled and beat her fist against the arm on the sofa.

Yasmine turned around to face Darian. "I never thought he was good enough for you anyway. And now he has another woman pregnant. He's no good. What a jerk! As far as I can see, today was a blessing in disguise for you. One day you will realize it, too."

Yasmine was an attractive Mexican woman with smooth brown babylike skin and an accent in her voice that enchanced her natural beauty. She grew up in Santa Ana, California, and was the oldest of three siblings.

Darian sniffed and blew her nose. "Well, I need to call Bill and submit my resignation before I return to my new life. I can have my furniture placed in storage until I decide what to do about it."

"What are you going to do when you get back to New Orleans?"

Darian pulled off her black boots and curled her feet under her. Her blouse was hanging outside her jeans and her face was wet. "I'm going to check on a dancing school for the girls, and I have to put some stability back into our lives." She sighed heavily. "I need it as much as the children do. How could Wade do this to me? I stood by him when he had nothing."

"He still has nothing if you ask me. It's best that you

find him out now, rather than marry him and get a surprise." Yasmine took a big bite out of her second slice of pizza.

"I guess you're right. But it still hurts."

"Apparently you two were not as close as you believed. Now, I'm going to pour us a glass of wine. You can use one, and I didn't buy that pizza for you to cry over Wade."

They packed until eight that night, and on Monday morning Darian sat on the sofa with a tearstained face. She looked at the vacant walls, boxes stacked in every corner, and it was like saying good-bye to half of her life. She watched Yasmine as she carried two cups of coffee and sat next to her.

"Bill Landers was very understanding. I explained that I would be raising the children."

"Bill's a good guy. What time will the storage people get here?" Yasmine asked and coughed. "I didn't realize this coffee was so hot. I burned my tongue."

"Be careful, girl." For the first time during the entire weekend, Yasmine got a smile out of Darian. The doorbell rang. "That's the movers, Yasmine. Open the door for me."

"Do you think you will ever come back to L.A. and live?"

"At first I had considered it. But right now, the way I feel I don't ever want to see this city again. But I have had some great times here. Wade was a big part of that, but what a waste. I can't believe him."

"Well, for what it's worth, you are a great woman. This is just a temporary setback. I know you feel like crap, but things will improve."

The storage movers loaded the last chair on the truck. Darian looked around her apartment once more. "I'll miss this place," Darian said, tears burning her eyes.

"I'm going to miss coming over, watching movies, and eating junk food on the weekends," Yasmine said as tears escaped the corners of her eyes.

They both looked around the apartment once more as they walked through the door and closed it behind them for the last time.

Chapter 8

It was a rainy Monday morning in November. Darian and Nikki had taken Shelby to school. They returned home, Darian did the laundry, and Nikki helped make the beds. Each time Darian went into Monique's room, she noticed that she would experience frightening flashbacks of Monique dying from a horrible heart attack. It seemed as though Monique was with her in every room she went to.

Darian stepped into the center of Monique's room wondering if she should redecorate it with a few pieces of her own furniture. She had given the girls their room back and she slept in the small room next to them. It was too soon for her to occupy Monique's room. She watched Shelby when she walked past her mother's room. She would stand and stare into it as though she were there.

"Darian," Shirlee yelled from the front door.

Darian felt as though she was coming out of a deep trance. She jumped at the sound of Shirlee's voice. She walked back to the living room, where Shirlee was placing a bag on the dining room table.

"On my way over, I stopped at the Café Du Monde

and bought some beignets for breakfast, and then I decided to stop at Loretta's French Market to buy some seasoning so you can cook something besides pork and beans and hot dogs. I knew you would have asked for pralines since they're your favorites." Shirlee rubbed her hands together to warm them as she looked around the room. "It looks nice in here. Where's Nikki?"

"Nikki, Grandma wants to see you," Darian yelled down the hall.

Nikki ran into the living room wearing red overalls and a yellow T-shirt. She jumped into Shirlee's arms, kissed her on the cheek, and ran back into her and Shelby's room.

"Nikki's in a hurry. What's she doing back there?" Shirlee asked.

"Playing with her dollhouse." Darian poured two cups of coffee and took them to the dining room table.

Shirlee followed Darian from the kitchen. "How's the children getting along?"

Darian looked at her mother for a few seconds. Today was Monday. Shirlee hadn't seen her grandchildren since last Thursday. Darian didn't know if she should throw her out and tell her not to come back, or just simply ignore the question. "The children are just like they were when you saw them last week, Mama. Nothing's changed. Nothing." She bit into her beignet.

"Didn't Shelby give you my message Saturday? I was ill with the flu and I didn't want to bring the germs over here. I figure you have enough to handle without the children getting sick."

"No, Mama, Shelby doesn't tell me a damn thing unless it's something to make me miserable or angry," she said with disgust. "She says as little as possible to me. And she still thinks that Monique died because I came here. Isn't she's a little young to be so mean and angry? Anyway, I don't know what to do with these children. I keep thinking that maybe if I move them into a different neighborhood it may be better for them and they wouldn't hurt over so many memories. I don't like this house or the neighborhood anyway. But I just don't know." Darian took a swallow of the coffee and coughed. She had made it too strong. "I need to add more water."

Shirlee listened as she coughed and cleared her throat. She could still feel tension in the air between herself and Darian.

"I don't think you should move the children, Darian. This is their home and Nikki was born here. Give them more time, Bay. What are you going to do with your life, Darian?"

Darian sat back in her chair and pondered for a while. *So now she's worrying about my life.* "I don't know right now. I suppose I could get a job as a buyer in one of the large department stores. I have money saved, and I received my pension statement in the mail, so I have enough money until the children have accepted the fact that Monique is gone and won't be back. I don't want to put them through too many changes so soon. And I won't go back to work until they are all right with me leaving them every day. It's going to take a lot of work with Shelby. Mama, soon I will move us into a different house."

"You do what's best, Bay."

"I hear the mailman." Darian strolled out of the dining room and returned with a stack of mail in her hand.

Shirlee looked at Darian's face. Sometimes it was like looking in the mirror when she was younger. The light brown complexion and the color of her hair. Monique looked like their father with a darker complexion. She and Darian had Shirlee's curly hair.

Shirlee picked up the two cups and went to the kitchen and placed them in the sink. She stood there and looked out the window. Monique used to sit on the grass, read a novel, and watch her children play. Sometimes she ran and played in the grass, tumbling to the ground. Shirlee wiped a tear and followed Darian back to the dining room. Darian opened the mail.

"What's all that?" Shirlee asked.

"Monique's mail. I need to see if there are any bills to be paid. Tomorrow I'm going to Shelby's school and let her teacher know she can contact me for anything."

"That's good, Darian. I hadn't thought of that. One of these days the children are going to thank you." Shirlee knew that the children needed Darian more than they needed her. Neither she nor Jefferson had the education to help with their homework, nor the patience. Yes, Darian was just what the children needed. "Monique didn't have much money struggling alone with the children. But she does have a small bank account. The bankbook must be someplace in this house, probably in her bedroom somewhere. I'll be helping you with them, too. If there are bills in the stack to be paid, give them to me. I don't want you spending all your money," said Shirlee.

"Thanks, Mama." They heard a knock at the back door. "That must be Miss Idele. She comes every morning to see if I need her." As Darian rushed to the door, she answered the phone. But it was a wrong number. She opened the door for Miss Idele.

"Come on in, Miss Idele. Mama's in the dining room."

"Darian, you have some more of that coffee? It looks strong enough to grow hair on your chest. It's just what I need."

"Sure, Miss Idele. I'll get you a cup." Darian went to the kitchen.

Shirlee pulled her mirror from her purse and

checked her hair. She looked at Miss Idele and smiled. "It's a little windy outside, you know. I don't want my hair standing on top of my head."

"What difference does it make, Shirlee? You look in a mirror all day when it's not windy," Miss Idele teased and laughed, her gold teeth flashing.

"She's adapting well, don't you think, Miss Idele?" Shirlee whispered.

"It's too soon to know, but she's trying. She would never let Monique down. But, Shirlee, don't push her too hard. Darian is not Monique. She'll take care of the babies but she won't take orders from you unless she thinks she needs to," Miss Idele said, scowling.

"Here's the coffee, Miss Idele. Are you ladies going to stay here with Nikki?"

"Sure, Bay," Shirlee answered. "Do you need me to do anything while you're gone?"

"No, but thanks. Just take care of Nikki for me."

"This coffee is good, Shirlee. But I got something better. I bought a large bottle of that good corn liquor from Old Man Jack last night. I say we get a taste. It is good in coffee."

"Okay. Let me get Nikki. She'll play with that dollhouse all day. These days, Miss Idele, I need something with a kick to it. Sometimes I don't know if I'm coming or going," Shirlee said and went down the hall to get Nikki.

"I'm ready, Miss Idele. I tell you Nikki runs like a little chicken."

They left for Miss Idele's house, Shirlee holding on to Nikki's hand.

As they walked into the living room, like always, Shirlee felt as though she were misplaced in a flower garden and momentarily blinded by the gaudy colors. The drapes were old with green leaves that stood out too bright, the large rug in the middle of the room was green and yellow with flowers, the sofa and love seat had the same green leaves that were in the drapes. The small house was clean, and warm with care, but the brown rocking chair, the old piano, and the large vase of assorted silk flowers were too much for a small room.

"Have a seat, Shirlee, while I get some glasses and a tea cake for Nikki." Idele went to the kitchen and left Shirlee standing in front of the picture over the mantel.

The gold frame had faded into a rust brown. There were five members of the church including Pastor Black standing in the middle. His large nose protruded like a sore thumb, and his round, large eyes seemed to be staring back at Shirlee.

"Shirlee, you're looking at that picture like they are looking back at you. Come here and have a drink." Miss Idele poured some in each cup. They were sitting in the dining room while Nikki sat on the floor eating her tea cake and watching cartoons on TV.

"This picture has a story to it, Miss Idele, and every time I see it I remember when my girls were young. I didn't let my gentlemen callers stay overnight. But one day I went to Pastor Black's office at the church to turn my raffle ticket in for that refrigerator. My refrigerator was hardly getting cold, and I couldn't afford a new one because I had just paid five thousand dollars to a plumber, and everything was going wrong. Ronald's pension was good but I had to spend it wisely to make it last. I had forgotton the ticket until I saw it in my purse. I looked at the date on it, and it was the last day to turn it in." Shirlee sipped at her corn liquor and placed the cup back on the table.

"I was young, you know. That old man said he would give me the refrigerator if I let him have his way with me. That was his exact words. And I said, 'what do you mean, Pastor Black?' That old man licked that big old pink tongue over his bottom lip, and told me that I could have anything I needed. Then I understood."

Miss Idele clapped her hands together and whooped with laughter. "So, did you do it?" she asked anxiously, and laughed out loud again. Her oval-set face softened into happiness, and the lines softened when she laughed.

Shirlee had envisioned the memory as though it were only yesterday. "He said no one would be at church for hours. 'Shirlee, you deserve to get what's needed for your children. A man in my position could do a lot for a young, wide-butt woman like you. You'll give an old man like me a reason to smile the rest of the week. Not that I'm not blessed anyway. But a man my age needs a little spice in his life. Not that the Good Lord hasn't already blessed me with it. And this could be good for both of us. It won't take long for an old man like me. Just ten minutes and you'll win that refrigerator, double doors with an ice maker, too.'"

"Miss Idele, I was afraid the Lord would strike me down for fornicating in his church. Then I said, 'I don't know, Pastor Black. Did you say it had double doors and an ice maker?'" Shirlee stopped talking for a few seconds.

"Go on, Shirlee. This is getting good," Miss Idele said, her long dress dipping down between her thin legs and touching the floor.

"Well, that fool began begging and I started to feel sorry for him. I could picture the double-door refrigerator in my mind. I got tired of waiting for the ice to freeze inside my old refrigerator. Besides, it was only for ten minutes, so what could it hurt?"

"Shirlee, you'll kill an old woman with all this suspense. Go on, child."

"Okay, Miss Idele, I said to Pastor Black, 'I got to go

home soon. Is it bad if we do this in the church? I mean, will I get bad luck?'"

"He said, 'Shirlee, the Lord knows his children is gonna sin sometimes. We can pray together for forgiveness. All you have to do is pray whenever you sin. The Good Lord hears all prayers. And, Shirlee, I've prayed for a long time for this day. I feel you every time I see you, Shirlee,' he said, taking on a passive tone, beads of sweat developing across his forehead, his tongue slithering."

"And?" Miss Idele asked.

"I got down on my knees and closed my eyes, and Pastor Black got down beside me. He said for me to repeat after him. I did. Then we got up and I stepped out of my shoes, raised my dress, and started to pull my panties down. He told me to stop. I asked why. Then he asked me to raise my dress high so he could see how pretty I looked standing in my panties. His mouth fell open, his dark face shone.

"'Now, pull your panties down nice and slow, Shirlee. I want to remember you just like you are now,' he said in that slow, deep voice of his.

"I couldn't believe he could make me feel all hot and bothered, but he did. And I was stupid enough to believe a man of fifty years old would get tired after ten minutes. I lay on the sofa, legs spread apart. He was a big man. I couldn't believe my eyes when I saw it. I've never seen a man so big before. He slid in me, he started slowly, groaning like a big old bear. Then he would slow down and start up again. He held me like he was riding a train on a railroad track, trying to stay on because if it fell off the track, that would be the end of it, and he didn't want it to end. And then he would yell, 'Bring it on home to Daddy.' Whatever the hell that meant, it went on for over an hour. Once he finished with me I jumped up, grabbed my purse, and flew out of there. It was cold that day and I didn't realize I had left my panties until I was halfway home. But I didn't go back. This picture was taken that same day."

"And the refrigerator?" Miss Idele asked.

"Two days later it was delivered at my house, double door, ice maker, and all. He even threw in a small microwave oven as a bonus. But I've never done anything like that again. Now you know why I always look at that picture when I come over."

"Good old Pastor Black, the pillar of the community. He died a happy man. Had nine children, and was found dead in the church office with his pants down to his ankles. I wonder who left him there?" Miss Idele said and sipped the last drop of her coffee.

"Yes, and we better get back before Darian gets home."

Darian turned the corner on Galvez Street and arrived at school at precisely two o'clock. She paused in front of the school, surveying the buildings that needed painting. As she neared the entrance she saw Shelby peering through the window. Darian motioned for her to come, and smiled when she saw Shelby skipping down the hallway so cheerfully. She was happy to see Darian.

On the way home, Darian said very little to Shelby, but she did ask her about her day. She was thinking of all the things that she had to do. Yesterday she had found the children's birth certificates, and paid off credit cards with small balances. Monique was careful by not overextending herself in debts.

Darian parked the car in the driveway and Shelby jumped out, running ahead of her. Miss Idele and Shirlee were sitting in the living room watching television.

"Looks like it's going to rain," Darian announced as

she stepped inside the house. The children ran off to their room.

Shirlee felt her heart race, and it was hard to breathe every time she thought of Monique. And today wasn't a good day. Hot flashes woke her in the middle of the night, and once she calmed down and fell asleep, she had a recurring dream of Monique. Before she could answer Darian, she closed her eyes and took a deep breath. She hadn't mentioned the problem to Jefferson for fear that it would worry him. "The weatherman did say we might get some showers today."

"Mama, can you and Miss Idele stay with the children until I go to Hibernia Bank on Canal Street?"

"Sure. I haven't anything better to do today. I came over to help you," Shirlee said.

Darian went into the bathroom, combed her hair, and applied lipstick. She looked into the mirror, and poked out her bottom lip to make sure the lipstick was evenly applied. Her jeans were tight, which accentuated her slender, round hips. The red sweater fit neatly over supple breasts, and she wore a pair of navy blue boots.

Chapter 9

Darian walked out of the house alone for a change. She desperately needed a break without the children, Shirlee, and Miss Idele. She missed having time alone to hear herself think. Although there were a hundred thoughts occupying her mind, for now she felt young and carefree again. If only she could drive off into the sunset and never come back to the responsibility she had inherited.

Driving down Canal Street, looking at all the tall buildings, she felt refreshed and inhaled the air down her lungs.

She drove into the crowded parking lot and pranced inside the bank. All heads turned, her sandy-colored, windblown hair cascading wildly down her neck. The frosted highlights danced in the sun. Darian's hazel eyes scanned the lobby as she saw the new accounts department. Luckily, there were no lines to stand in.

The tall gentleman dressed in a brown suit saw her when she walked in. Her lustrous face glowed with a stunning beauty that caused him to turn around and watch her every step. She sat straight in a chair with her head slightly tilted with an air of authority that made him want to grab her shoulders and shake her loose of the haughty, arrogant aura that flowed along with her, and he would enjoy doing it. He imagined himself playing with the curls that had tumbled on her forehead.

After the gentleman had finished his transaction, he had to pass Darian to go out the door. She looked calm, cool and unruffled. As he got closer he could see her face clearly. Recognizing her, he stopped in his tracks. "Darian? Darian Cantrell?"

Darian was still waiting for the new accounts clerk when she turned around with a questionable expression across her face. Besides her family and Miss Idele, no one knew she was in New Orleans but Vickie, so who had called her name?

He just stared at her. God, she was prettier close up if that were possible.

Without a word, she looked at him, and froze. "Brad St. James?" she asked, her eyes smiling with recognition. She stood up and extended her hand.

"Are you here to stay?" It was almost as though he was asking her to stay.

"Yes, I am, and how are you, Brad?"

"Good. I'm sorry about Monique. As a matter of fact I just found out this morning. I was hoping that you were here. And you're going to stay."

Feeling the heat in her face, she pushed her hair back. "I've inherited Monique's children. So, yes, I'm here forever." He was so tall she strained her neck by looking up at him. He looked taller than she remembered. Feeling his eyes so intensely on her made Darian wonder what was he thinking.

Brad looked at his watch. "I have a meeting at three-thirty." He pulled a business card and pen from his jacket pocket and handed them to her. "Why don't you give me your phone number and we can do lunch or dinner soon?" At first she hesitated; then she began to write. The front of the card had his employment title and number. He was superintendent of the New Orleans School District.

It was odd seeing Brad after so many years. When they were in school he was the class clown, always making jokes and never completing any assignments. After they started college, he got serious about his future. Now he had a terrific career. And boy, was he good-looking, with distinguished, piercing brown eyes.

Brad said good-bye and strolled hurriedly to the door, then turned and looked at Darian one last time. He found himself captivated by her charisma. As he remembered her, she was one of the smart girls in school that every boy wanted to say he had bedded just once. But it never happened with Darian. She still maintained a grace and casual confidence that made all eyes savor every step she took. Just like it was when they were younger. Looking at her, Brad felt that old stirring in his heart.

Riverwalk Trail ran for a quarter of a mile along the water, and was always crowded. The shops and restaurants were countless, music flowing out of bars into the streets. Darian decided to park her car and take a stroll down Riverwalk, looking at the new shops. She decided to buy the girls a gift. A toy store was at the corner and Darian bought the girls each a doll. The children deserved it. She had been out long enough and headed for her car.

She did not drive into the sunset. It was time to go *home.*

Darian pulled up in front of the house at the same time Shirlee and Shelby were going inside the house.

Miss Idele and Nikki were inside watching TV. Nikki ran to the window when she heard the sound of car doors shutting.

Darian got out of her car with gifts in her arms and went to Shelby where she waited at the door. She saw a bandage on Shelby's left arm. "What happened to her, Mama?" Darian asked and placed the bag on the front porch.

"It's nothing serious. She and Nikki were running down the hallway and Shelby fell and landed on her arm. She'll be okay." Feeling a wave of dizziness, Shirlee went back inside the house and took a seat on the sofa.

Darian kneeled down in front of Shelby and held her in her arms. "Does it hurt?" she asked, searching Shelby's face. She saw a tear and wiped it with her hand. "Don't cry. Here, open your present."

Shelby's eyes were round and excited. "Can I play with her now?"

"Yes. Here's another one. Which one do you like best?" Darian asked.

Shelby selected hers and ran inside to give Nikki her doll.

Chapter 10

"By the way, I talked to Mabel yesterday. She says she spoke with Brad and he was glad to see you. So you and Brad ran into each other?" Miss Idele asked with a teasing glint in her soft dark eyes.

"Yes, I saw him at the bank."

"Well, let me tell you something, honey. You better grab that man with all you got. I suppose there's plenty of women in New Orleans that want him."

"I suppose, but I've got two children that I have to learn to raise," she said, half frowning. Her tone was sarcastic, her words sounding dispirited. "I think this is the first time that I have no direction in my life. It's like I'm only existing day to day, Miss Idele, and it goes against everything that I believe in. Even as a child I had a plan. Now it's to wash dishes three times a day, cook dinner, and clean the house." She threw her hands up in the air as though she was ready to give up.

"It won't be this way always, and when these children get next to you, crying for their mama, and wanting to have their way about everything, you're gonna pray for a man to calm your nerves and give you something to smile about." Miss Idele waved and walked out the door.

"Yeah, right," Darian yelled behind her.

Darian had fallen into a light sleep when she heard voices around her.

She opened her eyes and the girls were standing in front of her.

"I thought you were dead like mommy," Shelby said. "We were scared."

"I'm sorry, you guys. I was just tired, I'm not going to die. Now, I'll warm dinner and make a salad." Darian went into the kitchen while the children waited on the sofa.

Darian watched Shelby's face relax. Every time she napped, would they think she was dead? Now she was certain that Shelby was still insecure, and afraid that they would be left alone. She went back to the living room and turned the TV on, pulled the shades down, and closed the drapes. "Dinner will be ready shortly." She started to go back to the kitchen. "Oh, and, Shelby? I'm not going to die, and I'll never leave you and Nikki."

Shelby shook her head, and her smile widened.

Darian called the children to the kitchen. She sat at the table and ate with them. She wanted to make sure that they ate as a family in the evenings. The children were giggling and talking as though they were one big, happy family. Nikki wanted to sit in the chair next to Darian, and Shelby sat opposite her.

"Who wants dessert?" Darian asked.

"I do," they both answered at once.

Darian got up and gave them each a small bowl of vanilla ice cream.

After dinner she washed the dishes, and wished for the dishwasher that she had in her apartment. It was seven o'clock and Darian gave the children their bath and let them watch TV until eight-thirty.

Darian lay on the sofa and read a book, but she

couldn't seem to concentrate. So much went through her head. She had deposited Monique's life insurance check, plus she still had her own savings account. She closed her eyes and for an instant, she wondered what Wade was doing. Yasmine said that so far he hadn't gotten married. Well, hell, what did she care? He wasn't worth the salt on his bread, whatever the hell that meant. It was one of Miss Idele's old clichés.

She got up and went to the kitchen to get a pen and paper. Darian began jotting down the children's reactions when they thought she was dead. If she wrote a book about how death affected small children, she could stay home. At least until the children were more secure. She continued writing and two hours had passed before she stopped, but she felt better.

The phone rang and it was Shirlee. "Hey, Bay, how is things over there?"

"Everything is fine, Mama. The children ate dinner and are in bed. I'll be glad when Shelby and Nikki are old enough to wash the dishes."

"It will go faster than you think. But you will have a dishwasher before they're old enough and you know it."

"You're right, I will. Are you feeling all right, Mama?"

"Of course I'm all right. Why do you ask?"

"You just didn't seem yourself, that's all," Darian said with a hint of concern.

"I'm fine, don't worry about me. Girl, I'm as strong as a horse."

Shirlee placed her hand over the receiver so Darian couldn't hear her. "Jefferson, keep your hand from under my dress until I get off the phone," she whispered, and giggled.

Shirlee knew he wanted her, but lately, she couldn't have sex and enjoy it unless she knew that Darian and the children were all right. "Darian, I can take Shelby to school and pick her up tomorrow."

"Thank you, Mama. That will help me tremendously. Nikki was sneezing today so I can keep her inside."

"Good. I'll be there in the morning."

Darian hung up and shook her head. She heard Shirlee tell Jefferson to wait, and she heard her giggle. Darian sighed, and for an instant she felt sorry for herself. When was the last time she had sex? She thought of Brad, but she wasn't ready to date again. She trusted Wade and he lied. Now she had children, and no man would want her. Besides, she gave Brad her phone number and he hadn't called. Darian was sure he wouldn't call. He was just being kind by asking for her number for old times' sake.

Chapter 11

Thanksgiving was a week away and Canal Street was already decorated festively with Christmas decorations.

It was happening slowly, but Darian was getting into the holiday mood and had made a Christmas list for the children.

Darian had done some researching at the library for her children's book, and written down every experience she observed from the children. Darian wrote down every time Nickki would forget and ask for Monique.

It was time to sell Monique's house and start fresh. Darian thought it would help the children to live in a different house, and away from the sad memories of Monique's passing. Monique had her name quit-claimed off the deed and added Darian's name so there would be no problem selling the house.

"Maybe it's better if you and the children moved to a different neighborhood. Just find a Realtor and get started," Shirlee said happily. Once Darian made up her mind, there was no changing it. So Shirlee decided to do it her way. After all, she was the one who took the children.

"Where is everybody?" Miss Idele called from the

kitchen. She always walked across her backyard and into Monique's house.

"We're in the dining room, Miss Idele," Darian yelled. "Come in here and have a seat."

Miss Idele walked in. Her long skirt touched her ankles, a pink bibbed-apron over her skirt, and a flowered flannel shirt under her apron.

Darian was smiling and stopped when she saw the disappointment on Miss Idele's face. "When you and the children move away, it'll be like losing family. But you and the children need to make a fresh start. There's too many memories here. Lord knows I'll miss you," she said with a faraway look in her eyes.

Darian got up and placed her arm around Miss Idele's shoulder. "Miss Idele, you won't have a chance to miss us. I'll still need your help, and I'll need a babysitter just as much as I do now. The only difference is that I have to come and get you."

"They're not moving for a while, Miss Idele. People are busy during the holidays. This house probably won't sell until after the New Year. Besides, who has time to house-hunt now?" Shirlee commented.

The children were playing inside because it was too cold outside.

"They're getting attached to you, Darian," Shirlee whispered.

"I know." Darian went to the kitchen and returned with a glass of water.

"Shirlee," Miss Idele whispered. "It looks to me like Darian is gettin' attached to the children, too. She's not making them wash their hands ten times a day, afraid they would leave fingerprints every time they touch her. I thought she would make the children wash the skin off their little hands. You know old crazy Lucy used to do the same thing to her grandchildren."

"Miss Idele, how many times do I have to tell you

that I don't give a snap damn about those old crazy people you knew back in the day? Darian still has a little ways to go. Now we've got to find her a husband with a job."

"In case you haven't noticed, she's a little hard on men since she caught that fool cheating in California. She needs more time." They stopped talking as Darian entered the room.

"You've got to take the girls to dance class, so I better go and catch some of the Christmas bargains," Shirlee said and picked up her purse off the floor. She pulled out her mirror and applied red lipstick carefully across her full lips.

"Hey, what about next week you guys go with me to see the girls dance?" Darian suggested. "You should see Nikki's class. They do everything except what they're told. Vickie is meeting me there today."

"I'd love to," Shirlee answered. "What about you, Miss Idele?"

"Just tell me what time and I'll be ready."

Nikki started to whine and said her head was hurting. "Let me see what's wrong with this whining child," Darian said. She felt Nikki's forehead. "Honey, you have a fever. No wonder your head is hurting." Darian looked at her watch and rushed to the bathroom to get baby aspirin and gave Nikki one.

"You better leave her here with me, Darian. I'll take her to my house so she can lie down. Now, hurry before Shelby's late."

"You're a doll, Miss Idele." Darian grabbed Shelby's hand and together they ran out the door.

"Come on, Nikki, let's go home." She grabbed Nikki's hand and led her out the back door. "I have a fresh bag of cookies, and you can pick the ones you want."

Darian and Shelby chatted and sang all the way to dancing school. The sun was barely coming out, but

Darian decided that she would not let anything spoil her day. She saw Vickie waiting at the door for her. She stood as though she was modeling her tight white jeans and shiny black boots. She really had the sensuality of a model, Darian thought.

"Vickie, I'm so glad that you could meet me here today. Nikki's not feeling well so it's only Shelby today. The girls are learning to love their dance classes," Darian said as she and Vickie walked inside and took a seat in the front row. "I told Mama and Miss Idele that I'd bring them next week."

"I haven't anything else to do. Anyway, I needed to get out of the apartment today. Bernard and I had an argument. I want a baby and he doesn't."

The class started, and Darian couldn't keep her eyes off Shelby. She saw Shelby look to see if she was still there. Miss Goodman was a nice teacher that understood and reassured Shelby that she wasn't alone at school.

Nikki watched Miss Idele fill a cup with apple cider.

"I want the big one," Nikki whined.

"No. You're only a little girl," Miss Idele said as she looked at Nikki with a critical eye. She went to her bedroom and came back with a pillow and placed it under Nikki's head for comfort.

Miss Idele sat back on her old green, flowered chair that faced the pictures on the wall. The old black-and-white photographs were of all dead family members. Miss Idele frowned, her narrow face twisted in pain. The arthritis in her left leg had flared up. This morning she rubbed Biofreeze on it, starting at her knee and on down to her ankle.

She got up again. "Stay here and watch the TV,

Nikki, while I go to the kitchen," she said, not giving Nikki a chance to answer. She stood at her stove and wondered what to cook for dinner. She pulled out her large black pot and lit the old black-and-white gas stove. Miss Idele poured a pack of red beans in the pot, enough for Darian and the girls. It had become a habit to include them in her dinner plans. Darian was still learning to cook, but the girl was trying, Miss Idele thought, and smiled as she thought of Darian becoming a stay-at-home mother.

Miss Idele wasn't paying attention when she placed the multicolored dish towel on the stove and went back to the living room. She watched Nikki sit up and turned to face her again. "You're getting twitchy, baby. Let's go to the front porch for a while until you get sleepy."

Nikki scooted off the sofa and ran to the door. They went outside and sat on the swing chair that was on the front porch.

After a while Miss Idele watched Nikki as she sat close to her, and her eyes closed. Suddenly Miss Idele smelled smoke and wondered where the smell was coming from. She quietly laid Nikki's head on the cushion, leaped off the chair, and started for the door. But surely the beans couldn't be burning so soon, and there was enough water in the pot, she thought. She peeked at Nikki again and her eyes were open. Nikki started to get up but Miss Idele stopped her. "I'll be right back, you stay here."

Before Miss Idele got inside the house, she saw the blaze coming from the kitchen. "Stay outside, Nikki," she yelled, but was too frantic to look back and see if Nikki had done what she was told. Suddenly she heard a loud pop and an explosion that shook the small house as the blaze blasted out of control. Miss Idele tried to fan with her apron, unable to get to the kitchen for water. She barely got out of the house safely before she was smothered in the smoke. She scrambled out and heard sirens and fire trucks, and called out Nikki's name, but got no answer. She ran to the side of the house. No Nikki. "God, where is Nikki?" she asked out loud. She was turning around in a circle, agitated and blind with fear for Nikki's life.

Everything happened so suddenly, as the firemen jumped from the trucks and pulled Miss Idele away from the house.

"Let me go. Nikki's in the house. She's a little three-year-old child," she yelled, and pleaded for help. Her face was distorted with raw terror. "No! No! You must get her out of the house." She fought with all her might to pull herself loose from the fireman, but he was too strong and held her too tight.

"It's already too late, miss." The fireman held his head down and closed his eyes.

Miss Idele fell to her knees and screamed. "That poor baby was burned alive. Oh Lord, I told her to stay outside, but somehow she must have run inside when I was trying to put the fire out." How could she not see her? Miss Idele kept asking herself. She rocked back and forth, crying uncontrollably. "What will I tell Shirlee, and Darian?" she screamed out loud.

Walking back to the car, Darian complimented Shelby on how well she had danced. She held her hand as they skipped the rest of the way to the car. Shelby was tall for a child of six and was growing taller.

"Come on and get in, Shelby, and buckle your seat belt. Why don't we stop and buy Nikki some candy since she's not feeling well?"

Realizing that she had never been around many children, and knew so little about raising them, she shook her head and sighed. It was so much to be responsible for. But she was now determined to learn how to raise Monique's children properly.

Shelby started singing a song from one of the characters in their Barney video. Darian looked up as she was driving and saw a dark, smoky cloud. She parked the car in front of the Circle Food Store on St. Bernard Street and bought the children their candy and ice cream.

As Darian started driving again, she turned the corner where they lived and she saw more smoke and the New Orleans fire trucks. People were standing around, some crying and asking for the Lord's help. Darian felt as if she were in someone else's body. She stopped the car and leaped out, leaving Shelby inside. "Stay here, don't get out of the car."

Darian ran through the crowd. When she saw Miss Idele's house in flames she stopped and looked around at the crowd, surveying each face as she searched for Nikki. She ran to a fireman. "Where is the woman who lived here?" Then she recognized Miss Idele in the crowd, but she didn't see Nikki. "Where is Nikki?" Darian asked Miss Idele frantically. "Is she inside?"

When the fireman took her arm, she froze in her tracks. Darian attempted to pull away, but the fireman held her firmly. Everyone was staring at her, and she still didn't see Nikki. By the sight of Miss Idele's appearance, Darian knew that Nikki perished in the fire. She heard voices crying out, people yelling, chaos seemed to be everywhere. Like a crazed woman, she was turning around in circles, looking for answers, her eyes still searching for Nikki's face.

"I am sorry, but only the old woman made it out alive." The fireman looked at Darian's distraught expression and felt her intense pain. He held her up as her legs were buckling beneath her. She watched dismal trails of smoke weaving upward and disappearing into the air.

"Miss, miss?" the fireman called out.

She saw everyone, and she saw no one. Darian blinked, closed her eyes tightly, and saw Nikki's face, what she must have felt, how she must have screamed in pain, and how Monique must be watching her now. She had failed miserably.

Darian opened her eyes and blinked fast as she heard everyone yell out Nikki's name and applaud. Miss Idele screamed as the little girl toddled out of her house next door.

Shelby jumped out of the car and ran to greet Nikki. Darian's head jerked around as she heard Nikki crying. Both girls ran to Darian and threw themselves against her, as all three fell onto the grass. Darian stayed down on her knees and hugged both girls. She cried and looked up at the sky, realizing again that God is real. She had seen the series *Touched by an Angel* on the television every Sunday night before it went off the air. Monique had been Nikki's angel, and led her home to safety. Darian was sure of it.

Chapter 12

Shirlee drove up at the same time the house had disintegrated into ashes. She ran from her car and spotted Darian with the girls on the lawn, Miss Idele crying hysterically about everything.

When the fire had started, Nikki was frightened and ran home to hide inside the closet. Shirlee held both hands to her face and cried when she saw Miss Idele's house.

"We thought Nikki had burned to death, Mama. But she had run home and hidden in the closet."

"How did it happen?" Shirlee asked, still shocked over what she saw. It was just three hours ago and everything was all right. She felt a chill pass through her as she waited and prepared herself for what she was about to hear.

"Mama," Darian cried ecstatically. "Everyone is safe now."

Shirlee had become panic-stricken and for a moment she couldn't breathe.

"We just got back, Mama. I stopped to buy Nikki some candy . . ." Unable to continue, she began sobbing again. "I thought that I was too late and had lost her." She held both girls' hands. "Let's go inside, Mama." Darian looked around her and saw that the neighbors were beginning to go their separate ways. She helped Miss Idele up off the ground and led her into the house. Her body shook like a leaf on a tree. She looked older and very tired. "Miss Idele, would you like to lie down?"

"No. I'll just sit in the chair." Darian gave her a glass of water.

Shirlee went into Monique's room and took a seat on her bed, wishing she were there. When she heard Darian and the girls she went back into the living room. She paused in the hallway when she heard Shelby ask what happened to Miss Idele's house.

Shirlee went back to the living room and sat on the sofa. She felt sick, her head hurt, and her breathing became labored.

The doorbell rang and Darian answered. It was Vickie. Darian waved her in and told her what had happened.

"I just ran into Beatrice in the store. She told me what happened."

"I'm so glad you are here, Vickie. It's like a nightmare, and Nikki is fine. She only has a headache; she and Shelby are in their room. She was a smart girl for coming inside when she saw the fire."

"I'm sorry about your house, Miss Idele," Vickie said.

"So am I, girl. So am I." Miss Idele held her head back and closed her eyes.

"Hi, Shirlee," Vickie said.

Shirlee couldn't speak. She held one hand against her chest; her face was red and stained with tears. She held her free hand out to Darian for help.

"Mama, are you all right?" Darian asked. "Mama, Mama," she yelled again. Darian kneeled on the floor in front of Shirlee.

"My chest hurts. Call the paramedics," Shirlee choked out in a whisper. Beads of perspiration were forming on her face.

Miss Idele ran over to Shirlee and held her hand. "Keep quiet, I'm here with you."

Darian ran to the phone and dialed 911, then ran back to Shirlee and held her hand, crying and pleading for Shirlee to stay with her. "Oh, please don't die, Mama. Mama, please hold on. I couldn't take it if you leave me, too."

The girls ran into the living room, but Vickie grabbed their hands. "Come, let's go to the bedroom so you guys can change." To take care of the girls was all she could do to help Darian. Besides, they were too young to be around so much excitement in one day. They had lost so much to be so young. But still, they were lucky, and had family who loved them.

The paramedics came and examined Shirlee. They placed her on the stretcher and began working furiously, racing against time.

Darian was frantic and prayed inwardly as she watched.

"It's her heart. We have to take her to the hospital."

"I'm going with you." Darian rushed to the bedroom where Vickie was and gave her Shirlee's home phone number to call Jefferson. "Tell him to hurry, please, Vickie."

"Miss Idele. Please eat and lie down. You need to rest," Darian ordered. She ran out the door and jumped inside the truck with Shirlee. *What if it was only she and the girls left, what if Shirlee died?* she thought with horror. There were so many questions, and no answers. Was their family being tested to see how much they could bear?

Darian looked at her mother's face and could see

that she was frightened. Her eyes were still closed and her lips were dry and feverish.

"Miss, move aside so I can help her." Reluctantly Darian moved but kept her eyes on Shirlee.

Only minutes had passed, and they were pulling into the emergency parking lot. The paramedics jumped out and Darian was right behind them. They rushed Shirlee inside and all the time Darian was holding her hand, talking to her, pleading with her to stay alive. A nurse ran out and led the way for them to push her behind the closed double doors.

"Wait out here, miss," the nurse said to Darian. She was firm and didn't give Darian a chance to object.

One of the paramedics gently took Darian's hand, leading her away from the door. "They'll let you in soon. I'm sure she'll be all right."

"I can't lose her. She's all I've got."

"Come on, John," his partner said.

"Thanks for being here. Do you really think she'll be all right?"

"Yes. God bless, miss." He walked out as Jefferson rushed through the door like a twister sweeping through a small town.

"What happened, Darian, and where's Shirlee?" he asked as he looked around the waiting room. He had never been so scared before. Looking at Darian's face, he knew it had to be bad, real bad.

"I don't know. It looks like a heart attack, and Miss Idele's house caught on fire today. We thought Nikki had burned to death. Mama got too upset."

Throwing his hands in the air, Jefferson sat down, shaking his head in dismay. "Good God, what happened? I have to find out if Shirlee is all right." He got up and started to the door.

"Wait for me," Darian yelled and ran behind him. Jefferson turned around to face her. "What?"

"They said to wait out here. No one has told me anything yet." She folded her arms stubbornly and placed them across her chest.

"I'm going in to see my wife now." He took long strides and disappeared through two swinging doors. Once he was inside, a nurse stopped him "Look, someone has to tell me if my wife is all right. You can't just keep people waiting."

"Do you mean Mrs. Foley?" The nurse took her glasses off and wiped them with a tissue.

"Yes," Jefferson answered, his eyes surveying the room. He turned around and Darian was behind him. She looked like she had been through the worst day of her life. No wonder Shirlee had to be rushed to the hospital, Jefferson thought as he watched Darian wipe the tears off her face. She had been crying since he arrived.

Darian felt an excruciating headache coming on, and her stomach was upset. Everything was moving too fast for her. The children, Miss Idele's house on fire, now her mother was ill.

Jefferson and Darian waited impatiently, both eyeing every doctor and nurse that passed. Darian's mind went from Shirlee to Miss Idele, Monique, and Nikki.

Jefferson couldn't wait any longer and went behind the curtain where the doctor was examining Shirlee.

Jefferson was behind the curtain for ten minutes and went back to Darian where she stood looking like a frightened child. "Now the doctor says she has to stay overnight for observation. If she remains stable she can go home. She had a panic attack. When that happens, sometimes your heart beats fast, or with some people, they can't seem to breathe normally and start to sweat and get dizzy."

"As long as it wasn't a heart attack. I know what a panic attack is, Jefferson," Darian snapped at him.

Jefferson had to take a step backward. For the first

time he had felt sorry for Darian. She was scared, vulnerable, and in just a matter of seconds she was her old self again, sarcastic and arrogant.

When Darian and Jefferson went to Shirlee's bed her eyes were closed, but she wasn't asleep. "Are you okay, Mama?" Darian was bending over her and Jefferson sat on the opposite side of the bed.

At first Shirlee merely nodded, finding it difficult to speak. "No, I'm not yet. But the doctor gave me a shot to help me rest. When I open my eyes, I see Miss Idele's house. Now she'll have to find someplace to live. Maybe she can live with that crazy old cousin of hers. When I close my eyes, it's like shutting the memory and pain away. I just don't think I could have faced another death." Tears were dripping from the corners of her eyes. "I don't think that I will ever be the same again." Shirlee opened her eyes and looked at Darian's face. She looked tired, drained; her hair was in disarray, and her eyes were red and swollen. But Darian was strong like her father. She would take charge and forge ahead.

"Since I know you are all right, I'm going down the hall and call Vickie to check on the girls and Miss Idele."

"Go on, Darian. I'll be here with Shirlee," Jefferson said, facing his wife. He gently touched her teary face. "It's going to take a while, but we'll work it out together, baby. Tomorrow, I'm going to take you home and take care of you." He kissed her cheek.

"You always take care of me, Jefferson." She closed her eyes and squeezed his hand. With all that had happened, she still felt lucky to have Jefferson. He walked into her life when she needed him the most and she hadn't regretted marrying him for a second.

Darian looked at her watch and saw it was seven. "I

appreciate your help, Vickie. How's Miss Idele? Is she sleeping?"

"No, Darian. She's driving me batty and she talks to herself. I think she'll have to go to an old folks' home pretty soon."

Darian sighed. "I'll give you a call back." She hung up and went back to her mother's room.

As Darian walked in, Jefferson was still holding Shirlee's hand. She took her seat next to the bed.

"How are the girls?" Shirlee asked.

"They're all right. Vickie says Shelby has been asking questions about Miss Idele since she wasn't there when the fire started."

"Bay, you look tired. Why don't you go home?" Shirlee said to Darian.

"I'll stay with your mother, Darian. The doctor just left before you came in and said she'll be fine. She just needs to rest." And Jefferson decided that he would speak to Shirlee about getting some counseling. But he would wait until she got home.

"You need some rest, Darian. Besides, the girls need you."

"You're right. The girls are probably afraid. And Vickie says Miss Idele is acting strangely. I'll call Vickie to pick me up."

Darian hung up. She went to the emergency entrance, paced up and down until she saw Vickie's gray Mustang stop in front of her. Darian opened the door and slid inside the car.

"Auntie Darian," Shelby said between hiccups. "What happened to Miss Idele's house?"

"It caught on fire. That's why you should never play with matches. Now Miss Idele is going to stay with us tonight."

Darian turned in her seat and looked at Shelby. She was so beautiful, her pink lips and sandy hair. She looked at Nikki, her thumb in her mouth as she slowly closed her eyes. She didn't take her daily nap that she was used to.

Darian was glad that they were almost home. She rubbed the stiffness in the back of her neck and closed her eyes, too. She felt as though she had been hit in the head with a hammer. Her head pounded in each temple and she wondered if it would ever stop.

"Darian, Darian, you're home," Vickie said and touched her shoulder.

"Did I doze off?"

"Yes, for a few minutes. Come on, let's get the girls inside the house."

Still smelling the smoke from Miss Idele's house, Darian and Vickie wouldn't look at it. It smelled almost as though the house was still on fire. "You have flowers inside that were placed on the porch for Miss Idele."

Darian nodded and climbed out of the car to open the back door and picked Nikki up in her arms. Once they were inside, Darian put her to bed.

"Come on, Shelby. I want you to lie in bed and I'll turn the TV on." When Darian went back to the living room, Vickie was seated on the sofa. Darian slumped down beside her.

"You know what I think?" Vickie asked.

Darian curled her feet under her. "What do you think?"

"I think that I should stay here with you tonight. We can stay up all night and talk like we used to. You have a tremendous responsibilty, Darian, and from the looks of it Shirlee won't be in any condition to help."

"Tell me about it. I don't know if I have the strength to stay awake all night."

Vickie eased out of her shoes and went into the

kitchen. She came back with a bottle of wine and two glasses. "We both need this and it should help you relax."

"We've got to move from this house. So I'm placing it on the market tomorrow. That's the first plan I have."

"I know you're still hurting right now, Darian, and thinking that Nikki was dead had to be terrifying. Hell, I get chills from just the thought of it. You gave up your life and a wonderful career for your sister's kids. Maybe if you had a warning you would have accepted it easier. But Shirlee didn't tell you. You had to walk in on a conversation to know it. That wasn't fair to you but you stayed. And you're making the girls a good mother, too." Vickie filled their glasses and sat next to Darian.

They touched glasses and savored the wine as it flowed down their throats.

Vickie poured another round as Darian blew her nose, wiped her eyes, and threw the box back on the coffee table, knocking a small bowl of mints to the floor. Vickie hopped up and picked up the mints that had fallen under the table.

"Now drink up. Tomorrow is another day, and there is plenty to do. You're selling and buying homes, and writing children's books. Honey, you have a lot to write about."

Darian sipped. "I sure missed you, Vickie."

"I know, girl."

Chapter 13

"Do you feel better, Mama? Yes, the girls are all right." Darian heard Vickie snore as she slept. Her mouth was open and the wineglass was on the floor beside the sofa where Darian stood. She frowned as dizziness came over her, causing her to feel light-headed. The floor felt as if it were moving under her feet. She ran her tongue over even, white teeth. Her mouth was dry. As soon as Darian hung up, she would rinse her mouth.

"I need to talk to you, Darian. Do you think that you can come over today?" Shirlee asked.

"Mama, does this have anything to do with your health? I can't bear to hear any more bad news today. I've had enough to last the rest of my life."

Darian sound depressed, and Shirlee wished she could gather her in her arms like she did when she and Monique were children. She used to tell them not to worry about anything; Mama was there to take care of it. But so many things had happened that Shirlee had no control over.

"No, Bay. I don't feel ill at all, at least not physically ill. How's Miss Idele?"

"Wait a minute. I forgot that she was here and she's usually awake by now."

Darian peeked in the bedroom but the bed was neatly made and Miss Idele was gone. Darian went back to the phone. "She's gone, Mama."

"She probably got up early and had her cousin pick her up. She'll call you later. Don't worry about her. You have your hands full with the girls."

"Okay, Mama. I'll be there when the girls are up and dressed." Darian pressed her hands against both temples as she felt her head pounding again. This time it was because of the wine. She lay on the opposite end of the sofa where she had slept last night. Just one more hour, she thought, before the children got up.

Vickie yawned, then stood up and stretched her body. She looked at Darian as she moved around on the sofa. "You kept kicking me with your long legs last night. But I was too tipsy from all the wine to get up and go to the bedroom. Gee, what time is it?" Vickie asked and slumped back on the sofa. "Bernard should be home tonight. But he gets paid well driving trucks."

"It's eight o'clock and I hear the girls. I was hoping that they would sleep later."

"I have to make a pot of coffee," Vickie said.

"No, don't. Why don't I run out to McDonald's and buy breakfast and coffee? I'm starved and I don't feel like cooking."

"Good. That's faster anyway."

"I am hungry," Shelby said. Vickie stood in front of the sofa.

Darian got up and went to the bathroom. The girls sat side by side on the sofa, both staring up at Vickie. "You girls stay with Vickie and I'm going to buy breakfast for everyone."

Darian was back in half an hour with two large bags in her hand. She placed their breakfast on the table.

After Vickie finished eating she went to the bathroom and came out with her hair combed and lipstick on.

"I'm going home, but just call if you need me for anything." She looked around the living room and grabbed her purse and jacket off the chair.

Darian hugged her. "I don't know what I would have done without you. Guess I better go to Mama's house and see what she wants to talk about."

Vickie left. Darian showered and dressed the girls. She picked up the plates and wiped the table off.

Outside, Darian turned her head to avoid looking at what was once Miss Idele's house. Darian started a conversation with the girls to divert their attention from the house.

The girls ran to Shirlee's door and rang the doorbell. Shelby rang it first and then Nikki started to cry because she didn't get a chance to. Darian lifted Nikki up so she could reach the bell. Shirlee opened the door and they followed her inside.

"Hey, what's happening, Darian?" Jefferson asked.

Darian looked at him for a few seconds before she spoke. What did he think was happening? "Hi, Jefferson," was all she said.

Jefferson nodded. Now that Shirlee was all right and Darian didn't need him any longer, she was back to being a snob. Was she ever happy? He looked at the girls and smiled.

"Come on in here and I'll turn the TV to cartoons," Shirlee said as Darian followed her into the den. The girls hopped on the sofa. "Come in the kitchen with me, Darian. I need a cup of strong coffee," Shirlee said.

Darian followed and took a seat at the table. Shirlee filled her cup with coffee. "Want a cup?"

"No. I bought breakfast at McDonald's this morning

and had some." She waited until Shirlee was ready. Darian noticed that Shirlee's face was pale against her dark hair.

Facing Darian, Shirlee took a seat at the table and sipped her coffee. "Darian, I wanted to talk to you about giving me the girls and you going back to Los Angeles. I realize now that it's my obligation to raise Monique's children. God knows he punished me enough for not taking them in the first place. You shouldn't have to be tied down with such a large responsibility. Yesterday was an eye opener for me. When I found out that Nikki could have burned in the fire, I realized I could have lost a grandchild. It still kills me when I think of losing Monique. It's the worst thing that could happen to a parent." She sipped her coffee again and placed the cup on the table. Tears rolled down her face as she fiddled nervously with the napkin. "I guess having grandchildren live with me would make me old and I wanted the freedom that I didn't have when I was younger. Now I feel older than ever. And I wasn't fair to you."

Stung, Darian just stared at her. She didn't know what to say. And she could just pick up, pack, and leave the pain and tribulation behind her. It would be so much easier than looking at Miss Idele's house.

"I don't know what to say. Well, I can't go back to my job. I've already lost my position as manager, but I can go back as a buyer. I can live with Yasmine until I find an apartment." She had been so sure that she would never see L.A. again. She would get her hair trimmed, her nails painted, and pull out her professional clothing. She held her hands in front of her looking at her chipped fingernails.

"You're free to go, Darian."

Darian stood up. "I should go and pack. I can be ready to go in about three days, maybe two." She hadn't felt such excitement since she left L.A.

"Come on, girls, let's go home." Darian kissed Shirlee on her cheek. "Thank you for giving my life back, Mama." Darian rushed out of the house fearing Shirlee might change her mind.

When Darian and the girls got home she ran to her room like a windstorm through the house. The girls followed and sat on the bed. They were unusually quiet and Darian sat next to them. Shelby took Darian's hand and looked at her face. The three just sat there, no words spoken between them.

It was almost as though they knew she was leaving. Had Shelby been eavesdropping on the conversation between Darian and Shirlee? *Well,* Darian thought, *they'll just have to get over it.* Besides, she and the girls weren't that close, and Darian wanted desperately to get her old life back. She went to the closet and pulled out her suitcases. She spun around and the girls were on her heels. "Wouldn't you girls like to watch TV?"

"Why are your suitcases out? Are we going on a trip?" Shelby asked. Nikki was sucking on her thumb and stood closely beside Shelby.

"Don't worry about the suitcase, Shelby. Come on so we can watch cartoons."

Darian waited, and Shelby stared at her, making no attempt to move. Tears were rolling down her cheeks, and when Nikki saw that Shelby was crying, she cried, too.

Darian clicked her tongue and sighed heavily. She had to pack and leave. Her home was L.A., and she wanted her freedom back and be relieved from the responsibilities that weren't hers. Shirlee had finally realized that as the children's grandmother, she was responsible for them. Darian looked at the girls again and pushed the suitcase back inside the closet. She perched on the edge of the bed, the girls beside her.

Her heart was aching, and the excitement she had felt only minutes ago had dissipated in the air. Darian felt a tear roll down her face, just as the girls did. Who was she kidding? Then she looked at the two sad faces that were sniffling their noses beside her, and knew that she couldn't leave them. How could she be happy when they were so sad? No, she couldn't leave Monique's daughters.

"Come on, girls, let's go back to Mama's house."

Jefferson looked peculiarly at Darian when he opened the door a second time in less than an hour. She and the girls walked right past him, all three looking sober as they marched seriously to Shirlee's bedroom. Darian and the girls sat on the bed beside Shirlee. "I can't do it, Mama. It's too late."

"But I want you to be happy, Darian. The girls will be well taken care of." Shirlee rearranged the pillows and sat up in bed.

Darian nodded in answer. "Not now, Mama. Everything has changed and I won't be another person to walk out on them. It would be like everyone they got close to left them. Being left alone could scar them for the rest of their lives. Besides, I'm placing the house up for sale first thing tomorrow morning. I keep telling myself that I should have come home more often."

"You came home every year, Darian. You helped Monique out financially, and came right home when she needed you. You've been more help than you think, Bay. But if you want to go, I'll take the girls. I just thought that you should know."

"Well, I know and I'm staying."

Darian stood and Shirlee got up and stood behind her, stroked her hair, and kissed her on top of her head.

"Thank you, Mama."

* * *

Darian went to the girls' room, but they weren't there. She heard a movement down the hall and went to see what they were doing. Darian stopped at the door when she saw Shelby and Nikki lying in the middle of Monique's bed. Shelby was lying on the pillow, and Nikki lay close to her. Darian watched and listened but they weren't saying anything.

"Girls, I thought you wanted to watch *Barney*. It's on and you guys are going to miss it." She wondered why they wanted to lie in bed with no TV or toys to play with, and they looked so sad.

Darian stepped inside the room and saw that Shelby had been crying, and she felt as though the wind was knocked out of her. Shelby's tearstained face was still wet with tears. Darian knew that it was time to try and reassure the girls that they weren't alone, and she wasn't leaving.

"Mommy won't ever come back to us. Who will Nikki and I live with? Who'll take care of us if you go home like Shirlee told you?"

So they were listening, Darian thought. She felt her heart jerk. What she must have put them through. At that moment she realized that she had never kissed the girls, or said that she loved them, or that she would take care of them. She just assumed they knew, or maybe she thought it wasn't important.

Darian shook her head in dismay, and realized she still had a lot to learn about parenting. She had never been the maternal type, but it was time she learned. She should have been more sympathetic toward the children and talked to them when Monique died. But instead, she had been more concerned about going back to L.A.

Darian walked to the edge of the bed and took the

girls' hands. "Come into the living room so we can talk." She picked up Nikki and carried her when she saw her face frown into a cry.

Darian sat on the sofa with Nikki on her lap. "Here, Shelby, sit next to us."

Darian took her hand. "Shelby, I'm going to live with you and Nikki so I can take care of you, and try to make you two happy. You and Nikki are not alone. I love you girls."

Shelby looked up at Darian's face. "You love us?" she asked, surprised.

Darian kissed her on the cheek. "Yes, very much." As Darian continued she was amazed at how easy it was to say "I love you" to the little girls. In the past, the children were only a thorn in her side. "You and Nikki shouldn't be afraid because I'll be here always."

"Okay," Shelby answered.

Nikki nodded her head and took her thumb out of her mouth. "Okay, too."

"You won't leave us ever? You promise?" Shelby asked.

"I'll always live here with you and Nikki."

Darian pulled Shelby closer and placed her arm around her. She remembered how safe she felt when her mother used to hold her and Monique close to her.

"Can me and Nikki sleep with you tonight?" Shelby asked. "We want to stay close to you, Auntie Darian."

"Okay, you guys can sleep with me tonight."

"Every night?" Shelby asked again.

"Every night? I don't know about every night, but you can tonight."

Chapter 14

Thanksgiving Day was rainy, cold, and windy. Darian and the girls had dinner at Shirlee's house. The girls were happy and it was clear to everyone that Darian and the girls had bonded. They were constantly talking to her, sitting close to her, and kissing her when she gave them permission to do what they requested.

The girls were playing in the backyard, and Darian helped Shirlee in the kitchen.

"Mama, let me help you with that." Shirlee was taking the food to the dining room. She sipped from her glass every chance she got. Darian had noticed that Shirlee seem to be drinking a lot lately. It was only one o'clock and Shirlee was already drinking. Darian made a mental note to mention it to Shirlee when they were alone. But she didn't want to spoil the holiday. The girls were ready for turkey.

They sat and waited while Jefferson blessed the table. Darian cooked the stuffing as best she could, and Shirlee baked the turkey, cooked candied yams, and green beans. For dessert, Shirlee baked sweet potato pies and an apple pie for Jefferson.

After dinner Shirlee and Darian cleared the table

and went into the kitchen alone. "Sit down, Mama, we need to talk," Darian ordered. "I didn't want to spoil the day but I have to say it."

"What is it, Bay? You're scaring me, Darian." She picked up her glass of vodka and orange juice.

"Mama, you have a serious problem."

Shirlee faced her. "What are you talking about, Darian? What kind of problem do I have?" she asked. She wasn't ready for any more bad news.

"Mama, what I'm trying to say is that you're drinking too much. You've had a glass in your hand all day. I know you've lost a daughter. But I need you now. The girls need you, too. You're taking the easy way out by becoming steadily more inebriated every day."

Shirlee turned around in her chair. "By becoming what?" She looked totally baffled as she glanced at Darian.

"By getting drunk, Mama. Drunk. Can you understand that?"

"Well, hell, then, say that. Don't come up in here with all those college words. And I'm not drunk. I just take a drink to take the edge off. It's hard to get up in the mornings without thinking of Monique. Sometimes I hear her calling my name in my sleep. But I guess I'm only dreaming," Shirlee said slowly as the words lingered on her tongue.

Tears streamed down Shirlee's face. "My chest gets tight and I think my blood pressure is up, too."

"Yeah, drinking will make your blood pressure high," Darian snapped. She looked as though she wanted to cry, too, and she needed Shirlee's help. Shirlee's drinking was just another burden on her shoulders. And Miss Idele wasn't there to help since she lived with her cousin.

"Mama, I don't want to make you angry or spoil your holiday, but you are spoiling ours."

Darian started to cry, and Shirlee placed her glass back on the table. She sighed and reached across the table and took Darian's hand. "Bay, don't get all upset. I'm sorry and I know you need me." She got up, walked to the sink, and emptied her glass. "Come on, Bay, don't cry. And you're right. I have been drinking more lately."

Shelby and Nikki went into the kitchen. Shelby started to cry and so did Nikki. "We want to go home," Shelby said.

Darian jumped up from the table. She kneeled in front of the girls and kissed both of them on their foreheads. "It's okay, don't cry. It's okay." Finally they calmed down.

Shirlee went to get more napkins and stood at the kitchen sink. She didn't hear Darian behind her as she poured vodka into her glass.

"That's it, Mama. The girls and I are leaving." Darian spun around on her heel, taking long strides marching out the kitchen. As she walked out she could hear the glass fall to the floor. Darian stopped, then continued to get the girls and leave.

"Come on, girls. Let's get your jackets. We're getting out of here."

Shirlee rushed into the dining room and just stood there, speechless. She watched Darian rushing around putting the girls' coats on, grabbing her purse and car keys. "You're really leaving, aren't you?"

"Good-bye, Mama." Darian and the girls rushed out the front door.

Jefferson had gone outside and stood on the porch watching as Darian drove off.

She had had it with everyone. Today was Thanksgiving Day, a day to give thanks and pray for their loss, not to get drunk. And she wouldn't watch her mother stumble around the house with a damn glass filled with vodka in her hand. *If she insists on getting drunk, she'll do it without me and the girls.*

Darian gave the girls some Jell-O and put them to bed by eight-thirty. As she walked down the hall she lingered in front of Monique's room. The room was still unoccupied by anyone. But the girls had started to play in there. Darian walked through the house as loneliness crept over her. She disliked everything about the house.

She sat on the sofa with a magazine in her hand and a cup of coffee on the coffee table in front of her. The house was so quiet that she could hear her own breathing. Unable to concentrate, Darian tossed the magazine aside.

If only Miss Idele was here. Maybe tomorrow she would visit her. God, how she missed her. "Oh, gee," Darian whispered. What a melancholy mood she had settled into.

"Thanks for making my day, Mama," she whispered out loud.

The Saturday after Thanksgiving, Shirlee, Miss Idele, and the Realtor were at the door at the same time. Darian rushed to the door, and the girls followed. "Hi, Mama and Miss Idele, come on in." Darian peeked her head out the door. "And you must be Miss Price."

Shirlee and Miss Idele embraced the girls and took a seat on the sofa. Miss Price sat in the chair opposite them; the children were close to Darian, one on each side of her.

"Miss Idele, you know where the coffee is," Darian said.

"I sure could use a cup of coffee." Miss Idele got up and left the room.

"Miss Price, let me show you around the house," Darian said and moved aside. Shelby and Nikki stood so close to Darian she almost tripped over them. She had lost weight and had to pull up her jeans around her waist. Lately, she had to force herself to eat.

"Although it's small, this is the master bedroom," Darian said. They were standing in Monique's room. She felt Shelby pulling at her hand. "What is it?" Darian asked and frowned.

"This is Mommy's room, not a master's room." Shelby looked confused.

"I know, love. But for now we'll pretend it's the master bedroom."

Miss Price followed Darian around the house. When they got to the kitchen, Shirlee was pouring a cup of black coffee.

"What a cute kitchen." Darian led her down the hall, and Miss Price stopped in the living room looking at the ceiling, the carpet, and the paint. She was about five feet and wore large round eyeglasses and her hair in a short natural. Her feet were short and fat, looked as though they were stuffed in her shoes. "Do you want it sold as is, or are you willing to paint it, honey? Everything else looks to be in good condition, Miss Cantrell." She jotted down more notes on a writing pad, and readjusted her glasses on the tip of her nose.

Darian was surprised that she remembered her name when she didn't call her honey again. "Sell it as it is," Darian answered. "I want it sold as soon as possible."

Shirlee listened, but said nothing. She would miss this old house where her grandchildren had spent most of their short lives. Miss Idele always yelled from the back door as she came inside. The laughter that

used to resonate through the house with loud cheery
energy was only a memory. Now as she looked around
she felt cold, and shivered, feeling the warmth dema-
terializing that was once so alive. Shirlee wiped her
eyes and stood at the window. She refused to look next
door at the vanished house.

"How soon can you find another house for us? I
want to live in a higher-scale neighborhood."

"That may cost more, honey. Unless you settle for a
two-bedroom house."

"I've considered paying more. Oh, and a brick
house if you can find one."

Miss Price adjusted her thick eyeglasses. "New
glasses are so hard to get used to. I'll try and find what
you want. You know, Miss Cantrell, there is a cute little
house in Elysian Fields. Let me go back to my office
and I'll call you with some additional information. In
the meantime, I'll take one more look at your kitchen
and get the ball rolling."

"Go right ahead. I'll stay in here so the girls won't be
in your way."

Miss Price went to look at the bedrooms again. She
took her time to write more notes. "Sometimes I miss
something when I walk through the first time."

"Go through as much as you need to. Now, you girls
go and get your coloring books from your room,"
Shirlee suggested. The girls looked at Darian before
they would move.

"It's all right. Go ahead and come right back."

"Why are they acting so strangely, Darian? They're
acting as if they are afraid to leave you," Shirlee said.

"Looks like they've gotten taller since I've been
away," Miss Idele said.

"They have, and ask about you almost every day,
Miss Idele."

"They've been like that since I promised that I

would take care of them." Darian sighed, and rolled her eyes up at the ceiling. "They're afraid they may lose me, too. But they're young, and I'm sure with time they'll be all right."

"Darian, I haven't touched another drink since Thanksgiving. I know that I have to face problems with a clear head."

"Mama, if it gets too rough maybe you should see a doctor," Darian advised.

"I don't need to see no brain doctor. And I wouldn't know what he's talking about anyway. Besides, I'm doing all right myself."

"I'm glad you've stopped drinking. Me and the girls need you."

Shirlee held her head stubbornly and looked in the opposite direction. She didn't care what Darian said; she was not going to see a doctor to tell all her business to.

"John Davis took his son to see one of those brain doctors. They say the boy got crazier and shot himself in the head. So maybe you're right, Shirlee."

"I know I'm right," Shirlee hissed between closed teeth.

Miss Price came back into the living room. "All right, honey. I got all I need. I can sell your house for a good price. I see the city has cleaned up the burned-down house next door and just in time, if I must say so myself. Crap like that could make your house hard to sell."

Shirlee could feel the muscles in her neck tightening as she listened to the woman speak of Miss Idele's house as though it really was no more than a piece of crap. She had to shut her eyes to prevent placing both hands around the woman's neck. When Shirlee opened her eyes again, she saw Darian looking at her strangely.

Miss Idele looked at the woman as though she was

insane. "That house used to be my piece of crap. I think you should know that before you say more."

"Oh, I'm so sorry. I didn't know."

"Well, you should have asked. That's why this world is so messed up today. People don't respect other folks' stuff."

"I'm truly sorry. You're right. I should have asked." Miss Price turned her attention back to Darian. "Now, I'm going back to my office and give you a call about the house I have in mind." Miss Price hurried out of the house. Darian watched as she took at least four steps compared to her one. Her legs were too fat for the long skirt she was wearing.

"I think Miss Price is nice," Darian commented when she closed the door.

"Well, I think she's gay myself, and she's not attractive at all. Did you see the way she looked at me? And her shoulders are almost as wide as Jefferson's are. And she walks like a duck," Shirlee replied.

"And she better stop talking about people's houses looking like crap. If my cousin Big Joe was here, she would have gotten shot."

"Now, Miss Idele, there you go with those old crazy cousins of yours," Shirlee said. "Did you see the way that woman was watching me?"

"No, Mama. I didn't see her look at you. But she does walk funny." Darian heard Shelby breathing heavily. "Shelby, do you feel all right?" Darian asked with concern. "Doesn't she have asthma?"

"Yes. Miss Idele mixed that goose grease and honey together. Give her a teaspoon of it. Monique keeps it in a small coffee can in the top kitchen cabinet."

"Goose grease and honey? You must be kidding?" Darian asked, eyes wide with laughter. "She's not going to like it."

"Darian, old folks been using that remedy for years.

In an hour it will make her breathe easier. She'll take it because she's used to it. You younger people don't know anything unless it's in a book."

"Okay, Mama." Darian got up and the girls followed. She gave Shelby a teaspoon of the honey remedy and went back to the living room.

"I used to give some goose grease to my cousin, and it helped. I need to run next door and get my sweater. It's getting cold in here," Miss Idele blurted out.

Shirlee and Darian looked at Miss Idele, then looked at each other. Darian felt like she wanted to cry. Nothing would ever be the same again. Losing her house was too much for Miss Idele, and Darian wondered how long it would be before they lost her. She pushed the thought from her mind.

"Shelby, Nikki, I'll turn the TV on cartoons and you two lie down and watch it." Darian knew her mother wanted to talk to her alone, so she took the girls to their bedroom.

When she came back, Miss Idele was in the kitchen refilling her cup with coffee. From the back, Darian could see that she had gotten thinner. Shirlee was standing at the window staring as though she was in a daze. Then she looked at Miss Idele's old driveway.

"Mama?"

"Oh, I didn't hear you walk in. My mind was far away."

"I know where it was. All the way next door. I'll be so glad when I can move away from here. As long as we are here, I'll never be able to make a fresh start for the girls and me."

"What happens if that funny-looking Realtor can't find you a house before this one is sold?"

"I'll rent an apartment until she does. I can't stay here much longer. There's too many memories."

"I know, and I haven't been much help lately to you or the girls. I'm sorry about Thanksgiving, Darian. I ruined it for everyone. After you left, Jefferson and me had the worst fight we've had since our marriage. He only drinks beer and when he's had enough he quietly goes to bed. But me, I had to act like a fool with mine." Shirlee got up and walked around the living room. It was small as were all the rooms in the house, but it was neat.

Shirlee stood in front of the fireplace and looked at the pictures of her family. She went back to the sofa. Nikki was crying and Darian rushed to check on her.

"This coffee is nice and strong," Miss Idele said, taking a seat on the sofa.

"Drink up, Miss Idele, so we can go home."

Chapter 15

The house was the third one on Tureaud Street. The lawn was well manicured with green grass and a red rosebush near the steps.

Darian's smile widened as she stood in front of the redbrick house, each child by her side. She went to the driveway and looked along the side of the house. She could see the white-painted garage in back. Darian could easily imagine herself inside the house with her furniture set in place. This house in a different neighborhood could be a new beginning for her and the girls.

"Miss Price, this house is mine." She was so excited that she could hardly wait to go inside and see the rest.

"Why don't we go inside and have a look around?"

Darian stepped inside the living room, and her eyes roamed over every corner of it. "Oh, I just love the beautiful crafted bookshelves in the corner, and the large window." She ran to the ornately carved fireplace and ran her hand across the top. "I love the color of this living room, too, Miss Price. I'll say it's the color of pistachio green."

"That's a good choice of words to describe it, Darian. I probably would have said a mixture of mint and olive green," she said, looking at Darian's excited face and gleaming, bright eyes.

"My furniture will go perfectly with the color of the walls." Darian was twirling around in a circle like an excited child on Christmas Day. It had been a while since she felt so young and happy. "Come on, girls, let's check out the kitchen." They were behind her, laughing with excitement. "Look, girls, this is where we'll eat." Darian pointed to the small table in the corner.

"Take your time, honey. We still have two more houses you can see."

"Oh, this kitchen is lovely, just the right size for us." She looked at the view from the window that captured the sunlight. "I can sit in here and read, cook, and still watch the children." Darian ran her hand over the granite counters that were practically new.

Darian and the girls walked down the hall and stopped to look into both bathrooms and bedrooms. She nodded her head and smiled. Then she took the girls to the backyard.

"This fence is good for the girls," Miss Price was saying. She sat on the steps while Darian walked around the yard. She watched her peek inside the garage.

Darian pulled an orange from the tall tree, dry leaves crackling under her feet.

Miss Price watched the girls running after each other. They were having fun.

"We don't have to go any further, Miss Price. And I don't have to see another house. I'm ready to make an offer. I definitely want this house. Don't we, girls?"

"Yes," the girls yelled out.

They went to their cars, and Darian followed Miss Price to her office to make an offer on the house. She would have the storage company bring her furniture.

"Are you girls all right back there?" she asked, glancing through her rearview mirror.

"Yes," Shelby answered. "But my head hurts again."

"As soon as we get home, I'll give you some medicine to make you feel better."

"Can we watch TV, too?" Nikki said.

"Okay." Darian turned right and parked in front of the real estate office.

The transaction in the real estate office was efficient. It was easy to work with Miss Price. Darian wrote a check for five thousand dollars as a deposit.

"I'll call you in a day or two, Darian. But I'm sure your offer will be accepted. My client wants to sell fast." Miss Price walked Darian and the girls to the door. "Your nieces are so well behaved."

"Thank you, Miss Price."

"Call me Barbara. Miss Price is so formal."

"Thanks, Barbara, and I'll talk to you soon."

They were home and Darian decided to let Shelby lie on the sofa instead of putting her to bed. She retrieved blankets and pillows and turned the TV on.

It was past two o'clock and time for Nikki's nap. She stood against the sofa, thumb in her mouth.

Darian went back to the bedroom again and got another pillow. After she got Shelby settled in she laid Nikki on the other end of the sofa. She could always sit and read or write notes for her book.

Darian laid her head back and closed her eyes, visualizing what the new house would be like after she decorated. She felt giddy by the thought that she had bought her first home. And she never would have thought in a hundred years that it would be in New Orleans.

Chapter 16

It was December and the weather was below freezing and the skies were dark gray. As Darian walked through the French Market she stopped at Café du Monde and bought a Café Brulot. It's said by the Orleanians that it's a glorification of the bean's purpose in life. Darian hadn't seen any coffee as dark in Los Angeles. After drinking Café Brulot most of her life, she was disappointed when she drank the drip coffee in L.A.

She watched as a young woman prepared it by her tableside. Darian had missed this treat on cold days. After the coffee was mixed, the waitress poured, and Darian sipped leisurely from the brulot cup.

Darian had just finished her Christmas shopping. She sat comfortably and watched passersby as they carried large shopping bags filled with Christmas gifts, just like she had. She looked at her watch, glad she still had thirty minutes before it was time to pick Shelby up from school. Shirlee stayed at the house and kept Nikki while Darian got lost in the crowd of shoppers.

Darian bought two doughnuts for the girls. She looked at her watch again; it was time to pick up

Shelby. But she knew that once she and the girls were all settled in the new house, she had to do more than taxi the girls around; she had to get back to work. Darian had always been a career woman. She missed the excitement of being a buyer.

She sighed. After the holidays she would take the girls to the Aguariumi Zoo Cruise. They would love that. But first it had to get warmer. Shelby was getting ill quite often with one cold right after another.

Darian parked her car and went inside to get Shelby.

"Did you have a good day, Shelby?" Darian asked as she drove down Galvez Street.

"No. My chest hurts," Shelby whined and loosened her seat belt.

Darian heard the buckle. "Keep your seat belt on, honey. We're almost home."

"Why didn't you bring Nikki?"

"She's home with Mama. Why didn't you tell me that you weren't feeling well this morning? I would have kept you home," Darian said gingerly, concerned. "I made some strawberry Jell-O."

She parked the car in the driveway and walked around the passenger's side to open the door. Judging from Shelby's whining and her red glowing face, Darian knew she wasn't feeling well.

"What's she so unhappy about?" Shirlee asked as she watched Shelby walk right past her. Her lower lip was pushed out into a pout.

"She's not feeling well and wants to go outside and play. If her chest hurts like she says it does, I'm keeping her inside where it's warm."

Shirlee grabbed her purse off the floor. She was wearing a pair of tight jeans, a purple sweater, and white sneakers. She smoothed her hair back on each side and stood in front of the long mirror that hung on the wall. "You take care, Darian. I'll call and check on Shelby tomorrow. But if you need me for anything today I'll be home."

"Thank you, Mama. I'm going to sign the final offer for the house tomorrow."

"That's good, Bay. But I wouldn't get too friendly with Miss Price if I were you."

"Why? She's a nice lady." Darian looked skeptically at Shirlee. She still wasn't her old self. Monique's death had taken a toll on her.

Shirlee swung her purse over her shoulder, placed her hands on her hips. "She's anything but a lady. That woman looked at us like she wanted to snatch our clothes off and eat us alive. Now, I'll see you tomorrow. Oh, I spoke to Miss Idele today, and it took her a while to remember who I was. She's getting worse, Darian. She's old, that's all."

"But it's happening so fast."

"I know, but it happens like that with some old folks. She's not that old, though. But Alzheimer's runs in her family. She said that her mother got it when she was forty-five." Shirlee shook her head and ambled out the door.

Darian ran behind Shirlee.

"Wait! Wait, Mama. Don't leave yet." Darian ran to the bedroom and got her purse. When she came back into the living room, Shirlee was waiting for her.

Shirlee looked bemused as she watched Darian coming back with her purse swinging over her shoulder, and wearing a frown.

"I forgot to pick out a Christmas tree. It just may radiate some Christmas spirit in this house. The girls would love it. It won't take long," she yelled over her shoulder.

"Go. I'll just sit right here and finish looking

through this *Ebony* magazine." Shirlee went to see what
the girls were doing. Shelby had fallen asleep, and
Nikki was lying at the foot of the bed with her thumb
in her mouth. As Shirlee walked down the hall, as
always, she turned her head to avoid the view of
Monique's room. She had tried her damnedest to go
inside and face the turmoil to learn to live with the reality, and grieve so she could move forward. But she
was still grieving. How could she face the future if she
didn't deal with the past? All of a sudden, Shirlee felt
seized by a feeling of agelessness. If only she could
enter Monique's room to say one last good-bye. She
felt her eyes water and looked up. "God, what I
wouldn't do to have another day with my baby."

Darian selected a green, six-foot tree. She had seen
the Christmas decorations and lights on the shelf in
the hall closet.

She stood back watching the young man tie the tree
on top of her car and tipped him five dollars.

Darian decided to stop by and visit with Miss Idele
at her sister's house. Shirlee had said that the woman
was cold, and didn't have very much to say the last
time she visited Miss Idele.

Darian parked in front of the house and rang the
doorbell. The door opened abruptly, and a tall, heavy-
built woman answered. Her face was expressionless;
she didn't smile and waited for Darian to speak.

"My name is, Darian, Shirlee's daughter."

"And?" she asked.

Darian looked into her eyes. She couldn't imagine
Miss Idele living with this cold old bat. "And I'm here
to visit Miss Idele. I just wanted to know if she needs
anything. I find it odd that she hasn't called lately."

"Probably because she doesn't remember your

phone number. I had to place the old woman in an old folks' home."

Darian gasped, and her brows came together into a frown. The woman had confirmed what Darian suspected.

"Idele's mind comes and goes. All she talks about is those old crazy cousins that I've always hated. Anyway, in the middle of cooking herself some breakfast, she almost started a fire. It was her second time and that broke the camel's back. The old woman don't have too long anyway. Everybody's got a hole in the ground, you know. And that's the gospel truth. Now, I have work to do." She slammed the door in Darian's face.

Darian sat on the steps for a few seconds to digest what she had just heard. "I'm going to miss Miss Idele," she whispered.

In less than an hour Darian had dragged the tree to the door, but before she could open it, Shirlee and Nikki came running outside. Nikki was laughing and jumped up and down. Shelby had been asleep but Nikki must have awakened her because she stood in the living room and watched.

"That's a nice tree," Shirlee complimented. She picked up her purse again and looked at her watch as she walked around the tree again. "Was it expensive?"

"No. I got a good deal, only eighteen-fifty. But I like the shape of it. I went to see Miss Idele, and her sister has placed her into a home."

"I know, but all we can do is visit her so she'll know that she still has friends." Shirlee went to the door. "I'm going home so I can cook my husband's dinner."

"Thanks for all your help, Mama. I don't know what I would do without you."

Surprised, Shirlee's eyes watered as she looked at Darian. Their eyes locked for seconds before Shirlee nodded. Darian had never said anything so warm or loving to her since she had been home. *Had the children changed her?* Shirlee thought as she eased out the door. She looked up as rain hovered over her head.

"So, do you girls like the tree?" Darian asked. She stood in front of the girls and watched as their eyes lit up. Nikki jumped up and down. They ran around the tree laughing and chattering at the same time.

Darian went to the hall closet and pulled out two large boxes of decorations. "I need help with this tree. Who's going to help me decorate it?"

Both girls yelled in unison. It took nearly two hours, but the job was done. Nikki placed her decorations at the bottom and Shelby filled in empty spaces in the middle of the tree, and one side they hadn't touched.

After the girls were put to bed, Darian flopped down on the sofa exhausted, and fell into a deep sleep. She was awakened by the ringing of the phone.

"Hello, Darian."

She held the phone, surprised that it was Brad St. James on the other end. "Hi, Brad. You surprised me."

"Did I really? I ran into Vickie at the gas station and she told me about the fire. I feel so sorry for Miss Idele. I used to see her shopping in the French Market."

"How have you been, Brad?"

"Good, busy. I just put my son to bed."

His son? *Have he and his wife reconciled and now he's calling me?* Maybe he was just calling to say hello. "How old is your son?" Darian asked, feeling all interest in this conversation declining.

"He's eight, and a smart boy if I have to say so myself. You have two girls to raise now?"

"Yes. It takes some getting used to," she said dryly.

"You'll do all right, Darian. Just give it some time. Motherhood will just fall into place."

"That's what they keep telling me." Darian rolled

her eyes up at the ceiling. *What in hell does he want? He has his wife.*

"When my ex-wife and I divorced, I got custody of my son. I wanted to raise him, you know, teach him how to be a man. She was too weak with him and he got away with too much."

Darian's ears perked up and her spirit lifted. She was wrong about Brad again. "I agree. A boy needs his father. How often does she come to see him?"

"She moved to L.A. So now the visits are getting slender. She merely calls him once or twice a month. She was married six months ago and now she's pregnant again. So now Tye hardly hears from her. I know you're trying to adjust with the kids and all the changes in your life. But when you are ready I would love to take you and the girls to a movie and dinner."

"I'll be moving into a new house after the holidays. What are you doing for Christmas?" Oh, why did she ask him that? She wasn't ready to date. But with Brad it wouldn't be a date. It would just be two old acquaintances talking about the days when they were younger.

"My mother invited us for dinner. But we can come over in the evening. Is that all right with you?"

"Sure. I'll give you the address."

"I'll call and get it when we're ready to come over. I look forward to seeing you again, Darian."

"Me, too. See you on Christmas Day."

Darian sat back, relaxed, and closed her eyes. What would it be like seeing him again? What would they talk about? Her past relationships, his? She had too much going on in her life to get involved with any man. She didn't even feel the need for a man. She closed her eyes and reminisced about her and Brad dating back in the day.

Brad was her first love, and the only boy that Darian had dated in high school. Both got good grades and went to college. While they were in college, they drifted apart, stopped dating, and went their separate ways.

It was Mardi Gras month, and she remembered their first kiss. The air in the streets smelled of romance and excitement. People were dancing in the streets and following parades for blocks. Darian had caught six necklaces and wore them around her neck. She looked for Monique because they had to be home by eleven.

While looking for Monique, Darian ran into Brad. "I called you twice, Brad, but you weren't home," Darian said and blushed as he held his hand out to her. She was cold, and the wind had blown her baseball cap off her head. Brad picked it up and replaced it gently on her head.

"I think if you didn't have so much hair your cap would stay on. I've been looking for you at least an hour. Your sister went home. She says to tell you it's too cold out here."

"She does that every year. If it's under thirty degrees, Monique can't take it." Darian looked at her Timex watch. "It's only nine-thirty. I still have until eleven before I have to be home."

Brad placed his arm around her waist as they walked and watched the parades, the tourists, the sober, and the intoxicated. They laughed at one man that took his pants off and threw them at one of the floats.

As Darian and Brad walked she looked up at him. He was tall, his face the color of dark brown sugar. Brad's eyes were dark, and because of his accident during football practice, he had a scar above his brow on the right side of his forehead, but it had gotten smaller. He wore tight jeans over his lean, muscular build. All the girls liked Brad, but his eyes were filled with Darian.

Darian and Brad stopped at Jackson Square and took a seat on a bench while watching everyone go by.

Trying to keep her warm, Brad pulled Darian close to him. He still held her hand, and when a float passed that she wanted to see, Darian leaped off the bench, and so did Brad. She felt his hand slowly and gently circling her small waist, his face close to hers, his lips gently brushing against her face as he captured her lips. Her heart was thumping fast, and her knees weakened. Brad's full mouth covered hers as she heard his breathing deepen, and felt his tongue explore the inside of her mouth. He tasted sweet and he was so gentle. An unfamilar excitement had taken over her body, and her thoughts, as she felt butterflies float inside her stomach. This wasn't the first time Brad had kissed her, and the thought of sex had slipped into her mind and frightened her.

She sighed and wondered now if it could be as thrilling and passionate as his kisses. As though she was coming out of a daze her eyes sprang open. She blinked and pulled away. *I won't fall in love with him,* she thought.

He was still a nice-looking man and had done well for himself, Darian thought. But she wasn't a kid anymore, and she had responsibilities. She had so much to do. There was no time for falling in love with anyone. Wade found his way into Darian's thoughts with his lies, and left her with a broken heart. How long had he cheated on her? Her mind went back to Brad again. Maybe they could become friends.

She closed her eyes, slipping into a deep sleep.

It was early Christmas morning, and the house was tranquil except for the crackling of the burning fireplace that Darian had lit. Still in her blue and white flannel pajamas, Darian was in the kitchen making hot cocoa for the girls before she woke them up to open their presents. She was haggard from wrapping so many gifts the night before. Shirlee scolded her for spending so much money on gifts. She even accused Darian of spoiling the girls. But how could she not spoil them? They had lost their mother and had no father.

"For God's sake, Shelby, you frightened me to death," Darian scolded and turned around to look at her. She was facing the stove when Shelby came up behind her.

Shelby giggled. There were more tiny footsteps coming closer. They were Nikki's.

Leading them to the living room, Darian took both girls by their hands. "Come on and see what Santa brought you two." The girls screamed and ran to the tree.

Darian helped by passing out the presents. She gave Nikki six boxes. It was such a pleasure watching the sparkle in their eyes, the smiles on their small faces. When they weren't paying any attention to Darian, she looked up and whispered, "How did I do, Monique?"

It was noon, and Darian stood at the front door watching the neighbor's children on bikes, skateboards, and roller skates in the middle of the streets. She smiled inwardly. It brought back so many memories of the childhood that she and Monique had shared. Of late, so many memories and recollections of the past were coming back to her. However, today was Christmas and the girls were happy.

Darian stepped outside. Her intake of breath sounded like it hissed as the cold December air covered her from head to toe. She folded her arms and ran back inside and gathered wrapping paper that covered the living room floor. She hit her toe against the red fire truck that she had bought for Shelby's doll.

Darian was in the girls' room when she heard the doorbell ring. She ran to the living room and opened the door. Shirlee entered with a pot in her hand. Jefferson was right behind her with his arms full of presents.

"So I was the one that bought too many presents for the girls," Darian said as Jefferson dropped the boxes on the sofa.

"I still have more to unload," Jefferson replied.

Shirlee placed the pot on the stove and stood in front of Darian. "Bay, you look tired. Maybe coming over here was better than you and the girls coming to my house."

"Yes, it's better. The girls can play with their toys. I've been up since five-thirty so I lay on the sofa while they played. Then at seven they wanted pancakes for breakfast. I think Shelby has a virus or something." Darian frowned and pushed back a straying hair from her face.

Darian heard Jefferson ringing the doorbell again and rushed back into the living room as Shirlee followed.

"My goodness, Mama. Did you buy out the store?" Darian asked, and the girls grabbed their presents and started to open the boxes. Wrapping paper was all over the living room floor again.

Jefferson sat on the sofa and Shirlee sat beside him. "We're going to see Jefferson's sister later today. But I told her it would be after dinner."

Darian looked at her mother. She and Jefferson were dressed in black leather pants, but Shirlee was wearing a black sweater and boots. She was a size 14, and in Darian's opinion, her clothes were too tight. But she had dressed that way as long as Darian could remember, and Jefferson seemed to like it. In spite of the way Darian felt about their marriage, he was devoted to her mother. The age difference didn't seem to matter, and as Darian glanced at Shirlee and Jefferson, she could feel the love they had between them.

The girls were running all through the house, toys in the middle of the floor and yelling as they pushed Nikki's fire truck from one room to the other.

"I wonder if I made a mistake by buying that damn fire truck?" Darian asked. As soon as Darian started to complain, they heard a loud clamor where Nikki had pushed the truck against the table, and a bowl fell to the floor. Shelby screamed as she stepped on a piece of straying glass that cut her foot. Darian picked Shelby up and carried her to the bathroom to clean her foot, and wrapped a bandage around it.

"Soon you'll know what to buy, and what not," Shirlee commented. "Jefferson, why don't you pour us a glass of wine? I'll sweep the glass up," she said as though it was an everyday occurrence.

"Sure, baby." Jefferson went to the kitchen to get the wine from the refrigerator.

"Hey, I could use a bowl of that gumbo."

"So can I, Jefferson," Darian said. "Why don't I warm it up so we can eat? The girls were too excited to eat their breakfast. All they've been eating is cookies, candy, and nuts. I better go check on them."

In the kitchen, Darian ignited the fire on the stove to warm the gumbo. She thought that she heard Shelby and went to check on her. Darian looked at Shelby, worried, and placed her hand over her forehead. It was warm. "Shelby, are you ill? Sit up, honey." Darian's mouth fell open as she saw the small blisters on Shelby's face. "Mama, Mama, come here quickly," Darian yelled.

Shirlee and Jefferson ran into the bedroom. "Lord, what is it now?" Shirlee asked, holding Jefferson's hand.

"Look at her face, Mama. It wasn't like this earlier."

Darian didn't know what to do. She was so tired of problems. It seemed as soon as one problem was solved, another quickly took its place.

Shirlee sat on the edge of the bed and examined Shelby's face, pulled up her T-shirt, and looked at her chest, back, thighs, and legs. "Well, it appears that Shelby has the chickenpox. Have you seen the children's shot records? They have to have them for school, and I'm sure that Monique kept a copy someplace around here."

"You're asking me? How am I supposed to know about school records for shots? So, what am I supposed to do now, Mama? I don't know one thing about chickenpox."

Shirlee stood up, hands on hips, and looked at Shelby. "Just settle down, Darian. She did get her shots taken because I went with Monique so I could watch Nikki. I had just forgotten. So she'll only have a light case of it. Now, for the bad part, in about ten days, Nikki may have them, too."

"What do I do? I'm not prepared for this, no one told me anything." Darian took another look at Shelby, gently rubbed her face, and kissed her on top of her head.

"We'll be eating soon," Shirlee told Jefferson.

"Okay. But I don't know what all the fuss is about. Kids are supposed to get chickenpox," he murmured under his breath.

Darian stood up again. "They do not, Jefferson," she snapped. No one asked him anyway, she thought. "Do you really think that Nikki will get the chickenpox, too? Two small kids sick at the same time?"

"Darian, it's really not a terminal disease. Plenty of children will have chickenpox. Look, Bay, you've gone through so much and so have I. When Nikki gets it, we'll take care of the children together. Believe me, worse things can happen."

Darian looked at the red blisters on Shelby's neck. Shelby's face was polka-dotted all over with small blisters. The doorbell rang, and Darian jumped. "Now, who could that be?" she snapped and rushed to the door.

Lord, will I react this way every time one of the children gets sick? she wondered.

Darian swung the door wide open. "Brad." She looked at her watch, surprised. Where had the day gone? "Hi, come on in."

"Is this a bad time, Darian? I can come another time," he said hesitantly.

"No. I mean yes. It is a good time. Have a seat." She was flustered as she sat down next to him.

Brad sat on the sofa but he could see that Darian was obviously upset. He looked toward the kitchen where he heard movements.

"That's Jefferson, my mom's husband. They bought gifts, gumbo, and desserts for us. And we just discovered that my niece has chickenpox, and I have no idea what to do about it. But my mom is pretty calm since my sister and I had it as children."

Darian took his leather jacket and hung it up in the hall closet. He was well dressed, wearing all black. When Darian sat next to him she glanced at his eyes. Light brown eyes set deeply into the smooth chocolate-colored face. His hair was black and neatly cut, as though he had just left the barbershop. Brad was a tall, robust man over six feet, blessed with wide shoulders and good looks. He flashed her a smile that would melt most women's hearts. Age hadn't changed him much. She could recognize him a block away.

Still wondering if he came at an inconvenient time, he felt relieved. "My son just got over chickenpox, and my neighbor's kid has it now. I can tell you what to do." He held his hand out to her. "Lead the way so I can see the little one."

Darian was amazed that he knew more about children than she did. She gladly took his hand and from that moment she felt confident that he could help. They walked hand in hand to the girls' bedroom. Shirlee was looking inside the medicine cabinet. She heard a strange man's voice and walked back to the bedroom with some aspirins in her hand. "Who is this?" she asked and stopped at the door. She stood back to get a closer look at Brad. Damn, he was a chiseled hunk of a man, too. *Looks like Darian got someone to keep her warm during the winter nights,* Shirlee thought.

"Mama, do you remember Brad? We dated while we were in college."

Shirlee stared at Brad for a few seconds. "Are you Louise's boy?"

"Yes, I am. My name is Brad." He held out his hand. "I was telling Darian that my son just recovered from chickenpox." Brad sat down on the edge of the bed. "First you need some calamine lotion for the itching and acetaminophen for pain."

"No calamine lotion or that other stuff in the medicine cabinet. Tell you what, Jefferson and I will run to the store. We'll be right back."

Darian followed Shirlee back to the living room. Shirlee headed for the door and turned around again. "You better keep him around, honey. He can be some help to you." She started to walk out the door and stopped again. "Hey, wait a minute. Did he say his son had chickenpox? I hope that doesn't mean he's a married man?" Shirlee had one hand on her hip waiting for Darian to answer.

Shirlee looked so ridiculous that Darian had to laugh. "No, Mama, but he's raising his eight-year-old son. Now, please leave already."

Rushing to get to the store, Shirlee waved her hand at Darian as though there wasn't anything else to say, and rushed out the door where Jefferson was waiting.

"Let Darian entertain her company without her mother hovering over her. That girl needs a man to help her raise those children. Can't you see how nervous and jumpy she was? The girls will take a nap soon. Darian and Brad can talk, and maybe she might relax a little." They were walking to the car.

Darian sat on the edge of the bed next to Brad. Shelby looked as though she was frightened.

"You'll feel better soon, Shelby. Brad's son had chickenpox, too. But now he's well again. You won't be ill for very long." Darian kissed Shelby on the cheek for reassurance.

"Who's the little one sitting on the bed with her thumb in her mouth?"

"That's Nikki. She's only three years old." Darian looked at Nikki and smiled. "She'll be four next month." Nikki was very quiet after Brad came into their bedroom.

The girls looked at him as though he was an intruder.

"I really respect what you're doing, Darian. Monique was lucky to have you for a sister."

"Thanks. I needed to hear that. It wasn't easy and I gave up a great career. But what could I do? The kids were my only sister's children. I can have a great career here, too."

A half hour had passed when Darian heard Shirlee coming through the front door. She ran to the living room and met her.

"I left Jefferson in the car since you have help with Shelby. You didn't tell me that you were expecting company," Shirlee said and gave Darian the brown bag.

"Well, it's not like I'm on a date or anything, Mama. He's just a friend."

"You have two children, Darian. Take my advice, make him more than just a friend."

"I can't date anyone right now, Mama. I'm not ready and by the way the girls are reacting, they're not ready either. Nikki's in bed as though she's afraid to move."

"They will get used to him if he keeps coming around. You better catch that man and keep him. I can tell that he likes you."

"But, Mama, you only just met him. This is only the second time we've seen each other since I have been home. The first time was briefly at the bank."

"I don't care. He looks at you that certain way. Anyway, a man that tall and good-looking, you better grab him. Does he have a good job?"

"Yes, Mama."

"Well, don't be foolish. Now, I'll call and check on Shelby later." Shirlee went back and said good-bye to Brad.

Darian sighed. Sure, Brad was good-looking and nice, but she wasn't looking for romance right now.

"Here is the medication we need," she said and sat next to Shelby.

"Rub it all over her body," Brad instructed.

Darian did as Brad advised, but by the time she was finished, Shelby was fast asleep. Darian went to Nikki and pulled the blanket up to her shoulders. "Looks like they're asleep."

"They were up before daylight. Why don't we go to the living room?" Darian suggested.

She sat next to Brad with her wineglass in her hand. "What should we drink to?" She held her glass up.

"To old friends and happiness," Brad said and clicked his glass against hers.

"I like the sound of that."

They sipped their wine, and Darian felt his eyes intensely on her. She glanced at his muscular arms.

"Life is full of irony. I would never have thought we would be sitting together again. If my life was like it used to be, I would have arrived in New Orleans on Wednesday and back to L.A. on Sunday. One never knows what the future may produce."

"No one ever knows. But you make the best of it. When I married I thought it would have last forever. Tanya was loving in the beginning. We met at the school board Christmas dance and got together the day after. We knew each other in college but nothing happened. I went to work and there she was. I fell head over hills in love. But as the years passed I still wondered why we didn't stay together. We had great chemistry."

"Here, let me refill your glass," Darian said and shivered. The conversation was getting too intimate. She remembered Tanya with the big derriere and voluptuous breasts. That's what all the guys wanted when they were younger.

"Would you believe I always thought we would get married and have a couple of kids?" He waited for her response, as she looked speechless. Her face was so perfectly sculpted. Brad couldn't draw his eyes away from her.

Darian's brows knitted together. "I didn't know, Brad." She sat back and curled her feet under her. "You should have used a little persuasion on me."

"I should have. I regretted it every time I thought of you. After my son was born our lives had gotten too complicated. Tanya stayed home with the baby and complainted about how lonely she was. I didn't understand why, and tried to do everything to make her happy. I owed her that much. The next thing I knew she was leaving the baby with my mother. I'd come home and she wouldn't be there."

He looked so sad and Darian touched his hand. It was big and warm. *Why are we talking about the past anyway?*

"When my son was three years old she packed her suitcase and left him with my mother. She moved in with another man. She said that he was exciting, and all I did was work. But I had a house note and a wife and baby to support. I took my son from my mother and now I'm raising him with my mother's help."

"That's some story. But lucky for your son, he has you for a father." As long as Darian could remember, which was so typically Brad, he was always the good guy. Maybe one day it would pay off for him, she thought.

"So, tell me about your life in Los Angeles."

"It was mostly work. But I loved L.A. The weather is never really cold. I used to laugh at women that complained about the weather. It wasn't winter, as we know it. They didn't know what cold weather was. I worked as a buyer. The last day I was there I had earned the promotion of my dream with a big office, a view of downtown. Next thing I knew, I'm responsible for my sister's children here in New Orleans."

"And your love life?" Brad asked with a teasing glint in his eyes. He could sit there and look at her all night, the way she curved her mouth when she smiled, the pear-shaped face and kissable lips.

Darian cleared her throat. "I fell in love, but it's over now. When I went to L.A. for a weekend, he was at his apartment with another woman. But it could have been because I have Monique's children. But everything happens for the best. I may never find a man that wants a ready-made family. I was under the illusion that it was good between us. We had our careers and we were always together." Her heart was sinking but she kept her head high. She had already cried enough over Wade. She took a deep breath. *Don't you dare, girl,* she thought to herself.

"You don't have to talk about it now, Darian." He reached over and squeezed her hand. "Being with someone that knows your history will make you think about the past."

"Well, now I'm in a completely different world, and in the most unimaginable way. But I'm here, and I'm staying."

Brad sprawled his long legs out and under the coffee table. "Two children are not so many that would prevent a man from marrying you. All he has to do is love you."

Darian sighed and looked into his eyes. For a fraction of a second she needed his arms around her. She had never felt so lonely.

"Your're still hurting, aren't you?" he asked, looking deeply into her eyes.

"Not like I used to. I've accepted the children to love and take care of, but it's a tremendous responsibility. I've never thought of someone else depending on me." Now she felt Brad stroking her hand. It felt nice, warm, and a little bit sexy. "Would you like something to eat?" Darian asked.

"No, thanks. I ate too much at my mother's house. She even baked a sweet potato pie for me and Tyc to take home."

"Well, now that you know there are children here, you can bring your son along the next time." Their eyes met and locked until Nikki stood in front of Darian. Saved by Nikki, Darian thought.

"Hi, little one. You sure are a cute little girl," Brad said and turned back to face Darian. "It's time I go now, baby. I'll call and check on Shelby tomorrow." He stood up and started to walk toward the door.

"Thanks, Brad." Darian stood on the tip of her toes

and kissed him on the cheek. She felt him squeeze her hand again, and he looked at her face as though he wanted to speak, but instead he turned on his heel and left.

Darian released a loud sigh of relief and picked up Nikki. She kissed her on the cheek. "Let's go and see if Shelby is awake."

She stood at the bedroom door and heard Shelby stir. Darian turned the lamp on and sat on the edge of the bed. She sat Nikki at the foot. Shelby was awake but made no attempt to get out of bed. "Are you hungry, honey?"

"Yes. I want some gumbo. But I don't want to stay in bed by myself," she whimpered. Her face was puffy and the tip of her nose was red and runny.

Darian looked at her for a few moments. "You know what, you guys? It's Christmas and we should be able to see the Christmas tree. How about I make the sofa into a bed and we can sleep on it tonight?"

Shelby sat up straight in bed. "Okay."

"Okay. So let's go to the kitchen so you two can eat. While you're eating, I'll make the bed for us. Then we can watch TV and see the lights on the Christmas tree."

Shelby wasn't feeling very well but her spirits lifted a bit as she walked into the kitchen and sat next to Nikki.

This Christmas was different than any before. Darian always came home for the holidays to spend time with her family, but the loss they had endured took a toll on all their lives. As Darian glanced at Shelby her small face was enlivened with her suggesting that they could all sleep together near the tree.

Darian was indeed sinking into motherhood. If Monique were looking down at her she would be proud.

Chapter 17

It was the morning after Christmas and the ringing of the telephone caused Darian to jump out of a deep sleep. Not used to sleeping on the sofa, Darian had forgotten where she was, and who was in bed with her. Shelby had kept Darian up late into the night, and she was exhausted.

The phone rang again and she climbed across Nikki, jumped off the sofa, and ran to the phone. Why didn't she place it by the bed? It was Barbara Price, the Realtor. Darian frowned as her voice boomed loudly against her ear.

"Hi, Darian. I hope you and your family had a merry Christmas."

"Thanks, Barbara. We did but poor Shelby has chickenpox. Nikki will probably have them next."

Nikki overheard the phone conversation and started crying until Darian pulled her into her arms.

"You need some good news, honey. I called to inform you to start packing. The house is yours."

"Oh, thank you, Barbara. This is the best Christmas present." Darian beamed with a warm smile. "I've been praying for some good news about the house."

"You wanted a thirty-day escrow and it looks like that's what you're getting. I'll stay in touch, sweetie."

There she goes wih that sweetie and honey stuff again, Darian thought as she laid her head back against the sofa. The phone had awakened the girls, too.

"Thanks for calling, Barbara." When she hung up and put Nikki down on the floor, she jumped up and down joyfully. Finally, something good had happened in her life.

Darian was lying next to the phone when it rang again. "Hi, Brad. Shelby isn't feeling well, but you did help yesterday."

"You have my phone number, so call if you need me. It only takes ten minutes to get there."

"I will, Brad. Oh, the Realtor called and my loan was approved."

"Soon you'll be in your own home. That's good news for you and the girls."

"You bet it is. It's exactly what I needed to hear." Seconds passed as silence fell between them. "I want to see you again, Darian."

She didn't know what to say. And she wasn't sure she was ready to start dating Brad. She needed someone to hold her, tell her that she was loved, but she couldn't risk it again, not now when she had so much going on in her life. "You have my number, Brad, and you know where to find me." Damn, why did she say that? She shook her head; it was too late to retract the statement.

"Good, I was hoping that you would say that. Anyway, call if you need me."

That was the end of their conversation, but she had to admit, it was nice to have Brad so concerned about her and the girls. She thought of the night before when they were sitting on the sofa and he held her hand. She felt comfortable with him and they had something in common. He was raising his son, and she had her nieces. He was so gentle with Shelby, and Darian could see that he understood what it was to be a parent. She had no doubt that Brad was a good father.

Darian picked up the phone again and dialed. "Good morning, Jefferson. May I speak to Mom?"

"Sure, Darian. How is Shelby?"

"She had me up all night. And she's still not feeling well, but I'm keeping her warm and in bed."

"Hello, Mama."

"What is it, Bay?" Shirlee asked with interest.

"My loan for the house was approved. The house belongs to me. Barbara called to tell me a few minutes ago. As soon as I get some boxes I'm going to start packing."

"That's wonderful. I can't tell you how happy I am for the news. Now, do you need me for anything today?"

"No. I'm all right. I'm staying inside, but I'll call if I need you." Darian hung up and sat on the sofa with the girls.

They were still in their pajamas, and Darian sat on the sofa sipping a cup of green tea. It must have been at least thirty degrees outside and she had turned the heaters on to keep warm. The living room was cozy with the Christmas tree in the corner; toys sprawled in the middle of the floor, waiting to be played with.

It began raining. Thunder and lightning resonated through the small house. It was one day closer to the New Year. Since they were moving, Darian had no choice but to pack Monique's clothing. *I'll donate them to the Goodwill,* Darian thought.

Darian was up at eleven that night and again at one. Shelby cried and complained of the itching all over her body. Her head hurt; she was cold and cried for Monique. As Darian held Shelby in her arms, her heart warmed over for the child.

Shirlee told Darian to mix oatmeal in the calamine lotion. At three in the morning Darian was dabbing it all over Shelby's body. She fed Shelby some warm tea and placed the little girl in her lap, rocking her back and forth until she was asleep.

Darian covered both girls. Thank God Nikki slept through all of it. Darian eased under the covers and was asleep instantly.

She jumped and reached groggily for the phone before it woke the girls.

"You sound ill, Darian. Are you all right?" Shirlee asked.

"I didn't get to sleep until four this morning. Shelby kept me up because she was itching during the night. I don't want to wake them."

"Go back to sleep while you can. I'll be over this afternoon." Shirlee smiled as she hung up the phone. Darian had done remarkably well adjusting to motherhood.

Darian peeked out the window as Shirlee drove up the driveway and slammed the door as she walked away from her car.

Darian opened the door and went back to the sofa. She was sleepy, and rubbed her eyes. "Hi, Mama."

Shirlee stepped inside the house and closed the door behind her. She gazed at Darian's appearance. "You look like a young girl with that ponytail, Darian."

"Thanks. I'll take that as a compliment since I have a sick child on my hands."

"It was a compliment. So stop frowning. I keep telling you it causes wrinkles." Shirlee inadvertently touched the small lines across her forehead.

Shirlee looked in on the girls, then went back to the kitchen and made a cup of coffee. She was unaware that Darian was observing her. She wore no makeup and her face was pale. She looked as though she wasn't getting much sleep either.

Darian grinned when she also noticed that Shirlee had been there for half an hour without looking into a mirror or freshening her lipstick and patting her hair in place.

"Stop that running before you fall and break your neck, Nikki," Shirlee yelled.

Nikki pouted. Her bottom lip trembled as she started to cry. Darian picked her up and sat on the sofa next to her. Shirlee sat in the chair opposite them.

"Okay, Mama. You're not wearing any makeup and you yelled at the baby. So what did Jefferson do to make you so angry?" Darian sat back, crossed her legs, and waited for Shirlee's reply.

"That idiot? I could just kick his ass out in the streets. We went to a party last night. He was drinking liquor like a thirsty billy goat. I told him that I was ready to go home. I mean, there were too many young, flirty women there and they were falling all over the men. Well, not that I'm old, you know. I'm only fifty now—"

"Fifty-two, Mama," Darian corrected with a smirk. "Fifty-two."

Shirlee frowned and rolled her eyes at Darian. "Like I was saying, I wondered what Jefferson was doing in the kitchen so long. I went in there to see for myself. He had this little tramp pinned up against the wall so tight, one could swear they were having sex."

"Well, were they?" Darian asked.

"Hell no. I'm not in jail, am I? If that would have happened, and with me right there in the same house, his ass would be six foot under," she hissed, then pulled her small compact from her purse and looked into the mirror. "I need to color my hair." She ran her fingers slowly through her hair. "I can see a few gray hairs mingling and making a home up there."

"You look good, Mama. And as for Jefferson . . . he's still young, you know."

Shirlee glared at Darian furiously. "You just love to wash my face with the age difference, don't you? Haven't I been through enough? This is the first Christmas without Monique." She wiped a tear with the back of her hand. "I've suffered enough and one would think that you and Jefferson would have more compassion." She blew her nose and dabbed at her eyes. "What a year it's been. I'm looking forward to the New Year. But who am I kidding? A new year won't take this pain away from my chest every time I think of Monique. I'm suffocating with pain."

"You're absolutely right, Mama. You have been through enough and it was insensitive of me to say that. Have you eaten anything today?"

For a moment Shirlee couldn't answer, and closed her eyes to choke down the tears. "Yes. I ate already. But thanks anyway. Now, tell me about Brad. Does he want you two to get together?"

"We didn't discuss *us*, Mama. Though he did say he wants to see me again. I've got too much on my mind right now. But I am excited that the escrow is only thirty days so we can move soon. Can you stay here for a few minutes so I can go out and find some boxes? I was so glad to hear Barbara's voice."

"Sure. I don't want to look at Jefferson's face today anyway."

"I'll bet he's sorry, Mama. That's if he remembers."

"He said that he was sorry, but I'm still angry as hell. And did you say Barbara? So you two are on a first-name basis, huh?" Shirlee asked with disapproval. "You better be careful with who you pick for a friend, Darian. If I were you, I'd keep that one at a distance." Shirlee pushed her mirror back inside her purse and placed her purse on the table.

"Mama, you don't realize how you sound when you talk like that, and I'm not going to sit here and listen to you moan and complain about everyone and everything."

"Okay, miss. Since you know everything, I won't tell you any more. But when she slaps you on that narrow ass of yours, don't come hollering for me. I won't say I told you so either," Shirlee said, pointing her finger at Darian.

"Lord, Mama," Darian said as she went to put some shoes on. She peeked in on Shelby and saw her reading a book.

Shirlee and Nikki were sitting on the sofa when Darian came from the bedroom with her Coach purse hanging from her shoulder. "Nikki, go and get me a tissue from my bedroom." Darian turned around to face Shirlee. "I didn't want her to hear. But Shelby was crying last night and asked for Monique, but she hasn't mentioned her today. They still don't realize that she's gone for good."

"I imagine the poor child really felt sick last night. Poor baby. It's hard on a child when they lose a parent. It was difficult for you and Monique when Ronald died."

Darian nodded in agreement. "Do you need anything from the store?"

"No." Shirlee glanced at the baggy sweatpants, an ugly oversized T-shirt, and no makeup, not even lipstick on her lips. "I certainly hope Brad doesn't see you looking like you've just finished mopping the floor."

Darian blew her hair from her face and mumbled as she pranced out the door.

Darian drove down Bourbon Street and turned the corner when she saw a stack of boxes on the side of the Circle Food Store. She stopped, and pushed as many boxes that would fit inside the Volkswagen. She would never get used to driving a small bug. She had sold her BMW the day before she left Los Angeles. Darian had planned to go car shopping that weekend. But there was no reason to rush out and buy another car. She had to manage her money wisely.

The boxes were stacked so high she couldn't see out the back window. Now, if she could just get home without being stopped by some cocky policeman.

Darian hissed between her teeth as she parked in back of Jefferson's pickup truck. Why couldn't he just park on the streets so she wouldn't have to move again? Guess he came over to beg Mama's forgiveness. She laughed to herself and took the boxes out of the car and went inside.

"Hi, Jefferson. Heard you went to a nice party last night." Darian looked at Shirlee and smirked.

"Yes, it was all right. *Smart-ass,* Jefferson thought to himself. *She'll never get a man with that snappy tongue of hers.* "Can we go home now, Shirlee? Baby, I swear I had too much to drink last night, that's all. Don't I always give you the highest respect?"

Darian stood in the hall laughing at how well he could beg when he had to. What happened to that tough-man, construction-worker attitude? He needed to shave that nappy hair off his face. He looked as though he had been intoxicated for a week.

"Mama, if you and Jefferson have something to do, I'm in for the day."

"Come on, Shirlee. Let's go home and talk this over," Jefferson pleaded.

Shirlee got up and grabbed her purse. "Oh, all right. I'll call you tomorrow, Darian."

"I'll be here." Darian walked them to the door. "Come on, Nikki. Let's go see your sister." Darian sat Nikki on the opposite twin bed and uncovered Shelby so she could check her body. "How do you feel, Shelby? You don't feel as hot as you did last night."

"I'm hungry, and I want to play with my toys." Shelby sat up in bed and rubbed her eyes.

"Good girl. Do you want some gumbo?"

"Yes. Can I take my dolly and sit on the sofa?" Her eyes were puffy and red; her face was thin and pink with spots on her cheeks.

"Okay, but you can sit on the sofa with this blanket covering you. I want you to keep warm and get well. Hey, girls, we're moving to that new house. Remember?"

Shelby nodded her head, and Nikki did everything she saw Shelby do.

After lunch Darian started going through the house to get rid of everything she didn't want. It made no sense to take Monique's furniture when she had her own. Shirlee could come over and pick out what she wanted, and maybe they could have a yard sale. There were keepsakes that she would keep for the girls until they grew old enough to appreciate them. She would cherish the thick photograph book that was kept in Monique's room.

Darian sat on Monique's bed and looked at the old photos. Monique had all the classic pictures of when they were children. So many happy memories that made her feel sad. The phone rang, and Darian was thankful for the interruption. She touched her face; it was wet with tears.

"Are you all right, Darian? Or could you use some company for a while?" Brad asked with hope and concern.

She held the phone for a few seconds before she responded. "You called at a good time. I was sitting in Monique's room looking at photos. I sure could use your company, Brad."

"Sure, baby. I can be there in fifteen minutes." Brad

brushed his teeth and combed his hair. His son was playing with his cousins at his grandmother's house. He was lucky that both grandmothers lived in New Orleans.

Brad couldn't seem to get Darian out of his mind. Darian didn't know it yet, but she was a good mother to her nieces. Brad was sure that she could be a good wife, too. But it was too soon to discuss marriage. She had the warmth and the loving qualities that he was searching for. He had noticed the way she took care of Shelby. Darian had given up everything to raise her sister's children. She was a remarkable woman, not to mention that she was attractive, too. He had known her as a young girl years ago, but spending time with her on Christmas night, he wanted to get to know the woman. He was thirty-eight; it was time he dated a woman that was interested in a future together. Darian was what he had been searching for.

The doorbell rang and Darian ran to answer. "Hi, come on in," she said as Brad stepped inside. He held her hand and gave her a big bear hug.

Darian sighed. "I needed that. Would you like something to eat?"

"No. But I would like to say hello to the girls," he said and followed her to the sofa where the girls were playing. Brad examined Shelby's face and shook Nikki's hand. He laughed when she pulled her small hand from his.

"We can sit at the table in the dining room so we can hear each other speaking. Sometimes I can't hear myself thinking when the girls are playing." She led the way.

Brad trailed. Looking at her ponytail bouncing from

side to side made him smile. She had the face of an angel, and the class to go along with it.

They sat down, both on the same side of the table. Darian looked twice when Brad selected his seat. "I have some boxes so I can start packing tomorrow."

"Need any help?" he asked.

Brad hadn't changed at all. It was as though no time had passed between them. He was still easy to be friends with. Some men made her nervous, but not Brad. "It's nice of you to help, but right now I just want to sit and relax. With Shelby ill I haven't been able to sleep through the night for days. Why are you smiling?"

"Do you remember the argument we had at school about Loretta Thomas? You were so angry with me. You socked me in the chest and knocked the wind out of me. Do you remember that?"

Darian could feel her face bloom. She placed her hands against her face. "Do I ever. I would get so jealous when I saw you with another girl. Everyone knew how easy Loretta was. I didn't know I had knocked the wind out of you. Though you did deserve it," she said, lifting her chin. "What made you think of that?"

"You were wearing your hair the same as now. Your ponytail always made you look younger. I remember when Jacob Henderson used to sit behind you and pull on it."

She touched her hair as though she'd forgotten to comb it.

Brad moved her hand from her hair. "Leave it alone. I like it that way, and you still look very young. Anyone else would think you are babysitting for someone older."

Darian blushed. He was sitting close to her, too close. She hadn't realized how lonely she really was since she had returned home.

"Do you ever see anyone we went to school with?" Darian asked.

Brad looked as though he was trying to remember. "I saw Ken Drew two weeks ago. He works at the courthouse. But I forget what he does there. Anyway, he looks about ten years older than we do."

"You and Vickie are the only two I have seen since I've been home. I'm very lucky to have friends like you two," Darian said. "Can I ask you a question, Brad?" Her tone changed to a serious one.

"Yes, what?"

"Are you dating anyone in particular?" She cringed inwardly, waiting for his response.

"I've been dating but it's not anyone in particular. I have not met anyone that I would want to get serious with." *Except you*, he thought. But he didn't want to take her too fast or frighten her either.

"Why do you ask, Darian?" he asked, his head tilted. He looked into her eyes and they were so serious, and yet so soft. He and Darian hadn't stayed in touch through the years. But they were together now.

"I just thought I should know."

Brad put his hand up to stop her from explaining. "It's all right, Darian. But if I were seriously dating someone, I wouldn't be here with you. When I'm involved, believe me, I really get into the person. No lies, no games."

Darian nodded in agreement. He made it sound so simple.

"Now that we have that off our chests, do you have anything cold to drink?" Brad asked. They looked in each other's eyes, and he held a lock of her hair between two fingers. It was as soft as a feather. "Pretty," Brad complimented. Every time he looked at her he wanted to touch her hair and brush his lips against hers. The effect she had on him was magnetic; it was hard to keep his hands off her. She was simply enthralling. This was going to be hard, he thought.

"Come on in the kitchen with me. We can see what you want to drink. My mother brought so much of everything over here on Christmas Day. We still have gumbo, desserts, and sodas. Oh, and I have apple juice."

Darian opened the refrigerator. "Here, how about a glass of wine?" She gave Brad the bottle to open and took two glasses from the cabinet.

They went back into the dining room. It was small with a wooden table and four chairs and a large painting on the wall of different shapes of mountains and trees, in all green and brown.

"When I started at the school board and earned enough money, I was able to afford a house for me and Tye. But it can use a woman's touch. One day soon you and the girls should come over and I'll throw some hot dogs on the grill. We can do something with the children together. I would like that, Darian," he said and looked into her eyes to see what reaction he would get from her.

"The girls would love it, and so will I."

She felt Brad's eyes on her, but she had nothing more to give him. It was still too soon. Her expression remained impassive.

Brad touched her hand. "How's the book coming along?"

"It's okay. I'm still working on it. But I have more research to do, and some revising. I take notes of the questions that the girls ask. I can only write at night."

They talked for hours until Brad looked at his watch.

"It's four and I promised Tye that I would take him to a movie. Working long hours, I try and make it up to him on the weekends and holidays."

Darian walked with Brad outside. He kissed her on

the cheek, and her blood raced to the top of her head. What was she feeling?

Brad held her hand longer than necessary and let go after she gently took a step backward. He wanted to kiss her long and tenderly, hold her in his arms, and tell her that he would make a safe and loving life for her and the girls. But still, it was too soon.

As Brad drove back to Tye's grandmother's house he couldn't stop thinking of Darian. He would take her slowly, easily, and when the time was right he would ask her to marry him. Whatever it took, he would win her heart. He would make her happy, as he was certain that she could make him happy, too. Brad hadn't been so sure of anything in his life. He wouldn't lose her again.

Chapter 18

"Well, here we are again. Just you and me on New Year's Eve," Vickie complained as she filled her glass with wine. "I said last year that I wouldn't be caught alone again on New Year's Eve. Bernard won't be home till morning, and I didn't want to be alone. New Year's Eve is when lovers should be planning their future together, Darian." Vickie folded her arms against her chest like a disappointed child.

Darian sat on the sofa next to Vickie and placed her arm around her shoulder. "Oh, Vickie, we're not the only two that are alone tonight. What if we were stuck with men that we're unhappy with? Honey, I would rather be alone."

"Yes, I guess you're right. Bernard better be serious about giving up that position as a truck driver. When he gets home we are going to discuss having a baby. If he says no again, I don't know if I'm going to stay in this marriage. He still says that he's too old."

"I hope you can convince him, Vickie. You went into the marriage knowing he didn't want children, though forty-four years old for a man is not that old."

"No, it's not too old at all. Where's Shirlee and Jefferson tonight?"

"She was angry at Jefferson a few days ago, so I would say they're probably at home making up, if you know what I mean," Darian said, and laughed. "My mother doesn't make it a secret about how she likes to satisfy her man."

"In a way that's good. My mother doesn't tell me anything about her boyfriend. Everything is a secret with her." Vickie sipped her wine. "Do you remember Eric Black?"

"Wasn't he the one that started calling you Black Beauty?" Darian asked.

"Yes, that's him. I ran into him yesterday at the mall. He's fat and country-looking. He asked about you."

"You were so angry when he called you Black Beauty, but it's only because you were the darkest and the prettiest girl in our class. You have that dark pretty skin and your face is one that other girls hated you for. So why did you get so mad, Vickie?" Darian placed her empty glass on the coffee table in front of her and popped a mint into her mouth.

"It was just a shyness thing, girl."

"But most of us wanted to be you. You got all the boyfriends."

"Well, whatever. How many glasses of wine have we had?" Vickie asked. She was looking at her empty glass.

"Too many. But what else is there to do?" It was straight-up twelve midnight, New Year's Eve, and the phone rang.

Darian got up to answer and brought the phone back to the sofa.

"Happy New Year, Darian."

She hesitated, surprised by his call. Brad's voice was so rich and tantalizing. Somehow, she knew he would call. "Happy New Year's to you, too, Brad. Vickie and I were having a glass of wine. She's staying overnight."

Vickie moved closer to Darian and began yelling into the receiver.

"Happy New Year, Brad," she said loud enough so he could hear.

"Sounds like she's had more than one."

"She has. How's everything going?" Darian asked, wondering why he was home tonight.

"My son and I went to a dinner party. Now he's eating a slice of chocolate cake and listening to fireworks."

Vickie hit Darian on the arm, and Darian rolled her eyes at her.

"I hope the new year brings you happiness, Brad."

"You, too, baby."

They hung up and Darian turned back to Vickie. "Why do you think he's alone?"

"If he's anything like the ones I've dated, he's not alone. Some woman is probably in the bathroom getting undressed."

"Could be, hmm?" Darian answered, pondering over it.

"But who knows? It was thoughtful for him to call. At least that's what he told me. Anyway, he did call."

"We'll find out soon enough," Vickie said devilishly.

"Brad's a good guy. But I don't know what's going to happen with us."

"I know it's soon for you, but do you feel anything at all for Brad? I mean, a good man trying to raise his son alone? He has a home and a good job. How can you not feel something? It's not normal to be around a man with such sex appeal and not feel anything for him, or at least wonder what's he's like."

"I have other priorities." Darian placed her glass on the coffee table in front of them. She contemplated a way to explain it to Vickie. Her eyes became soft and faraway as she thought of the last conversation she had with Brad before he left her house. He kissed her on the cheek and made her insides jitter. It was a quick kiss with a shocking aftereffect.

"I've always had a secret place hidden away in my heart for him. But right now my plate is running over with more than I had ever imagined handling."

"Okay, now that you've skated around my question, how do you feel about Brad?" Vickie asked with smiling eyes. "You're talking about what you have to do first, but, girl, he is a good catch." She folded her arms and waited for Darian to answer. "Well?" Vickie laughed.

Darian threw up both hands. "Okay, yes, he's sexy, sexy, and sexy. Is that what you want to hear?"

"Yep, that's what I wanted to hear. Darian, you better watch out, I bet he's a handful between the sheets."

"Oh, shut up, girl. I'm tired and tomorrow I'm going to be hungover from all this wine we're drinking." Darian held up the bottle. "Look, it's empty."

"Oh no, you mean we've finished the whole bottle? I'm going to bed, Darian. It's already New Year's Day." Vickie looked at her watch. It was past 2:00 a.m.

"We're sleeping in the twin beds. I put the girls on the sofa bed in the third bedroom."

Vickie stood up and fell back on the sofa again. She held her arms out for Darian's support.

Darian leaned down and grabbed her arm. "Come on. We can help each other." But Vickie was no help. Darian acted as a crutch as she led her to the bedroom.

"Auntie! Auntie!" Shelby screamed as loud as she could. She stomped her feet and cried. Nikki was beside her and crying, too.

The voices seemed far away, but the crying seemed to get louder, nearer. Darian thought she was dreaming until she felt someone shake her. She opened one eye and felt dizzy, closed it tight, and tried again. She tried to raise her arm, but it was too heavy. Her entire body was limp. Her head ached from too much wine the night before.

"Auntie?" Shelby cried out. Tears streamed down her face.

Darian sat up and tried to focus on the girls' faces. "What's wrong, Shelby?"

I hurt all over," she whined.

Darian got out of bed and looked at Vickie but she was still asleep. Her mouth was open as she snored; she was still fully dressed.

Darian shook her head; her mouth was dry. "Come on, girls. We don't want to wake Vickie." She took the girls' hands and led them into the living room. She sat them on each side of her and placed her arms around their shoulders.

"Now, girls, sit here until I get back and get your breakfast." *Today is a cold cereal day,* she thought. She went back to the bedroom and covered Vickie with a blanket, then went to the bathroom to wash her face. She looked at her image in the mirror. Her eyes were red, curls were all over her head, and damn, the floor under her was still moving.

Darian went back to the kitchen and brewed some strong coffee, and gave the girls a bowl of cornflakes. After the coffee was ready, she lay on the sofa with a full cup of coffee. Darian thought, *If I survive this day I'll be lucky.*

The house was serene and peaceful. Since Shirlee had taken the girls to the Circle Movie Theater, Darian packed the rest of Monique's clothes. She knew that Shirlee wouldn't like being reminded of Monique.

Getting rid of Monique's personal possessions was too painful. Darian gave some items to the Salvation Army. Now with the girls away, she had time to complete her packing. They would be moving into their new home in three days.

Fortunately, the financing on both homes was closing at the same time. Another single woman and a couple of kids would be occupying Monique's house.

The phone rang and Darian leaped over three boxes to get it. "Hello," she answered.

"Hi, Darian, it's Yasmine."

Darian smiled into the phone. "Hey, girl, what's up?" She took the phone and sat on the arm of the chair. "It's good to hear your voice."

"Someone from the storage company phoned me this morning, and regrettably, your furniture won't be there until the day after you move in. I hope it's not too much of an inconvenience."

"It's all right. We have enough beds to sleep in so I can wait for the rest."

"Also, you have a company check that Bill mailed to you yesterday."

"How's Bill? He was so understanding when I spoke to him."

Yasmine laughed. "You know Bill. But since he's not in your face all day, I think he's getting more work done."

"I hope you fly out when you're on vacation, Yasmine."

"You can count on that. I want to do the Mardi Gras."

"Good, you do that. I'll call you as soon as we move in and get unpacked."

Just as Darian hung the phone up, Shirlee and the girls walked in.

Shirlee carried Nikki to the bedroom and laid her in bed. She went back to the living room where Shelby was telling Darian about the movie.

"I'm tired. Nikki was sleepy and wouldn't walk to the car. I had to carry her into the house." Shirlee went to the kitchen and returned with a tall glass of orange juice in her hand. She flopped down on the sofa.

"I'm sleepy and my head hurts," Shelby whined. She laid her head against Darian's shoulder. Darian felt her forehead with the back of her hand. "Maybe you're tired," Darian said. It was Shelby's first time out since she had recovered from the chickenpox.

"I sure appreciate all the help you give me with the children, Mama. Raising kids isn't easy, but it's not as bad as I had imagined it would be. Although it's a lot of work." Darian slumped down on the sofa. "I'm tired from all the packing."

"How long has Brad been away, Darian?"

"It's been over a week now. I only spoke with him once since he left, and that was the week of New Year's. But he'll be home tomorrow."

"You never listen to me. He's a good man. Any woman would want a man like him, good-looking, good job, and good sense most of the time. What else can you ask for in a man?"

Trying to keep calm, Darian sighed, shook her head, and counted to ten.

"Now, let me cut to the root of the matter. When he gets home, take him to bed and make sure you give him something that no other woman can, or know how—"

"Mama, what on earth are you talking about?" Darian looked at Shirlee as though she didn't know her.

"Look here, Darian. Your father and me were married for fifteen years. That man never cheated on me once. On the weekends he stayed home with us. Ronald knew no woman out there could do what I did. I made that man beg for more," Shirlee said, standing in front of the mirror, pulling her sweater tighter against her full breasts. "This sweater is too big."

Darian threw both hands up. "Mama, I really don't want to know what you and Daddy did. Please, give me a break. I have enough on my mind."

"Okay. But I have a thirty-seven-year-old husband. Today is Saturday and you know where he is?"

"No, Mama. I really don't."

"Well, I'm gonna tell you. He's at home waiting for me. If you want to make Brad crazy about you, Mama will tell you what to do. I'm going home and take care of my man." Again she stood, went to the wall mirror, and looked at her sweater.

"It looks like my derriere is getting bigger. These jeans are already a size fourteen, and since the holidays are over I'm on a diet." Shirlee's jeans were tight and looked as though they were painted to fit her small waist and around her curvy hips.

"Don't forget what I told you, Darian. I saw the way Brad looks at you and he's gentle with the girls. You two complement each other. When he comes over again you better lay it on him good, girl. If you know what I mean." Shirlee winked one eye at her daughter, and then strolled leisurely out the door.

Darian sat back and looked at the closed door. "I don't believe she said that," she said out loud. But the truth was, she did like Brad.

Miss Idele looked in the mirror at the old brown, faded dress, but why did it matter when she was moved into a home for old folks? Some were unable to speak, some died, and some talked too much, but they all were dying. Miss Idele pinned her long braid on top of her head and frowned. Her front gold teeth didn't sparkle the way they used to. She placed both hands in back to tie her apron, but she wasn't wearing one. She had spoken to one of the employees about returning her aprons, and told them she had never dressed without one. It was a part of her just as her clothing was. Just one more thing to depress her. That old woman, Anna, said she had a man last night, and teased Miss Idele about not having one. "Honey, you see Mr. Herman over there? See, the one with the slight limp when he walks? He comes to my room at night, and we don't just sit and play checkers, if you know what I mean. He's seventy-eight, but he's got something that makes me sleep well, and it's better than those old sleeping pills the nurse gives me."

"So why are you telling me?" Miss Idele asked.

The woman changed her expression to a mean sneer. "Because he's my man. I just want you to remember that. He visits two other rooms at night, and I'm not too happy about it."

"Shame on you, old woman. I haven't had a man in twenty years and don't want one," Miss Idele said and walked away. That was her first night at her new home. Miss Idele, still standing in front of the mirror, sniffed at the smell from the kitchen. The cook probably burned the oatmeal again, she thought. She gazed into midair as though she was trying to remember something. "Burn the oatmeal? No, it's not the oatmeal. Something's burning," she whispered. Her mind was playing tricks on her again. It was her house burning. "Lord, help me. Nikki's in the house and it's burning," she said out loud. She closed her eyes tightly and could see the fire burning her house, and she had to save Nikki's life.

Miss Idele grabbed her purse, but forgot that she wasn't wearing shoes. She went outside, looked down at her feet, and in her mind she heard Nikki's voice. The poor child was scared. Darian didn't want to raise

Monique's daughters and Shirlee wouldn't take care of them. Lordy, her house was burning and Darian was at the dancing school with Shelby, and left her responsible for Nikki.

Miss Idele waved her hand to get the taxi driver's attention. She got inside the car and pulled out her small coin purse to pay him. "You have to take me to save Nikki."

"Where is that, miss?"

She gave him the address and he sped off. When the taxi arrived at her destination, she hopped out. "Wait here till I get back." She went to the back door of Monique's house like she had for years. Except for the television going in the girls' room, the house was quiet when she entered. She stopped in the hallway and listened to the burning fire, blinked, and saw it getting nearer. Oh, she had to hurry and get Nikki out. Time was running out and the fire was so close that she could feel the heat.

Miss Idele tiptoed into the girls' room and Nikki was asleep. She picked her up and rushed out the back door. Once she got back outside, her feet were frozen and her toes were so cold that they curled downward.

The taxi driver opened the door so Miss Idele could assist Nikki inside the car.

"Hi, Miss Idele. Can I go to your house?" Happy to see Miss Idele, Nikki sat close to her.

"Take me to Piedmont Street. It's only eight blocks away." Her mean old cousin was out of town for a week, and if she didn't start another fire, Nikki would be safe from any harm. Maybe Darian would agree to raise Monique's children. "Wait a minute," she whispered. She had gotten confused again. Had her house caught on fire before Monique died or after? First she would bake Nikki some cookies and would remember about the fire afterward. "The fire? Oh." Goodness, too many things were going through her mind at once. And why was she standing in her cousin's kitchen and not her own? She tried to remember how she got there. She went into the kitchen to bake Nikki's cookies.

"How was the movie?" Darian asked as she sat on the sofa drinking a cola.

"It was funny, but Nikki kept talking when I tried to hear it."

"She's your little sister. You have to help her understand."

Shelby got up. "Can I have a cookie?"

"Yes. See if Nikki is still asleep. She may want a cookie, too."

In less than five minutes Shelby was back. 'Nikki's not here. I looked in all the closets, under all the beds, and she's not even in the bathroom either."

Of all the days Nikki wanted to play hide-and-seek. Darian was exhausted.

"Nikki, where are you hiding?" Darian yelled.

Nikki didn't answer. "Nikki, you get in here right this minute." Darian sighed and went into the girls' room. But Nikki wasn't there as Darian waited. Darian stood in the middle of the room, then looked under the beds, inside the closets, and ran frantically from room to room. Darian ran outside and called Nikki's name. She checked the backyard, ran into the garage, still no sign of Nikki.

Darian bit down on her fingernail and saw blood. Tears spilled from her eyes.

She ran inside the house and grabbed the phone. "Mama, did you take Nikki home with you?" She waited for Shirlee's reply, and was afraid for her heart.

"Did I take her home? No, Darian. I left her asleep in

her bed. What's going on?" Shirlee squealed through the phone.

"She's missing, Mama. I can't find her any place. I better call the police."

Darian wanted to look one last time, but when she went back to the girls' room, and then to the back door, she froze. She hadn't noticed that the door was ajar the first time she'd gone out to look for Nikki. Someone had been inside. "Nikki . . ."

Miss Idele gave Nikki cookies and milk. She looked at the child's bright eyes lighting up with happiness. It was as though Nikki missed her just as much as Miss Idele missed the child, and she wondered why it was all taken away. Sitting at the table next to Nikki was as if she were babysitting as usual.

The room was quiet, peaceful, but the fire was playing tricks with her mind. She could feel the flames coming closer, and ran to the sink to fill a pot with water and splashed it on Nikki. "I won't let you burn, child." She watched Nikki as she shook with fear, not able to speak or scream. She cried out and reached for Miss Idele to take her out of the chair. "I almost lost you once, but Miss Idele will save you this time, child."

"Miss Cantrell, how often had you checked on the child before you missed her?' the officer asked, as he jotted notes on his writing pad.

"Not even twenty minutes. Like I said, my mother put her to bed when they returned home. Twenty minutes later she was gone," Darian said. She turned to Brad and laid her head on his shoulder and cried.

"What was she wearing?"

Darian inhaled and blew her nose. "A pair of jeans

and a red T-shirt. Her tennis shoes are in the bedroom, so she had no shoes on. I wonder if she's hurt
or hungry?"

"She'll be home soon, baby," Brad said.

"I don't know about that. The little girl that was
missing a few months ago was never found," Shirlee
said and burst into tears.

Jefferson held her in his arms. "Don't think like
that, Shirlee. Nikki will be found."

After the officers finished taking a report they left.
Darian, Brad, and Jefferson went out searching for
Nikki. Shirlee stayed home with Shelby. She didn't
mention to anyone that her heart was beating fast, and
she was getting weak.

As Brad cruised slowly down the streets, Darian
looked at every child's face in search of Nikki. "Pretty
soon it's going to be dark, and more difficult to see
Nikki. I don't know if she left alone or if someone took
her. I can't believe she's alone, Brad."

Brad placed his free hand on Darian's knee. "We'll
find her, baby."

"You know, she was Miss Idele's favorite. She loved
Shelby, too, but she was crazy about Nikki. When her
house burned down, she was more concerned that
Nikki was safe." Brad's hand was still on her knee, and
Darian placed her hand on top of his.

They drove around for another hour and came to
the conclusion that Nikki wasn't lost alone. If she had
been out alone, someone would have reported it to the
police. Or taken her away, Brad thought.

When Darian got home, she jumped out of the car
and ran into the house. "Has anyone called, Mama?"

"Not a soul. I'm just sick with worry, and I can't live
through another death." Shirlee held her hands to her
face and cried.

The doorbell rang, and everyone jumped and

looked at each other. Darian pulled away from Brad and ran to the door. She placed her hand on the doorknob and hesitated. Was it bad news, had they found Nikki dead . . . or alive?

Brad moved Darian's hand and opened the door. Shirlee was right behind him.

There were two police officers, and Jefferson came in behind them.

Darian wondered why it wasn't the same two officers that had taken the missing person report. She was sure that she would collapse, and so did Shirlee.

"Good evening, folks. Have you seen your neighbor that used to live in the house that was next door?" the officer asked.

"What?" Darian asked. "We placed a missing person report for my niece. We haven't seen Miss Idele . . . is she missing, too?"

"Yes, we got a call an hour ago. They say she wandered away from the nursing home and needs to be medicated."

"Oh my God, Mama, you know what that means? Miss Idele probably has Nikki with her."

The two officers looked at each other.

Shirlee took a deep breath. "If she has Nikki, she'll take care of her. But I wonder where they are?"

"What's going on here, miss?

"My niece is missing, too. I think that maybe she is out there somewhere with Miss Idele."

"So now we have to add kidnapping a child and hope that we find her. They say the old woman is clearly out of her mind. Miss, may I use your phone?"

"Yes, help yourself."

Darian turned to Shirlee. "I wonder where can they be, Mama?"

"Darian, you don't know if she has Nikki," Jefferson said.

"But she has to, Jefferson. This is too much of a co-incidence. But if they are at that old bat's house she would have called us already."

"Yes, if she was in a sound mind. But since she is out of her mind, she could be hiding anywhere," Brad interjected.

The officer finished his conversation on the phone and turned his attention back to Darian.

"Officer, we're going to the house where Miss Idele used to live," Darian said and grabbed her purse.

"Miss, you can show us where she lives." The officer placed his cap back on his head.

"Mama, you don't look well. Can you stay here with Shelby?" Darian asked with concern.

Shirlee was standing near the door. "I can stay, just bring Nikki back." She went back to the sofa and sat next to Shelby.

"Darian, I better stay with Shirlee," Jefferson said.

Darian nodded in agreement and ran out of the house. She jumped in Brad's SUV, and they took off with the police car behind them.

"I want to go home with Darian," Nikki said at the table. She was curled up in the chair. Her face was dirty with cookie crumbs and a runny nose.

"Don't be scared, Nikki. I had to put the fire out so it won't burn my house down like before." Miss Idele gave Nikki a wide smile and stepped closer to her, but Nikki drew her feet up closer under her.

"Nikki, why is your dress wet? You've been a bad girl, and probably been outside playing in the rainwater. Now I have to dry your pretty little shirt. But don't be afraid. Miss Idele will take care of you."

"I want Auntie Darian and Shelby," Nikki cried and placed both hands over her face.

"Now, Nikki, you stop that whining." She snatched Nikki's wet shirt off. "I'll put your shirt inside the dryer," she murmured to herself. "I don't know why people waste good money on dryers. I used to hang my clothes on the clothesline in my backyard. Folks don't need a clothes dryer taking up space in the house." She closed her eyes tight, trying to prevent seeing the fire burn. It was always there with her. Closing her eyes and seeing fire had become part of her, and kept her confused. It lit up high above her head. She ran to the stove, her heart racing fast inside her chest. She opened the windows for some air and bumped into the cabinet, the stove. And for moments she had forgotten where she was. She was turning in circles feeling as though she was inside someone else's body. Why was she inside her cousin's house? she wondered. "Oh, where is my boy?" she asked with fear of losing him. She held her hand out to Nikki. But the little girl closed her eyes and held her head between her knees.

"Come on, child. I have to find my boy before the police shoot him. We have a long way to travel, Nikki."

The doorbell rang, and she heard voices, and someone banging hard on the door. "We have to hide, Nikki. It's the policeman looking for my brothers." She ran around the living room, losing her mind. Her clothes were dirty, and she still wasn't wearing any shoes.

"Miss Idele, are you there?" Darian yelled. "We want to help you, Miss Idele."

"Auntie Darian, I want to go home," Nikki yelled.

"Was that a child's voice?" one of the officers asked.

Nikki was crying out loud and calling Darian's name. But she was too afraid to move away from the chair.

Darian kicked at the door. She balled her hand into a fist and banged hard. "Miss Idele, do you hear me? Open the damn door and let her out," Darian commanded. "You better stop this nonsense and open the damn door."

Miss Idele backed against the stove and screamed. She had laid her hand flat on the hot burner. She grabbed a wet dish towel to wrap around her hand, and heard the door being kicked open. The officers, Darian, and Brad ran inside as if they were going to war. The police officers had their weapons drawn. It was so hot inside the house, the heat slapped them in their faces.

"Holy shit. You can smother to death in this place," the officer commented.

Darian grabbed Nikki and held her close. "Are you all right, honey?" She pushed Nikki back to see if she was hurt, and she wasn't. She was just trembling with fear. But Darian didn't believe that Miss Idele would have hurt Nikki if she were thinking clearly. But the poor old woman was just crazy.

Brad took Nikki in his arms and carried her outside. She felt hot, sticky, and wet. Brad wasn't sure if it was caused by the heat or if water had drenched her clothes.

The police officer handcuffed Miss Idele and helped her inside the car.

"She's only an old woman. Must you handcuff her like she's a criminal? Where are you taking her anyway?" Darian asked.

Miss Idele cried out in pain. "My hand is burned something awful."

The second officer helped her out of the car. "She did burn herself pretty badly."

"We're taking her to the hospital, miss."

"Thank you, officer."

"And you, little one. It's time to go home." Brad and

Darian drove off with Nikki's thumb in her mouth and curled up on Darian's lap.

As it turned out Shirlee had her medication in her purse. She took some, and she was feeling better. She and Jefferson went home but Brad stayed until Darian fed Nikki some hot soup and put her to bed.

Darian walked him to the door. He kissed her on the cheek, and then the mouth. The kiss lasted for minutes, and left Darian out of breath. "Wow," she whispered to herself, and said good night.

Chapter 19

A month had passed, and it had been a hellish day, and to make matters worse, Nikki had gotten the chickenpox and was feeling lousy. She cried the entire time they were moving into the new house.

The movers had put the last piece of furniture, and every labeled box, in its place.

"Is she finally asleep yet?" Darian asked, exhausted from all the packing, moving, and now unpacking.

Shirlee helped with the girls. "No, she's not asleep yet but she will be soon. I rubbed calamine lotion all over her body and gave her a baby aspirin, and fed her some chicken soup. Shelby is sitting on her bed playing with her dolls. Every once in a while she looks out the windows into the backyard. All the beds are made, too." Shirlee walked around the house. "Moving is so tiring. But this is one time that I'm glad I could be some help."

"I love this house and I know the girls will love it, too. You made a good decision, Darian. I'll feel better coming over here to see you. It used to break my heart every time I got out of the car and didn't see Miss

Idele's house. By the way, I visited her yesterday. I think she recognized me for a minute."

"I don't know if I can see her again."

"She's an old woman, Darian, and she didn't hurt Nikki."

"I know, and she didn't know what she was doing, but it's going to take a while before I can see her again."

"You wait too long and she won't remember you at all. After her house burned down, she had a breakdown."

Darian was unpacking a box in the living room. "As soon as I finish this box, I'm going to take a break and find something to eat. I haven't eaten since morning."

Shirlee looked at her watch. "I don't have to pick Jefferson up for another hour. I'll run out and get a couple of Po' Boy sandwiches for you, and some soup for the girls." She picked up her purse.

"Thanks, Mama." Darian got up and kissed Shirlee on the cheek. "I don't know what I would do without you."

Shirlee felt her eyes tearing. She looked at Darian again as she pulled a box of lightbulbs from a box. Watching her on her knees, her hair combed back into a ponytail, and wearing a T-shirt and jeans, she looked so young, so pretty. Shirlee decided that both her daughters were just as pretty as she was. She opened her purse, pulled out her mirror, and took one look, then ambled out the door.

When Shirlee returned, she blew her horn so Darian could run out and get the sandwiches. As Darian went back inside, she looked into the brown bag and there were two Po' Boy sandwiches made with hot sausages, two slices of lemon pound cake, and a Coke. She placed the bag on the kitchen sink, peeked at the girls, and went back to work.

Night was nearing; the wind was blowing vigorously

as Darian felt every bone in her body ache. As she sat at the kitchen table, the phone rang and she answered.

"Hello."

"Hi, girl, are you beat?"

"Yes, Vickie, I'm beat while you're at work flirting with cute guys," Darian said and frowned into the phone.

"You do know me too well."

"Hey, why don't you come over and give me some decorating suggestions?" Darian asked.

"Okay, I'll be there early tomorrow morning to help you. Bernard will be home day after tomorrow. In two weeks he starts his desk job."

"Good. I can use the help. See you in the morning."

"Hey, Darian, don't hang up yet. I'll stop by Starbucks and pick up coffee and pastries for breakfast. You know that's why I'm in a size twelve. But so what, I'm happy," Vickie said.

"And that's all that matters. So hang up and go back to work. I'm busy."

Darian warmed the soup for the girls and went to their room to check on them. "Aren't you hungry, Shelby?"

"Yes. But I want to walk around our new house."

"Come on and eat dinner." She closed the blinds and picked up Nikki. Her job was never done, she thought.

After dinner, Darian made a bed on the floor for Nikki; she and Shelby sat next to her. The carpet was thick and the house was warm. Darian turned the TV on so the girls could watch it as she soaked in a hot tub of water.

Darian lay in bed, but the busy day and the thought of so much to do prevented her from sleeping. She got up and went to the living room, flipped on the TV, and lay down on the floor. The phone rang and she jumped up again. *I wonder who that could be?* she thought.

"I'm back."

His voice was deep, sexy, and she was happy and surprised to hear it. Brad, she thought. "Brad, it must be eleven o'clock in Los Angeles. How is everything going?" She wondered how much longer he would be there.

"Yes, it is eleven in L.A. But what do I care? I'm home."

Darian couldn't speak for a few seconds. "You're what?" she managed to say.

"I'm home. I got back tonight."

He sounded so sexy, and she did miss him. But she was afraid. Should she even take the chance on dating now when her life was still in such turmoil? But Brad was no stranger to her. The last time he kissed her it rocked her world. "I moved today."

"I hope it was an easy move, or are you dog tired?"

"I'm okay, but I'm happy it's over."

"Okay, I just wanted to say good night before I went to bed."

"I'm glad you called and I'll see you tomorrow." She hung up.

She went to Shelby's bed and pulled the covers over her shoulders. Suddenly, she had an urge to kiss Shelby's rosy cheek. But instead, she sat on the edge of the bed and watched the girls as they slept comfortably. How could she not love them or even hesitate wanting to keep them safe? Looking at Shelby's face was like looking at Monique's face when she was that age. There were times she felt Monique's presence next to her.

It was early Saturday morning. The doorbell rang and Darian was surprised to see Brad standing there with two large bags in his arms.

"I have more in the car," Brad said and handed her one of the bags. They took the two bags in the kitchen. Brad went out to his car and came back with two more bags.

"Brad, what are you doing?" she asked. The bags were filled with food.

"I went shopping for food and thought of you. I knew with you moving and Nikki's chickenpox, you needed food in your refrigerator." He set the last bag on the kitchen counter. Before she could protest he grabbed her in his arms and kissed her. This time it was long and gentle. "There. Now I have to take my food home. It's in the trunk of my car."

Her eyes were dazed and her heart rate quickened as she looked up at him. *What am I going to do with you?* she wondered. She wanted to take a step back but her feet wouldn't move. He simply took her breath away.

Finally, a slow smile played across Darian's mouth. Her eyes had softened and she took a step forward as though she couldn't help herself. She brushed her lips against his with both arms circling his neck.

"I better get out of here while it's still safe," he whispered against her ear. Brad kissed her one last time and held her hand. Darian walked him to the door.

When Darian went back into the kitchen to empty the bags, there were steaks, chicken, ground turkey, cold cuts. He had purchased four tall bags of food for her and the girls. She pulled out a box of Gummy Bears and Shelby's round eyes lit up when she saw them. "Here, give this one to Nikki. Maybe it will make her happy, too."

Darian smiled to herself. "What a guy he is, and he wants me," she said and smiled again. She was in a dreamlike daze when the sound of the doorbell interrupted it.

It was Vickie with a bag from Starbucks in her hand.

"I tried to get here sooner but I stayed up till after midnight reading a novel." Vickie followed Darian into the kitchen. "Let me look around."

"Go ahead. I'll be putting this food away," Darian answered.

"You went shopping already?" Vickie peeked over Darian's shoulder. "Who kept the girls?"

"No one. Brad went shopping. Shocked the hell out of me," Darian said, flabbergasted at the thought of it. He'd caught her totally off guard.

Vickie's mouth fell open. "You are not kidding, are you?"

"No. He came over and rang my doorbell with a large bag in each arm. What can I say? The man wants me," she said jokingly.

"Now, that's what I'm talking about. He's a man, a real man. Not some chintzy moocher that is always trying to use a woman. The men that I used to date would come to my house and eat my food. Now, what else happened when he came over?" Vickie asked anxiously.

Darian had emptied the last bag. "Nothing. He kissed me and left."

"Get your coffee and come on." Vickie led Darian back to the table where they could see a view of the backyard.

"I have a lot to think about, Vickie."

"What's there to think about? You know you like him. I mean, what's there not to like?"

"Yes, I like him. He just caught me at a point in my life when everything is still a little upside down."

"Silly, that's when it always catches you, upside down, or inside out. But what difference does it make? He's a good man, so stop worrying about the past and go forward. Most of all stop comparing him with that jackass Wade. You have a new life here, Darian."

"He grabbed me into his arms and kissed me like

we're lovers. All I could do was kiss him back. What do I say when I see him again?"

"Nothing," Vickie answered. "Absolutely nothing, so enjoy it. You have a man to help raise the girls, Darian. Take it, girl, and run with it."

Darian listened and sighed. "Maybe you're right. Now come on and look through the house. Afterward, we can start lining the kitchen cabinets since it's what I hate most."

"Will your house ever be free of chickenpox?" Vickie asked teasingly.

"I hope so. Nikki cries when she itches. And it's worse at night. Come and look at my bedroom."

It was raining torrents outside, but Darian kept the house warm. At four-thirty, Darian and Vickie decided to call it a day. "Lining the cabinets and unpacking the dishes was the hardest, but we're finished. I'm so glad you helped me, Vickie. Let's relax in the living room. I have some cold cuts. Want a sandwich?"

"No. While I'm still standing I'm going to go home and relax."

Darian walked Vickie to her car. "Drive careful, girl."

"I will. You get inside before you're soaking wet. Get some rest. I have an idea that you are going to have a visitor tonight or tomorrow night." Vickie rolled her window up and drove off.

Chapter 20

It was Mardi Gras time, and the air was cold and damp. The streets were crowded with tourists eager to experience the forbidden pleasures of the city of sin, enjoying the foods, drinks, and dancing in the streets, partying into the early dawn. Mardi Gras catered to all tastes impartially. Drinks, drugs, they were all available. The city was wild with a ring of excitement, yet romantic, with the taste of love permeating the air.

Darian was driving down Claiborne Avenue on her way home from taking the girls to the doctor's office. The girls were over the chickenpox, and got a clean bill of health.

Shelby and Nikki looked out the window, pointing out necklaces and bracelets that had been tossed in the streets the night before.

It was noon, and Darian was anxious and nervous to return home and open her mail. She had sent her manuscript to six agents, had gotten rejections from three, two in the same day. Now she wondered what was waiting at home for her today, if anything at all.

Pulling up into the driveway, Darian saw the mailbox crammed with mail. The lid was up with a brown envelope hanging over the top. She knew instantly it was another rejection from an agent.

Darian and the girls went inside the house. She went to the kitchen and filled three glasses of apple juice, and sat the girls at the table. She went back to the living room, sat on the sofa, and the large envelope lay on the coffee table in front of her. She stared at it, picked it up again, and placed it back on the table, her heart flipping with anticipation of another rejection.

Finally, after she placed the empy glass back on the table, Darian grabbed the envelope. "Open it," she whispered to herself. "Just open it already." She slowly tore the envelope open and began reading. Darian gasped with one hand against her chest and continued to read the letter again. It felt as though her eyes were jumping all over the page. She hopped off the sofa, jumped up and down, and ran to the phone to call Shirlee. "Mama, you sound terrible. Have you seen a doctor?"

"No. I sound worse than I feel. Besides, I mixed some honey and baking soda for the cough and it's getting better."

Darian rolled her eyes up. Shirlee would always use the old remedies instead of modern medicine. "Guess what, Mama? I got an agent for my book," she blurted out excitedly.

"No, you didn't, girl." Shirlee beamed, proud of Darian. "You are actually going to get your book published."

"Yes, I am, Mama. I'm looking at the letter in my hand now."

"That's wonderful, Bay. I knew you would."

Darian heard Nikki crying. "I have to go, Mama. Nikki is crying." Darian hung up quickly and went to the girls' room. Nikki was sitting in the middle of her bed, tears running down her face.

Darian picked her up. "What's wrong, sweetheart?"

"She's just being a baby," Shelby replied.

"You two come in the living room with me and play cards while I cook dinner."

Just as Darian went back to the kitchen she grabbed the phone.

"What's going on, good-looking?"

Listening to his voice, Darian blushed all over. "I got an agent, Brad. I'm so happy you called so I could share the good news."

"Congratulations, baby. We'll have to celebrate," he said mischievously. "I just wanted to say hello before I go to my meeting. I'll call you later."

She knew Brad wanted her; she could hear it in his voice, and saw it in his eyes the last time they were together.

"I'm so glad you two came over," Louise said. Tye kissed her and ran to the kitchen. Louise, his grandmother, always had something good to snack on. She did everything to make Brad and Tye happy. They were her life.

Brad and his mother took a seat in the den. He had lived in this house as a child. His father bought it when Louise was three months' pregnant with him. The house was made of red brick with a well-manicured yard.

Louise sat on the sofa and listened to her son as he spoke. He was a kindhearted man, and would make the right woman very happy. Brad had good character, and he was so handsome. But he was a better man than his father was. Louise's husband had broken her heart repeatedly before he died.

Louise knew she was too attached to him, but after the way Tanya, Tye's mother, had hurt him, Louise did everything she could to make up for the hurt and pain he'd endured. She hated Tanya more than she thought she could ever hate another human.

Tye was going to be as good-looking as Brad was. Louise felt proud to have a handsome son and grandson. No other mother was as lucky as she. Anything she wanted, Brad provided it for her. Louise bragged to all her friends about her son and grandson.

"What are you doing tonight, Brad?" Louise asked curiously.

"Tonight I'm going to see my girl," he said and winked at his mother.

Louise frowned, her brows furrowed together. "Your girl? You've been keeping secrets from your mother, dear. Who is the lucky girl? I hope you don't get too serious too soon."

"Darian Cantrell. I really care for her, Mom. So I hope you don't mind if Tye stays with you tonight."

"Cantrell, Cantrell," she pondered. The name sounded familiar. She kept trying to place the face with the name. Her back stiffened; frown lines developed across her forehead as she remembered. It couldn't be whom she was thinking of. "That wouldn't be Shirlee Foley's daughter. She's such an ignorant, uneducated woman, the tramp. I heard one of her daughters died. Must have been dreadful for Shirlee. But I guess she keeps busy with that stud of a husband." Louise stopped in midsentence when she saw Brad watching her, paralyzed, no words emerging.

"No, no, you couldn't be talking about Shirlee's daughter. It can't be, she's no good for you, son. She's just not good enough. You can't date someone like her around your son. She may have gone to college, but she's still Shirlee's daughter."

Her tone was calm and even, but the words hit hard enough to stick inside his head. Brad stood up. "How can you be so judgmental about someone you don't even know? It amazes me that you could speak of people with such viciousness. Yes, I am speaking of Darian. I intend to keep seeing her," he snapped furiously and grabbed his jacket.

"Wait, Brad. It was one thing when you had a little fling with her in high school. But this is different and you have a son now. You need a decent woman coming from a more appropriate family. She may seem like a nice woman now, but you just wait. She'll be no better than that vagrant, money-hungry Tanya. You didn't listen to me about her either." Louise was momentarily blinded with anger. Why couldn't he ever see things her way? But she had to control herself and calm down until she could convince Brad to stop this nonsense.

"I'm leaving now, Mom. We won't speak of this again." Brad slipped into his jacket and started to walk to the door.

"Brad, use your head, you're an intelligent man, a good-looking man. You can get anyone you want," she said as convincingly as she could. But she was fuming inside and would have to take a Prozac, thanks to Shirlee's daughter. Just when she decided to stop taking the Prozac, another problem arose that upset her.

"Mom, I am using my head. It's Darian I want." Brad left her standing and slammed the door as he walked out.

Louise had to figure out a way to stop this idiocy before it got out of control. She was sixty-four years old, but she was still clever enough to protect what was hers.

Once Brad was outside he took a deep breath to try and clear his head. The vicious words his mother had said still rang in his ear. She was so used to having everything she wanted and shaping it to be perfect in a nonperfect world. Well, he would not tolerate her interfering in his life. In time she would learn to love Darian. How could she not? he wondered as he backed out the driveway.

Brad rang Darian's doorbell at exactly eight-thirty, as promised. He held a dozen red roses in his hand. Although he was anxious to see Darian, his mother's words had lingered in his heart. But tonight was his night with the woman he loved. Funny, how fast it happened. He had to admit that through the years he wondered what it would be like to be with Darian, since he already knew the girl. She opened the door, her face glowing, eyes dreamy, and lips curved into a slow smile.

Darian took his hand and led him inside. "The flowers are beautiful," she said. "You make yourself comfortable and I'll put these in water." She noticed Brad's free hand behind him.

He smiled. "This is champagne for the big-time writer." He held the bottle in front of her.

It was amazing that he was so thoughtful. "You think of everything, don't you?" she asked in a sincere voice.

"Where you're concerned, I try." He followed her into the kitchen. "Are the girls asleep?" he asked, leaning against the door and watching Darian as she placed the roses in a clear, tall vase and took two glasses from the cabinet for the champagne.

"They're asleep. I put them to bed at eight every night. That way I can hear myself think and write." She brushed past him as they started for the living room.

The room was cozy and decorated in all neutral colors. Darian had made a fire in the fireplace. When Brad called and asked if he could come over, she took a quick shower and dressed slowly. She even applied lipstick and washed and set her hair.

"You look lovely tonight, Darian."

The skirt was short and fitted closely to her hips. It seemed that every time Brad gave her a compliment, her cheeks burned and she felt giddy inside. She hadn't felt that way since . . . since. She didn't want to think of it. This was here and now, this was Brad and her new life.

"Shall we open the champagne?" she asked.

"Yes."

Brad held his glass up. "Let's drink to your book, and to a new year for us, just the two of us, Darian." They clicked their glasses, and sipped their champagne. What did he mean? Should she go along with him? As she looked into Brad's eyes she decided to take the chance and see where his head was.

Brad took the glass from Darian's hand and placed both glasses on the coffee table.

She felt his hand touch the back of her neck, his sweet, hot lips against hers. His tongue tasted sweet like the champagne as he kissed her gently and slowly. She felt his hand stroke her neck as waves of pleasure started to make her insides quiver.

"I want you, Darian. I want you so much," he whispered, and ached for the taste of her.

Darian opened her eyes and without giving it any more doubt she led him to her bedroom. It was time to love again, time to forget and start anew. She flipped on the dim lamp and closed the door as she felt his hand around her waist. He stood in back of her, his hard body molded to hers and gently moving his lips up and down her neck. He was so warm, she thought her legs would buckle under her. One large hand against her stomach, she jerked when it gently stopped at her breast. Darian felt his deep passion.

He couldn't hold back any longer and carefully removed her blouse, unzipped the back of her skirt, and led her to the bed. He undressed and watched her lie on her back with her hands above her head. Her perfectly sculpted body curved in all the right places, her breasts standing high, the pink nipples sprouting like pink rosebuds. The girl had it going on, he thought.

Brad finished undressing and lay next to her, kissing her lips again and again, his tongue teasing softly around her nipples. He felt her legs rubbing against his hard thighs, and she lifted up against him. Brad heard her low moans against his ear, her lips against his and her soft hands caressing his back. He couldn't wait any longer and reached for the condom that he placed on the nightstand and skillfully slid it on. He entered her as she released a deeper moan, and her breathing became brisk. Her hands were circling his back. Her legs were high around his waist. They were lost in each other, mingling like longtime lovers.

Darian couldn't stop and wanted this moment to last forever, his strong hands, so large, so delicate, and so soothing. She needed everything that he gave her, and he went slowly and deep.

Darian felt his body tensing. He moaned, kissed her, and relaxed. They held on to each other. She looked into his eyes as he smiled at her. A smile that told her he was pleased.

"I love you, Darian. I love your looks, your touch, your intelligence. I love everything about you," he whispered.

Darian saw him looking deeply into her eyes. "We've wasted so much time going our separate ways. I love you, too, Brad."

"Are you ready to make a commitment? I'll be good to you and treat you right. I love children, too. You need someone to help take care of you and the girls. I want to be your man. You deserve the best, and the best is me because I love you."

"Brad, I won't be with you because I need help raising the girls. I can do it alone. But I do love you because of who you are." She closed her eyes, felt his fingers going through her hair, touching her neck, and gently pulling her closer against him. She had just said that she loved him and felt shaken, as the words flowed so easily out of her mouth. And she was afraid of being hurt again. But she was never afraid to take chances.

Darian and Brad lay in each other's arms talking for hours before she felt herself under him again. They couldn't seem to get enough of each other. Finally, at three that morning they stood in the living room saying good night.

Darian went back to bed. She curled up in the same spot where she and Brad had made passionate love. She laid her head on his pillow and fell asleep with a smile across her face.

"Hi, Mama. What are you doing here so early?" Darian asked and moved aside so Shirlee could pass.

"I didn't get out of the house on the weekend. But I feel better so I thought we could go shopping together. Where is Nikki?"

"She's in the kitchen eating a bowl of hot cereal. She didn't eat breakfast before I took Shelby to school."

Shirlee went into the kitchen and came back with Nikki in her arms. She looked at Darian sitting on the sofa. "Are you okay, Bay?"

"Yes, Mama. I was up late last night, that's all." She didn't dare tell Shirlee she was up till three in the morning with Brad.

"What were you doing up so late?" As she looked at Darian she saw a dreamy glint in her brown eyes.

"I'm all right. Brad and I watched television till midnight."

"Just TV? You could have done better than that, Darian."

"Oh, Mama, don't start." Darian saw Nikki's doll in the corner and got up to give it to her. "See, you couldn't find your baby this morning."

"Why don't I dress Nikki while you get ready? I want to catch some of the sales."

"That's a good idea. I may see something that I like, too."

When Darian went back to the living room, Nikki was standing at the door with her thumb in her mouth, and Shirlee was applying her lipstick.

"I'm ready, Mama," Darian said.

Shirlee parked the car at the Elmwood Mall. They went in and caught lots of bargains. Darian bought jeans, red boots, and two sweaters. She also bought sweaters and T-shirts for the girls.

As they walked back to the car, a tall man was unlocking the door of a black BMW parked next to them. As he turned around and saw Darian he stopped and stared as though he knew her. Darian smiled and he smiled back. He watched her until she got into the car.

"Can you believe that, Mama? He didn't move, just stood there and stared at me so boldly," Darian commented.

"You can't flirt and smile at these white men out here, Darian. This ain't California, you know. It hasn't been that long that blacks started coming to this mall. Their women don't like us and all the men will do is sleep with you and act as though they don't know you in public."

"Mama, that was a long time ago. Times have changed."

"Not that much. You take a pretty, young Creole woman like yourself and they will be all over you like white on rice." Shirlee turned right and drove out of the parking lot.

"When I was about fifteen years old I went to school with a girl named Brenda. She was a black, pretty, dark-skinned girl. She was only fifteen years old, too. But one day she met this white boy named Sammy. I don't know how it happened, but she started sneaking around with him."

"How do you know that for sure, Mama?"

"Not only me, everyone knew. Anyway, she told me that she was somewhere, I can't remember where. But Brenda saw him with one of his white friends. She spoke to Sam but he acted as though he didn't know who she was. The next day he had the nerve to wait in their hiding place for her."

"Did she meet him?" Darian asked as she looked in back to make sure that Nikki was all right.

"No. But it was too late for Brenda. She found out that she was pregnant. Times were hard in those days. Her parents sent her away."

"What happened to the boy?"

"Nothing. He was white and she was black. Her parents wasn't fools enough to confront his parents, because they would only deny it anyway. No way would a white man pay child support for a half-black baby. It would be a disgrace to his white family. Poor girl, no telling what he did to her. I hear those people do crazy things when they have sex. I don't know what that boy did to make her keep going back. But she did until she got pregnant."

Darian shook her head. "They don't make love any different than we do, Mama. Why would you think so?"

"Is that what they taught you in college? I read that four or five of them make love in the same bed, and at the same time, together. Gee, that's how people get all kinds of diseases these days. You could get AIDS like that. It's just not safe, or natural either."

"Mama, where do you hear things like that? Don't you know that all races are doing the same things now? What you're saying is just old-fashioned and ridiculous. Whites and blacks are getting married and have been for years. They don't worry about what people say about it as long as they love each other. A friend of mine in L.A. just married a Mexican. And he's one of the nicest people I know. I have a few Mexican and white friends myself. We work, party, and eat together. The world has changed," Darian said, shaking her head in dismay.

"Yes, and not for the best. And why would your friend marry a Mexican anyway? Miss Idele said all of them have the same names. José and Maria, that's all they call themselves. Now, something is crazy about those people. What kind of sense does that make? I'm telling you, Darian. They're a different breed is all I got to say. Stay with your own kind and life would be easier for everyone."

Darian whooped with laughter. She was certain that Shirlee would never change.

"We should sleep with our own race, Darian. We understand each other and know what we like. We sleep with one partner at a time. Now, I didn't finish high school, but I have enough sense to stay with my black men." She felt proud and held her head high with dignity.

"Did Jefferson tell you that, Mama?"

"Hell no. Jefferson doesn't have that much sense. Sometimes that man acts as though he don't know diddly-squat. And sometimes he says I'm the smart one in the family."

"He must have meant the smart one in your house,"

Darian answered with a smirk across her face. She loved teasing Shirlee.

"Watch your mouth, girl. I'm still your mother."

"Sorry, Mama. Anyway, Shelby will be out of school in thirty minutes."

"Okay. We'll pick her up on the way home," Shirlee answered.

The weeks passed fast, and Darian and Brad were deliriously in love. They took the kids to movies, dinner, and on boat rides. The girls got along well with Tye. With Brad it was like an act of faith that they had gotten together as though time had waited for them.

Darian and Brad were standing in the kitchen. She was facing the sink and he stood behind her, his hands holding her waist as he nuzzled her ear and neck.

"My mom has invited us to lunch on Sunday. Do you think you can make it?" Brad asked between kisses on her neck. He inhaled her sweet scent and gently blew the straying curl that danced down her neck.

"Really? You've discussed me with your mother?" Darian asked. She closed her eyes when she felt his warm lips against the back of her neck.

"Of course I've discussed you. You are my woman, aren't you?" he whispered.

Darian closed her eyes. Lord, he was working her, and she felt as though she was slipping into a pleasurable dream. Finally she managed to speak. "I'm your woman one hundred percent. Now, what did she say about me?" She turned around to face Brad, but instead of speaking she kissed him on his lips.

Brad thought of the change his mother had made regarding Darian. "She knows I love you. She wants to get to know the woman that has her son's heart."

When Darian opened her mouth to speak, he grabbed her into his arms and kissed her deeply.

She gently pulled away. "You make me forget what we're talking about when you kiss me that way," she said in a whisper.

"Good." Brad toyed with the buttons on her blouse until it was open, and caressed her nipple. "What time will your mother bring the girls back?" he asked, never taking his hand away. Her nipples bloomed like a flower coming alive. He loved watching her when she enjoyed his touch. Her lips parted, and her voice became a mere whisper.

"They'll be home in an hour."

Brad guided Darian into her bedroom. "An hour is all I need, for now, that is."

"Good," she whispered, stepping out of her jeans and lying in the middle of the bed. She waited for his touch.

Sunday came fast, too fast as far as Darian was concerned. She wasn't ready to meet Brad's mother. Since she had agreed to, Darian wanted her approval.

"You look great, Darian," Vickie complimented. Darian stood in the living room; the girls were playing in the backyard. Vickie walked around her slowly. "I wish I could be sitting there when you walk in that old snobbish witch's house. I saw her a few months ago and it was same as always. I spoke to her and I had to make her remember who I am. She pretends she doesn't know me. Anyway, she will be nicer to you since you are dating her son. Me, I only speak to her just to aggravate the hell out of her."

"I certainly hope she likes me."

"That purple pantsuit fits perfectly. I love the boots,"

Vickie said and looked at her watch. "It's time for the girls' lunch."

"I already made tuna sandwiches. I owe you one for babysitting. It's the weekend and I don't want to bother Mama," Darian said, picking up her purse. The doorbell rang and she looked in the mirror one last time and rushed to the door. She flung it open and Brad was standing there dressed in a gray sweater and jeans.

"Every time I see you, you look more beautiful than before. That's another reason why I love you, Darian." Brad smiled and kissed her on the cheek.

"Thanks." She held his hand and they went inside.

Vickie walked into the living room. "You two look nice today."

Brad hugged Vickie. "Thanks for babysitting. I won't keep her out too long."

"You better not. My husband is working days and will be home when he gets off."

Brad turned into the driveway in the middle of the block. The house looked large, made of red bricks with two tall trees on each side. The pavement that led from the car to the house was dark and looked newly paved. The large windows had drapes hanging.

Brad rang the doorbell and a tall dark brown woman opened the door. She smiled and stepped back so Brad and Darian could come in.

"Mama, this is my special girl, Darian," Brad said with pride. She examined Darian from head to toe and sucked in her breath.

Louise extended her hand. "It's time I meet the woman who keeps my son away. Just call me Louise." She led Darian into the living room. "Where's Tye?"

"He went to see a movie with his school buddy, Mom. I'm picking him up on my way home."

"This is a beautiful home, Louise." Darian looked at the oil painting, the large cathedral-shaped windows and high ceilings. She and Louise took a seat on the sofa. Brad sat in the chair facing Darian.

"I've met your mother but I don't see her often. Would you like a glass of wine before lunch?" Louise asked.

"Yes, thank you," Darian answered. It was odd how relaxed she was. She hadn't wanted to meet Brad's mother but now she felt calm. She glanced over at Brad and smiled. Darian watched Louise as she went into another room to get the wine. Darian leaned over and whispered to him, "She's very friendly and attractive, Brad."

"She'll love you, sweetheart. Mom is warming up to you already and that's not easily done by Mother." Brad was amazed when Louise apologized to him for the awful things she had said about Darian and Shirlee. After all, if Darian made him happy, that was all that mattered. Brad was so happy, so proud of the two women he loved most in the world.

"All right, here's the wine." Louise sat back on the sofa again. "Brad told me how courageous you were for taking on your late sister's two small children. I commend you for that. Your sister was very lucky to have you. But I'm surprised that your mother didn't take the girls."

"My sister wanted me to take them. Maybe because I'm younger."

"But one day you may want to get married. How can that happen when you already have two children?" Louise asked, amused at Darian's shocked expression.

Louise looked at Brad as he shifted in his seat.

"If and when I get married, he'll have to take all three of us. But I'm not worried about that now. It's too soon." Darian looked at Brad as he nodded with approval.

"I see. But one day you'll have to give it some thought."

Darian gave Louise a soft smile. "When that day arrives I will give it some thought. But not today."

"Well, Brad, what do you think about ready-made families?" Louise asked.

"Mother, first of all the entire conversation is a little premature. But if you must know, since I have a son, I love the idea. Is that what you really wanted to know?"

"Oh no, son. Since you two haven't been dating very long, I guess it could be a premature conversation." But that wasn't the answer that Louise wanted. "Now, ready for lunch?"

Brad and Darian went into the dining room together. He gave Darian a quick kiss on her cheek as he pulled her chair from the table.

"Here we are. I made a nice cobb salad and some homemade dinner rolls."

Darian admired the white lace tablecloth, and fresh flowers in the center of the table. From what Darian had gathered, Louise had impeccable taste.

"The bread is scrumptious, Louise."

"Thank you, Darian. When Brad lived at home and my late husband was alive I used to bake every weekend. But it seems so useless baking now that I'm alone."

"My mother baked more when when me and my sister were home."

"I'm surprised to hear that Shirlee was a domesticated mother."

"Why would that surprise you?"

"Oh, she just looks like a woman that doesn't have the touch for things like cooking, or raising children."

Brad cleared his throat as his eyes shot daggers at Louise.

Darian looked into Louise's round eyes. She decided that she didn't like the woman, and her rudeness was indefensible. What kind of life could she and Brad have with Louise in their lives? All of a sudden Darian wanted to go home. She realized that she wasn't really welcome in Louise's house. Darian was sure that Louise didn't think that she was good enough for Brad.

Darian looked at Brad, and as though he knew what she was thinking, Brad laid his napkin on the table. "Are you ready to leave now, baby?"

"Yes, I'm ready." She had never been so ready to leave a place as she was that very moment. She looked at Louise again. She could have sworn she had a smirk across her lips. There was something evil about this woman.

"I'll see you after I take Darian home. We have a lot to talk about, Mother."

"Indeed we have," Louise answered and looked at Darian as she held her head high with a haughty wave of her hand that caused Louise's mouth to fall open. Odd, how she saw herself in Darian. She was quick, and smart. But Louise was smarter, and she had to stop Darian before she and Brad got too involved.

Louise nodded. She knew he wasn't pleased with her. But what did she care? He would thank her later.

Brad opened the door so Darian could get inside the car. When he got in, Darian looked at him and sighed.

"So much for your mother liking me. She's trying to break us up, Brad."

He looked at Darian, but she didn't seem to be too disappointed. "I know, baby. But it won't happen. No one can break us up. When I love a woman I love her all the way." He placed his finger under her chin and kissed her on the cheek. "I swear, baby, no one will break us up."

Louise peeked from the window at the warm affection that Brad and Darian shared so openly.

* * *

Louise knew the moment she heard the doorbell ring that it was Brad. He must have taken Darian home and hurried back. The day was a total waste, and she was in no mood for an argument over a woman she wanted to forget. She got up from the large reclining chair and slowly walked to the living room to open the door for Brad. Brad still had a door key but never used it. Maybe he thought that he would interrupt her with a gentleman friend. But that would never happen. After her late husband, she had no use for a man in her life.

Louise opened the door, and taking long strides, she went back to the den. Brad followed her.

He was too angry to sit still. Brad stood in front of Louise. "Mother, when you invited Darian for lunch I thought you really wanted to meet her and wanted to share my happiness. I didn't think that you would use such malicious tactics just to have what you want." Waiting for her response, he paced in front of her, both hands behind his back.

"I did it for you, Brad. Why waste time with her when you can do better for yourself? If you just want her for sex, then have it and get on with your life. I was rude because I was thinking of you and Tye."

"You're a liar. You did it for yourself. You want me to be alone with no life just like you are. But you can't rule my life, Mother."

Louise jumped off the sofa. "You dare to call me a liar? I'm still your mother, Brad. I won't tolerate it in my house." Her disposition had turned sour.

Brad stepped back. "Then I won't come to your house anymore."

"What! What do you mean by that?"

"If you have so little respect for me, then I won't be back." He stood over her angry enough to drive his fist through the wall.

"Look, Brad, you're making too much out of this. So

I made a mistake. I did it for you and Tye. I want him to have the best stepmother possible. We're so close. Would you really let someone like Darian tear us apart?" She looked hurt, tired.

"That someone you're speaking of happens to be very special to me. Like it or not, Mother, she's in my life and my heart. You stay out of my business or you'll lose me for good. After Dad died, you made the mistake of making Tye and me your entire life. You have friends and should make a life of your own." He stood facing her and when there was no reponse he continued. "Mom, you're a strong woman, but let me advise you, Darian is just as strong. She won't allow you to walk all over her."

"I saw that today, Brad," she snapped disgustingly. She had to admit that Darian was brighter than she had expected. "But she's not the kind of woman you need. That mother of hers is boorish. So she couldn't have raised her girls to be any different. If you continue to see her long enough you'll find out for yourself." She folded her arms.

"Let me say with all candor, Mother, you're not infallible yourself. You think about that." He turned on his heel to walk away but Louise was up again and shouting.

Louise squinted her eyes tightly, which was a habit when she was angry. She couldn't digest her son's defiance. Well, she wouldn't have it. She didn't tolerate her husband's and she wouldn't take it from Brad either. "Don't you ever come into my house again and speak to me that way. You know nothing about that woman."

Brad turned his back to her to walk away. "Goodbye, Mother. I mean what I said. You keep it up and I'll stop coming around." He was done with it.

Louise's words stumbled to a halt as she jumped at the sound of the slamming door.

As Brad backed out the driveway he saw the drapes move to one side. Louise was peeking from the window. She knew nothing about Darian, he thought. So what gave her the right to judge?

Brad's father was a hardworking man, a good father. But Louise was the boss in their household and his father catered to her every wish. She was so dominating, and inflexible. Brad often wondered why his father tolerated her selfish, uncompromising ways. Well, Brad thought, he was in control of his and Tye's lives.

"Did the girls do as you told them?" Darian asked. She looked in their room, and went back to the living room and sat on the sofa next to Vickie.

"Yeah. They're well-trained children. Shelby wanted to play house. I thought it was too cold outside for them." Looking at Darian's long face, Vickie crossed her legs and waited for Darian to tell her about her lunch date.

"So, did you have a good lunch, or what? It couldn't have been as bad as the gloomy face."

Darian nodded her head. "It was awful and she hates me, Vickie. She's a real pill, I'm telling you. A real bitch is more like it." She kicked off her shoes and turned to get a full view of Vickie.

Vickie sat up straight. "What did she do, girl?"

"She showed her ass today. I can't imagine why she hates me so. She hates my mother even more. Would you believe she asked me how can I get married with two children? In her words, who would want me? What difference does it make as long as Brad loves me?"

Trying to make sense out of what Darian had told her, Vickie sat quietly. "Maybe it's not just you she doesn't like. It could be that she doesn't want to share

Brad with anyone. She's probably very possessive, controlling, and evil as hell."

"If she doesn't lose him to me it will be to someone else," Darian mused. "At least I love him. And he loves me, too."

"That's exactly what she's trying to prevent."

"I feel bad about everything, Vickie. Finally I find a man that loves me, and his mother hates me."

"I know you feel bad. But you and Brad are adults. Don't worry about what that old bag of bones says."

Darian laughed. "I don't want to put Brad in the position to choose between me and his mother," Darian said and laid her head back on the sofa. She sighed and closed her eyes. "My stomach hurts from the stress. And I probably won't sleep tonight."

"What did she serve for lunch?" Vickie asked.

"She made a nice salad, and baked dinner rolls. But I can't remember how it tasted. I was so busy trying to keep calm, I ate but didn't taste anything, except anger." Darian ran her fingers through her hair and blew the curls that sprang to her forehead.

Vickie laughed, got up, and put her coat on.

"How is work?" Darian asked, trying to forget lunch.

"I love working there. I get off one hour before Bernard. We are really enjoying each other since he's home. But he still doesn't want a baby. I want a child so badly, but I'm not pressing him about it."

"Maybe he might change his mind one day."

Darian followed Vickie to the door, and stood there until the silver Camry drove off.

Darian changed into a pair of jeans. As she looked in on the girls again, she smiled to herself. Nikki would be four years old tomorrow and it would be her first day in preschool. She would have Shelby at school at eight-thirty, and take Nikki to the other building for preschool.

By seven that evening, Darian had bathed the girls and cooked dinner. They watched TV with her. Darian could hear Brad's footsteps and the doorbell rang. She smiled expectantly.

Darian sighed and open the door for Brad. He stepped inside and gave her a tender kiss on the mouth.

"I need to speak to you, Darian." He took her hand and led her to the dining room. They sat at the table facing each other.

Brad didn't let her hand go. "I don't know how to apologize for my mother's behavior. But I think we have something good going. I don't want you to have second thoughts because of what happened today."

Darian smiled as she saw so much love in his warm, intelligent eyes. "I agree with you, Brad. We do have something good between us. The scene at your mom's house was intense."

"I know, baby. But I wanted to be sure that we understand each other. If you ever need to ask me anything, Darian, just ask. I want us to always understand each other. This isn't a short-term relationship for me. We have our children to think of and one day I want a family."

Darian pulled her chair closer to him. She ran her fingers through his hair, and dived deeply into his kiss. She knew without a doubt that this was her man.

Chapter 21

Two weeks had passed since Darian or Brad mentioned lunch at his mother's house. But it didn't concern Darian because she and Brad were so close that it really didn't matter who objected to their relationship.

It was now September. Darian had taken the girls to school and stopped in the French Market to do some shopping.

As Darian walked out of the store she enjoyed the warmth of the sun, the breeze lightly prickling her skin, and blowing through her hair. As she walked she saw a beat-up brown Buick parked too close behind her car. Before she got inside she walked around her car to make sure there were no dents in it. Why would some numskull park so close? she thought. From the age and condition of the old car it couldn't be covered with any insurance. It was obvious the driver didn't care. Darian stood beside her car and looked in all directions, but no one came to the car. Luckily, no one was parked close in front of her or she would have been stuck.

Darian was anxious to get home and check her mailbox for the contract from her agent. She jumped inside her car and drove off. It was time to pick the girls up from school and go home.

As Darian parked the car in the driveway she saw a passing car. She blinked. Could it be the same car? She couldn't see the back of it, but it looked just like the parked car at the mall. "Couldn't be," she said out loud.

"Couldn't be what?" Shelby asked and looked up at Darian.

"Nothing, nothing. Hurry, get inside," Darian ordered. She locked all the windows. She thought of what she was doing and felt utterly ridiculous. It couldn't be the same automobile; after all, she only saw the back of it.

"Girls, give me your jackets so I can hang them in the closet." She turned the TV on and went to the girls' room. Then she remembered she'd forgotten to check the mail. But when she checked there wasn't any mail.

Darian listened as Shelby answered the phone. "It's Brad," Shelby said, giving it to Darian.

"Hi there," Darian said happily.

"Hi yourself. Guess who wants to see you again?" His voice was deep and clear.

"Who? You?"

"Yes I do, but there's someone else. My mother called me here at the office and wants you to give her one more chance."

This wasn't the news that Darian wanted to hear. She didn't have a good feeling about Louise or seeing her again. Everything had been going so well for her and Brad. But after all, she was his mother. "What do you think, Brad? Is she sincere this time?"

"Yes. We had a lengthy conversation about you. She knows how I feel." He sighed into the phone and waited for her answer. Brad wanted so much for Darian and Louise to become friends.

"Okay. When?"

"Not us, dear. You."

"Alone?" She didn't want to face that woman alone. Besides, what would they have to talk about? Darian shuddered and looked aimlessly ahead.

"Yes. Tye and I will stay with the girls. He wants to come over."

"Should I call her?" Darian asked.

"Yes, please, for me, baby."

"Wait a second." Darian took the phone from her ear. "You girls stop making so much noise. Now keep quiet so I can hear."

"Okay. Why don't you and Tye come over for dinner and we can talk about it?"

"Six all right?" he asked.

"Six is good." Remembering her last visit, Darian hung up and wondered what Louise had up her sleeve.

"Girls, stop running through the house," Darian yelled, rushing to open the door for Shirlee. Almost knocking Shirlee over, the girls ran into her.

"I guess they're glad to see you, Mama. Come on in the kitchen while I make lunch. They've been running and playing since we got home."

She took off her jacket and followed Darian to the kitchen. "Has Brad said anything about his mother yet?"

Darian sat at the table opposite Shirlee. "As a matter of fact I just spoke with Brad. Louise wants to start over. I don't know, Mama. Maybe this time we may hit it off."

Darian's appearance didn't go unnoticed by Shirlee for a minute. Her expression flickered with indecision as she sat there forcing a smile.

"Just remember one thing, Bay. She only wants to

see you again because of Brad. Don't let your guard down with that one. I've met her a time or two, and she's a live witch. She thinks that she's better than anyone else. I'll bet she hasn't had a man since her husband died. Little did she know his hands were under a few skirts. Maybe that was better than being with a cold blanket like her. Be careful with that one. That woman looks mean." Shirlee crossed her legs. She hated the fake, highfalutin type like Louise.

Darian nodded her head. "Would you like a grilled cheese sandwich, Mama?"

"No. I ate last night's leftovers. Jefferson bothered me about smothering pork chops and rice. That old heavy food make me full for two days." She squirmed in her chair as she tugged at her jeans to pull them loose around her waist.

"You look fine, Mama."

"I ran into silly Vickie in the bakery yesterday."

Darian laughed. "Why do you call her silly?"

"Because she is. Running to Los Angeles and back here again. She has a good man and was flirting with a pretty-boy in the bakery."

"She told me that she saw you when she called me yesterday. Let me get the girls so they can eat. We can go back into the living room."

Darian sat the girls at the table and went back to the living room. "When was the last time you saw Louise, Mama?"

"It's been a while. I think I ran into her at Jefferson's cousin's house. They're just like her. That's why you've never seen any of them in my house. Jefferson and I ran into Louise. She looked at Jefferson as though she wanted to eat him alive. But I knew what she was thinking."

"What was she thinking?" Darian asked with interest. Shirlee had an answer for everything.

"She was trying to remember the last time she had some, of course." Shirlee looked at Darian as though she should have known why. "After all, Jefferson is a young, strong man. Since the old men are incapable, Jefferson is what the mature woman needs."

Darian laughed out loud. "You're funny, Mama. Don't ever change." It was as though she had lived in a box and never came up to date in today's world. She was always wearing tight sweaters and jeans. Shirlee looked into the mirror and played with her hair. "Lord, I get so tired of dyeing the gray." She pushed the mirror back inside her purse.

"I'm trying to build my nerves to call Louise today."

"Don't be nervous, Bay. You are one intelligent woman. If anyone can put her in her place, it's you. She's got to respect you for that much. You've got more class than she has."

Darian smiled. "Thank you, Mama."

Shirlee picked up her purse off the coffee table. "I better be going. Be sure to keep the girls warm. I feel a chill in here."

"It should be warm soon. I turned the heater on when we got home," Darian said, walking Shirlee to the door.

"Hello, Tye. Girls, Tye is here," Darian yelled. But before the girls made it to the living room, Tye took off running to their room. He was tall for his age, but so was Brad.

"They're becoming pretty close, wouldn't you say?" Brad asked, pulling Darian closer into his arms, her soft curls against his face. "You're all I think about, baby," he whispered in her ear.

"I better be," she replied. "Sweetheart, this will have to

wait for later. Right now I have to go to your mother's house." Just the thought of Louise made her shiver.

"I hope that after today, you two won't be strangers any longer," Brad said.

"Me, too, love." Darian pulled away from him so he could get a full view of her. "How do I look?" she asked.

"Good. You look good with or without clothes. Preferably, without."

"Wait till tonight," Darian answered with a teasing smile that curled up the corners of her mouth. She was dressed in a brown pantsuit and light blue blouse. She picked up her brown Donna Karan purse that matched her boots, and kissed Brad once more on the lips. "I'll be back in about an hour. So you just sit tight and relax." Darian opened the door, blew him a kiss, and strutted out.

Brad watched her through the blinds as she got into the VW. If only she knew how much he loved her. To make it even easier for him, his son loved her and the girls. Maybe his mother had realized how lucky he really was. In the past, he had dated women with no children that couldn't comprehend why he couldn't spend every moment with them. Darian knew he had to spend time with his son, and there was homework during the week. Tye only had a father; Nikki and Shelby only had Darian. They were a perfect match, and enjoyed spending time with the children. One day, she would be his wife. It was amazing how quickly they fell in love. He had selected women so carefully because of Tye. Darian would be his last, and Louise had better get used to it.

Darian stood at the large double doors and waited for Louise. She frowned and smoothed her hair back just as Louise answered. Why was she so nervous? she wondered. But she knew that she loved Brad and wanted Louise to understand what she and Brad had would last. Getting her approval would make their relationship so much easier.

"Hello, Darian. I'm so glad you could come." Louise stood aside so Darian could enter. She watched Darian closely. "You look so pretty, dear. And I love the color of your sandy hair. If I was looking for you in a crowd, you and your beauty would certainly stand out." She gave Darian a warm smile and led her into the living room. "Red would look good on you, too. I only like red on certain people. Do you ever wear red?"

Darian wondered why only on certain people. "Yes, I do wear red sometimes." Darian followed and watched Louise walk with such grace, her head held high, her gray hair cut close and neatly combed. So far, her spirits hadn't dampened. So far, she thought.

They got to the sofa. "Have a seat, dear. I made us some chamomile tea. I'm up in age now so I thought it best to cut the caffeine."

Darian almost laughed out loud when she saw the silver teapot on the shiny silver tray. She thought of Shirlee and the difference between the two women. Shirlee would have walked out of the kitchen with two coffee mugs in her hand.

"Chamomile tea is fine, Louise."

"What did you do when you were in Los Angeles, Darian? Lemon?"

"Yes, please."

Louise gave Darian her cup and waited for her reply.

"I was a sales manager over the buyers in a large department store chain located in Los Angeles and San Francisco. I loved working as a buyer. I worked hard to accomplish everything I have."

"One has to be smart to take on such responsibility," Louise said as she sipped her tea.

"I had no husband or children, so the job was my life," Darian said proudly.

"My Brad is a very smart man. I've always been proud of him. My grandson will be just like his father."

Darian saw Louise's eyes light up with such love and admiration for her son and grandson. "I'm sure you are proud of Brad and Tye."

Louise placed her cup on the table and refilled it. "I wanted to apologize to you in person, Darian. We both love my son and we don't want to see him hurt or disappointed. He has to have a decent mother for his son, too."

Darian placed her cup on the table. "I understand, Louise. But you can't think that I'm not decent when you don't know anything about me, just as I couldn't judge you by one visit, although I must say with all candor that I had no intention of ever coming here again," she said slowly, and distinctly.

Louise was taken aback by Darian's assertiveness. It was odd that she reminded Louise of herself when she was younger. Louise threw her hands up in the air. "Well, now that we understand each other, I would like for you to come and visit me more often."

"Sure, I will." Darian was sincere, but she would make a mental note to keep the first visit in mind. As Shirlee reminded her, Louise couldn't be trusted. And Darian wasn't completely convinced that she would ever accept her and the girls. Today she was so nice that it was uncanny. What had made her change her mind?

After the ice was broken, the two women chatted as though they were friends.

Darian looked at her watch. "I've enjoyed myself, Louise. But your son is babysitting and we planned to take the children to a movie." Darian stood up and Louise walked her to the door. To her surprise Louise held out her arms and embraced her warmly. She could have sworn that Louise shivered as she hugged her, and it didn't feel comfortable. How could she feel so differently about her so suddenly? Darian wondered. Maybe Louise was doing it for Brad's sake. After all, she wanted her son to be happy.

"Now, you come to see me again, and make it soon."

"You can visit me, too, Louise. Have Brad bring you over."

Still not sure if she liked her or not, Louise watched Darian as she backed out the driveway. Louise went back to the sofa and remembered happier days of Brad as a child. The years had been so precious, no one interfering or taking him away from her. Brad gave her the perfect grandson, which only made Louise love him more, if that were possible. She had gotten his wife out of his life; now she had to figure out a way to remove this Creole bitch. It seemed as though everywhere she went there was always one in her way, taking up breathing air from the good, decent folks. Louise rested her head on the back of the sofa. "Why should I lose my son and grandson to her?" she hissed out loud. Her eyes squinted with anger, and closed tightly as she was certain they would pop out of her head. Her fists lay at her sides, and her breasts heaved. "You got a fight on your hands, Darian, and I hope you're prepared for it." Oh, how excited she felt to know that she would deal with someone as intelligent as she was. Yes, Darian would wish she were never born when she was finished. But she had to think of a way to get rid of her, run her and those bastards she was raising back to Los Angeles. And Shirlee? Just let her get in the way. It would give her more pleasure to take care of both of them. Those people were just taking up breathing air on this planet. After all, she had killed her husband and with her expertise no one even suspected her. She asked him several times to leave those Creole tramps alone, but he was hot for them. Once he had his first one, he couldn't stop. That night he came home and told her that in a week he would move out for one of them. Louise got angry and two nights later they were at the table eating dinner, just the two of them. She had gotten rid of his medication. But she had to think of a reason to excite him so he would need it for his weak, treacherous heart. His heart was so weak that all she had to do was think of a way to frighten the hell out of him and with no medication he could have heart failure. They sat at the table. She only had three nights and he would leave her. It made no difference that she didn't love him, but he would not leave her high and dry for another Creole woman. What was it about them that made him so hot inside? Watching him across that table, she hated him more than ever.

Louise watched her husband eat dinner as he reminded her that he was leaving on Saturday. She went to the kitchen and rushed back with a long carving knife in hand. She lashed out at him, but before she could stab him he jumped out of his chair. She raised the knife to push it into his black heart. His hands went to his chest, and he fell to the floor. Louise shut her eyes tightly as she could remember his every movement as though it were yesterday.

With one hand he reached up to her. "My medication, please, Louise. My chest hurts."

She stood over him. Just as she started to get the medication a thought hit her. *Let him die.* She could always say that he had left it in his car, and after she ran out to get it, it was too late. Louise smiled and her eyes lit up with excitement. "Get it yourself. On second thought, get to the phone and call your Creole bitch. Tell her to help you." She watched as he begged, and tears were trickling down his face, his chest twisting in agony. She watched his eyes roll up so that she could only see the whites. Louise sat in her chair and finished eating her dinner before it got cold. Oh, how she hated eating cold food, she thought. And as she finished, her husband expired. Her husband's death was a long time ago. Now she had to protect her son before he made the same mistake. "Creoles," she said out loud and shook her head in dismay.

Louise went to the kitchen humming a song and repeating the lyrics over and over . . . "I'm going to get even with a Creole." It was the same song she hummed the night her husband died. She washed the dishes and danced around the table humming her song.

The next morning she felt fresh, and the sun was shining.

Darian arrived home. Before she could stick the key in the lock, Brad opened the door.

"Did you hear me drive up?" Darian asked.

"No, not really. My mom called me on my cell phone to tell me you were on your way back. She sounded happy." He took her hand. "Come on and tell me about it." He sat on the sofa and pulled her down beside him.

Darian looked around to see if she saw one of the children. Without realizing it, she had fallen into the habit of saying hello to the girls when she came home and checked to see if they were all right. They were now her girls.

Brad followed her eyes. "The children are fine. They've been playing since you left them."

"Okay, give me a kiss first," Darian teased. She loved seeing him happy, and she knew that he was anxious to hear about her visit with Louise.

Brad kissed her. "Now, talk to me," he said breathlessly.

Sensing the effect she had on him, Darian smiled. "What did Louise say when she called to tell you I had left?"

"She apologized again for the first meeting. She says that you remind her of herself when she was your age. I knew that she would love you."

"Now, is that good enough for you?" Darian asked and traced the V-shape of his sweater with her index finger, teasing him with featherlight touches.

"She'll love you, sweetie. You just stay around for a while."

"Oh, I plan to, Brad. I plan on being around as long as you want me."

The kids ran into the living room and jumped on the sofa between Brad and Darian.

Darian and the girls walked Brad and Tye outside. Brad whispered in her ear, "One night this week we'll have to see each other alone, and soon." He gave her a warm embrace.

Chapter 22

The next day was Monday all over again. Low clouds shrouded the windows of Darian's house. The morning breeze swept across her face as she opened the door and looked outside.

Darian cooked oatmeal and toast for breakfast, dressed the girls, combed their hair, and drove Shelby and Nikki to school. As she drove, she looked at her watch and saw it was only eight o'clock. If she was still in Los Angeles, being the career woman that she used to be, she would have been in her office two hours already. She always arrived two hours earlier than anyone else except Bill Landers. There was a title of an old movie, *Gone Are the Days*, which was now her life story. Nothing was what it used to be. She hadn't realized how carefree her life had been. The eating out at restaurants with Wade and her coworkers, and cooking was out of the question, shopping all day on Saturdays, it was all gone. Her life was now completely different. Darian sighed at what used to be.

She came straight home. But as she turned the corner she saw the brown Buick behind her. She drove up her driveway as the car slowed. Darian strained to see his face clearly, but couldn't. His dark wool cap was pulled down above the sunglasses. She couldn't describe him to anyone if she tried. Darian hurried into the house and checked the windows, but they were locked.

Darian sat on the sofa, her purse still hanging on her shoulder. She picked up the phone to call Shirlee but changed her mind. What could she tell her? She couldn't even see the man's face, hair, or the color of his eyes. She didn't even know how tall he was. Then it finally hit her; his face was hairy and in need of a shave. But that still wasn't enough, and how many men needed a shave that lived in New Orleans? She couldn't give any accurate description of him.

Darian paced the floor and stopped, she looked out the window but saw no sign of the car. Maybe the man lived near her house. Or maybe he hadn't even noticed her at all. It had to be a prudent explanation, Darian thought. The doorbell rang and she almost jumped out of her skin.

Darian peeked out the window, and to her surprise it was Brad. The moment she opened the door, he kissed her and she had forgotten about the rusty brown Buick.

She gently pulled away. "What are you doing here?"

"I came to make love to you, woman." He held her close and kissed her again feeling the passion seething inwardly. When he let her go, she noticed he was dressed for work in a navy blue suit, a light blue shirt, and a blue-and-beige-striped tie.

"I take it you're on your way to work?" she asked between kisses, feeling the fire burning through her body.

"I was. But I called and told my secretary that I would be late. I need you, baby." He led her into her bedroom. She wrapped her arms abound his neck and kissed him hard and hungrily. Piece by piece he undressed her; her clothes fell to her feet. Darian lay on her back and watched as Brad undressed and quickly pulled a condom from his pants pocket and slid it on carefully. Her body tingled, nipples perked, as she looked at his length. When he got on top, the scent of his body made her shiver with desire. He was masculinely graceful, like an athlete. His chest was hairy, and the muscles in his strong legs were hard. His eyes were closed, and Darian heard him mumble her name softly.

Her smooth, soft body made him want to savor every moment. He felt her breasts heaving full and soft against his chest. He moaned when he felt her legs part for him. She lurched upward as his mouth covered her breast. With his other hand, he reached behind her, seized her round, firm butt, and entered her. It was as if he were drowning inside her and never wanted to come out.

Darian sucked in her breath, her arms holding him tightly, circling around his back, sliding down his buttocks as she quivered for more. She trembled at the feel of his thrust, her body stretching to accommodate him as he plunged deeper inside her. She drew in her breath and moved sensually, her body glistening with a veil of perspiration. Lust blazed as their bodies sought to quench the flames engulfing them.

She heard herself groan deeply, felt her body moving faster, upward, clinging to him until he called out her name. He stiffened inside her.

"Oh, baby, I needed you," Brad whispered and rolled over, pulling her over with him. She laid her head on his chest. "I want you all the time, Darian. But with the kids it would be easier if we lived together." He felt her body stiffen and wondered if he had said the wrong thing. Was he rushing her? he wondered.

"It would be easier, but harder for you to get up and

be at work on time." She heard him laugh, and felt his fingers mingling through her hair.

"Well, we have time. When we're ready, we'll know it. Just don't marry any one else, understand?" Brad asked.

Darian raised her head and looked into his eyes. "You're the only man I want, Brad."

"Good. Now, come and take a shower with me. I have to keep my job if you are going to marry me one day."

They were in the shower, and again, they made love. Afterward Brad dried Darian's back, and then she grabbed her robe and went into the living room to wait until he was dressed. For them, the living room was safer than her bedroom. He dressed and held her hand as they walked to the door, then kissed her good-bye and rushed out for a full day at the office.

An hour had passed and it was time to pick up the girls. She went into her bedroom, slipped on her jeans and sweatshirt, and ran to her car. Now that Nikki had started to day care, that gave Darian more time to take care of herself.

"My stomach hurts. I want to go to bed," Nikki whined.

"I'm sorry your stomach hurts. We'll get Shelby and go straight home. Darian held her hand and went to Shelby's classroom where she was waiting at the door.

"Why is Nikki a crybaby?" Shelby teased. "She cries all the time."

"Stop it! Stop it!" Nikki shouted.

"Both of you stop it. Now come on so we can go home."

As Darian drove, she kept looking through her rearview mirror to see if the brown Buick was following, but thank God it wasn't. It was just a crazy coincidence that she saw it twice in one day.

Once they arrived, Darian went to the mailbox and thumbed through her mail. Bingo, the white envelope was from her agent. She ran into the house, opened it, and pulled out her advance check. "Yes! Yes!" she yelled loudly and ran to the phone. "Are you coming over, Mama?"

"Yeah, Bay. I'll be there as soon as I leave the nail shop."

"Good."

Darian hung up. First, Brad visited and now her advance. What a beautiful day, she thought. "I think I'm a woman in love," she whispered to herself. She stopped; surprised that she could actually say the words out loud again. Wade only broke her heart, but not her will to love again.

Holding her doll against her chest, Shelby skipped into the living room, her sand-colored braids bouncing down her back.

It was odd how Darian felt as though the girls were hers now and not just a responsibility that gave her no choice. But she never knew what it was like to have someone's life in her hands. In her prayers, Darian had asked God to show her how to be a mother with no resentment lingering inside her.

Darian looked in on Nikki, but she had fallen asleep. The doorbell rang and she sauntered into the living room finding Shelby's hand on the doorknob. "Stop it, Shelby." Darian opened the door and led Shelby back to the sofa. "When the doorbell rings, always wait for me to open it. Don't ever open the door for anyone unless I ask you to. Do you understand me?" She sat Shelby on the sofa and sat next to her.

"You're teaching her right, Darian," Shirlee said.

She stepped inside and took off her brown leather jacket.

Shelby kissed Shirlee and ran off to her toy box.

"Where's Nikki?" Shirlee asked.

"She complained of a stomachache, so I gave her lunch and put her to bed. She must be tired because she fell asleep. Would you like something to drink, Mama?"

Shirlee threw one hand up. "Oh no. I had two cups of coffee while sitting in the nail shop with Dee. The girl who does my nails drinks more coffee than anyone I know." Shirlee flashed her fingernails in front of Darian. "But she does a good job. Darian, your hair needs trimming and your nails could stand a little color, too."

"I like the clear polish. What do I need with painted nails to clean a house and take care of two small children? When I had a job I went to the nail shop every week."

"Suit yourself. But do get your hair trimmed. Anyway, how was your meeting with Louise?"

"All right. She was nice. Brad says she is mean to all his dates since his father died. She's just afraid some woman will take him away from her."

"One day he will want to get married again. She'll just have to share him and get over it. He's a man, and a man is not going to sit around and stay single because of his mother. He has his own life to live."

"I think she knows it now," Darian said. "As long as Brad wants me, I won't be put off because of her."

"When I was a kid, Creoles had it hard. The dark-skinned blacks didn't like us because of our complexion; the white people didn't like us because we're a black race. Maybe because Louise is dark-skinned she's still holding it against us. With her I guess old habits die hard."

"I'm not sure she feels that way, but it's a good

point, Mama. I'll keep that in mind. But Vickie is dark-skinned and we love each other. She wasn't intimidated because of her complexion and we've been friends since junior high school."

"You and Vickie are younger. Neither of you experienced any racism. I hope you never do. But remember one thing, Darian; it's still going on. Now, what are you going to do with your book advance?" Shirlee crossed her legs and her boots shone; her makeup was flawless and freshly applied.

"I plan to put it in my savings account. I had money left over when I bought this house." Darian was quiet for a second. Then almost jumped out her skin. "Did you hear something, Mama?"

"No. It's probably Shelby playing with all those toys you bought them."

"I better go and see. Maybe Nikki is crying." Darian jumped off the sofa and rushed to the girls' room. "Shelby." Darian called out Shelby's name three times on her way to the girls' room.

Shelby finally answered and ran to the living room. "Here I am and Nikki is still asleep."

Darian had one hand over her stomach, the other hand trembling uncontrollably. She was still unglued by Miss Idele taking Nikki, and became frightened over a game the children played while hiding from each other.

"I'm so sorry, Mama. But I was so afraid the day Miss Idele took Nikki." Tears spilled down her cheeks. Her eyes watered. One mistake, one slip and she cried. "I didn't want to let Monique down again."

Shirlee's heart bled for Darian. All this time she had no idea that Darian felt she had let Monique down. To think she carried such dreadful guilt in her heart had to be agonizing. She had no idea how well she was taking care of the children.

Shirlee went to the sofa and perched next to her. Darian laid her head on Shirlee's shoulder. Shirlee held Darian's head close to her. "Bay, you've been like a mother to Monique's children. The only thing you have to do now is stop overprotecting the girls. Didn't it ever occur to you that Nikki was playing hide-and-seek? You automatically thought she was hurt."

"I know it's a game, Mama, and I'll have to do better."

"Wait here." Shirlee left the room and came back with a box of tissues in her hand. "Here, Bay, wipe your eyes."

"I was so happy this morning. Now my day is ruined."

"Darian, your day is not ruined. Wait till the girls are fifteen and eighteen, then your day will be ruined. Right now they're still babies. Well, I have a headache and I'm going home. You know, I think that I'll go uptown and do a little shopping first. I need a new pair of jeans." Shirlee reached inside her purse and pulled out her mirror. "I have to buy something for the lines in the corners of my eyes."

"I thought you had a headache and where's uptown, Mama?"

"Uptown on Canal Street, girl. That's where it's always been. And some fresh air might make my head stop hurting."

Darian walked Shirlee to the door and locked it. The phone rang, and she answered. "Hi, Jefferson, if you're looking for Mama she just left."

"I wasn't looking for Shirlee, Darian. While driving to work this morning, I saw a store with swimming pools for small children. I'm on a break and wondered if I could drop by. It would be great for the children this summer."

Wondering what Jefferson really wanted, Darian

held the phone for a few seconds before speaking. He had treated the children well, but Darian never felt that he had any real interest in the girls. "Okay, Jefferson. But Mama is here almost every day. She can drop it off if that's convenient for you."

"I'm only ten minutes from your house, Darian."

"Okay, come on over." Darian stared at the phone before hanging it up. She went into the kitchen and took a can of apple juice from the refrigerator. About the time she grabbed a pen and paper to jot down what she needed from the supermarket, she heard Jefferson's footsteps approaching the door.

Darian swung the door open and Jefferson was standing there.

"Hey, where's the kids?" Jefferson asked as he looked inside the living room.

"They're in their bedroom playing with their dollhouse Mama bought. I believe it's their favorite toy."

"Well, here, I don't have much time before I have to be back. Remember, Darian, call me if you ever need anything. If one of them were a boy, I could play football with him or do something that a boy needs a man to teach him. But with the girls, I can't really do anything with them."

Darian nodded in understanding.

The door was ajar and they were standing in the living room. Just as Jefferson started to turn around and leave, Darian called his name.

"I appreciate this, Jefferson. I know the girls will love it, too."

"Shirlee says you and Brad are getting seriously involved?"

"Yes, we are," Darian answered, wondering where this conversation was heading.

"I hope it works out. You certainly deserve the best." He moved closer to the door. "Anyway, I better go."

Because his jeans were so tight, he had to force his hands inside his pockets. His long black knee boots were dusty, and the sleeves of his white T-shirt were rolled up with a book of matches tucked inside the fold of one sleeve.

Darian watched him until he drove off in his pickup truck. It seemed that Jefferson was full of surprises. Every time she wanted to dislike the man, he did something to stop her. Since it was still chilly, she took the small swimming pool to the garage. She looked around the yard. Soon, she would plant flowers and maybe grow some strawberries for the girls.

The next day Darian took the girls to school. On the way home, she stopped at a small clothing store. Walking out of the store, she decided to go to Gentilly Woods Mall. The mall was small and always packed. Taking her time, she browsed from store to store. She went into a clothing store and looked around. She placed a yellow blouse against her, and noticed the time. She had to pick up the girls, and left the mall to go back to her car.

"Watch out, lady."

The voice sounded far away, vibrating with warning. The sound of the skidding brakes and burning rubber permeated the air around her, and got her attention. Darian felt a large, hard hand grab her left arm roughly, jerking her aside. Her purse fell off her shoulder but she managed to hold on to it. The brown Buick was speeding toward her. It was no doubt that his aim was at her with such forceful, fast speed.

The gentleman held Darian in his arms. Feeling his body against her, she pulled away, her hair in disarray. She stumbled off balance, her eyes squinting from the sunlight shining brightly. She looked at the man's face as he sat her on the curb, where people were standing and surrounding her. She heard whispers and everyone asking if she was all right.

At first Darian was unable to speak, so she nodded, and closed her eyes while taking a deep breath. "I've seen the car before. Did it look like an accident to you, sir?"

"No, I'm sorry to say. Whoever it was wanted to kill you. He was driving too fast for an accident, miss." The man took a seat on the curb next to Darian.

"I agree," Darian choked out. She felt dizzy and rested her head against her knees, feeling the throbbing in her left temple like the beat of a pounding drum.

"Miss, can you drive home?" the gentleman asked. He was short with wiry gray hair, brown-skinned, and looked to be in his late fifties. "You should report this incident to the police department. He may try it again."

"What? Again?" she repeated, shaken. "I didn't get your name?" Darian asked. Finally, she was able to stand. The gathering crowd was beginning to disperse in different directions.

"It's Mr. Jones." He pulled out a business card and scribbled his home phone number on the back. "Here, in case you need a witness."

"Thank you so much, Mr. Jones." But why would she need a witness? The dizziness had subsided, but her head was still pounding. It was getting past the time to pick the girls up, and she ran to her car.

Still in a daze, Darian drove off too fast for such busy traffic. She hit her brakes hard to prevent running the red light. She felt tears streaming down her face. Who was this man in the brown Buick? What had she done to make him want to harm her? "Kill me?" she whispered, ready to panic. If only she knew who it was, what he wanted?

Darian turned into the school parking lot, jumped out of her car, and looked around to see if she saw the car. She ran to Nikki's room first.

"I'm sorry that I'm a little late. I had an errand to run," Darian said to Miss Horn. It was difficult to get the words out.

"It's all right, Miss Cantrell. I'm always here at least an hour after the class leaves."

Darian hurriedly picked Nikki up in her arms and dashed to Shelby's room. She saw Shelby standing impatiently at the door.

"I'm hungry," Shelby complained.

"I know, honey, sorry I'm late." Darian was glad that Shelby's teacher was speaking with another parent and only waved at her. She rushed the girls to the car.

She hurried the girls as they ran into the house. Nikki thought they were playing a game and laughed.

Darian ran through the house to check the windows and doors, like she had for the last couple of weeks. She dialed Brad's work number and told him what happened at the mall. After she hung up, she gave the girls each a peanut butter and jelly sandwich and a glass of milk. They were instructed to go to their room and play.

Thirty minutes had passed while Darian paced the living room. Every time she heard a car she ran to the window and glared out. Finally, she heard Brad pulling up into the driveway.

Darian ran to the door and almost jumped into Brad's arms.

"It's all right, honey. Now, slowly tell me what happened." He led her to the sofa and sat close to her.

"Two, maybe three times, I can't remember right now, but I've seen that brown beat-up Buick in different places. The first time I saw it, I was shopping and it was parked too close behind me. When I got home I thought that I saw it pass but I wasn't sure." She sighed out loud and ran her fingers through her hair.

"Take your time, baby. Have you seen his face?"

"No. I can only see this wool cap pulled down and he wears sunglasses, too. I don't understand. Why me, Brad? Why does he wants to hurt me? I don't know of any enemies that I have here, or any place else for that matter. Maybe he has mistaken me for someone else. Or maybe he's just crazy."

"Why didn't you tell me about this before, Darian? You could have been hurt, or killed."

She held his hand tightly. "I just didn't think anyone wanted to hurt me." She looked into his eyes, and then fell back into a shadow of misery. Her body was stiff, and every time she heard a car she jumped and felt a thump inside her chest.

"I'm going to call the police department so an officer can come out and take a report," Brad said, reaching for the phone. "Don't worry, baby. We're going to find out who this bastard is and what he wants."

Darian grabbed his hand. "What can I tell them? I don't even know what he looks like."

"We need to report it anyway. Now sit back and try to relax." Brad made the call and Darian listened.

All of a sudden she realized that someone out there really wanted her dead.

"Let me check on the girls." She went into their room. "You guys want a cookie?"

Shelby jumped up and Nikki followed, running into the kitchen behind Darian.

"You guys have been very good today." Darian wiped the corner of her eye. "In a few minutes we can watch TV together and talk about what you did at school today." She kissed both of them. Darian heard the doorbell and rushed back to the living room.

When Darian got to the living room, two New Orleans police officers were seated and waiting for her. One was tall, and his eyes lit up as she ambled into the room. The other one was white with gray eyes, wearing a solemn expression. Darian looked at them and took a seat next to Brad.

Darian introduced herself and waited to be questioned.

"Miss Cantrell, I'm Officer Jamison, and my partner is Officer Hicks. Now, you want to tell us what happened?"

Darian reached for Brad's hand. "I went shopping at Gentilly Woods Mall today. As I walked out a gentleman grabbed my arm and pulled me back to the curb. A car would have hit me if it weren't for Mr. Jones who saved me. I saw the car passing my house earlier."

"What kind of car was it?" Officer Jamison asked.

"It was an old brown, beat-up Buick in need of a paint job. Oh, and the top of it was rusty."

"Good. Now we need a description of the man."

"I couldn't see him clearly. He wears a brown cap pulled down too far. And he wears sunglasses, too. I've never seen him out of the car, so I can't even tell you how tall he is." Darian looked at the officers as they exchanged glances.

"Did you write down his license number?"

"I never had a chance to write it down." She felt defeated, knowing she was no help at all.

Officer Jamison moved around as though he was getting impatient.

Darian felt foolish, but what could she tell them? She looked at Officer Hicks, and he gave her a warm, sympathetic smile.

"So, Miss Cantrell, in essence, you have nothing to

help us with," Officer Jamison said. His manner had become abrupt. He sighed again. He could abide that pretty face, but her empty head was wasting their time.

"Under the circumstances, she's telling you all she can remember. If she sees a passing car, she hasn't the time to get a pen and paper to write down anything," Brad intervened.

"I'm sorry. We will turn in the report but that's all we can do," Officer Jamison said and stood up.

Officer Hicks stood up, too. "Miss Cantrell, when you leave the house, take a pen and paper with you and be prepared. Leave it on the seat in case you see him again, and call us right away."

Darian nodded absentmindedly. "Thanks for your time, and I'll remember to do as you said. But what if I'm killed in the meantime? Would that make it easier for the police department to pick him up?" Shaking a lock of light brown hair off her forehead, she stood with both hands on her hips; her face was red with frustration as she looked at both officers. Officer Hicks's mouth lifted into a smile. She was a saucy one, but cute. "I hope it doesn't go that far, Miss Cantrell." They walked out.

Brad walked outside with them. When he came back, Darian was still sitting on the sofa.

"They were a big help," Darian said and sighed with resignation.

Brad sat next to her. "We'll figure this out, baby. In the meantime, you and the girls stay inside." He held her hand. "Does your mom know?"

"No. I don't think she needs to."

"I think she does, Darian. She may know someone with the car or she may have seen it before."

Darian shook her head. "I've noticed that every time something frightens her, she gets heart palpitations.

I was afraid that I was going to lose her after Monique's death. I can't tell her, Brad."

Brad stood up and pulled her close to him. "I understand, baby. I have to go back to the office, but I'll check on you later. Please give some thought to you and the girls staying at my house."

Darian nodded and circled her arms around his neck. "What would I do without you?" she whispered. "But I'm not running away from my house because of a fool running loose."

Brad pulled away so he could see her face. "I'll never want to know what you would do without me, Darian."

Her eyes searched his. He had become part of her life. And to think she hadn't intended to fall in love again. She didn't think that she needed a man to lean on. But Brad was different and she needed him.

"Why isn't Tye in bed this time of night, Brad? Isn't tomorrow a school day?" Louise asked as she followed Brad and Tye into the living room.

"Go take your clothes to the bedroom, Tye," Brad said.

He waited until Tye had left the room. "I need a favor, Mother."

"Sure. What is it, son?" They were standing in the living room and Louise took a seat in the large leather chair.

"Somebody tried to run Darian down while she was at the mall today."

"What? Why?" Louise asked. "Can't the girl be mistaken? Surely no one would hurt her for no reason at all."

"Apparently someone wants to. She has seen the car at least three times. We called the police today but they can't do anything because she can't describe the man."

Louise placed one hand over her mouth. "How could she not have any idea who it was? Maybe it's an old boyfriend from her past." She got up and stood in front of the large oak bookcase. "You could get hurt. I knew she was bad news when you brought her over here. Why place you and Tye in the middle of her mess? It's hard for me to believe she has no idea who it is, Brad."

Louise knew from the beginning that Darian was trouble, and was sure that she had slept with the man who wanted to see her hurt. Louise sighed deeply. If only she knew the man. She felt the excitement of the possibility that Darian could be hurt or killed. And again, she thought of the night her husband died, and smiled. She was always the only one that had durability in her family. Never any action was taken unless it was hers.

"This mess is going to cause me to worry all the time about you and Tye. And all because of her." Louise clicked her tongue at the top of her mouth. "Creoles," she murmured.

"Mother, please. It's not an old boyfriend, and you don't have to worry about Tye and me. Just calm down," he said and sighed. He should have known it would be a mistake telling Louise.

"You shouldn't go to her house until the man is arrested," she hissed.

Brad put both hands up in the air and sat next to Louise. "You worry too much about me and Tye. I can take care of us and Darian, too."

"Take care of her? She's the one that's involving you. If something happens to you and my grandson, I won't forgive Darian." She grabbed his hand and squeezed it tightly before she let go again.

"Will you take Tye to school for me tomorrow?" he asked and kissed her on the cheek.

Louise looked at her son's face. He looked so much like his father. She meant it, if anything happened to Brad, Darian would have hell to pay.

"Sure, I'll take Tye to school tomorrow. I'll get up early and make him breakfast."

Brad stood up. "Thanks, Mom. No matter what happens, I know that I can count on you." He touched her hand and started to the door.

"Brad?"

"Yes, Mother."

"Why don't you bring Darian and the girls over a week from Saturday? I guess it's time I get to know them. I'll cook a pot of gumbo."

"Sounds great, Mother. We'll be here."

In spite of everything that happened today, Brad walked out of his mother's house with a wide smile.

Darian and the girls stayed inside the rest of the afternoon. After she had put the girls to bed, she was skimming through a magazine when the doorbell rang. She looked out the window and saw Brad's black Lexus SUV. Smiling, she opened the door.

He stepped in with a black suit and an overnight bag in hand.

"What are you doing?" she asked, confused, and looked into his dark brown eyes.

"Staying with you so I can get some sleep. Now, I'm taking my clothes to your bedroom." He gave her a brown bag with a bottle of wine. "Woman, don't just stand there. Put the wine in the refrigerator." He walked right past Darian as she stood in awe. *Get some sleep?* she thought with a shy smile.

Darian put the wine in the refrigerator and followed Brad to her bedroom.

As they entered, he grabbed her around her waist. "Are the girls asleep yet?"

"Yes," she whispered.

Brad ran his left hand under her blouse; the other hand unzipped her jeans and slid into her black lace panties. He heard Darian gasp.

"Oh God, Brad," was all she could manage to say. She was still standing when he opened her blouse and pulled her bra straps down her slender shoulders. He lifted one leg to free her of her jeans and kneeled in front of her as he freed the other leg. Kissing her smooth thighs, he yanked the jeans completely off.

"Lie on the bed, Darian," Brad whispered, his baritone echoing like a silky saxophone.

Darian did as she was told, and watched with anticipation of his strong and gentle touch. The touch of his hands massaged her like magic.

Brad slipped on a condom and mounted her. "Love me, Darian," he whispered. When he felt her body melting into his, experiencing bliss, he could wait no longer. Brad cherished the intimacy between them. It was the first time all over again.

Chapter 23

A week had passed and there were no signs of the brown Buick. The warm sun poured into the kitchen where Darian was cooking oatmeal for the children. She was in a pleasant mood. The weather was nice, the flowers bloomed, and she hummed and moved around the kitchen. She smiled as she watched a blue jay fly from tree to tree in search for food.

"Is it time to go to school yet?" Shelby asked as she walked up behind Darian.

"No, Shelby. It's Saturday, today we are going to visit Louise. She's Brad's mother. She invited us over for dinner."

"Will Tye be there?"

"Yes. Louise is Tye's grandmother."

"I want a grandmother," Nikki whined and tugged at Darian's blouse.

"Mama is your grandmother, silly," Shelby answered.

Darian placed three bowls on the table. "Now, Shelby, don't call your sister silly. Tye calls his grandmother grandma, but you and Nikki call your grandmother Mama. But she's still your grandmother."

Darian had high hopes that the day would go

smoothly. The last visit was pleasant enough, even though they didn't really like each other, but Darian would settle for just being respected, not judged.

She went to her bedroom, opened the closet, and pulled out her gray slacks and a blouse to match. She heard the girls pushing their chairs away from the table, and she went back to the kitchen.

Darian felt anticipation because this was Louise's first time meeting Shelby and Nikki. Darian wanted to dress them impeccably. Surely she would fall in love with the girls so beautiful and well behaved.

Brad and Tye were ringing Darian's doorbell at precisely one o'clock. The girls ran to the door with Darian.

"I have three beautiful girls," Brad said. He kissed Darian and ruffled her hair.

Darian and the girls laughed out loud. She locked the door as Brad led the girls to his SUV.

In the car the girls were singing. The ride was short and Brad pulled into his mother's driveway. Her long white Lincoln was parked to make room for Brad's SUV.

As they stepped out onto the pavement, Darian smelled Louise's small rosebush, its sweet scent permeating the air. It was spring, Darian's favorite time of year.

Louise was waiting, her short black hair shining like black silk. The purple, simple dress went beautifully with her dark skin. She smiled and looked down at the girls.

Brad, Darian, and the children almost looked like a happy family. *No, they will never be happy*, she thought to herself. *After Brad finishes playing with her he'll move on to someone better.* In the meantime, Louise had to make Darian and the girls welcome. After all, it was the southern thing to do. Besides, she still had to make amends for the first visit. When it was over, Brad would know she tried to be the good hostess, and mother. She looked at Darian, and knew she was in love with her son. She could see it in her wicked, light-colored eyes. Louise hated light eyes. Anyone with light-colored eyes couldn't be trusted.

"Hello, Louise. It's nice of you to have me and the girls over," Darian said. "Look at how excited they are."

"They'll have fun," Louise said and kissed Brad on his cheek.

"Tye, take the girls to your room and show them your toys. He has the same room that Brad had before he left home."

Darian followed Louise into the house. The kids had already run inside with Nikki toddling behind them.

Darian followed Louise to the den where she always sat when she was home.

"Brad tells me your new house is cute."

"Yes. Luckily my sister's house was already paid for. Otherwise I would have had to use my savings."

"Come on, honey, let me show you my old room. That's where the kids are now." Brad led Darian by the hand and Louise went to the kitchen.

Darian stood in the room. The bedroom was decorated for a boy with sports posters on the wall, and a radio on the nightstand. Tye and the girls ran out the door. "It looks as though it was your room," Darian said and reached for Brad's hand. She walked around the room and looked at his desk and the stocked bookcase.

When Brad and Darian went back to the den, Louise was waiting with a platter of crisp vegetables and a bowl of ranch dip. "Come, sit next to me, Darian. You can always sit next to Brad later." Oh, how she hated the girl.

Darian smiled and sat on the couch next to Louise.

"Brad told me about the incident when you were shopping in the mall. Is there any potential danger for the children or Brad? I wouldn't want to see anyone hurt."

"Louise, I hope none of us are in danger, especially Brad and the girls. Since I reported it to the police department I haven't seen the car. Whoever it was, it seems he only wants to harm me."

"It's frightening. I would be afraid to leave my house. I'm just too old to worry about such things in this stage of my life." Louise smiled, and then frowned with worry.

"Mother, it's nothing for you to worry about. Let me and Darian take care of it." He regretted that he told Louise about the incident.

"Okay. I'll try not to worry too much. But don't tell me not to worry at all, Brad. You have a son, and when you get to be my age, you worry."

Darian held her head down. Just one more reason for Louise to hate her, she thought with disappointment.

"Mother, the gumbo smells great. I'm starved."

Louise laughed at her son. "We can eat right now if you want."

Together, Louise and Darian went to the kitchen. "The children can eat in here, Darian. This is where Tye and I eat when he's here." Louise took a stack of bowls from the cabinet. "I haven't seen your mother in a long time. How is she?"

"She's well. Mama is so much help to me. She comes over almost every day to help with the children. Her husband bought the girls a small swimming pool for the summer. I don't know what I would do without my mother."

"We can prepare the children's dishes first," Louise

said. She took the top off the rice and gave Darian a large spoon for the gumbo. "I take it you and your mother's husband get along well? Since he is closer to your age."

Darian stopped and looked at Louise for a second. "Jefferson and I get along well enough. I mean, we're not very close but we respect each other. Respect is all that I expect from anyone."

They were getting to know each other because they both wanted the same thing for Brad and Tye.

"Now, I'll fix Brad a bowl and you can go and get the children so we all can eat."

"I'll do that," Darian answered.

Louise watched as she walked out of the room. "I'm really trying, Lord," she said to herself, and closed her eyes so hard that her face distorted into a twist.

The three adults were at the dining room table. Darian admired Louise's exquisite taste. A silver platter sat on a white lace place setting in the middle of the table, white china bowls stacked beside the silver platter. Darian looked at the expensive oil paintings on the walls trimmed with wood frames. But as Louise placed napkins on the table, for the first time Darian noticed her dark-colored fingernails that looked to be those of a smoker. Maybe she had stopped, but not before the smoke discolored and stained her nails.

"The gumbo is delicious," Darian complimented. "My mother is a good cook, too."

"I take it she taught you how?" Louise asked.

Darian looked at Brad. He was sitting next to her. "She tried, but I still have a lot to learn. When I was in Los Angeles I worked long hours and ate out too much. But now that I have the girls to raise, I'm trying."

"It takes practice, baby. You are doing pretty good," Brad said and kissed her on the cheek.

Louise gritted her teeth together as she watched the

two lovebirds. And every time Brad looked at Darian he smiled. "Oh, the young," Louise said. "You two remind me of my younger days. So much in love." But what did she know about being in love? It had been so long, and she'd forgotten the feeling. Louise had hated her husband the last year of their marriage.

"Does it show that much?" Darian asked, smiling. She embraced Brad and their eyes locked as two people in love.

"Yes, it shows. I've been watching you two since you arrived. And Tye and the girls seem to be getting along very well, too. Your girls are adorable."

"Thank you, Louise," Darian answered with pride.

"Mother, this has been a good day, hasn't it?"

"Yes, son, it has. Now, you two take your time while I get that apple pie out of the oven." Before Louise could get up, a loud clamor resonated from the kitchen. Nikki was crying and everyone in the dining room jumped from their seats and raced into the kitchen, Brad taking long strides in front of Louise and Darian.

Darian entered the kitchen and gaped as she looked at Louise's shining floor with gumbo splattered all over it.

"Lord, Nikki, what happened?" Darian asked as she ran to the table where the children were sitting.

"I told her to wait, but she got up anyway," Tye said.

"My God, Darian. Do your girls have any home training at all? I just waxed my floors yesterday," Louise yelled loudly. Her round eyes were wide, and deep creases across her forehead were enough to cause Darian to stare at her. She sounded angry; her voice was cold enough that Darian felt a chill creep up her back.

Darian felt the hairs on her arms stand high; her eyes burning with tears as embarrassment seized her, she looked helplessly at Brad. "As a matter of fact I don't train my girls. You train animals, so I teach my girls. I'll clean up and take the girls home. I'm so sorry we came."

Everything was going so well, but she was wrong. Louise would never think she and the girls were good enough. Darian looked at Louise; she looked too shocked to move.

"For God's sake, Mother. She's only a child and you've frightened her to death." Brad touched Darian's shoulder. "It's all right."

"No, Brad, it's not all right. You know I teach my girls," Darian said more to Louise than to Brad.

"Okay, baby. But accidents do happen."

Brad gave Louise a disgusted look and took crying Nikki in his arms. "It's okay, honey. It's okay."

"Mother, I'll help Darian clean up, and then take her home."

"But you didn't finish eating," Louise reminded him.

"I lost my appetite after your outburst. Just give me something to clean this mess up with." Brad looked at Darian again. "We can stop somewhere on the way home and buy dinner."

Darian nodded in agreement.

Louise stopped him by shaking her head. "Stop. Everyone take your seats and finish dinner. I can clean up myself. It's not that big a deal." She had to stay calm until she thought of a way to get rid of Darian.

"No, Louise. I think it's best that I take my girls home," Darian replied firmly. "Come on, girls, it's time to go."

Louise looked at the displeased expression on Brad's face and knew instantly that he was angry. "No, Darian, wait please. Look, I know I overreacted. But I didn't mean it that way. The words just rushed out of my mouth without thinking. My late husband used to tell me all the time that I get too angry too easily.

Except for this incident, the girls have been good since you all arrived."

Brad looked at Darian as she held Nikki in her arms. "Do you feel comfortable enough to stay, baby?"

Darian looked at Louise and back at Brad again. "Okay. You and I can clean up and finish eating. I'm just so sorry," Darian said, looking straight at Louise.

Darian placed Nikki back at the table and helped Brad. Once they finished, Brad and Darian went back to the dining room.

"Is the child all right, Brad?" Louise asked.

"Yes, Mother, she's only four years old."

"Just turned four in January," Darian said. All she wanted was for this day to end. It would be a long time before she returned to this house again, if ever.

No one said very much during dinner. It was as though they all felt the same, eat and leave.

Darian excused herself and went to the restroom. Standing in front of the mirror, she pictured the ugly twist of Louise's face. She was truly a mean woman, she thought. And if she and Brad married, she would stay away from Louise. Shirlee did say she couldn't be trusted. Now Darian was certain of it.

Brad was waiting for her in the den. "Are you all right, Darian?"

"I really would like to go home, Brad. But we can wait until Louise is finished."

He sat close to Darian and held her hand. She looked sad and disappointed. It had been a long nerve-racking day. To relieve the tension, they would have to leave.

Louise waltzed back into the den. "Anyone want a glass of wine?"

"No, thanks, Louise. The girls are probably getting tired and I really should take them home," Darian answered.

"Okay, Darian. But I hope you will forget this incident and bring the girls back again." Louise sat beside Darian. "I'm really sorry for getting so angry." She placed one hand under her chin as though she was pondering what to say next. "You know, I wasn't angry at the child. After all, she's still a baby, but I think the noise scared me more than anything. So what do you say, Darian? Come back soon and bring the girls again."

She had to be kidding. But Darian forced a smile for Brad's sake. She turned around to face Louise. "All right. I will come again." *Like hell she would*, Darian thought to herself. The day was going so well until the ruckus started in the kitchen, and Louise seemed to care more about her floor than Nikki's feelings. "I do appreciate you inviting my girls and me over." Darian picked up her purse. All she wanted was to go home.

"I'll get the girls," Brad said.

"He's very attentive, isn't he? His father was like that, too. You're a lucky woman, Darian."

"I know, Louise, and I don't take it for granted either."

"You're a smart young woman." *Why did I say that?* Louise thought. Maybe because the girl had a sarcastic tongue and was a challenge, and Louise would love the challenge since she detested weakness. Looking at Darian, she saw she was no pushover.

Brad returned to the den with Tye and the girls. "Ready?" he asked Darian.

"Yes, I'm ready." She had never been more ready in her life.

Louise watched the way Brad handled Darian and the girls. At that moment she realized if he married Darian, he would always defend Darian, and Louise would always be wrong. All of a sudden she felt completely left out of his life. Would Brad just toss her aside? How could she let Darian steal her family?

* * *

The children laughed and talked in the backseat, but Darian and Brad were quiet.

"It wasn't so bad, was it?" Brad asked. He looked over at Darian and smiled.

"No, not in the beginning. I'm not sure if I want to go back. She acted as though the girls and I came from another planet. I think she feels we are beneath her, Brad."

"That's not true. Mother has had her way for so long and it's hard to change. But she knows she has to, Darian."

Like hell she did, Darian wanted to say. But enough had been said for one day, and she was too tired to argue.

Once they were home, Brad helped Darian and the girls inside. He walked in and turned the lamp and heater on. The girls ran to their room, and Tye followed.

Brad pulled Darian down on the sofa beside him and kissed her tenderly. "I've waited for this all day," he whispered in her ear.

"So have I. When you kiss me like that I forget all my problems."

"Good. I'll do it again, and again." And he did, even better.

"I better leave now while it's safe." He kissed her neck, and her lips. "It's always so hard to leave you. Tye, time to go," Brad yelled.

He and Darian laughed out loud. Tye ran into the living room, the girls behind him.

"Why can't we stay here tonight, Dad?" Tye asked.

"Because I have work at home to take to my office."

Darian and the girls walked them to the door and said good night.

Chapter 24

"Did the girls enjoy themselves?" Shirlee asked.

"Yes, very much. They played in the backyard until it got too cool. Then they played in Tye's bedroom, which used to be Brad's," Darian said.

"Darian, while the girls are at dancing school next Saturday, why don't we go shopping?" Vickie suggested.

"All the parents have to stay. The instructor would have a fit if I left."

"Bay, I can take care of the girls. After the class is over we can go to lunch," Shirlee said. She was sitting with a magazine in her hand.

"Are you sure you don't mind, Mama?"

"Of course I don't. Besides, Jefferson has to work next Saturday. But for now, I better go home. I woke up with a headache this morning." Shirlee picked her purse up off the table.

"Are you all right, Mama? Your face is beet red."

"Yes, Darian. I'm just hot, my face is red because I had a hot flash. That's what fifty-two-year-old women do." She pulled her sweater tighter around her waist.

Darian and Vickie exchanged glances, then looked at Shirlee again and laughed out loud.

"Laugh all you want to. But your day is coming." Shirlee strutted out the door and waved good-bye on her way out.

Darian went back to the sofa where Vickie was sitting. "I have something to tell you," Darian said and curled her feet under her.

"What, girl?" Vickie's eyes were wide.

"I'm in love again and I'm completely over Wade. All the fears of being in love again have disappeared."

"Taking on a family was a pretty tall order, Darian. It took you a while to accept it. But Wade was lying even before you left L.A. I told you Brad was a nice guy. Why don't the four of us go out together one evening?"

"Good idea, Vickie. Maybe we can go dancing one Saturday night. Brad will love it. Lately, we've only been taking the children out."

"Bernard still says no about us having a baby. He has a twenty-year-old son. But I want a child, too." Vickie's happy expression was changed to sadness. "I've tried everything to try and convince him, but so far nothing is working."

"Before you guys were married he didn't want children."

"I know. But I thought that after a year of marriage he would change his mind. But I don't know, Darian. My clock is ticking fast." Vickie got up with her empty glass in her hand.

"We can speak to Brad and Bernard about us going out together," Darian said. "And stop worrying about having a baby for now. Who knows, he may change his mind." Darian walked outside with Vickie and stood on the porch until Vickie drove off.

It was morning, and the sun peeked through the blinds. "I don't want to miss school," Shelby cried.

"I don't want to go. Can I stay home with you, Darian?" Nikki asked.

"Yes."

"And, Shelby, you can miss school for one day. My head hurts badly and my stomach aches." Darian flopped down on the sofa. "Go and get a pillow off my bed, Shelby."

Shelby stomped out of the room. Nikki ran to her room and came back with her doll in her hand.

Shelby stood in front of Darian with the pillow in her hand. She placed it on the sofa and traced the black and red lines on the pillowcase with her index finger.

"You like the colors in the pillowcase?" Darian asked.

"Yes," Shelby said and laughed out loud. She was happy again.

Darian phoned Shirlee to tell her that the girls would stay home today. She had a terrible sinus headache, and going out would only make it worse.

It was cool outside and the blinds were closed to prevent the sun from streaming through. Darian pulled the blanket up to her shoulders. She couldn't get warm enough. Her hair was combed back into one braid. She had a half cup of tea on the coffee table in front of her.

Shirlee rang the doorbell and waited. As Darian opened the door, Shirlee breezed aimlessly inside the house like a winter storm. She noticed that Darian's face was pale, and put her hand against Darian's forehead. "You have a slight fever. It must be the flu."

"I think so, too. When Monique and I were kids I still remember Uncle Buck always bringing us chocolates."

Shirlee pulled a small brown bag from her purse and gave Darian a bottle of Flonase to spray up her nose. "Buck died when you were eight years old. That man left his sperm at every woman's house he went to. He had children ranging from ages three to twenty-five. He had three by Susie Mae, and the others were from every other woman he slept with, which were many."

Shirlee slipped her shoes off and sat in the chair opposite Darian.

She looked at Darian again. Her face was red and her eyes were puffy. "Does it still hurt?"

"Yes. But it's getting a little better. Now I feel weak because I got up at three this morning and took a Benadryl on an empty stomach." She sat up on the sofa and closed her eyes against the dull ache, laying her head back.

Shirlee made the girls lunch, and opened a can of chicken noodle soup for Darian. "Come on, Bay. You need some food in your stomach."

Darian tiptoed lightly to the kitchen where the girls were eating lunch. "The girls are so quiet."

"They finished and went to their room. Toys were everywhere," Shirlee commented.

She got up and slipped into her long blue coat sweater that stopped at her knees. "If you're not feeling better tomorrow, call me and I'll drive the girls to school."

"I'll go out with you so I can get my mail." Darian stood up and slipped into her bathrobe. When she stepped outside she reeled off balance as the bright sun momentarily blinded her. She blinked twice before she could see clearly again.

The mailbox was on the side of the house near the driveway. Darian got the mail as Shirlee opened the door and stopped. Darian read each envelope and when Shirlee made no attempt to get inside, Darian stopped and looked at Shirlee's face.

Shirlee's mouth was open, and as Darian followed

her eyes the brown Buick was coming up the driveway speeding with a straight aim at both of them.

Darian grabbed Shirlee, jumping away from the car in fear of getting killed. Shirlee tripped, and as she held Darian's arm they both fell to the ground.

Just when Darian was sure the car was going to hit Shirlee's car, it stopped, only inches away, and backed out into the street. The car took off speeding, the motor loud, black clouds of smoke and a trail of dust rising into the air.

"Thank you, God," Shirlee said as she lay on her stomach and covered her eyes with both hands. Her heart rate quickened with raw fear. She could taste the blood on her bottom lip from biting into it.

Darian got up first and extended her hand out to help Shirlee up. Excruciating pain throbbed in each temple as she puked up on the grass. "Are you all right, Mama? Come on so we can get inside."

"Am I all right?" She dusted off her clothes. "Who in the hell was that? Do you know who it was?" she asked angrily. "The bastard could have killed us. I wish my pistol was inside my purse."

"Do you need to go to the hospital, Mama?"

"No. I don't think so. Just get me inside so I can lie down for a few minutes. What I really need is to know who that was."

Darian helped Shirlee to the door and walked her inside. "Lie down, Mama. I'll get you a cold glass of water." Darian stopped to thank God that the girls were asleep, and not outside. *My God, what if they had been outside?* This was getting too dangerous. *Now he knows where I live,* Darian thought.

"And a wet towel, Darian. I need a wet towel to place against my forehead."

Darian got the cold glass of water and ran to the bathroom to get a towel. When she got back Shirlee was stretched out on the sofa, her eyes were closed, and one hand lay against her chest. Darian ran back into the kitchen and checked the windows and doors to make sure they were locked.

"Here, Mama. This should calm you down a little. Take deep breaths. That's it, breathe in and out."

"You're damn right when you say a little. It won't help knowing a crazy fool is on the loose. Have you ever seen that car before?"

Darian felt her hands tremble uncontrollably. She ran to the bathroom to vomit until her stomach was empty. "Did you recognize him, Mama?"

"Hell no." Shirlee rubbed her thigh. "It hurts. I must have fallen on it. Now answer my question. Have you seen him before?" She took the towel from her forehead and opened her eyes, waiting for Darian's answer.

"Whoever it is, Mama, he tried to hit me two weeks ago."

"What?" Shirlee huffed. "And you didn't tell me? Have you made anyone angry?"

"No, Mama. I haven't been around anyone but you, Vickie, Brad, and that mother of his."

Shirlee sat back against the sofa. "I'm calling Jefferson and telling him to bring his daddy's old shotgun over here. You and the children need some protection. On second thought, maybe you and the girls should come stay with me."

"That's not the answer, Mama. What if it goes on for months? What if he stops as soon as I come home and starts again? No, I have to stay home. I better call the police again."

"Again? What happened the last time you called?"

"Nothing. They took the report but I couldn't describe the man, so they did nothing."

"Call them now. I bet I'll set fire under their asses,"

Shirlee said and took her shoes off again. "Call them right now," she demanded.

Evidently the police officers patrolled the neighborhood, because the same two officers came. Darian gave her report, and the same one took notes and asked questions.

"Can anyone describe the man this time, if it was a man?" he asked.

"Now, what difference does it make if it was a woman or man? My daughter and the children are in danger. I fell to the ground by trying to prevent that low-life fool from knocking my brains out. This is the second time my daughter has called you. We didn't recognize the maniac, but you damn well better catch him." Shirlee leaned forward in her chair as she talked. Her face was red, and she pointed her finger as she spoke.

Officer Jamison motioned with one hand. "Miss, what do you expect for us to do? We've been casing the neighborhood and haven't seen the car yet. You need to give us something to work with."

"I expect you to do police work and find this man," Shirlee snapped and folded her arms.

"Miss, we understand how frustrated you must feel, but it's hard to look for someone when you have no idea who it is. Like I said, we have passed your house a few times to see if we saw anything out of the norm. We've looked for a brown Buick but so far we haven't seen one."

"Well, what are we supposed to do? Do you expect us to wait and let him hurt one of us, or even our girls, and then say, 'Hey, let me see your face, or incidentally, are you a man or woman?' Is that what you officers think we should do as he's killing us? Well, that won't happen. I'm going to bring my husband's shotgun, and when I shoot him I'll be glad to hand him over to you.

That should help with your police work. I'm too old to be dealing with some nutcase rippin' and runnin' like a damn fool. My family is in danger."

The officers exchanged glances in frustration.

Darian rolled her eyes up at the ceiling. "What should we do next?" she asked. "I have two small girls in the house with me. They have to go to school."

Officer Jamison shrugged. "I hope that we find the car before anything else happens, Miss Cantrell."

"In the meantime, keep your doors and windows locked," Officer Hicks said. "With luck, we will catch him."

"Ha! Luck?" Shirlee asked. "Luck has nothing to do with it. Sorry, but we weren't born with a star over our heads, so we're not lucky." A definite edge had developed in Shirlee's voice.

Officer Jamison sighed. He was tired of this crazy-talking Creole. "Miss, now wait a minute. We'll do all we can, but you can't go around carrying your daddy's old shotgun to shoot people. Have you ever shot a gun before, do you even know how?"

"Look, my daddy taught me how to shoot a jackrabbit a mile away. If I have to, I can aim and hit that fool square between his eyes from the end of the block. I can shoot a gun as good as y'all, and from the looks of it, I'll get the bastard before he's caught by either one of you."

Shirlee folded her arms in front of her and rested her back against the chair.

Exasperated, Officer Jamison looked at Officer Hicks and sighed. He seemed to be enjoying the entertainment here. It was so much easier when they had made the trip the last time.

"Miss, all I have to say is don't go around flashing a gun. Call us again if he passes by." The officer got up and started to the door, leaving Hicks behind him.

Officer Hicks got up to leave and stopped at the chair Shirlee was sitting in. He kneeled down to whisper in her ear, "Don't shoot unless he's in the house, then call us." He winked his eye at Darian and gave her a long, lustful smile, then walked out the door.

Officer Jamison lit a cigarette and took a long puff, leaving trails of smoke weaving after him.

"Well, they were a lot of help," Shirlee said.

"What do we do next, Mama? I can't live jumping every time I hear a noise."

"Teach you how to shoot is what we're going to do. I'm afraid to leave you alone." Shirlee sat in the chair trying to figure out a solution.

Darian heard a car and ran to the door, but it was a red Ford parking across the street. She went back to the sofa and curled her legs under her. Luckily the girls were napping because her head hurt more than it had earlier. "Go home, Mama, and get some rest. I don't want to worry about your health, too. He never comes twice in one week. This time he waited two weeks."

"Yeah, but what will he do next is what scares me. You won't come and stay at my house. So I don't know what to do, Darian."

"Mama, this is my home."

"But you still have a room at my house, too."

"I know, and I appreciate it. First, I need to sit still so my head will stop hurting. Tomorrow I can think clearly."

"Okay, but tomorrow I'm bringing that old shotgun over. Jefferson has a .32 at home, too. It may be easier to use."

Darian was getting nervous enough to puke again. Why was this happening to her?

Shirlee stood up with her purse in hand. "Keep the doors and windows closed and locked."

"I will, Mama. Let me walk you out again." They

walked outside and Shirlee ran to her car. Darian went back inside, ran to the bathroom, and leaned over the toilet.

Her stomach twisted in knots as she choked and puked. Tears stung her eyes, and she remembered Monique dying in the same position, and there wasn't anything she could do to help her. Would the vision ever leave her mind? She was profoundly depressed and frightened for the safety of her family.

Still in the bathroom, she sat on the floor with her head against the wall, her eyes closed, her forehead moist, and her body aching all over. The thought of Shirlee bringing a gun into the house didn't seem real.

She went to her bedroom and crawled under the covers. Two hours had passed when she opened her eyes. Shelby and Nikki were standing beside her bed.

"Get up, Darian," Nikki said.

"She doesn't have to, Nikki," Shelby said and pushed Nikki away from the bed.

"You girls stop it," Darian whispered and scowled. She was afraid if she spoke too loudly her head would pound. She looked at Nikki's pouty bottom lip and got up very slowly. "You guys go and get your dolls and get into bed with me. I'll turn the television on." The girls ran out of the room as Darian grabbed the remote and flipped on the TV.

They came back with puzzles, dolls, and coloring books.

"You guys have to play on the floor with the coloring books and puzzles." Darian turned over in bed and closed her eyes. Five minutes hadn't passed before the phone rang. She sighed, sat up in bed, and answered.

"I'm all right, Mama," was all she said.

"What are you talking about, Darian?" Brad asked.

"Sorry, I thought you were my mother."

"You answered by saying you're all right. Has anything

happened?" Brad asked with concern. Then he thought about the brown Buick and dropped his pen on his desk.

"Me and my mother were walking to her car and that idiot drove real fast up the driveway. He stopped suddenly and drove off. I already had a terrible headache. Now it's worse. Who is he and what does he want with me?"

"I'm coming right over."

"No. You can't keep running backward and forward from your job in the middle of the day, Brad."

"I don't care about that. Why don't you and the girls stay at my house until he's caught? You're being stubborn and hardheaded."

"Now you sound like my mother. This is my home and I won't let anyone run me away from it." She sighed and lay back on the pillow. "Besides, running won't solve the problem."

"Since you're staying here you must have some idea who it is. Could someone have followed you to New Orleans? Why would anyone want to harm you?"

"You asked me the same questions before. I have no idea who it is. Maybe someone is just playing a game. Or maybe it's some hoodlum having fun. I don't know who it is," she snapped, an irritated edge coating her voice. "And don't speak to me as though I'm lying." For an instant she thought of Louise, but she had seen the Buick before she had met Louise.

"Look, it's just that I don't understand why it's happening to you."

"Well, I don't either, Brad."

"Then why don't you want to stay with me until it's over? My house is large enough with four bedrooms and three baths."

"I've been to your house and I know how spacious it is. Besides, we hadn't made any plans to live together or get married. We're still trying to get to know each other. And what would your mother say? She already hates me."

He couldn't argue the comment about his mother hating her. "I'm concerned about you and the girls, not about what my mother would say. Are you sure that this is not some man from your past? Maybe you can't remember because there wasn't anything to it, but it was taken seriously. Try and concentrate, Darian."

"Brad, I assure you that I don't know anyone that would try and hurt me, or want me dead. If you don't believe me, then this is where it ends for us. Now, you try and concentrate on that." She hung up. Did he really think she hadn't considered everyone that she'd had an affair with? Or maybe he didn't believe her. The phone rang again but she didn't answer; instead she went to the kitchen and grabbed a Coke from the refrigerator, and cursed under her breath, stomping back to her bedroom.

"The first time I laid eyes on her I knew she was trouble," Louise said. "But I've tried to accept her because you wanted me to. She's keeping something from you, Brad. She knows who's threatening her. Otherwise, why would someone want to harm her, and more than once? She has those two innocent little girls in the middle of her wrongdoings. I worry all the time about you and Tye, and I can't even sleep at night." Louise dried her hands on her white-bibbed apron. She took a seat in the den where she could face Brad. He was sitting on the brown leather sofa. Why couldn't he understand that she was worried about his safety?

"Don't worry, Mother. I can take care of myself. Right now I'm worried about Darian."

"You shouldn't be. She doesn't seem to worry about

placing you right smack in the middle of her past. She's no good, Brad. You've seen that tramp of a mother she has. Apples don't fall too far from the tree." She shook her head and wiped moisture from her forehead with the back of her hand.

Brad stood up. "What's that supposed to mean?" he asked, feeling anger taking over the conversation. He was still angry with Darian, and couldn't believe she had hung up on him, but she had. He loved her and only wanted to keep her safe. He was her man, and supposed to protect his woman. But instead, she slammed the phone down in his face. He pondered over their conversation. Well, maybe he shouldn't have questioned her as though she was at fault. Maybe he could have been more sympathetic.

"Out of all the girls you've had, what makes her so special?" Louise was saying. His father had a poor judgment of women. Always sneaking up some Creole's dress. Brad had to be smarter. She would make him understand.

"Tye, come out here," Brad yelled.

"Mother, this conversation is over. Like I said, I can take care of myself."

With his jacket in one hand and a Spider-Man toy in the other, Tye came running into the den. "I'm ready, Dad." Tye was tall and handsome with chocolate-brown skin and brown eyes. Louise complained about him being too thin and not eating enough. But Brad always said that Tye ate plenty.

"I don't know what to say to make you understand. Darian has too much baggage in her life." *She's from the wrong side of the tracks.* But of course Louise couldn't say that to Brad. Making him too angry would only send him into Darian's arms. She had to be careful with what she said about the woman. Maybe Brad would get tired of her and life would go back to the way it was before Darian showed up.

"Bye, Grandma," Tye said and kissed Louise on the cheek.

"Would you like to take some dinner home for you and Tye? I always cook enough in case you two are hungry."

"No, Mother, but thanks. I have a couple of steaks for us." Brad walked out the door before Louise could say another word. He had heard enough for one day.

Chapter 25

Darian had been in and out of bed all day. Finally, the pain in her temples had subsided, leaving her weak. To make matters worse, the girls had been whining about going outside.

Darian's brows knitted together, her hands on both sides of her temples. "It's too cold out today, Shelby, and it may rain."

She sat up in bed. "It's more fun here in my room. You guys sit down and I'll read a good story." She began to read the dinosaur book, but it only made her head pound unmercifully. The phone rang and Darian answered.

"Yes, Mama. The doors are locked and I'm reading a story to the girls."

"Do you feel better, Darian? God knows you have a reason to be sick."

"I've been in bed all day. As a matter of fact, I'm still in bed. And I can't seem to get warm enough."

"Well, Jefferson is off tomorrow and he says the pistol is better than that big old shotgun."

"Okay, Mama. I agree that I do need some protection. But I just hate the thought of having a gun in the house."

"You won't hate it if that fool gets any closer to you."

"Okay. So I'll see you tomorrow." Evening was approaching when she got up, showered, and made soup and sandwiches for dinner. It was not a day for cooking.

After dinner she gave the girls their bath, and at eight they were in bed. Darian flopped down on the sofa and sighed. Brad hadn't called her back. Maybe she should call to apologize. But he kept pushing her and she was ill. She held the remote to the TV, but didn't turn it on. Instead, she grabbed a magazine from the coffee table, flipped through a page or two, then tossed it back.

Only eight months she had been in New Orleans and it seemed as though it had been years. She was tired, depressed, and still trying to figure out who was trying to harm her. No one that Darian could remember. It just didn't make any sense. The insanity had gone too far, and her stomach did somersaults every time she thought of it.

The phone rang and interrupted her thoughts, but she welcomed the intrusion. It was Brad. "Are you still angry with me, Darian?"

"No. But I'm frustrated. I was trying to think of everyone that I knew, but I'm getting nowhere. There are no boyfriends, no one I know that would want to harm me. What do I do next?"

"What about your sister?"

"I can't think of anyone that would hurt Monique, except her husband, but he was beaten to death in prison."

"I know a sergeant at the police department. I'll give him a call tomorrow and see if there's more they could do. Are you sure that you don't want to come to my house?" Waiting for her to yell like she had earlier, Brad held his breath.

"No. Staying with you wasn't in our plan."

"Darian, I'm not asking you to move in permanently. It would be only until things cool down a bit."

"I know, love, and I do appreciate the offer. We'll see how it goes for a couple of weeks and then I'll give it some thought."

Brad raised his brows and shook his head. "Okay, baby. At least think of staying with me until it's over. Just give it some thought."

She hung up and smiled. Darian went to her room. She could no longer keep her eyes open.

It was morning when Darian woke up again. She sat up in bed and felt no more pain in her head. It was time to start breakfast for the girls.

When it was time to take the girls to school, Darian walked outside first. She went back inside and got the girls. As she drove them to school she noticed every car that passed by; there were no signs of the brown Buick. She glanced in the rearview mirror constantly.

After she parked, Darian walked the girls to their classrooms.

When Darian arrived home she jumped out of the car and ran inside the house. She cleaned the kitchen and made the beds. The doorbell rang. She jumped and a glass fell from her hand and shattered on the floor.

She peeked through the blinds and her eyes opened wide. It was Louise. "Wonder what she wants," she whispered to herself.

She opened the door. Louise was standing with her black purse folded under her arm as though she thought someone would grab it. She was dressed in a black pantsuit and a white blouse that buttoned up to her neck.

"Come in, Louise. This is a pleasant surprise,"

Darian said out of graciousness. It was just the polite thing to say, even if she didn't mean it.

Louise stepped inside and Darian led her to the sofa.

"You look very nice, Louise. Can I get you a cup of coffee or tea?"

"No, dear. I'm on my way to the Chamber of Commerce meeting and just happened to be driving through the neighborhood. Brad mentioned how stressed you've been and he seems to be just as worried. I just wanted to say hello and that I'm so sorry you're going through so much. It just doesn't seem fair. You've taken on a large enough responsibility, and now this madman is taunting you."

Yeah, right. Sorry my ass, Darian thought. "Thank you so much, Louise. But sooner or later the person is going to get caught, or get tired of playing this game."

Louise looked around the living room. "You have good taste, Darian. Brad mentioned that to me." She sat up straight and dabbed her forehead with a white handkerchief.

Darian didn't dare smile, and she knew Louise's only concern was for Brad's safety, not hers or the girls. Darian couldn't seem to keep her eyes off the top of Louise's blouse. It looked too tight around her neck, and no matter how she tried to ignore it, her eyes seemed to find their way back.

"Well, I know we started off on the wrong foot, but I realize how much my son cares for you, and so does Tye."

Louise stood up. "I really have to rush off, but I had to see you before I started my day. You've been on my mind since Brad left my house last night." She placed her hand on Darian's shoulder. "Please let my visit be our little secret. I wouldn't want Brad to think that I was being a nosy old woman, when I really visited out of concern for you."

"I'm sure he wouldn't have any reason to think that you're not concerned for me," Darian said and smiled.

Taken aback, Louise looked at the expression on Darian's face, but she was unable to make a comment. Darian looked at her as though she knew she was lying.

Darian walked Louise to her car. Louise climbed inside her long white Lincoln that was at least fifteen years old. But it shone and was well kept like a new car.

As Louise drove off she thought of her conversation the night before with Brad. Darian peeking out the door before stepping outside did not go unnoticed. Maybe with a little luck the man would soon finish his job before Brad asked Darian to marry him. She prayed that Darian would get frightened enough to go back to L.A. Too bad she had to be a Creole. Louise was certain that Brad had fallen in love with her. After seeing her new home, Louise decided that at least the woman was clean, and in spite of how she felt about Darian, she had to admit that she was a smart and educated woman. But she was still a Creole.

Driving down Industry Street, Louise thought of her mother and father. Her father worked in a factory. He was very dark, medium height, and a hardworking man. Louise had two brothers, being the only girl; John, her father, always told her that she was his heart, his beautiful daughter. Her mother stayed home and had dinner on the table every evening at precisely six. Everyone said Louise resembled Clara, her mother. Louise was fourteen years old when John walked out of their lives. Louise was devastated. He left his wife and children for a Creole woman. He didn't pay child support and the oldest son dropped out of school to work and help support the family.

Louise remembered her mother's telephone conversation with her father, begging for money to help with food and rent. But John completely cut his children out of his life. Louise remembered the cries late into the night from her mother's bedroom. Three months later they had to move into her grandmother's two-bedroom house.

One day Louise and her cousin were walking home from school when Louise decided to stop by her father's house, and tell him what she thought of him. She had so many questions. How could he just walk out of his children's life and not look back? What kind of man was he? After she convinced her cousin to go with her, Louise stood in front of the house for twenty minutes before mustering enough nerve to knock on the door.

Finally Louise knocked, and a naked man answered with a bottle of beer in his hand. Her father's wife was stumbling behind him, also butt naked. They were inebriated, and had been drinking all day. Louise couldn't understand what they were saying. Every time she asked for her father they would laugh and laugh until they were speechless.

Louise ran to her father's job. Her cousin was frightened and ran home. Maybe if she told him what she saw he would leave his wife and come back home. They could live in a bigger house and become a family again.

"Who told you to go to my house, Louise?" he asked angrily, after she told him about the naked man and his wife. He slammed down a stack of time cards on a table and stormed out the door without looking back at her. When John saw Louise behind him, he yelled for her to go home, and never go to his house ever again. She stayed far enough behind and followed anyway.

After John went inside his house, Louise heard yelling, bottles breaking against the walls, and loud blaring. Then everything was quiet, the yelling stopped.

The door wasn't closed. Louise quietly tiptoed, peering through the door, and saw her father stretched out
on the floor. His white shirt was soaked with blood. She
ran inside and screamed at the top of her voice. Her
stepmother was sitting on the sofa, blood on her hands
and smeared over her naked body as she cried and
rocked back and forth. Louise took a step closer to her
father. His face was twisted in pain, and more blood had
covered the front of his shirt, red, red blood. She
touched him, felt the warm blood stick to her fingers,
and in the palms of her hands. She felt ill, her body
trembled, and she vomited as she ran home.

The next morning was the saddest day of Louise's
life. Her family got the news of what happened. His
Creole wife had stabbed him to death. Her boyfriend
took the broken bottle from her hand, but it was too
late. She had stabbed John in his throat. She was
drunk and went mad out of her head. Since that day,
Louise hated all Creoles, and had never forgiven herself for her father's death. It was she who killed him.
She shouldn't have gone to his job to tell him about
his wife. She had another Creole whore to deal with.
But she would sit back and let the stranger run Darian
back to L.A.

Darian had just finished mopping the kitchen floor
when the doorbell rang, and she jumped, dropping
the mop to the floor.

She looked through the blinds and saw Brad's car.
She opened the door and hugged him tightly.

Brad kissed her long and passionately. "Boy, what a
welcome," he whispered against her ear.

"I'm sorry for yesterday, but I was so upset, and I'm
so tired of this crap. Hey, why aren't you at work?"
Darian asked.

"Because I came to be with you." He took his brown jacket off. His tailor-made suit fit perfectly, and his sexy eyes locked with hers. He grabbed her again and led her into her bedroom. They got into bed and made slow, ravishing love. It was one of those days when Brad wanted to make love to her all day. She was so warm, and moaned every time he touched her. "We're so good together, Darian, and we connect so easily."

"I know," she said slowly, as she got on top of him. Feeling Brad deeply inside made her heart beat rapidly. It was like magic, like a fantasy that developed into real life, and it was all for her.

When Darian fell off Brad she lay in his arms. They held each other, touched, and kissed. His fingers moved from the fluttering pulse of her throat, slowly downward to her flat stomach, and rested there.

"Have you ever thought of getting married, Darian?" he whispered, and kissed her on top of her head.

"You mean lately?" She looked at his face as he stared deeply into her eyes. Darian held her head up, resting on her elbow.

"Yes, lately. I need to be with you all the time."

"But what will I do with my house, Brad?"

"Lease it, sell it. My house is large enough for a family of five." He looked over at the clock. "Don't say anything right now. We can discuss it further once that jerk is taken into custody. Come on and take a shower with me." He held his hand out to her.

Darian blushed and took his hand. Their lovemaking continued in the shower.

On the way to school to get the girls, Darian pondered over the prospect of marrying Brad. She did love him, so why not? But marriage was something she couldn't decide until she was safe again. She also had the girls to think of. Would they accept a man in their lives? Darian pulled into the school's parking lot, and as always, she looked to see if she saw the brown Buick. But it wasn't there. Was it possible he had found someone else to stalk?

Darian went to Shelby's classroom first. Then Nikki's, and she was waiting impatiently.

On the way home Darian drove down North Galvez Street. "Who wants a treat?" Darian asked as she looked through her rearview mirror at the girls.

"I do," they answered in unison.

Darian parked the car and went into McKenzie's Bakery. She bought a small chocolate cake. "After lunch you guys can have a slice."

When Darian got home she drove into the driveway, rushed the girls out of the car, and went inside the house and locked the door. She hated to admit it, but she didn't feel safe unless she was locked inside. Leaving the house made her feel vulnerable.

Darian phoned Brad to hear his voice.

"Baby, we need to go out so you can loosen up."

"Are you telling me that I wasn't loose enough today, Brad?" Darian asked and smiled.

"You were far beyond my expectation," he answered and smiled. "I spoke to an intern at my job. She's only twenty-one, still in college, and needs to earn as much money as she can. She says that she can babysit for us anytime."

"That's great, Brad. She's what we need. As a matter a fact, Vickie wants us to double-date sometime."

"Fine, let me know when."

"I think my mother is at the door. I'll call you when she leaves." Darian rushed to the door, and it was Shirlee.

"Mama, that big old shotgun looks heavy."

"It is heavy, but until that stalker is caught, it's better than nothing. Here, hold it against your chest."

Shirlee showed Darian how to position the shotgun in her hands. "It's not loaded now, but I will load it after you get the feel of it."

"How do I aim, Mama?"

"Goodness, Darian. Take the blasted shotgun and aim, and then pull the trigger. That's how I learned. And I broke my fingernail trying to get it off the shelf."

"I wish a broken fingernail was all I had to worry about." Darian tried again by aiming at a vase in the corner, the TV, and a picture on the table.

"How does it feel now?" Shirlee asked and stood back to give Darian enough room to handle it. "Here, point it at me and act like that fool is coming toward you." She stepped back, bent forward with hands on her knees. "Come on, I'm waiting."

Darian held the shotgun higher toward her face and looked right at Shirlee. "It doesn't feel so heavy now. And why are you bending over? You look utterly ridiculous."

"Don't worry about how I look. Whenever that jackass gets ready to make his move, it won't seem heavy at all. Don't aim at his head or his heart, hit whatever you can to stop him. Hit his legs, arm, any place that will stop him dead in his tracks. Remember to always tell the girls to run inside before you shoot. When you come inside to get the gun, lock the girls in their room. After they are safely inside the house shoot him as many times as necessary. Don't let him get close enough to take the gun from your hands. Now look at me again." Shirlee stood with her legs apart, and turned slightly to the side. "Now aim, fire."

Darian tried again, and this time the shotgun wasn't heavy at all. "I hope it doesn't come to this, Mama."

"I hope it doesn't, but it's better to be safe than sorry. We're talking about saving your life, girl. Now, let me load it." Shirlee took the shotgun from Darian's hand.

"Load it? This was just a mini presentation. It didn't teach me how to fire a gun," Darian said desperately.

"Right now it's all we can do until Jefferson takes you to the shooting range."

"Dad kept his gun away from us."

"Well, your daddy didn't have someone chasing his ass all over town either. Now it's loaded. I'll place it up high in this closet where the girls won't see it. Besides, they can't reach it anyway. It needs to be close by. Where are the girls?"

"Playing with their dollhouse. They'll play back there all day if I let them."

Darian and Shirlee sat on the sofa. "Mama, I wonder if he'll be back."

"I hope not, Bay. I know how frustrating it must be for you. That's why I brought the gun over. I thought it would be easier on you if you had some protection. I wouldn't worry so much if y'all stayed at my house. Jefferson says that starting tonight we're going to drive by here every night before we go to bed. We won't ring the doorbell. Just ride by to see if that tore-up Buick is around."

"All this time I didn't like Jefferson, but you always said it was because I didn't know him. I think it was his age that I really didn't like. But he's a nice guy, Mama. Though he'll never feel like a stepfather." Darian got up and peeked out the window at a passing car. "Brad called me and said he found a babysitter for us. But now that I'm thinking about it, maybe going out isn't a good idea. It's too dangerous."

"You need to go out, Bay. I should watch the girls until we're completely sure there's no more trouble."

Darian nodded in agreement. "I was concerned about it, too. I think you're right, Mama."

"Just tell me what night, and Jefferson and I can

come over. But of course you can't spend the night with your young man like you would want to," Shirlee teased.

Darian blushed, her face glowing red. "My young man is older than your husband. Brad will be thirty-nine on his next birthday." Darian got up and looked out the window again.

Twice in thirty minutes, Shirlee watched her staring out the window. She wondered how Darian acted when she was alone with the children. "Well, I better get home. Keep the doors and windows locked," Shirlee said as she got up and stood at the door. "I'll check on y'all later."

Darian stood on the porch and watched Shirlee as she got inside her car.

"Why did Shirlee run?" Shelby asked. The girls were standing next to Darian.

"She's in a hurry. Why don't you call her Grandma?"

"She says not to call her grandma. I don't know what to call her, so I say Shirlee." Shelby tugged at Darian's hand.

"Call her Mama. I do."

As Darian closed the door she heard a speeding car and stopped. Deep inside, she knew it was the Buick. She had gotten used to the noisy rattle as the car roared down the streets. And she was right. The car had stopped in front of her house, but the driver hadn't driven up the driveway like before. For an instant, Darian thought her heart had stopped. "You girls go to your room and play house." Darian ran to the closet and reached for the shotgun. But he stayed inside the car and she couldn't shoot unless he tried to come inside her house. Then another thought came to mind. It could just as well be a female, which made it even more puzzling.

She placed the gun back inside the closet and picked up the phone to call the police, but the engine roared loudly, and the car sped off. Besides, what was there to tell them differently? She still didn't know what the driver looked like.

Darian gasped, took a deep breath, and exhaled heavily. She sat down on the sofa and closed her eyes. Realizing that she might have to shoot him, she felt her body go limp. The weather was getting warmer. What could she tell a four- and six-year-old when they wanted to go outside and play in the yard? She had to keep the children safe inside.

Darian went to the girls' room to fold clothes that she took from the dryer.

"Get off," Nikki yelled. She stuck her thumb in her mouth and started to cry.

Darian went to her bed and sat Nikki on her lap. "What's the matter, sweetheart? Don't you feel well?"

"Shelby hit my foot."

"I didn't," Shelby yelled back at Nikki. "Mommy had clothes on my bed so I sat on yours, huh, Mommy?"

Darian's mouth fell open and she couldn't speak. Shelby had called her mommy.

"Are you our mommy?" Nikki asked.

Shelby looked at Darian, waiting for her answer.

Darian stood up. "You two follow me." They went into the living room and watched Darian as she picked up the picture with Monique holding Nikki on her lap, and Shelby standing by her side.

"Here, let's sit on the sofa." Darian held the picture up so both girls could see it. "This is your mother. She will always be your mother, and I want you two to remember that. She loved you guys very much, but I'm your aunt. Do you understand, Shelby?"

"Yes."

"I will always treat you guys like your mommy did. I'll always take care of you. I promise that I won't leave either of you. Now, if you want to call me mommy you can, but I don't ever want you to forget your real mother." Darian pointed at Monique in the picture. "I love you girls very much and I'll be the best mommy ever."

Darian felt the tears on her face as the girls nodded in agreement. Her heart felt heavy with so much love, she wondered if that was what a mother felt for her children. She kissed the girls on their cheeks and went to put the clothes away.

Chapter 26

"I wonder what's keeping Vickie and Bernard?" Darian said and looked at her watch.

"Sweetheart, if it was only the two of us, I still would have a nice time." Brad placed Darian's hand against his full, sexy mouth. "You look beautiful tonight, baby. I like you in black, and I like that low-cut neckline even better," he said teasingly.

Darian flushed. She had taken the extra time to make herself look good. Her black dress fit perfectly and showed off her legs. She even wore pink lipstick and gold earrings. In L.A., she'd taken the time to dress and look her best. After taking the girls, along with the chores, she didn't know how to manage both. Besides, no one was interested in her. But now she had Brad, and she was learning.

"I didn't think you could look any prettier but you do." Brad held her hand reassuringly. He couldn't seem to keep his hands off her.

There was a bottle of white wine in the middle of the table. The eight-piece jazz band in the corner played soft music as couples poured through the door. The club was small and jumpin,' and it wasn't long before all tables were occupied, and the dance floor began to come to life.

"Here they come," Darian said excitedly. She looked at Vickie's face and by the look of her, Darian detected Vickie's unhappiness. Bernard stood behind her as she scanned the room.

When Vickie saw Darian's hand waving to get their attention, the frown on her face relaxed into a wide smile.

"We finally made it," Vickie said. "Bernard, this is Darian. We've been friends for a long time. This gentleman is Brad. Please sit down, Brad. I'm no stranger," Vickie said.

Bernard leaned over and shook Brad's hand. They took their seats.

"I saw you on TV last week, Brad. I think you're doing a good job as superintendent of the New Orleans School District."

"Thanks, man. I believe in education for our children."

"This is a pretty cool place. I've never been here before," Vickie commented.

"It opened about four months ago, but this is my first time here, too," Brad said.

"You look lovely, Vickie," Darian said. She looked at Vickie's jet-black hair shining under the light. Her red dress fit every curve on her body; Vickie kept her body in shape and looked good in all of her clothes. As the night wore on, Darian noticed that Vickie laughed and joined in all the conversations.

"Come on, baby." Brad pulled Darian back on the floor to a slow song. They floated with the music. "Are you enjoying yourself, Darian?"

"Oh yes." It had been a while since Darian felt so beautiful and loved. "Going out without the children for a change was a good idea. We have to do it more often."

"But I don't want us to get stuck in a habit of not living it up and enjoying each other once in a while," Brad whispered against her ear.

The music stopped and when they got to the table Bernard had bought another bottle of wine.

"The band plays well," Bernard said and moved his arm around Vickie's shoulder.

Brad nodded in agreement. "We should meet up here again. First, we could go to a nice place for dinner and come here for the remainder of the evening."

"I would like that," Darian said. "It's so nice that we can double-date with our men, right, Vickie?"

"Yes, and it's about time."

Bernard was very warm and friendly. He was far more intelligent than some of the men Vickie had dated, Darian thought.

It was one-thirty and both couples walked out at the same time.

Bernard shook Brad's hand and kissed Darian on the cheek.

The couples said good night and went their separate ways.

"You know, for a while there I didn't think Bernard was as friendly as he turned out to be," Darian said and looked out the window of the SUV. She didn't want to spoil the evening by letting Brad know she was looking for the brown Buick.

"The Buick is not behind us, baby," Brad said. He reached across and held Darian's hand in his. The street was practically empty. He made a right on South Peter Street.

Darian sighed, looked at him, and smiled. "How did you know I was looking for it? You're beginning to know me too well."

"Because it's my business to know you, darling. And one day he's going to get too cocky and get caught. I'm sure you aren't the only person he's terrorizing. I've given it lots of thought. You're probably just one of the people he's stalking."

Brad parked the car in front of her house. Darian opened the door and Shirlee squinted her eyes to see them clearly. Jefferson was watching a debate about the war on CNN.

"What time is it?" Shirlee asked and slipped her feet inside her black flat shoes.

"Hope you guys had a good time," Jefferson said.

"We did. It was good to get out and have fun," Darian said.

Brad took a seat on the sofa next to Jefferson while Darian got their coats.

"I'll call you tomorrow, Bay." Shirlee started to the door before Jefferson could slip into his coat.

"Later, man." Jefferson shook Brad's hand.

After Shirlee and Jefferson left, Darian sat on Brad's lap and placed her lips against his. After twenty minutes of kissing and touching, they tiptoed into Darian's bedroom. Brad pulled her down on the bed and kissed and stroked her nipples. He could feel the protuberance of her breasts. Her body was flexible and moved in perfect harmony with his.

"What time do the girls wake up in the morning?" he whispered, burying his face against her neck.

"Around seven."

"I'll be out by five."

"Good," Darian whispered. It was always like the first time, and the more she had him, the more she wanted. Moments later he held her close, soothing her into a blissful sleep.

At five Brad was up and picked his clothes up off the

floor where he had hurried out of them the night before.

Darian lay on her side and watched him dress. "Want a cup of coffee?"

"No, thanks. I'm going straight home and get back into bed." He reached for her hand. "Come and lock the door."

Darian got up and slipped into her robe. When they got to the door, Brad kissed her long and tenderly. "That will have to last until the next time."

"Just until the next time," she said, closing the door behind him. Smiling, she went back to her bed. She closed her eyes as her body moved to the warm place where Brad had slept.

She was sound asleep when she felt two bounces on her bed. Darian slowly opened one eye. The girls were there, the TV was on, and Nikki's doll was staring in Darian's face.

There would be no more sleep for Darian, so she grabbed the remote from the nightstand and flipped the channel to the Barney show. The girls ran into their rooms to get more dolls and came back. Darian closed her eyes while the girls and their dolls jumped on her bed to watch cartoons.

"I don't want to go to school today," Nikki said and laid her head on Darian's shoulder.

"Today is Saturday. But you guys have to go to dance school. So let's get ready to start our day." Darian was still sleepy, but it was time to get up.

Chapter 27

Darian hung up the phone, made the beds, cleaned the kitchen sink, and washed a load of clothes. All of a sudden it hit her. Once she was married she'd have to do more laundry, and there would be more dirty dishes. She still hadn't gotten used to all of her chores and no sleeping on weekends. How could one's life change so drastically in such a short time? She released a melancholy sigh. She inadvertly shook her head and ran her fingers through her hair. But she knew that it was only because she and Brad had gotten close and started discussing marriage. More cooking, more chores. After they were married.

Darian sat on the sofa, the frown melting away from her face. She loved Brad, and she would be happy as his wife. Darian looked at her watch and grabbed her purse so she could pick up the girls. She stood at the door and scanned the room. Since she had been cleaning for hours, every room in the house sparkled.

As Darian drove past Elmwood Mall she decided she would stop to look at some slacks. She already had three closets full of clothes but hadn't been going any place to wear them. In two months her book would be published and she would be going out more often. Darian still hadn't made a decision about whether she would keep writing or get back into Corporate America. But deep in her heart she knew the girls still needed her. It was still too soon after Monique's death. And moving into Brad's home would be another adjustment for Shelby and Nikki.

Darian ran inside and got the girls. She had to go straight home to meet Shirlee.

"My chest and head hurt," Shelby complained.

Darian looked at her from the rearview mirror, and could hear her wheezing. "It's your asthma and it's windy, too. When we get home I'll make a snack, and then you have to lie down and rest, Shelby." The winds and cold weather had really taken their toll on her asthma.

"My head hurts, too," Nikki said.

"You will lie down and rest, too, Nikki," Darian said and smiled. Nikki never wanted to be left out.

Shirlee stepped out of her car when Darian drove up the driveway. She helped the girls out and unlocked the door.

"Darian, did you comb your hair today?" Shirlee asked.

"Of course I combed my hair. But it was windy when I came out to get the girls. I should have put it in a ponytail."

Shirlee looked at Darian disapprovingly. "You could wear a little lipstick, you know."

"Mama, I was in a hurry. I can't go aound with my nails polished and hair in place like yours. Now Shelby isn't feeling well, and you know Nikki starts to complain, too. Were Monique and I like the girls when we were kids?"

"Yes, Nikki and Shelby are just like you two all over again," Shirlee said and looked at the girls.

The phone rang, but when Darian answered no one was on the other end. "Wrong number," Darian said to herself. She went into the kitchen and opened a can of tomato soup for the girls. "Come and eat, girls."

"Darian, do you still have some goose grease and honey mixed? It's Shelby's asthma again." Shirlee poured orange juice for the children.

"Yes. I'll get it when she finishes eating. I laughed the first time Miss Idele mixed it but it does help. I have to take them to the dentist next week, too."

Darian and Shirlee went back to the living room while the girls ate lunch.

Shirlee opened the blinds and the sunlight illuminated the room, giving it the look of spring when flowers bloom and plants grow healthy and the birds are singing in the early mornings. So why did she feel so moody, tense, as though something in the air wasn't quite right? If only she could shake off the feeling of guilt for not raising the girls. It was beginning to haunt her again. But soon Darian would be married. She was lucky that she had met Brad again. Shirlee went back to the sofa and kicked off her shoes.

"I forgot the magazine I left inside my car. I bought it yesterday."

"What kind of magazine?"

"*Vogue.* It has a beautiful suit in it. Oh, and Brad gets off work early today. He should be here in a few minutes. Let me run out and get it so I can show you the one I'm thinking about buying. It's gorgeous, Mama. But don't ask me when or where I'll wear it."

Darian grabbed the car keys and ran outside. It had been weeks since the brown Buick passed her house and today, Darian forgot to look out the door before stepping outside.

She stopped in midmotion when she saw the brown Buick. She strained to see where the driver was. Darian started to turn around and run back inside the house, but before she could turn, someone had jumped out from behind the tall bush and covered her mouth.

"I've been watching you," he said with a raspy voice that sounded like he had a cold. "But you came out just in time, and you're the only one that needs to get hurt."

Darian's breathing became labored; she couldn't get enough air. Her mind whirled in confusion as she tried to fight her captor off.

"Stop it," he whispered. "You want the old lady to come out and see me stick this knife in your heart?" he said, and laughed when he felt her body stiffen against him. "You don't know who I am, do you, Darian? My hair has grown on my face and I'm much thinner. That's what jail time does to you."

"No. Who are you and what do you want with me?" Darian tried to turn her head to see if Brad was coming. Maybe if she kept the man talking Brad would be there soon enough to save her. On the other hand, if Shirlee came out to find out what was keeping her so long, they both might die. God, what to do? His voice was familiar but he was in back of her and she couldn't see his face. His body felt thin and tense. He had an odor like his clothes were old and unclean, and his hands felt rough against her throat.

"Come on, you're going with me."

He started to pull her to his car, but Darian fought, kicked, twisted, and turned in his arms. As he stood in back of her she felt his arms circling tighter around her neck, choking her. Darian's eyes watered, but she still tried to fight. Darian felt her body go limp against him as she held her hand back and tried to grab his arm for support. His hand was tight around her throat. She coughed, choked, and felt her legs weakening, her body falling against her will.

Inside the house, Shirlee waited, got a glass of water, and on her way back to the living room she peeked out the window. "God almighty," she said, jumping back, running into the children's room. "You girls stay in your room, and, Shelby, don't come out until I come back to get you. Do you hear me, Nikki?" Shirlee didn't wait for an answer. She closed the door and ran back into the living room.

Shirlee opened the closet and grabbed her daddy's old shotgun. She could shoot better with it than the pistol that Jefferson sent to Darian. She ran to the phone and dialed 911.

As Shirlee came outside she saw him grab a handful of Darian's hair.

Her neck jerked back. This time he made sure she couldn't move, and she groaned with pain ricocheting from her head down to her neck. She began to gag and felt herself slipping into darkness.

"You bastard, let my daughter go," Shirlee shouted and stepped down the steps, the shotgun pointed at his head.

The man snatched his cap off and laughed out loud. "Don't you know me, Shirlee? It's your long-lost—"

"Pete Jr.? Well, I'll be damned."

"Yes, Shirlee, it's me."

"What do you want?" Shirlee asked. "You've been riding around here in that old car looking like the crazy fool you've always been. Why?"

"I want what belongs to me. I came back to find my wife. This little bitch stole my mother's house and sold it, took my children. But you can have the little brats. You owe me for my mother's house. You had no right, Darian. You owe me twenty-five thousand dollars for the sale of the house. And you're going to give it to me. That house didn't belong to you to sell."

"Listen to me, Pete Jr. You left Monique and your children. You come back after four years to pick up where you left off. Now, if you want to live to eat your next meal, let my child go, and now. I'm telling you for the last time," Shirlee said, almost blind by the perspiration rolling off her forehead and into her eyes. Her finger felt wet, slippery on the trigger. She blinked, but could see well enough to point the shotgun between Pete Jr.'s eyes. If he made one move she was sure that she could shoot him in the head. She would not lose another child. "Monique got a letter from the prison saying you were dead."

"I know, Shirlee, but it was a mistake. I lived. They just forgot to contact my family to let them know. I'm here for what belongs to me."

"You should have died in prison, Pete Jr.," Shirlee yelled at him.

Brad saw the brown Buick and stopped his car five houses down the street. He got out and started to run toward Darian's house, then stopped. He had to have a plan. If he snuck up quietly in back of the man, he could jump him. Once and for all the creep would be caught.

Pete Jr. held Darian tighter when he heard Brad's movement. He had started to sweat heavily and had become agitated.

Darian tried to pull away, but she felt the blade from the sharp knife against her throat and froze.

Just for a fraction of a second Pete Jr. lost his balance and rocked backward.

Shirlee knew this would be her only chance when Darian's legs buckled, causing her head to fall forward.

"You chicken-livered, no-good animal, look at me. I

want you to see the bullet that's going to spill your guts. This is for Monique," Shirlee yelled.

His eyes widened and his mouth opened, but it was too late. The explosion from the shotgun was loud and powerful. Darian fell to the ground as she felt his blood gush onto her yellow blouse. She crawled away on her hands and knees, screaming.

The blast from the shotgun blew Pete Jr. two feet into the air and knocked him against his car. His head wobbled like an apple hanging off the tip of a tree branch, his limp, bloody body sliding down the brown Buick to the ground, blood spurting from what was left of his head.

Brad ran to the body as Darian ran into Shirlee's open arms. He picked up a piece of paper that fell unfolded beside the body. Brad looked at Shirlee and Darian but no one saw it. He pushed the paper into his pocket.

"Oh, baby, are you all right?" Brad asked Darian and held her in his arms. Everything was happening so fast. Darian looked up when she heard the sirens coming nearer. "Are you all right, Shirlee?" Brad asked.

"Yes, I just can't move, that's all. It feels as though my feet are cemented into the ground." Finally, and slowly, Shirlee sat on the steps, the shotgun on the ground in front of her feet. She was surprised that her heart was beating normally.

The police car skidded to a stop in front of the house. The same two police officers that were there before jumped from the car, pulling their guns.

"Looks like we don't need our guns," Officer Hicks said as he looked at Shirlee.

"No, you don't need them. Where were you when we needed you? We pay our taxes and when we need you cops, you're still out to lunch somewhere, and when will this piece of trash be removed from my daughter's property?" Shirlee asked, rubbing sweat off her forehead and wiping the palms of her hands against her jeans.

"We got here as soon as we could, miss," Hicks answered.

Officer Jamison ran back to the patrol car and called for the coroner's wagon.

"Okay, Miss Cantrell? Are you all right?" Hicks asked sympathetically. She was still trembling in her boyfriend's arms. Her wild curls had blown all over her head, dirt was smeared across her face, and blood was painted on her blouse like a canvas.

Answering yes, Darian shook her head back and forth as though she was unable to speak. Brad went into the kitchen and came back out with two tall glasses of water, and gave one to Darian and the other to Shirlee.

When Darian finished telling her version of the story, both officers looked at Shirlee.

"You shot the man with your daddy's old shotgun while he was still holding your daughter?" the officer asked in amazement.

"Yes, I told you two that I could shoot a june bug off the tip of your nose if I had to. My daddy and me have shot so many jackrabbits it's a shame to say so. I gave Pete Jr. what he deserved, and I'm glad I could do it. I gave him a chance to release my daughter, but he wouldn't. He won't be around bothering my family again. I didn't want to shoot. All he had to do was release my daughter, but he didn't."

That woman had a mouthful to say every time she spoke, Officer Jamison thought, as he listened.

The officer walked to the door and looked at the detectives and the coroner. He wanted to finish outside before Shirlee started telling her story all over again.

"You people can stay inside since we've already taken your statements." He went outside again.

"I'll put some water on for tea," Brad said.

"I must look in on the girls," Shirlee said. "They stayed in their room like I told them to." She managed to get up without trembling or collapsing on the floor. As she walked down the hall she had to stop and lean against the wall. All of a sudden, she didn't feel well. The activity of the day was overwhelming. But she kept telling herself she'd seen worse.

"I know what a traumatic day you've had, but it's over now, Darian. We can go on with our lives. Now you are safe," Brad said. He tried to comfort her in every way he could.

Darian shook her head. "I was just so afraid he was going to slice my throat. If my mother hadn't been here, I'm sure he would have killed me. He doesn't love his daughters and was absent from his duties as a father and husband long before he left Monique."

Officer Hicks pulled out his business card and scribbled on the back, and gave it to Darian. "If you need counseling, give Miss Huntly a call. She's really good." He wanted to hold her in his arms and tell her that everything would be all right. But it was too late; she already had someone. He walked out the door just as Brad walked in with two cups of tea.

"Here, drink this, darling."

"I don't think the girls heard anything. They're playing with their playhouse and the dolls. Tea, just what I needed." Shirlee sat down heavily in the chair that faced the sofa. She looked at her watch and saw she had another hour before Jefferson came home. She would have to take her blood pressure medication as soon as she got home. Her head was pounding as if she had been kicked by a horse.

"Sweetheart, can you stay alone until I come back? I just have a quick run to make," Brad said.

Darian was astounded that he would leave her now. What could be so important at a time when she was so upset?

"Yeah. Sure. I'll be all right," she answered dryly. *At lease I won't have to worry any more about my safety*, she thought.

Brad kissed her on the cheek. "Love you, baby," he whispered and rushed out the door. Did he hear a hint of anger in her voice?

"He loves you, Darian. He looks as though he could have killed Pete Jr. with his bare hands," Shirlee said. Men, she thought. At times even the good ones were empty-headed.

"Yes, I know. He still looks angry."

Louise opened the door, and Brad followed her into the den. She took a seat and smiled. "I started to go and visit Darian today, Brad. I thought we could get to know each other better. After all, you seem to be quite taken with her." Louise looked as though she was in a joyful mood. When she realized that Brad hadn't answered, she looked at his face. He stood with his elbow resting on the mantel that was lined with family photos above the fireplace. He just stared at her with creases lined across his forehead. At that moment he looked to be the picture of his father. The similarity was uncanny, and brought back the memories of the night he died.

Brad pushed his hand down into his pockets. "What's this, Mother?" He placed the folded check hard into her hands and watched the distorted expression on her face.

Louise held the check for thirty-five hundred dollars in her trembling hand. She knew instantly what it was, but how did Brad get it? Her dark face had begun to shine, and her eyes narrowed, but she tried to maintain some dignity. The check fell to the floor as she looked at Brad again.

"Where did you get this?" she asked, trying to find words to soften the blow, but there weren't any.

"You know damn well where I got it. That animal almost killed Darian. What if my son was killed, not to mention Darian's nieces?"

Louise wanted to stand but she knew her legs wouldn't hold her. "You've got to let me explain, son. Ida lives across the street from his mother's house. She saw him standing in front of the house. He had just found out the house was sold. She said he cried when he found out that sister of hers had died. You know that everyone thought he was dead, too."

"Her name is Monique. Please don't refer to her as 'that sister of hers,'" Brad yelled. "At least respect the dead since you obviously don't respect the living."

"All right, Monique. Ida said she didn't even recognize the man until he spoke to her. He really thought he would get money out of the house. When he found out that Darian had sold his mother's house, he was dangerously furious, mad enough to kill her. You're in love with Darian. So I had to do something to stop the nonsense. I ran into him coming out of a liquor store on the corner of New Orleans Avenue. I approached him and made the deal. He was glad because he needed the money bad enough, and I needed Darian and her family out of our lives. But after I had paid him, I realized that I was wrong, Brad. You know that I would never do anything to hurt you, or to harm her."

"Out of your life, Mother? You wanted Darian out of your life? But what I don't understand is how hypocritical you are. You called her and said that you wanted to know her better, and you led me to believe that you gave us your blessing," he said, and pounded the mantel with his fist. Louise jumped.

"It wasn't like I hired him to terrorize her, he was going to anyway. So I just sweetened the pot by paying him to . . . to do whatever it took to keep you and Tye."

Louise watched his eyes dart from side to side and for a moment she thought he might punch her. "Now, Brad, you have to believe me. I called the entire plan off. I even let him keep the money if he would just leave it be and move on. I offered him more money, but he said why settle for what I gave him when he could get so much more from Darian? Honey, you have to believe me. I begged and begged him to leave New Orleans, Brad." She began sobbing and placed her hands over her eyes.

"You are a liar and you're crying because I could have you arrested, or is this just another false, bullshit way of making me stupid enough to believe in you, to ever trust or forgive you? Well, it's too late, Mother."

Louise jumped up from the sofa. "Oh no, son, you wouldn't tell Darian about this. I could be arrested. And I tried to stop him but he wouldn't listen. That is the truth." She started to walk toward him and stopped when he raised his hand to stop her.

Brad looked at his mother's face. There were no tears, no remorse. "Never, I mean never call my house again, and never come near my son." He stormed toward the door when he heard her voice.

"You don't mean it, Brad." She ran behind him and tried to grab his arm, but he pushed her away and whirled on his heel.

"I'm not my father, and I won't go back on my word. You're the reason he's dead. You crushed his manhood and beat him down until he died."

Louise thought her heart had stopped as she listened to Brad speak about his father's death. Her first thought was he knew how his father died. But as the conversation continued, she knew that he didn't know. Brad didn't know how he ran from woman to woman.

"You're a liar, and you're mean and treacherous. I no longer trust you around my son. My father should have been strong enough to walk out of your life like I am today."

"Your father was weak behind those red Creoles," she yelled. "And my father was murdered in front of my very own eyes by his Creole wife." Louise started pacing the floor. "My father left his family for a Creole woman. I was only fourteen years old and went to his house. His wife had another man there and they were both naked. Do you hear me? They were naked," she screamed. She paced faster, her eyes wild, and she looked strangely around the room as though she'd forgotten where she was. She held her hands out in front of her and they were red . . . like blood, her father's red blood wasting from eight stab wounds in his chest and throat. Blood was everywhere . . . red, warm. She rubbed her hands hard against her dress. She had to rub the blood off, and she could smell it again just as she did the day it happened. She closed her eyes tightly to make the blood disappear. Calm, she had to stay calm. She had stopped taking her Prozac months ago.

"I fell to my knees in front of him and closed my eyes tightly, but I could still see the blood, smell it, and it was in my hands, between my fingers. Is that what you want Darian to do to you? She will, you know," she yelled.

"You're mad," Brad yelled and stared at her in disbelief. She had never told him how his grandfather died. Brad had heard that John had died from a massive stroke.

"I'm not crazy. I'm not crazy." She shook her head from side to side. "They're all alike, Brad, and she'll kill you and Tye," she yelled even louder, and stood up again. "You have to believe me. I was only trying to save your life, save you from those crazy Creoles." Louise turned around in a circle as though she was lost. "Where did he go?" she asked as she waited for Brad's response.

He knew she had lost her mind. "Where did who go?" Brad asked and took a step closer to her.

"Them." Then she gave Brad a warm smile; she was back. Her handsome son was standing in front of her. "Are you staying for dinner, son?" she asked softly.

She had kept it a secret. How could he not know? Sure, there were times when she had gotten hysterical, but this? He should have known. He had to take some responsibility for her behavior.

"Mother, I won't have you arrested if you get help. You are a very disturbed woman. You can't see Tye unless you agree to get help." Brad waited, but got no response. "I'm out of here."

"They're tramps, all of them, outsiders, strangers. They are below us," she yelled with such savage rage that Brad stopped in his tracks.

He didn't move. He just stood there watching, listening to her raving uncontrollably. "Who are you talking to, Mother?"

Louise's head jerked up, and she looked at Brad with ferocious black eyes. He was leaving her for a Creole. First John, now Brad. It was like déjà vu.

Louise was tired. Brad and Tye were safe since Pete Jr. was dead. She started to speak again, but the look in his eyes told her that he hated her. She had lost her son and might never see her grandson again. She had lost.

Louise started up the stairs. She held her head high

as she climbed step by step. She sighed deeply. So tired, she thought.

Brad watched her. But he didn't try and stop her. He knew that she was a sick woman. He looked around the living room as though it was for the last time. He would call Louise's sister in Kansas City and ask her to come out and take care of Louise.

Chapter 28

Brad was on his way back to Darian's house. He dialed her phone number with his cell phone. "Hi, baby, are you all right?"

"Yes. I'm just tired."

"I'm going home to get Tye and we'll be right over. Should I stop and get dinner for you and the girls?"

"That's thoughtful, Brad, but no. We are all right, I made sandwiches for the girls."

"What about you?"

"I couldn't eat if it was forced down my throat. Right now my biggest problem is my upset stomach. I'm just so happy it's over. I won't have to look over my shoulder every time I walk out the door."

"I know." But it wasn't over yet. Brad still had to explain his mother's part in it. He had loved Louise and thought that he knew her, but he was wrong. How many other skeletons were in her closet? It made him wonder if she ever loved his father at all. Now he understood why his father worked so late. The weekends his parents barely had any conversation at all. Deep inside, Brad knew they weren't in love, but only tolerated each other for the sake of marriage. Did either one of them know what real love was?

Darian went back inside the house as Shirlee was slipping into her jacket. Her eyes were red and she still was shaken by today's events.

"Mama, you're leaving? Are you composed enough to drive, or should I call Jefferson?"

"Honey, I can drive. All I want to do is go home, climb into my bed, take a shot of Johnny Walker, and get some sleep. Lord, I'm glad this is finally over. No more worrying about you and the girls in the middle of the night. Finally I can sleep. Now, when the girls are finished eating, you get some rest and try and forget this day, Darian. It's over."

"I'll be all right. But who would have thought that Pete Jr. was still alive after that horrible beating he got in prison? I wonder, how did they give Monique such incorrect information anyway?"

"I don't know, and don't care anymore. Prison doesn't care if you're dead or alive. I'll check on you tomorrow." Shirlee opened the door and Darian followed her. Darian looked at the spot where she had cleaned the blood from the cement. First, she used the water hose; then she went inside and came back with a pail of hot water and the broom. She scrubbed it hard against the cement and used the water hose to wash it away.

Shirlee stood with both hands on her hips. "It's clean, Bay. There's nothing left so come back inside the house." Shirlee attempted to help but thought against it. She didn't want to break another fingernail.

The girls ran outside and stood with Darian as they watched Shirlee back out the driveway.

"Where did the men go that were in our yard?" Shelby asked.

"Can we play outside?" Nikki asked.

"No. No. You girls play inside the rest of the day. Besides, Shelby, you said that your chest was hurting."

They went back inside. Darian heard Brad driving his car into the driveway, and she and the girls ran back to the door. He had changed into his jeans and a blue T-shirt. His still looked upset and strained. But Darian was sure she looked worse.

"Hi, Tye," the girls yelled and led him to their room so they could play with their toys.

Brad and Darian were alone, and he led her to the sofa. "I don't want to start our lives with lies and secrets, Darian." He pulled her closer to him and held her hand. He began by telling her what had been conspired between his mother and Pete Jr.

Darian listened, her hands rested on her lap. "She hates all Creoles enough to kill me and my nieces? How could one person have so much loathing inside?" She laid her head on Brad's shoulder and closed her eyes.

"Pete Jr. was already stalking you, and she gave him money to keep it up."

"Correction, she paid him to harm me."

"You're absolutely right. And I'll never forgive her. But you have to admit one would have to be sick to hate someone that badly. It never occurred to her that Tye or I could have been harmed just as well. Yet she thought that she was protecting us. Anyway, I called my aunt in Kansas City to stay with her. I told her that she needs help. I know that I should have her arrested, but help is what she really needs. So what do you say, Darian?"

Darian closed her eyes and pondered over the question. How could she have Louise arrested and still marry Brad? She didn't want to put him in the position to choose between her and Louise. Her only hope was that Louise would move to Kansas City permanently.

"Pete Jr. was already after me anyway, and it wasn't like she had looked him up, he had already planned to harm me. In spite of everything that happened I agree with you. She does need help. I don't want to start our lives by having your mother arrested. But I don't think it's a good idea to tell my mother. She's been through enough."

Brad nodded in agreement. "Early tomorrow morning, I'm going to call my aunt and see if she can convince my mother to relocate to Kansas City.

"I want to marry you, Darian. I want us to be a family." He held her hand in his. "Will you marry me?" Then he thought of his father with a fierce surge of satisfaction, hoping he had had at least a bit of happiness with his Creole lover.

Darian was sure that she heard her own heartbeat. Tears formed in her eyes as she looked at him. "I can't imagine marrying anyone else. I love you, Brad, and yes, I will marry you."

He kissed her tenderly.

"I have to select a wedding dress, but I'll start looking. And I have to find someone to lease my house, or sell it. Oh, goodness, Brad. So much to do."

"Sweetheart, calm down," he said and kissed her neck.

"Like you, I want to get married and put everything else behind us." Tears still spilling, she laughed and returned his kiss. "How can the worst day of my life turn into the best?"

"Because we love each other, darling." He had lost his mother, but found the love of his life. "I better go now. You look tired, baby."

"Tye, come on out," Brad called as he and Darian walked to the door. When he stepped outside, he realized that the blood had been washed away. There were no traces of the day's earlier mayhem.

Darian went back inside and changed into her pajamas. She and the girls were going to bed early that night. But she knew she wouldn't sleep.

Chapter 29

"Hi, Vickie. . . . You're what?"

"I'm pregnant and I'm so happy, Darian. You know what?"

"What, girl?"

"Bernard says only this one time. So it will be an only child. But I'm so happy that I cry every time I think of it."

"Of course you're happy. You sound happy-headed, Vickie, and I'm happy for you. Guess what?" Darian asked.

"What?"

"Brad and I are getting married."

Vickie jumped up off the sofa in her living room. "Get out of here. Are you serious, Darian?"

"Absolutely. Now, what are you guys doing this weekend?"

"We're going on a second honeymoon, you nut. I'm pregnant and you're getting married. What do you think we're doing?"

Darian laughed into the phone. She could picture Vickie standing with her hands on her hips. She changed the mood by telling Vickie what had happened with Brad's mom.

"How stupid, and all because of something that happened before you were born. Anyway, how do you feel about her now?"

"Relieved that Pete Jr. is out of my life. But I hope that Brad doesn't blame himself for what Louise did. Who would have predicted that she was crazy? I never want to see her again."

"I guess you're right. She's sick for sure."

But Darian did feel bad about Louise and Brad. How would Brad live with knowing what she had done? "Anyway, I have to give the girls their baths. I had a headache and was too mentally depressed to bathe them last night."

"I'll call you tomorrow, Darian."

Darian sighed and hung up. If only she would have known that Louise felt so strongly against their relationship. But what would it have changed? She was in love with Brad, and neither Louise nor anyone else could change that fact.

The next morning Darian was up early to get the girls ready for another school day. But she couldn't get Louise out of her mind. If she weren't going to marry Brad she would surely go to the police department and tell what had happened with Pete Jr. and Louise. Darian decided that she would never speak to Louise again. With hope, Darian wished Louise would move to Kansas City forever.

The day wore on and night had eased in on Darian before she realized how late it was.

Both girls snuggled against her and all three fell into a deep sleep. The next morning Darian stood in the shower while the girls were still asleep. Today was a new day and Darian felt blessed. The last few days were the past and she looked forward to better days.

She cooked oatmeal for breakfast, the girls' favorite, and filled her cup with instant coffee. The girls ran to their rooms to get their sweaters.

"Mama, make sure the girls are sitting on the sofa so they don't get their dresses dirty," Darian yelled nervously from her bedroom. "I hear Nikki whining and I don't want her to start crying this morning. Gee, I'm nervous enough as it is." She glanced at her reflection in the mirror. Her white suit fit perfectly, and her pearl earrings with two small diamonds in the middle sparkled. She had gone to the beauty salon and had her curly hair shaped and blown straight.

Today was Darian's wedding day, and tonight, she and Brad were going on their honeymoon. She was told to pack comfortably with kick-around clothing. Where they were going was a surprise for her. She'd tried and tried to make Brad tell her, but he would only smile, kiss her, make love to her, and say no.

Darian looked in the mirror one last time. Her white suit had a knee-length jacket to match, and she wore white step-in heels. She closed her eyes tightly and tried to imagine the long nights she would spend with Brad for the rest of their lives.

Darian decided that after being married a month, she would write a book about children adjusting to moving into a new home with their stepparents, and what adjustments had to be made. The girls had lost their mother, but thank God they hadn't seen Pete Jr., their father, or witness Shirlee shooting him.

* * *

In the Wyndham Hotel in New Orleans, Brad paced inside the small chapel.

Bernard and Vickie walked in looking happier than ever. "Is the bride-to-be here yet?" Vickie asked.

"No, but I'm sure she's on her way," Brad said. "Everyone we invited isn't here yet either." As they were talking, three couples from Brad's job, Vickie's mother, and Pastor Williamson came in. Other than Tye, Lenny, Brad's cousin, was the only relative that attended. Nikki and Shelby came in ahead of Darian, Shirlee, and Jefferson behind them.

Darian and the girls were dressed in white. Shirlee was dressed in a white suit with a tight skirt and a short-waisted jacket, short enough to reveal her round figure.

The music started to play as Darian met Brad in front of the pastor. Brad released an audible sign of relief. He wasn't worried about her not showing up; he just couldn't wait to see her. What a joy to marry someone that he truly loved, in every sense of the word.

Darian and Brad wanted a small wedding. Lenny stood there as Brad's best man, and the girls stood beside Darian holding white roses in their hands. Dressed in a white tuxedo, Tye held the ring for Brad.

Nikki was upset because she, Shelby, and Tye would stay at Shirlee's house while Darian and Brad went on their honeymoon. Shelby held Nikki's small hand.

Darian's voice trembled as she repeated after the pastor. As nervous as she was, she prayed that Nikki wouldn't cry out. Darian got through her wedding vows. When the pastor told Brad to kiss the bride, Shelby laughed out loud as everyone clapped their hands. Nikki cried. Tye was happy and stood by his father.

For the third time, Brad looked at the guests to see if Louise had decided to come, but she wasn't there. It was best for everyone that she stayed away. But still she was his mother and he had never imagined getting married without her. He had always envisioned her watching him with tears of happiness, and pleased with her daughter-in-law.

As Brad and Darian walked out of the chapel, it was apparent that it was the happiest day of their lives. Darian's arm was hooked into Brad's. Louise watched from her car. Her son looked so happy, and Tye was holding Nikki's hand. They looked like a family, the family she had lost. "Lord, if only that dreadful Pete Jr. had gotten killed without Brad finding out that I was involved," she whispered, and now it was too late. She doubted if Darian or Brad would ever forgive her. She was wrong; she should have killed Pete Jr. and stuffed that damn check down his throat so he would choke on it. The last few days she had thought of a hundred ways she could have killed him. Now all she could do was hope while she was away that one day, Brad might find some way to forgive her. Was that too much to hope for? she wondered, and drove off into the traffic. Her sister was waiting to make reservations to get a flight back to Kansas City. She sighed. The Prozac had kept her calm, and the doctor instructed Louise to take one every day. If only she hadn't stopped.

The wedding reception was held in a room across the hall from the wedding chapel. Brad and Darian danced first. Tye danced with her twice. When the music stopped, Brad and Darian went back to the table and laughed and talked with Vickie, Bernard, and Jefferson. Shirlee kept the girls company.

"You look beautiful, Darian. Aren't you glad the wedding is all over now?" asked Vickie. "The closer it got to the wedding, didn't you get nervous? I mean, right before the wedding, I started to wonder if me and Bernard were doing the right thing."

"You don't feel that way now, do you?"

"No. Bernard is the best thing that has ever happened to me."

Hand in hand, Darian and Vickie sashayed across the room. They stopped and hugged each other. "I'm finally glad that I stayed in New Orleans, Vickie. I'm so happy that you're here, too. You look beautiful in blue."

"You girls are walking around like two old hens. Come cut the cake, Darian. You can hug up with Vickie when you get back," Shirlee said.

"Okay, Mama, we're coming. I guess Brad will get used to Mama one day. Her white suit she's wearing is getting a little tight. She bought the shoes yesterday, and did more shopping than I for the wedding. But what can I say? Shirlee is Shirlee."

"It's easier than you trying to get used to Louise," Vickie said, and frowned as though she had a bitter taste in her mouth.

Darian and Vickie went back to the table. "It's time to cut the cake, honey. We have a plane to catch in three hours."

The cake was cut, and more dancing came after. Darian danced with Brad of course, and Nikki and Shelby danced together and ran back and forth with Tye and the other children. They ate as much cake as they could digest. Two hours later, people were leaving. Brad looked at Darian standing at the door hugging and saying their good-byes to everyone.

Vickie whispered in Darian's hear, "Don't come back pregnant."

"Are you insane?" Darian answered.

At last he could have his wife alone. Brad said it out loud again, *his wife*. It had a nice ring to it.

* * *

Shirlee and Jefferson were waiting in Darian's living room to take the children to their house.

Darian was in her bedroom, and placed the girls' suitcase on the bed. Tye's bags were in the living room.

The front door opened and closed. Darian knew it was Brad ready to leave for their honeymoon. She picked up the suitcase and went into the living room. The girls and Tye ran behind her.

"Come on, Jefferson. Let's go home. I'm tired and we've had a long day, but a good one. My baby is married." Like so many times, Shirlee thought of Monique and her eyes watered. Like today, she would have danced and cried at Darian's wedding. For so long it had been just the three of them.

"Come on, honey," Brad yelled from the car.

Darian looked around the living room again to see if she had forgotten anything.

They arrived at the airport two hours early. The lines were long; impatient people with young children in their arms, some running in and out of the lines. One woman yelled at her son for running a circle around her.

Finally, Brad and Darian were at the gate and in line to board the plane. Once they were settled in their seats and the plane had taken off, they ordered a glass of wine.

Brad reached over and held Darian's hand. "You are a beautiful bride, baby."

"Thanks. I wanted to be for you. We've been through so much together."

"Well, it's over now. We're a family now, and we'll go through more, but together."

* * *

The plane landed in Orlando, Florida. They checked into the Sheraton Safari Hotel where Walt Disney World was only a quarter of a mile away. There was a heated pool, with a unique, exotic African safari theme.

Brad and Darian stepped inside the large room. Darian whirled around on her heels, and looked around in awe. "It's awesome, Brad. I love it," she complimented, gliding into his open arms. "I love it, baby," she said in a honey-coated voice.

"Only the best for you." Brad looked at his watch; it was past midnight.

"Why don't we hang our clothes up and go to bed? We've had a long day and I want to be rested for tomorrow."

Brad smiled as he listened to her. "Do you really think we are going to rest once we hit that big bed?" He smiled mischievously and kissed her on her cheek.

"Probably not." She giggled.

Once they finished, Darian went to the bathroom and came out wearing a short, satin, light blue gown. Her eyes settled on Brad as he sat on the bed looking through the *Orlando* magazine. Darian gently took the magazine from his hand. "Let's go to bed, honey." Her voice was soft and seductive. She smiled when she saw the desiring glint in her *husband's* eyes. He wanted her.

He was enthralled; his eyes searched hers. Brad had already undressed down to his black underwear and was waiting patiently for her.

He pulled her down onto the bed and laid her on her back. He wanted this night to last eternally.

Darian's heart was racing fast, and she wanted him. She wanted this night to be a memorable one, too. She felt the cool breeze against her skin as her gown eased down her breasts, then her waist, and legs. Brad's warm hands caressed her. Everywhere he touched she felt his lips against her scorching, hot body.

He was unable to stop, or wait any longer. He was inside her, moving fast, then slowly as he felt her warm body against his, her legs circling his back, holding him inside her. This was their world, his and Darian's, together. This was where they forgot his mother, the shootings, and the threats on Darian's life. This was heaven.

The next morning was a repeat of the night before. They lay on their pillows. "Did you get enough rest?" Brad asked with a smile across his face. He kissed her on the forehead.

"No. But I didn't want to rest. I only wanted you. Have you realized that we have a lot of years ahead of us?" she asked.

"Yes. That's why I asked you to marry me." He grabbed her hand. "Now, come on so we can shower. Afterward, we can dress and go to breakfast."

"Good idea." Darian jumped out of bed and raced him to the bathroom.

At ten they were dressed and ready to explore their day. They went to the hotel's restaurant for breakfast.

They ate and talked about the children. Not wanting to spoil the day, they didn't speak of Louise. Once they were finished, Brad asked for the check. They started their outing by walking a block to rent a car.

As Brad drove down Orange Avenue, they saw flashy new skyscrapers, Egyptian revival buildings, and plenty of art deco facades. They went on to Universal Studios. By two, they had lunch and at four they went back to the hotel, made love, and went out to the heated pool.

The next day they went to Walt Disney World. The resort was divided into several sections. They went to the Magic Kingdom, and the rest of the week they went to U.S.A. Adventureland and explored all they could in the surrounding area. Darian bought gifts for the children.

The nights were blissful, and they hated when it was time to return home. But it was time to start their new lives together.

When they arrived at the airport and walked out with their luggage, Shirlee, the girls, and Tye were waiting. Nikki yelled out Darian's name, and Shelby and Tye ran straight into Darian's arms.

"This has been a long week, I'm telling y'all. And, girl, I'm tired," Shirlee said. She was wearing tight jeans and a white blouse that hung loosely on the outside.

"I have presents for you guys. Did you miss me?"

"Yes," they answered in unison.

"I sure did. Nikki cried about everything. She missed you, Darian," Shirlee said.

"What about me?" Brad asked jokingly.

"We missed you, too, son-in-law." Shirlee kissed him on the cheek.

Brad and Darian placed the luggage inside the trunk of Shirlee's car. Darian and the children got into the backseat, and Brad sat in front with Shirlee.

"Your renters called me, Darian. They needed the key to the garage. They've just been waiting until you returned so they can move in." Shirlee stopped at the signal.

"They can have it day after tomorrow. Everything is all packed and the movers will be there at nine tomorrow morning," Darian explained.

"Mama, did you pack the children's bags?"

"Yes. I packed them two days ago," Shirlee said jokingly. "They're in the trunk."

Brad laughed. "That bad, huh, Shirlee?"

"It was the first time I've kept them for an entire week, but it was fun. Whenever you guys need to get away, it's time I keep my granddaughters more often."

Darian was quite surprised to hear Shirlee admit that it was time she acted like a grandmother.

"Jefferson certainly enjoyed having the children around. He made it a real vacation by taking them to a movie, to the park, anything they wanted to do, he did it."

Shirlee parked her car in Darian's driveway. "I'll see you tomorrow, Darian. Hope you two had a good honeymoon."

"We had the best time, Mama." Darian's face heated as she thought of the passionate nights she had spent with her husband. As the children got out of the car, she kissed them again. It was time to start her new life as a wife and mother. A year ago, just the thought of being a mother was unimaginable.

"I won't be going in with you. Hell, I'm tired, Darian," Shirlee said, still sitting inside the car.

"It's okay, Mama. I appreciate you babysitting." Darian watched Shirlee as she backed out the driveway. Brad and the children were already inside.

When Darian went inside, the children ran to their room and Brad was sitting on the sofa.

"Baby, Tye and me are leaving so we can make more space in the girls' room. We want everything to be perfect for you and the girls. But I'll be here early tomorrow morning to start moving you into your new home."

"Okay. I'm going to spend some time with the girls and do some last-minute packing in the kitchen." Darian walked Brad to the door. He kissed her and yelled good-bye to the girls. Tye ran from the girls' room and followed Brad outside.

As Darian closed the door, she heard the running footsteps coming toward her. "I have a present for you guys." Darian grabbed the large bag and pulled out a Mickey Mouse DVD, T-shirts, and two Mickey Mouse books. Before she could say anything else they were jumping up and down asking for her to place the disc into the DVD player.

Chapter 30

It was their first night in Brad's home. Darian and Brad were exhausted from all the moving. But everyone was happy and excited. Brad and Tye played and teased the girls until it was time for bed.

Darian loved her new home, and the next morning she walked through the two-story, four-bedroom house. It was decorated with mint-green carpet and drapes. The kitchen was spacious with a connecting laundry room. Darian's furniture was placed in the living room and Brad's brown, sectional sofa was moved into the den. Brad and Darian's bedroom was large with a balcony and fireplace. Darian had watched the girls' reactions, but Tye kept them playing in his bedroom.

Louise had left a detailed letter in the mailbox. She had gone to Kansas City with her sister and was considering selling her house and living out the rest of her life in Kansas. She apologized again, and said she was taking her medication again. She asked for Brad's forgiveness and said that she would contact him later. Brad knew that once she was settled, he would visit her, but it wouldn't be soon.

After the children were in bed Brad and Darian went to their bedroom. Darian stood on the balcony while Brad went back downstairs to turn out the lights. He eased up behind her.

"Last night Tye said he's happy to have a mommy, and two sisters."

Darian smiled. In her wildest dreams, "mommy" was a word that no child would ever call her. But in her wildest dreams she never thought she would find Brad again.

"I'm going to be a good husband, Darian."

"I know you will, sweetheart. You're a good man."

They had been married for three weeks. Darian's book was selling well, and she had been book-signing and storytelling for the local bookstores. *No Turning Back* wasn't anything compared to the wonders of her new life. Life was good, and she was ready for whatever came next, as long as she had her family.

Acknowledgments

To my son, Darren, good luck on the book that you are writing. To my daughter, Cassandra, thanks for being you, and to my son-in-law, Chris Royal, thanks for doing a terrific job editing *No Turning Back*.

Thank you to my mother for always being there. Thanks to all my sisters and brothers for being in my life.

To Selena James at Kensington Publishing and a special thanks to Rakia Clark for being there when I need you.

And to all the authors I've met: thanks for your encouragement and continual support.

To the book clubs and fans, I thank you all.